Kay Brellend was born in north London and her first saga, based in the early twentieth century slums of Islington, was published in 2011. The opening novel in the *Bittersweet Legacy* trilogy came out in 2017. Published by Piatkus, this series was set in a north London sweet factory and on the Somme battlefields.

Kay's *Workhouse to War* trilogy is also set during the Great War. The series begins in the Whitechapel Union Workhouse and moves to the bustling markets of East London, between 1914 and 1918. It has all the heart, grit and personal connection that distinguishes her as one of the most exciting voices in the saga genre.

By Kay Brellend

The Bittersweet Legacy series

A Sister's Bond
A Lonely Heart
The Way Home

The Workhouse to War series

A Workhouse Christmas
Stray Angel
The Workhouse Sisters

THE
WORKHOUSE
SISTERS

Kay Brellend

PIATKUS

PIATKUS

First published in Great Britain in 2022 by Piatkus
This paperback edition published in 2022 by Piatkus

1 3 5 7 9 10 8 6 4 2

A CIP catalogue record for this book
is available from the British Library.

ISBN 978-0-349-42519-1

Typeset in Palatino by M Rules

Printed and bound in Great Britain by
Clays Ltd, Elcograf S.p.A.

Papers used by Piatkus are from well-managed forests
and other responsible sources.

Piatkus
An imprint of
Little, Brown Book Group
Carmelite House
50 Victoria Embankment
London EC4Y 0DZ

An Hachette UK Company
www.hachette.co.uk

www.littlebrown.co.uk

For Sandra, with love

Also, for all the people who were unfortunate
enough to spend time in a workhouse

Prologue

Christmas Eve 1915
Whitechapel Workhouse, Mile End Road, East London

'Merry Christmas, my dear.'

Having poured two large measures of Scotch, the fellow handed one to his companion and raised his own in a toast. Firelight glinted through their chinking glasses, tinting the whisky ruby red. 'And here's to a very happy 1916. God willing, this war will finally come to an end.' He sipped, smacked his lips, then sank into a hearthside armchair, sighing contentedly.

'Never mind the bloomin' war.' His friend downed her drink in two unladylike glugs. 'It would be better still if my husband popped his clogs before spring.' She winked. 'We could get married. After a decent time, that is. Not that Bill Gladwell deserves much respect or grieving, the way he's treated me over the years.' She perched on the arm of his chair. 'We could retire to the coast, eh, love?' She dropped a kiss on her boyfriend's balding crown, her salt-and-pepper ringlets curtaining his jowls.

Norman Drake smiled gamely, though he wasn't

intending to marry again. He was fond of his lady friend, but he'd no wish for another wife. One had been enough and his heart was buried in her grave. She'd passed away almost a decade ago and he had kept busy to stop himself pining. His employment left scant free time, and he'd adapted to his living arrangements. He had a cosy little domain: private, yet well situated, if he chose to immerse himself in East End hubbub. Occasionally he did when he had a day off, and would browse the teeming markets and join in the pub sing-songs. But he was content with his own company and found a weekly visit or two from his companion to be sufficient.

June Gladwell was an old friend of his late wife's, the two of them having grown up together in the backstreets of Whitechapel. June was a lusty woman and was up for a romp when the mood took them ... which wasn't as often as when they had first become a couple. They were both in their early sixties, though June was still youthful in body and mind. Norman hadn't aged as well and was feeling his years. He had arthritis that gave him gyp in the winter months. More worrying were the pains in his chest that came and went. No amount of liniment soothed those.

He tipped his glass and another warming swig of whisky slid down his throat. He rubbed his aching knees, moving his slippers towards the warmth in the grate.

June helped herself to the dregs in the whisky bottle and swiftly dispatched them. She ambled to and fro in front of the fire, the empty tumbler oscillating between thumb and fingers. It was Christmas Eve and she'd dressed up in her glad rags, hoping to persuade Norman to take her out.

'Sit down ... you're making me giddy, June,' he complained.

She did take the seat opposite but tapped her feet like a fidgety child. She felt exuberant and didn't want to waste time cooped up in this dreary place. Her glass found the table with a thud. Christmas Eve was for celebrating and she wanted to get tipsy and have fun. There was little enough enjoyment in her life, stuck, as she was, in three ground-floor rooms of a rotten terrace, with a crippled husband. She was sure Bill was clinging to his miserable existence just to spite her. Last time he'd been admitted to the London Hospital in Whitechapel the doctor had told her she must prepare for him never to come home. But he had. Drat him.

She flopped back in her chair with an exaggerated sigh. Norman looked older than his age and acted it, too. He seemed ready to doze off, not have a knees-up. The least he could do was break open another bottle of Scotch, or there'd be little point in her hanging around. She wasn't settling for toasting her toes by a Yuletide fire without a drink in her hand. She could go and meet her neighbours in the pub and belt out carols round the piano. She'd heard the raucous choir when walking along the Mile End Road and had been tempted to go inside and join the carousers, glimpsed through the frosted glass.

'Thanks for the drink then.' She flounced to her feet. 'You seem all in, ducks, so I'll say toodle-oo and let you have a little kip. I'll call again after Boxing Day, I expect.'

Norman started from his doze. It was difficult to keep his eyes open with flames doing a hypnotic dance about the logs. He didn't fancy being on his own on this special night so stirred himself. June was reaching for the feathered hat she'd taken off earlier and dropped on the table.

'Don't go yet, love. There's more tiddly in the sideboard.'

He eased himself out of the chair. 'I was saving a few brown ales for tomorrow.'

'Why don't we go to the pub?' she countered. 'We can get properly merry. The company will do you good. You're stuck in this place too often.' June wasn't settling for a bottle of lousy beer. She wanted port or whisky, and her glass refilled several times.

'I'm on duty,' he reminded her with a frown. 'If I toddled off without a by your leave, I'd be for the high jump.' He patted her cheek. 'And you don't want your neighbours gossiping, do you?' He made a cautionary noise, rolling his eyes. 'It wouldn't do for the two of us to be looking cosy, having a rare old time, while poor Bill's at death's door.'

'We've been together four years, ducks.' June snorted a laugh. 'The neighbours did their gossiping early on. My husband's been knocking on the pearly gates for years, and I reckon everybody knows it's about time he was let in.'

'People have gossiped about us?' Norman sounded surprised.

''Course they have,' she said airily.

'Aren't you worried about that?' Norman was wondering if *he* was. He'd trusted they'd been discreet enough for it to seem they were good friends through his late wife.

'I'm not worried,' she flatly replied. 'I've done my duty and treated Bill better than he deserved, considering the dog's life he led me. He's never been liked. He used to cause trouble, picking fights; he still would if he was able to.' June pinned on her hat. 'I've got a day of it tomorrow with my Ginny coming over with her lot. The grandkids will be running around, driving me potty. I'm taking it easy tonight and having a drink. Are you coming?' she challenged. 'If not, I'll go on my own.'

'Oh, I don't know ...' Norman sighed. 'It's irregular, you see ...'

'Nobody'll come here, anyway. Not on Christmas Eve.' She scoffed. 'Who the bloody hell would want to?'

'That's just it, love,' he said dryly. 'Nobody wants to come here at any time of the year, but the poor wretches do.' He stood up and clasped her hands. 'How about we entertain ourselves another way?' He jerked his head towards the box room that housed his bunk bed.

'I'll tell you what: we'll have a little drink and a sing-song in the Bow Bells then I'll let you unwrap your Christmas present tonight, if we're both still in the mood.' She jiggled her bosom at him and followed that up with a kiss on the lips.

Norman had felt a pleasant stirring as she'd shimmied and teased him with her tongue. 'All right – just the one drink, mind. Then straight back here in case I'm missed by the boss.'

While she waited impatiently by the street door for him, hands on hips, Norman took off his slippers and pulled on his boots. Then he found his hat and coat. Once he was dressed for outdoors he felt more amenable to a jaunt. In the six years he'd been a workhouse porter nobody had ever knocked him up for admission on Christmas Eve. June was right. Even the destitute would try and hang it out until after the holiday before entering Whitechapel workhouse. And who could blame them? There was no Christmas cheer to be had in this place.

Norman loaded a few more logs onto the fire to keep it alight for a warm welcome home. Then he unlocked the door, a livening blast of wintry air greeting him. He quashed his misgivings. It *was* against the rules to go out.

But he was sure he wouldn't be missed if he deserted his post for half an hour.

The woman stomped to and fro, muttering to herself in irritation. She returned to the building and rang the bell again then banged on the door with a gloved fist. Still there was no sight or sound of life from within.

A fine soft sleet had started to fall, icing the pavements and her large black hat. The two children with her were silent. The elder of them was perching on the step of the lodge, with an adult's long scarf wound around her neck and up over her fair hair, muffling her against the chill. The baby boy was in a wicker basket, his tiny body covered by an old cardigan used as a makeshift blanket.

'Ain't nobody opening up for yer?' A fellow called out. He was stumbling on and off the pavement as he approached, swigging from a brown bottle.

The woman turned her back on him and squatted down by the children. From a distance it might seem she was lovingly protecting her offspring from the elements with her bulky figure. But she wasn't their mother at all. She was a baby farmer who'd taken charge of these unfortunates, promising their mothers she would provide foster care. All Mrs Jolley loved was the money those desperate women handed over for their children's keep. She pocketed it with no intention of earning the trust put in her. Over the past year she'd taken in half a dozen infants. All had been disposed of apart from these two. They too had now become a nuisance, and she wanted rid of them.

The tramp wasn't discouraged by being ignored; he meandered over to stand swaying beside the little group. 'Have yer rung the bell?' Without waiting for a reply, he yanked on it himself. 'Need to give it a good ol' tug, missus.'

'Clear off. We're just having a rest and will be on our way shortly.' The woman kept her hat brim low, shielding her middle-aged features. Not that she thought he would remember her; he was so inebriated he probably wouldn't recognise his own face in a mirror. But she detested interference and didn't want him drawing attention to her. Not that many people were about. They were at home, dressing turkeys or Christmas trees. Or they were in warm taverns, getting merry. She wanted to be elsewhere too and wasn't hanging around for much longer. By the time the hostelries turned out she would be on the way to catch her train out of the capital to the suburbs.

'Porter's always in there,' he insisted, unwilling to give up on being obliging. 'Ol' geezer must be goin' deaf.' Propping one hand on the door to steady himself, the other gripped the base of the empty beer bottle, employing it as a battering ram.

The thud, thud, thud was driving her crazy. She sprang up, shoving her mannish features close to his bristly face. 'I said clear off. I don't need your help, you drunken fool.'

He looked affronted and threw the empty bottle into the gutter where it smashed. He wended on his unsteady way, muttering about ungrateful cows. At the corner he stopped, still feeling resentful, and peered back the way he'd come.

His hammering on the door had been fit to wake the dead. It hadn't brought the porter running. Nobody was home. But he would be back on duty at some time this evening, she was sure. She couldn't hang about waiting for him. She was impatient to start afresh without encumbrances in a new neighbourhood.

She looked at the shivering girl, sitting huddled into her shawl with her scarfed head almost touching her knees. It was fitting that Charlotte Finch should return here. Her mother had been an impoverished widow who'd died in the workhouse infirmary, giving birth to her. The baby in the basket had been a factory girl's bastard, offloaded at her parents' command before the neighbours wised up to their daughter's disgrace.

Mrs Jolley had no intention of introducing herself to the porter or giving any explanation for why she was abandoning the children. If she spotted a light go on inside, or heard the locks being drawn, she would hurry away. She crouched down by her foster daughter, shaking her shoulder to rouse her. 'You must stay here with little Peter and somebody will come and let you in, and take care of you. Do you understand, Charlotte?'

The girl gave a nod, barely raising her head.

The baby peddler gave a final clatter on the bell, aware she was doing so in vain. Without a backward glance she set off briskly for the station, praising herself for having taken pity on those two and left them alive for somebody to find. It was more than she'd done for any of the others.

The little girl raised her head, blinking against the ice blurring her vision. Through the sparkles she could see somebody coming. It was the same man as before. He was wobbling as he walked and stopping now and then to find his balance. Mrs Jolley hadn't wanted him to help with banging on the door. Charlotte would be thankful if he helped her. She was cold and hungry and her throat was very sore. She got up and used her small fist on the wooden panels, copying what she'd seen Mrs Jolley do. She hoped the man would hurry up and pull on the bell that she couldn't reach. She put her ear to the door as Mrs

8

Jolley had, listening for a noise from within. She couldn't hear anything other than the hiss of the sleet and a sound of singing, somewhere in the distance.

'You all right, nipper?' The tramp was picking a careful path closer to her on the ice. He was too drunk to remember he'd thrown down his bottle. A piece of smashed glass pierced through the newspaper stuffed into the hole in the sole of his boot. With a yowl he hopped, flailed his arms, and toppled over onto his back.

Charlotte stopped what she was doing and hurried over to him. She bent down, yanking on his arm, then patting his face because his eyes were closed. When he blinked them open she skittered back. He didn't smell nice or feel nice. His cheek had bristles that scratched her skin and she felt a bit afraid of him.

Jake Pickard continued gazing at the beautiful little child with big staring eyes and wisps of fair hair stuck to her damp forehead. She'd tried to help him up and had touched him with her soft-as-snow cold hands. He started to sniff and to cry in a long low whine.

Charlotte sped back to the step. She didn't know what she'd done wrong. She'd only tried to help him. But she was always doing something bad even when she tried to be good. She peeked at Peter in the basket then tucked the old cardigan around him. She was about to sit down but the baby whimpered, taking her attention. Then she heard the singing growing louder, and somebody laughing. The wonderful sound was a lure. She set off at a trot in the direction of that happy person to ask them to help.

'Oh, would you look at that! It's a Christmas angel come down from heaven.' June Gladwell removed her hand from Norman Drake's shoulder where it had been tapping in time to the music being pounded out on the piano. He hadn't heard her speak to him, nor did he notice when she stepped away to sashay towards the little girl standing just inside the doorway.

'Are you looking for your mum, sweet'eart?' The noise of the rowdy rendition of 'Hark the Herald Angels Sing' was drowning out her voice but she continued grinning tipsily at the flaxen-haired child who had a length of tatty scarf drooping from her head and bundled against her chest.

June crouched down so their faces were level and she could gaze into a pair of deep blue eyes set in a white face. 'My, you're a cherub all right, and pretty as a picture.' A smattering of ice crystals glittered on the girl's fair hair where the scarf had slipped, and failed to protect her from the snow. June swept the cold spangles away with her knuckles then reached for her hands. She'd barely touched those small chilled fingers when they were jerked free and the child darted outside into the corridor, beckoning June to follow.

Unbalanced, June wobbled on her heels, whirling her arms, then tipped backwards onto her posterior. She gave a shriek that drew Norman's attention, cutting short his carolling. He couldn't help but chortle at the sight of her, though she was displaying her bloomers in a most unladylike manner. He put down his tankard and came to help her up.

The less inebriated patrons tutted; those coarsened by Christmas spirit hooted with laughter, encouraging her to show a bit more leg.

'Ooh ... me bleedin' arse.' June's alley-cat roots broke through whenever she was under the influence. She gave herself a rub as she was hauled upright, and pushed her hat out of her eyes.

Norman had been having a rare old time, but he was on the way to being sozzled and June had had plenty to be making a spectacle of herself. 'Time we headed back,' he said, pulling out his pocket watch. He muttered a self-reprimand; he'd been gone from his post for well over an hour.

'Ain't going back till I've found the kid,' June slurred stubbornly.

Norman put an arm around her and managed to propel her into the corridor, hoping that the cooler air might sober her up. He'd have to walk her home right to her door, the state she was in. He rarely did that. Daft as it seemed, considering he knew her husband was a bed-bound invalid, Norman imagined the brute might jump out and bash him. He'd known Bill Gladwell in his heyday when the man had been capable of causing a riot. June wasn't exaggerating the rotten life she'd endured as his wife.

June wriggled free to attend to her hat with the fastidiousness peculiar to inebriation. 'I know I wasn't dreaming, Norm. I saw a pretty little girl and spoke to her.' She traipsed along the corridor, leaning sideways to see past the kink in it. 'Now where's she gone?'

'You'll be seeing stars in a minute.' Norman steadied her as she almost tripped over.

'There she is!' June waved. 'See! Told you!' She pointed triumphantly at the child, who was shivering and holding the scarf over her lower face as she peered round a corner.

'She's probably just waiting for her folks.' Norman tried to urge June towards the exit. It wasn't an unusual sight: kids loitering in pub corridors, or sitting outside on the step while waiting for their parents to finish drinking themselves silly in the warm.

The girl moved the muffling wool away from her face, revealing delicate features, framed by pale blonde hair. Now he had a better view of her, he recognised that pallid, heavy-eyed look. Sickness in the family was often the trigger for people entering the workhouse and ending their days in the infirmary. He moved closer and bent down to speak to her. In the wavering gaslight, he could detect blotches of feverish colour on her cheeks and blue hollows beneath her red-rimmed eyes. 'Are you waiting for somebody in there?' He pointed to the rowdy room. 'Mother's in there, is she?'

Charlotte shook her head. 'Mother's gone.'

Norman had inclined closer to catch her whispered words. 'She's gone in there for a drink, has she?' He indicated the saloon bar again. 'Shall I fetch her for you?'

'Gone to the train. Peter's crying. Come and see.' She tugged on Norman's sleeve. 'I banged on the door but nobody's there. Come and see.' She muffled her neck again, wincing, as though speaking was painful.

'You banged on a door, dearie?' June butted in. Curiosity was sobering her up more efficiently than the draught in the corridor.

'Is Peter your brother? Is he waiting outside?' Norman held the back of a hand to the child's clammy brow. She had a temperature. Perhaps she was delirious to say her mother was catching the train. In his opinion it would be kinder if parents left poorly kids at home, than drag them out to sit on a freezing pub step. All good intentions of 'only being gone a minute' disappeared after the first drink slid down. As he well knew; he'd intended having just the one. 'I don't think you're well, little one.' Norman sounded concerned. She looked underweight but that wasn't unusual for East End alley scamps. 'Is your throat sore?' He'd noticed her wince on swallowing.

She nodded and automatically opened her mouth for him to look at what hurt her. Charlotte had got used to doing this when her foster mother asked to examine her throat. Mrs Jolley would groan after looking at it and seem annoyed with her for being ill. But this man didn't mutter and tut, so she grasped his hand, trying to pull him towards the exit. It was warm and dry in here but she couldn't stay. She had to go back and look after the baby.

Norman had bent down on creaking joints to take a look in her mouth and had got a whiff of her diseased breath. His expression was grim as he straightened up. He'd spent time in the workhouse infirmary as an orderly and knew about diphtheria and the havoc it caused, raging through poor communities.

A blast of icy air reached them as some revellers came in. The little girl took her chance. Before the door swung shut she darted into the street, trotting back the way she'd come. Norman rushed out after her, urgently beckoning June into the sleety night. She obeyed without a word, having also sensed an impending calamity.

The streetlamps were illuminating relentlessly descending snowflakes. Norman proceeded as fast as he could, conscious the pavements were now perilous. June clung to his arm, moaning at him to slow down as she skidded on patches of white underfoot. He had a mounting, horrible suspicion that he knew where the child was heading. As they drew closer to the lodge he squinted into the blinding atmosphere, making out a fellow by the building with an arm raised, banging on the door. Norman's heart sank. His absence had been noted. The little girl leading the way was tiring and the couple soon caught her up. Norman firmly took her hand, helping her along those final yards.

'Do you know these children?' Norman puffed out to the local tramp.

'*Me?* No … I … don't,' Jake Pickard barked indignantly. He'd dragged himself to his feet after his fall, but not in time to stop the little girl running off. The condition he was in, he knew he'd no hope of catching her if he gave chase. As he'd lain supine, snow had melted on his face, sobering him up. 'The mother went off up there.' He jerked his head. 'Bold as brass, the cow. Left her kids behind in the snow.' He spat into the gutter. 'Shame of it.'

Norman quickly found his keys and opened up, bundling June and the child over the threshold. He picked up the wicker basket then went inside, slamming the door on the tramp, who was making a crafty attempt to follow them.

'Settle the girl close to the fire to warm up,' Norman ordered June. He put the basket down on the armchair and with stiff, unsteady fingers removed the wool cover, shaking the slush onto the floor. Norman stifled a groan. The little girl had said Peter was crying but this poor mite would never cry again. He looked about six months old and his sunken face was quite still and whiter than the grimy sheet he lay upon. Norman felt for a heartbeat beneath a bony ribcage but knew he wouldn't detect one. He hung his head in shame, swaying it from side to side. 'I should have been here.' He sent a tortured glance June's way. She appeared to be in a daze, gripping the mantelshelf for support. 'This boy might still be breathing if he'd been brought indoors sooner.' Norman covered his quivering lips with his fingers.

'The wicked bitch that dumped them outside is to blame.'
June rallied to splutter a defence. She was also at fault,
badgering Norman to go out when on duty. She gingerly
approached to look at the tot. 'He's just skin and bone. The
poor thing was too sickly to survive; his mother must've
known it.' She spat a tsk of disgust through her teeth.
'Fancy that! Scarpering and leaving innocent little ones
to fend for themselves on a night like this. Woman needs
horsewhipping.'

Norman felt equally outraged by such odious behaviour. Destitute parents often brought sick children here for
admittance to the infirmary, unable to afford a doctor's fee.
He'd never before found any abandoned on the doorstep,
although he'd heard of it happening in days of yore. The
woman's heartless behaviour didn't ease his conscience
over his own dereliction of duty. He deserved a taste of that
horsewhip himself.

'You're not to blame for this, Norman.' June gave his
shoulder an encouraging squeeze. 'You're a good man. One
of the best. And nobody'll know you weren't about when
the kiddies were brought here.' She glanced at the child,
huddled by the fireside. 'Was only us two talked to the
girl. And that old tramp won't be believed, whatever tales
he might tell. Pickard's always hanging about, gabbling on
about this and that. Nobody listens to anything he says.'

Norman knew that was true. Jake Pickard was a regular
sorry sight, mooching up and down, and drunk whenever he could beg, steal or borrow the funds to buy booze.
Norman had seen tykes chucking missiles and jeering at
him. Yet a vagrant had been the first to take notice of two
foundlings, then make an effort to protect them.

'I know what I did, June.' Norman stared at the girl

resting her cheek on her drawn-up knees and holding her hands to the embers in the grate. 'What a brave little thing she is; bless her heart for trying to get her brother help.' He sighed. 'I don't know how she did it when she's as ill as she is. I've let her down as well as the baby.' He closed his eyes, thinking things through. 'I imagine no father will come to claim them. Perhaps he's away fighting ... or could be he's perished in the war, and the mother can no longer cope. I reckon the surviving child is now no better than an orphan.'

'Don't care if her mother is a war widow, what she did is pure evil,' declared June. 'The coppers should be after her. She needs locking up.' The enormity of the tragedy had started June snivelling.

'Coppers can't help these two children,' Norman said sharply. He didn't want the police involved. The workhouse master was a stickler for keeping his business running smoothly to ensure the Board of Guardians were held at a safe distance. Any irregularities prompted an investigation and interference into the management of the place by the Whitechapel Union. Were Mr Stone ever to find out what had gone on tonight, Norman knew he'd be out on his ear. He wouldn't just lose his job but his accommodation, and at approaching sixty-three years of age, he was too long in the tooth to start seeking new work and lodgings. 'You can't mention this to anybody, June. I'll deal with it and put things right. First, the girl must quickly see a doctor, or she'll end up going the same way as her brother.' Norman bucked himself up; much had to be done and wallowing in regrets would waste time. He took June firmly by the elbow, steering her towards the door. 'You should go home now. I have to clear this mess up and concoct a tale to tell the master.'

June didn't seem as though she wanted to leave yet. She slipped her arm free, and made to uncover the baby again to study him for signs of life. But she tottered back at Norman's next words.

'I think the girl has diphtheria. Perhaps the boy had it too and it weakened him and that's why he died. It's a nasty infection, so don't get too close.'

'Gawdawmighty!' June croaked. 'Diphtheria! I've got me grandkids over tomorrow for Christmas. They can't catch a dose of that.' She shoved her hands deep into her pockets.

'Go home, June.' Norman led her to the door, opening it this time and making it clear she had to leave. She turned as though to wish him a merry Christmas, but seemed to think better of it. With a defeated shrug she hurried off into the quietly falling snow with barely a farewell.

'Can you tell me your name?' Norman asked the child while loading more logs onto the fire, stirring the embers with a poker until flames leapt up.

'Charlotte Finch.' The little girl didn't raise her cheek from its resting place on her knees.

'Well, Charlotte, you're not very well, are you, dear? You'll soon feel better once the doctor's looking after you.' Norman went next door into his bedroom and tugged a blanket off the bunk. He returned to the sitting room to carefully cocoon the girl with it. 'Now I'll make you a nice warm drink of milk. Then I have to go out. But I'll be back and bring the doctor with me.'

'Thank you,' she murmured.

Norman felt a tenderness wash over him at her politeness and stroked her damp hair. 'How old are you, dear?'

'Five,' she answered in a rasp.

'No more talking for now.' Norman had noticed her

screwing up her face in pain. He heated the milk in a pan in the kitchenette then put the cup down on the hearth beside her.

He carefully covered the tiny corpse with the woollen rag and while patting it down felt something in one of the cardigan's pockets. He drew out an old envelope. If the girl's name was Finch the garment hadn't belonged to her mother, he mused to himself, having read the scrawled name of Mrs Jolley and an address in Poplar. He thrust some fingers inside but whatever communication it had contained had been removed. He put the empty envelope into a drawer for proper perusal later, then picked up the basket. He would have to take Peter to the infirmary and report a dead child had been abandoned on the gatehouse step. The medical officer would deal with it from there. Norman was confident few questions would be asked and there was nobody to contradict his version of events.

Charlotte Finch was a different matter. Norman knew he should take her to the infirmary as well. But he didn't want to, and not just because the girl was old enough and bright enough to fully recount what had happened this Christmas Eve, landing him in hot water.

She was a lovely child; too fine to be stuck in an institution for the rest of her life. And she would be. Once inside, who would come to rescue her from that hellish place? Her beauty and her courage – and she had immense courage to run through the snow to get help for her brother – would wither beneath the workhouse regime. Her pretty hair would be shorn and she'd be put into an ugly uniform. If she survived and reached ten years old, Charlotte Finch would be a different child, browbeaten by inflexible rules and punishments until her spirit was defeated. If she reached twenty years old and was still an inmate, she would have forgotten she'd ever dashed through streets and heard people laughing and singing.

He had enough on his conscience without adding to it with the prospect of Charlotte Finch's life-long torment. He'd heard the old-timers in the workhouse who'd given up on protesting at their lot, howling pitifully for death to release them. It was the worst sound in the world.

A plan was hatching in his mind as he picked up the basket containing the baby's body. He glanced at Charlotte; she seemed settled, so he didn't disturb her with more conversation. He let himself out and hurried off towards the infirmary to start making reparation.

'I would say this unfortunate child has diphtheria. She will need to be hospitalised. I hope to God this isn't the start of another epidemic. Is her mother somewhere close by?' Dr Howes asked, closing his medical bag.

'I'm afraid she isn't.' Norman had not long ago gone to bang on the local doctor's door. The fellow had promised to come to the lodge as soon as he could and, true to his word, he had been close behind. Dr Howes had examined Charlotte and grimly confirmed Norman's fears about what ailed her.

Now the doctor was expecting more of an explanation for the presence of a sick child here in a porter's lodge, rather than in the workhouse infirmary. 'She's my granddaughter,' Norman started reeling off his rehearsed tale. 'My daughter isn't coping, you see. She has younger ones to care for. It's hard for her now her husband's in the navy. She asked me to take Charlotte and get her the care she needs. She doesn't want the others to catch the infection. I must help until Charlotte's better and can return home. I have some money

19

for your fee.' Norman had some savings, squirrelled away from frugal living. He'd gladly use them to make amends for what he'd done. He put the cash on the table for the doctor to take what he liked.

Norman *did* have a daughter with a brood of kids, living in Essex. And she did have a husband who'd enlisted in the merchant navy. Norman knew that much, though he and his only child had rather lost touch since the girl's mother died. Their visits and letters had petered out as his only child made a new life for herself in the countryside. She had always been an ambitious sort and had married well. Her father's lowly position, guarding the gate of an East End workhouse, was an embarrassment to her. 'I haven't seen Charlotte since she was a babe in arms. She hardly knows her granddad, but help's needed, so I've rallied round to do what I can for the family,' he added, in case the little girl denied their relationship.

'Yes ... commendable ... best thing ...' Dr Howes nodded sagely, pocketing his coins. This fellow had paid handsomely for his services, as he'd promised he would, so Howes would be accommodating despite the prospect of his wife's scowl when he got home. With guests due to arrive later that evening, she would be furious with him for going out to make a house call. 'Are you able to take your granddaughter to the London Hospital, Mr Drake? I can write a brief note of my diagnosis for you to hand to matron.'

'I'd be much obliged if you would take her yourself, sir,' Norman interrupted. He didn't want to disappear again, compound his mistake and risk even more questions being asked if he was discovered to be absent. 'I'm on duty, you see, and can't leave my post. If I was delayed at the hospital, I could jeopardise my job. Without a home and an income, I would struggle to care for my granddaughter.' He grabbed some cash from the table. 'Here, take some more for a cab to assist you ... it is a freezing night.'

Dr Howes waved away the proffered coins. 'Unnecessary. I have a jalopy,' he said. 'I'll crank the old girl and get her started, then please bring out the child. Quick as you can, when I call out. She needs to be kept as warm as possible.'

'Thank you, sir. I have time off next week and will visit the hospital to check on her recovery. The moment I hear she's well enough, back she'll come with me.'

Shortly after Dr Howes went outside, Norman could hear the sputter and bark of an engine being turned over. He lifted Charlotte to her feet. She'd been a good little thing, despite being in pain, letting Howes examine her without complaint. But since she'd settled back down by the hearth, the warmth of the fire seemed to have worsened her fever. Her head lolled against Norman's arm and he could hear her harsh breathing.

'It's all right, little one,' he crooned, wrapping the blanket firmly around her for the journey. 'Doctor's going to take you to hospital where they'll make you well. Then when you're better, I'll come and get you. You tell the doctors and nurses that Norman Drake is your granddad and that I'm going to take you back home with me.'

That part was true. It *was* what Norman intended to do. He had an address to follow up and was hoping that would lead him eventually to the girl's mother. If necessary, he'd shame the woman into taking her child and caring for her. But he regretted the rest of the lies he'd told, primarily to save his own skin. And he'd have to tell more, and keep telling them, to cover up his negligence and the death of an innocent baby boy.

Chapter One

Spring 1916

Lily Larkin stopped, turned around, and smiled at the woman trotting down the road in her direction. Beneath her breath she was groaning a curse. This was a meeting she'd been trying to avoid. She anticipated a question being fired at her and in answering it she would have to tell a lie ... possibly several. She felt uncomfortable doing that, yet deceit was unavoidable if she were to protect somebody dear to her.

'Been wanting to have a word with you.' Eunice Smith was holding a stitch in her side by the time she puffed up to stand beside Lily. 'I'm too old for haring about. D'you know, I turned forty-three a few weeks ago. My Bobby remembered me birthday, God bless him. He sent me a present from France. Lovely bit o' Brussels lace it is. Sewn it on me best blouse ... on the collar.' Eunice patted at her throat.

'Forty-three, eh? You're looking good for your age,' Lily continued, edging away. She liked Eunice but already could guess the direction of this conversation once the niceties were out of the way. 'Must dash. The lads will be back from the market soon and want their wages.'

'Oh ... hold on a mo, love.' Eunice grabbed Lily's elbow. 'I've had a letter from Bobby this morning. He's doing well enough, though he's got lice.' Eunice rolled her eyes. 'By all accounts, the whole platoon's scratching. Anyway, he wants me to find out if he's upset Margie in some way. He's sent her a letter but not heard back. Those two were always close pals, so it is odd. Then I was thinking to meself ... well, I've not clapped eyes on Margie for a while. Unusual that, cos I always see the gel walking up and down the road, to and from work.' Eunice settled her hands on her hips. 'She ain't poorly, is she? Lots of colds about fer springtime.'

'She's on honeymoon.' Lily trotted out a yarn, just as she'd promised she would if pressed to explain her best friend's absence. 'Quite a whirlwind affair, it was. Margie'd lost touch with this boy after leaving primary school. Anyway, they bumped into one another and got talking and it carried on from there.'

Eunice closed her dropped jaw. *'Margie's got married?'* she enunciated. 'And she never let Bobby *know* about it?'

'She didn't let anybody in on it. Well, I knew, but it was a spur-of-the-moment thing for them before he was posted. Just a quiet do with his family in Southend. She didn't want any fuss.' It certainly had surprised Lily when Margie laid out her plan to keep the gossips at bay. Lily understood why action was needed though.

'She's up the spout, ain't she? That's why she's married on the hurry-up.' Eunice smacked her hip in enlightenment. 'Well, I never did.'

'Shhh ... I'm saying nothing.' Lily pressed a finger to her lips. 'Margie'll tell you all about it in her own time, I expect. When she's back and swanning about as Mrs Green.'

'Mrs Green, eh? Fancy that.' Eunice shook her head. 'So

she's coming back then? Ain't staying down Southend way with her husband?'

'No point. He's already had his papers and is shipping out shortly. She'll be back at work next week. Now I've got to get going. It's non-stop when we're short-staffed.' At least *that* was the truth, Lily wryly thought, even if Margie was actually in North London and close enough to turn in for her shift at Wilding's costermongers. Instead, she was hiding out at a friend's place to give credibility to her make-believe marriage.

'Don't know whether to tell Bobby about this.' Eunice frowned. 'He'll start fretting about what's going on back home, I know he will. He needs to take care of himself.' She shook her head. 'Ain't just bombs and bullets they're up against now the swine are gassing our boys.'

Lily had been worried sick too, reading the reports of the Germans using chlorine gas to gain an advantage against the Allied troops. 'Might be best to skim over it in your letters for now. Let Margie break the news herself when he's back on leave, eh?'

'I always hoped Bobby would get together with Margie. Lost his chance now, though,' said Eunice dully.

Lily knew Margie had always longed for that to happen. But Smudger – as everybody called Bobby Smith, apart from his mother – had been besotted with somebody else, and that doomed affair had set in motion a horrible sequence of events.

'Oh, hark at me, should have enquired how you're doing,' Eunice tutted. 'How's your luck, Lily? Have you heard if your fiancé is getting leave so you two can tie the knot?'

'Greg hoped he might be back before Easter, but that's come and gone.' Lily sorted through the post every day, hoping to spot a letter from the man she loved, telling her to book the registry office now he had a date to sail.

'My Bobby's not been home once yet. Now bachelors are being called up, perhaps it'll give some of the serving Tommies a well-earned break.'

Lily smiled but didn't believe Eunice held out much hope of that coming to pass any more than she did. Things weren't going well for the Allies. Verdun, Albert, Artois were French towns known to every wife or mother who had menfolk stationed on the Western Front. A hint of an Allied victory was what families longed to hear about. What they got were notifications bearing regrets on having to inform them of a death; or conscription notices, because more men were needed to replace the mounting casualties.

'You keep your chin up, love, same as I'm trying to.' Bobby was Eunice's only child and the apple of her eye. She dreaded seeing an official-looking letter on her mat after the postman had been. 'I'll let you get on then. I know you're busy.' She trudged back the way she'd come.

Lily continued down the lane towards the High Street, mulling over their conversation. The constant worries about her fiancé and her brother, serving in France, were put from her mind. Her best friend's problems were more pressing right now.

Margie's fake news was out, and it would spread. Sooner or later it would have become obvious she was pregnant anyway. A baby wasn't something a woman could hide for ever, if she wanted to keep it. But a husband fighting in a war was a different matter. There was nothing implausible about a new bride being widowed when British Tommies were being buried on foreign soil every day, some with wives or children they'd only recently acquired and would never watch grow older. If Margie's tale held together, she would be treated with sympathy and respect rather than the insults directed at what some people considered the lowest of the low: an unmarried mother.

Lily reckoned whatever tale Margie told Smudger when he got back, he'd guess the truth. Margie was carrying her rapist's baby and it was just as well the monster was already dead because Smudger would have tried to kill him.

'Ah, yes. I have found the record. A general practitioner brought the child in with diphtheria, some months ago. Charlotte Finch had a severe fever then lapsed into a coma.' The hospital matron had read then summarised a long list of entries in a few sentences before returning the closed ledger to her desk. 'Your granddaughter has been very poorly indeed. She needed that long rest for her little body to fight off the infection.'

'Yes, Howes is my local doctor and obliged me by bringing Charlotte here on Christmas Eve.' Norman cleared his throat and turned his attention to the envelope clutched in his fingers. He pulled a piece of paper from it and held it out. 'This came for me yesterday, Sister. It says my granddaughter is finally on the mend. I'd like to see her, please.'

The matron took the letter and cast an eye over it that lingered at the faded signature haloed in grey. It appeared water had plopped upon the paper, making the ink run.

'Are you new, Sister? I haven't seen you here before.' Norman hoped being amiable might persuade this stern-faced woman to allow his visit, though he knew it was late. He'd wanted to drop everything and hurry over the moment the post turned up that morning, but there hadn't been an opportunity to slip away with the master making his presence known all day long.

'My predecessor volunteered to join the Royal Army Medical Corps.' The matron offered a tardy explanation for the regular nurse's absence and carried on reading.

'Ah, I see . . .' Norman responded politely.

'The consultant paediatrician sent this. He deems Charlotte well enough to be discharged in a couple of weeks . . . if there are no setbacks, of course. I see no reason for her grandfather not to be allowed to say a quick hello.' She raised an eyebrow. 'Earlier in the day would have been better, sir. But you may come with me.' The matron got to her feet and was soon out into the corridor.

'Work, you see . . .' Norman mumbled apologetically, hurrying behind the swishing skirts of the lithe woman striding noiselessly on parquet. He had a job keeping up with her on his sore, swollen feet. He felt excited yet anxious too, as though he'd just passed a first test. He hoped there'd be no more hoops to jump through before he was rewarded with a bedside visit with the little girl. After such a length of time, would Charlotte remember that he'd told her to call him her granddad? The poor girl could take fright and deny knowing him, and that would be closer to the truth than his claim that they were kin. The last thing he wanted was to cause a commotion, yet he ached to see her.

For several long months Norman had fretted Charlotte Finch would die and his conscience would never allow him peace. One child's death was a weighty burden to carry, but two? Impossible. Norman had seized every opportunity to visit the London Hospital, even though on each occasion he'd been told to go away because his granddaughter wasn't well enough for visitors. The closest he'd previously got to

Charlotte had been when the other nurse had taken pity on him. She'd ushered him through the corridors, pressing a finger against her lips whenever she turned to look over her shoulder at him. They'd stopped by a glass partition and he'd gazed at a small still figure lying beneath bedsheets on the other side. He'd not recognised the child and hadn't been allowed to loiter to search for something familiar in the gaunt grey face. Too soon the nurse seemed to regret what she'd done, and fearing the consequences she'd bundled him towards the exit with a promise that he would be informed when there was a change in Charlotte's condition. Yesterday, that promise had been kept. On reading the wonderful news, he'd wept, spoiling the letter. He'd felt ashamed afterwards because his relief had been as much for himself as for Charlotte Finch.

They passed through dull green painted corridors that smelled of cabbage-water and carbolic. Several pairs of doors were negotiated before the matron came to a stop by another set of doors upon which had been stencilled a colourful rainbow. She turned, raised her eyebrows to warn, 'Your granddaughter no longer needs to be isolated. This is the children's ward. She is greatly improved but still very weak.' Her thin lips twitched. 'She's obviously from robust stock, sir. I have witnessed healthy young adults succumb to lesser disease.'

'We are strong folk,' Norman croaked, licking his lips. 'Can I see her now?'

'Come in ... but stay calm and quiet. Children tend to get excited if they see a familiar face.'

Norman loosened his collar and the hat in his hands was rotated faster.

The matron led him forward, then positioned a chair

close to the bed. 'You may sit down by her side. You can have five minutes, then I'll be back.'

Norman did as he was told, his eyes on the pale oval face on the pillow. He did recognise her now, though her eyes and her cheeks were sunken. Her fair hair had been neatly looped into a topknot, to keep it out of the way, he imagined. He remembered having touched her pretty hair to soothe her. It had been cold and damp from the snow. She looked younger than the five years she'd told him she'd attained. 'Charlotte,' he croaked, taking her limp fragile fingers into his.

She opened her eyes and blinked at him, and for a moment Norman was terrified she might scream as she stared and stared with eyes that looked huge and black. He started to draw his fingers from hers and elevate his buttocks as though to quickly get up and leave, but she gripped at him with surprising strength.

'Do you remember me?' he whispered, hovering.

Her chin was dropped to touch the sheet in response.

He relaxed onto the seat and gave her a tentative smile. 'I'm Granddad ...' he said hoarsely.

She gave another nod to let him know she remembered. 'Come to take me home.'

'Soon ... when the doctor says so.' He squeezed her fingers, overcome with emotion. 'It's all going to be fine now, my love,' he gurgled. 'I promise.' He rubbed the back of her hand with clumsy arthritic fingers, then laid it back on the sheet. He stood up and hobbled outside before the sob closing his throat burst from him.

Chapter Two

July 1916

'You could be in for a long haul, my gel. This baby's coming arse first.' Sally Ransome's comment was addressed to the expectant mum, but the poor girl was rigid with pain and couldn't unclench her teeth to respond.

The worst of the contraction had passed and Lily managed to slip her hand free of her friend's frantic grip. She got up from her chair at the side of the bed and hurried over to speak to Sally.

Presently, she was donning a clean overall pulled from her bag of tricks. Other midwifery paraphernalia was contained within, yet to be revealed, but a rubber sheet, and a bar of carbolic soap had already emerged and been put to use. On turning up, Sally had immediately demanded a bowl of hot water to scrub her hands with the carbolic. Thereafter, she'd examined Margie, giving her verdict on the state of play. Once that was done, Lily had helped the handywoman ease the protective cover beneath her groaning friend. The gravel-voiced stranger had come properly prepared and apparently knowing what she was doing, despite the fact she didn't resemble any nurse Lily had ever met. The women who had staffed the workhouse infirmary had all been starchy, with little to say for themselves, unlike Sally.

'What d'you mean . . . arse first?' Lily hissed, wide-eyed. She'd started to relax but, sensing a hitch, her jitters had returned. For all Sally's cheerful tone, the woman was pursing her lips, contemplating a hard task in front of her.

'Baby's coming out the wrong way round.' Sally carried on rolling up her sleeves while explaining. 'Usually a woman drops a baby head first, but this one's letting the world know what it thinks of it.' She puffed a sigh, turning serious. 'I'm not going to try and turn the blighter round the right way. So it's a bit more of a to-do than a regular birth. Your friend's young and strong, and that's the main thing at times like this.' Sally glanced at Margie, fidgeting in discomfort. 'Just as well you fetched me when you did though. Breech delivery ain't the sort of thing a gel should have to deal with on her own. 'Specially when it's her first, and she's not got much of a clue what's going on.'

Lily nodded vigorously. Neither did *she* have much of a clue of what was going on. They wouldn't have gone to work at the crack of dawn if they'd an inkling of what was about to unfold shortly before midday. At seventeen years old and without mothers or older sisters to advise them about pregnancies and babies, Lily and Margie had had to rely on female friends telling them what to prepare for. Eunice Smith had given Lily the name and address of the local 'handywoman' and instructions to fetch Sally Ransome when Margie started feeling worse pains than the sort that came once a month. Sally wasn't officially a midwife: she delivered babies for working-class women unable to afford qualified medical attention. But she'd learned her trade from her mother, who'd nursed with Florence Nightingale at Scutari; a fact Sally would often proudly drop into a conversation. Today, she didn't feel like boasting and had told Lily she'd need her on standby for this and that when the real business started.

Lily reckoned it might be wise to find Sally an assistant who'd at least some experience of what was going on. Eunice was a mother herself and was sure to oblige, if asked to help. Lily voiced her suggestion quietly, so Margie wouldn't know she was nervous. Margie had always looked to her to be the strong one in a crisis and she didn't want to let her best friend know she wasn't feeling equal to such blind faith today.

Childbirth scared Lily. She might not understand all the intricacies of it, but she knew how difficult and dangerous bringing a baby into the world could be. Her beloved mother had lost her life giving birth to Lily's half-sister. For years, Lily had believed the little girl had also perished on that bed in the Whitechapel infirmary. Only later had it come to light that lies had been told to conceal a scandal. Her sister had survived, and Lily had been on her trail ever since.

But Lily refused to be distracted by her own worries right now. Her best friend was on the brink of becoming a mother and Lily prayed that whatever was to come ended safely and happily.

'Good idea, love, about fetching Eunice.' The handywoman had broken off rummaging in her bag to accept Lily's offer to recruit a mature pair of hands. 'I'll need plenty more hot water. Would you put some on to boil before disappearing down the road? I could do with some clean rags 'n' all. And if you've got a stack of old newspapers, fetch 'em; those'll be handy keeping the place tidy. There'll be a mess; nothing unusual about that. So don't panic when you see blood.' Sally gave a snuff-coloured smile. She had a pleasant face and a mop of incongruously blonde curls for a woman whose lined complexion put her age at more than fifty.

'If you take a look in that bottom drawer, you'll find sheets and nappies and a cotton baby gown. I've been saving up old newspapers for months. I'll get those.' Lily was thankful that Eunice had given them an idea of what to stock up on.

'Good gel, that'll save you some mopping later.' Sally ran a critical eye over the bedroom. 'Glad to see you keep the place clean and cosy. And well done for getting your friend back home. Wouldn't have liked trying to deal with a breech delivery in Wilding's warehouse.'

'Lucky I've got the van.' Lily rolled her eyes in horror at the prospect of having supported Margie walking home while the girl was racked with cramps. She'd got her friend into the vehicle's passenger seat then driven home at speed. Margie's contractions had been more spaced out then and Lily had used the intervals between to help her friend descend the basement steps to the flat. Once inside, she'd got Margie undressed and into her nightie, trying to keep their spirits up all the while with chatter. After Margie had settled in bed, Lily had raced to ask Sally to come as soon as she could. The handywoman had turned up close on Lily's heels, banging on the door within a matter of fifteen minutes.

'Why's the baby coming early?' Lily whispered. 'Margie's been fine up until now. We worked it out she still had weeks to go.'

'Babies make up their own minds when they've had enough time inside Mum. Or perhaps your friend got her dates wrong.' Sally patted her arm. 'Don't make no difference now, love. You get on with boiling up the kettle then rope in Eunice if she's about.' Sally crossed her arms. 'Ain't much to do now but wait for nature to take its course.' She delved into a pocket and withdrew a tin of snuff, sprinkling it onto the back of a fat hand then snorting. 'Get off me feet for a bit and store up me energy for later.' Sally sank into the chair by the bed, wafting her skirt up and down. 'Bleedin' hot day for all this running about.' She stretched out one stout leg then the other, displaying feet encased in sturdy boots.

Lily hurried into the kitchen and turned on the tap. She paced impatiently to and fro, nibbling on her thumbnail while waiting for the water to stop spurting and increase flow so she could swap one filled pot in the sink for an empty one. As soon as the kettle was brimming, she put it onto the stove. Then she carried on prowling the small kitchen, inwardly thanking her lucky stars that Margie hadn't been on her own when her pains started. But for a loose cartwheel needing attention, Joey Robley would have been at Chrisp Street market at that time of the day rather than at the depot. Lily had immediately abandoned the market stall when he hared up to garble out that Margie had real bad bellyache and needed help. Lily had left Joey and Eric Skipman running the show between them. She'd sped back to base in the van with her heart in her mouth and it hadn't yet returned to its proper place. Excitement and joy were mingling with her anxiety: her best friend was having a baby. A new life was almost here. When the panic was over and Margie held her baby in her arms, they would have a celebration.

Lily returned to the bedroom carrying a tin bowl filled with steaming water. She was greeted by a wail from Margie that wiped the determined smile from her face.

'Oh, no! I've wet meself.' Margie fell back against the pillows, embarrassed at having soaked her nightdress.

'No, you haven't. Don't worry about that, love.' Sally pushed the girl's fair hair back out of her eyes. 'I knew to bring that rubber draw sheet, see, for when this happened. Everything's as it should be and you're doing just fine. Baby's been having a swim in a bubble inside of yer belly. He don't need that water now, so out it comes.' Sally beckoned Lily. 'Things are moving again, so keep the hot water coming, soon as you can.'

'Where you going, Lil?' Margie's plaintive call stopped her friend bolting from the room. Margie lifted her head off the pillow, her terrified gaze on Lily. She struggled up onto her elbows. 'Is something wrong with me baby? You would tell me, wouldn't you?'

Lily scooted back to the bedside to make her lie down. 'Hush . . . you heard what Mrs Ransome said: you're doing fine.' She raised her eyes and received a reassuring nod from the midwife. 'Won't have too long to wait now, and you'll have your beautiful baby, Marge, then you'll think all this hard work's worth it. Probably won't even remember having these pains tomorrow.'

'Feel like I'm gonna die though, Lil . . .' Margie moaned.

'Enough o' that now.' Sally chucked Margie under the chin. 'You wait till your husband gets home on leave and sees his little 'un. Be so proud of you, he will.'

Lily gave her friend a fiercely encouraging smile. Worrying about gossip and the sham of a non-existent husband seemed like so much nonsense now. A healthy infant at a blissful Margie's side was the only thing that mattered. Her friend had a deformed right hand and ever since Margie discovered she was pregnant she'd fretted that her unborn baby might be similarly afflicted. 'I'd better get some more hot water on the go to help Mrs Ransome, love. Be all over and done with even sooner then, and next time I put the kettle on it'll be for a nice cup of tea.' Lily dropped a kiss on her friend's sweaty brow then determinedly quit the room. She headed towards the front door, not the kitchen. That senior pair of hands was urgently required and Lily hoped she would find Eunice in.

Lily was flying along the lane when she suddenly heard her name called by a familiar male voice. She twisted about, open-mouthed, squinting into shimmering July heat at the approaching figure. 'Smudger!' The very person she had been thinking about had materialised at the very moment she was heading to knock on his mother's door.

'Where you off to in such a rush?' He broke into a trot, and on reaching her side, gave her a peck on the cheek. 'Not got a smile for your old pal then? I've just been to the warehouse looking for you. It was all locked up, so I headed to Chrisp Street. Joey and the new foreman was on the stall; nice and busy they was too, so I left 'em to it rather than get in the way. Joey said Margie had the bellyache and had gone home. Eaten a bad shrimp or something, has she?' Having rattled that lot off, he barely paused before starting again, leaving Lily little time to get a word in edgeways. Not that she had a clue what to say to him, anyway. 'Gotta watch them dealers in Billingsgate, y'know. Ain't unusual for 'em to freshen up yesterday's catch.' He emphasised his point with a finger wag. 'This new lad, Eric Skipman, he knows the ropes when he's buying stock, does he? Noticed he's got good sales patter, but that's only half of it. Your skipper needs to be savvy dealing with the wholesalers, 'specially during the summer months cos stuff's soon on the turn.' Smudger had been the best foreman a costermonger could hope to employ and had every right to sound territorial about his old job, and knowledgeable about the market sharks and their scams and dodges.

Lily nodded, feeling dazed by his untimely arrival. She unstuck her tongue from the roof of her dry mouth to garble, 'Yeah . . . Eric's learning fast . . . he's a good foreman.'

'Drat. Was hoping you was all really missing me,' he said, mock-solemn.

''Course we're missing you,' said Lily. 'Missing every one of you and wishing you back home for good.'

'Brought you a letter from the guv'nor.' Smudger still called his old boss 'guv'nor', though over a year had passed since Gregory Wilding was running his costermonger business. His teenage fiancée had taken over and the general opinion was that Lily Larkin was doing a damn good job of it, too.

'Oh, thanks . . .' Finally Lily had something to really smile about. 'I've been waiting on the post. I've not had a word from Davy in weeks.'

'Don't worry; he'll be up to his old tricks somewhere.' Smudger knew Lily adored her twin, toerag that he was.

Lily would have liked to hear whether Smudger had bumped into her brother recently, but there was no time for questions. She hurried on down the lane with, 'Sorry . . . I'm in a bit of a rush, Smudger. Catch up with you later . . .' She feared that explanation wouldn't satisfy him or send him on his way.

'Where you off to?' Smudger pursued her.

'I'm looking for your mum,' Lily rattled off. It was lovely to see him, but excruciating bad luck that he had turned up right now. As she looked him over properly, it suddenly struck her why he was back home and she halted again. 'You've been injured!'

'Got a bit of a shrapnel hole in me back.' He explained the reason for wearing hospital blue uniform rather than his regular khaki.

'Oh, no! How bad is it?' Lily shot him an assessing look.

'All bandaged up under me shirt. The doc's a good sort; he don't keep us all cooped up in hospital. Been back in Blighty over a week and convalescing over Highgate way in a big house. But don't tell me mum that. She'll tear me off a strip for not coming by sooner. I wanted to be well on the mend first instead of frightening the life out of her. You know what a worrier my mother is.'

Lily couldn't see a way to avoid telling him she was in the midst of an emergency without resorting to blatant deceit. She felt too fog-brained and jumpy to even concoct any lies. Besides, this crisis involved Smudger too, because in a way he was responsible for what had happened to Margie.

'Reckon they'll be sending me back again in a week or two, now it's all kicking off round the Somme.' He quickly brightened up, not wanting to worry Lily. Her brother and her fiancé were right in the thick of it over there and he didn't relish having questions fired at him about how bad things had got. 'How are you, Lil? You've not got dodgy guts 'n' all, have yer?'

'No ... I'm fine. Nothing wrong with me.' Lily burst out, 'Look, Smudger, I can't stop for a proper chat now. I really need to speak to your mum straight away.' She charged up to Eunice's door.

'Well, you're wasting your time knocking. I've already tried. The old lady upstairs called out of her window that she's at the Women's Institute for the afternoon. Probably knitting socks or making jam for the troops ...' Smudger tailed off, frowning. Lily wouldn't be looking that disappointed if she was only stopping by for a chat. 'What's up? You don't seem your usual self, Lil.'

Smudger wasn't daft and neither was he inconsequential. He was the first friend Lily had made on the outside after leaving the workhouse. He'd always been kind and loyal, even if a while ago he had unwisely let his heart rule his head. Lily understood why Margie had fallen for him and why her best friend had been distraught to discover Smudger was besotted with a married woman.

'It's Margie ... she's having a baby, Smudger.' Lily sighed in defeat. 'The midwife's with her right now cos her labour's started. Mrs Ransome could do with some extra help, so I came to get Eunice ...' Lily hadn't finished her explanation when Smudger began running up the road towards the flat.

She yelled at him to stop and when he ignored her she sprinted to drag on his arm. 'Now calm down, or you'll make things worse, not better,' she panted. 'Margie's in a state as it is.' Lily hung on to him as he tried to wriggle free. 'Now you listen to me. I don't think she'll want to see you right now. Don't complicate things for her, please. She can't cope with any more.'

'I wondered if this might happen,' he croaked, shoving his fingers through his hair. 'When she never said nothing I thought to meself, thank Christ for that. That bastard ain't left any loose ends need tying. Every last memory of what he did's buried with him, that's what I thought.' He threw

40

back his head and growled in despair. 'Why ain't she ever said? She should've told me.'

'Why d'you think she never said?' Lily returned shortly. She lowered her voice, conscious of windows flung open on this balmy afternoon. 'Not something any girl is going to shout about, is it? Being knocked up by the man who raped her is something to forget, not to broadcast. She didn't want anybody to know.'

'I'm not anybody!' he roared. 'It's my fault! I'd've helped her with money if she'd asked. She only needed to ask.'

'I'd've helped her if it'd come to that,' Lily hissed. She put a finger to her mouth and jerked her eyes to a face looking at them out of an open sash. She dragged on his elbow, moving him on. 'She didn't want to go down that route.' Lily couldn't even utter the word abortion on a day like this, with the new life imminent. 'Margie wanted her baby,' she continued quietly. 'It is *her* baby. The father ... well, he's gone. And Margie's husband ... he's a dead war hero, name of Danny Green. Remember that, if anybody asks. Mrs Marjory Green is gonna do just fine bringing up her little 'un by herself.'

'We'll see about that.' Smudger started off again and this time Lily couldn't catch him up. She'd left the door on the latch and she was fearful he'd barge in, but he stopped and waited for her by the railings when he reached the flat.

'Come on then, if you're coming . . .' With a defeated shrug she led him down the steps. 'Stay quiet though ... don't let her know you're here. Not sure how she'll feel about it. And I'm not asking her either at a time like this. Margie's got to concentrate on what she's supposed to be doing, not fretting about you showing up out of the blue.' Lily blurted to him the *really* bad news. 'Thing is, the midwife said the baby's the wrong way round.'

Smudger's eyes widened in anxiety. 'Sounds bad. Margie's gonna be all right, isn't she?'

''Course she is.' She beckoned him into the quiet hallway. Lily's hopes that a miracle had happened and everything had been done and dusted while she'd been outside evaporated when a protracted groan issued from the bedroom. She bundled Smudger past the bedroom door and into the kitchen to prevent him bursting in. 'You stay in here and boil up pots of water and I'll do what I can to help Mrs Ransome take care of Margie.' She took up position on the threshold as he tried to dodge past into the corridor. 'You'll be in the way in there. You can help by getting the midwife the hot water.' Lily pointed at the pots stacked in the sink. 'All those need to be filled and put on the stove. Plenty to keep you busy.'

After checking over her shoulder to make sure he hadn't followed her, she stopped outside the bedroom. Part of her wished she could swap places with Smudger and stay in the kitchen, and it made her feel like a coward. Her face was damp with perspiration from having been dashing about. Using her pinafore, she dried her face and clammy palms. Then, taking a deep breath and pinning a smile to her lips, she opened the door.

Chapter Three

'Men ain't allowed! Get out of here! Your wife don't want you seeing her like this.' Sally Ransome had heard the door creak and whipped a glance over her shoulder. Once she'd overcome her astonishment at the sight of a young soldier hovering in the doorway, she'd scrambled to her feet and given him a blast. Childbirth was women's work and men had no business poking their noses in. Usually husbands were more than happy to pace about outside or hide in the pub with pals until summoned home to proudly admire the new addition to the family.

Lily hadn't noticed him either until then; she'd been too busy trying to encourage Margie to dredge up a little more energy. The poor girl was all in, yet things were far from finished. Thankfully, Margie wasn't yet aware of his presence. She had her eyes screwed up and an agonised expression contorting her face. Her harsh panting was echoing around Lily's head as she sent Smudger a furious look. Until that moment he'd observed her rule to stay out of sight, boiling water and leaving the pots by the door so that she could bring them inside as needed. But she knew why he'd burst in. Margie was really struggling now to push the baby out. Her groans had become more guttural and Lily was terrified that Margie might die in labour, as Lily's own mother had.

'Can't stay outside when she's crying like that,' Smudger sheepishly mumbled. 'It's driving me mad. There must be something I can do to help . . .'

Margie blinked open eyes that were stinging with mingling tears and sweat. She stared at him, trying to lift her head as though to improve her vision. Her head dropped back to the soaked pillow and her parched lips formed his name.

It was all the permission Smudger needed to step closer.

'Get up there and hold her hand then,' Sally growled, jerking a nod to the head of the bed. 'Only women allowed down the business end of things during a labour. You've done your bit, son, now I'm trying to sort it out.' Sally wasn't larking. She was red-faced and sweating, supporting an exhausted Margie to try and facilitate the delivery.

Smudger meekly did as he was told, whipping past to crouch at the side of the bed. He took one of Margie's hands, smoothing her damp fair hair out of her eyes. 'You all right then, Margie?' he croaked, then grimaced at having spoken baloney.

Lily found him a smile. He was as apprehensive as she was, and doing his best to be of use, as she was. If Margie was embarrassed at him seeing her like this, she was past showing it. She wanted him with her, that was obvious; the girl had tightly gripped his fingers the moment he touched her hand.

'Come on . . . you can do this, you know,' Smudger blurted. 'Gel like you can do anything. I know how strong you are, don't I?' He raised their joined fingers and clumsily kissed them. 'I want this baby, Margie. Honestly I do. We're gonna be a family. The three of us together. Soon as you're up 'n' about we'll be married – if you'll have me, that is. You'll let me take care of you now this has happened, won't you?'

Though his words had been muffled against Margie's forehead, Lily had heard the gist of his frantic proposal. She was primed to spring up and drag him out of the room if any of it upset Margie.

Lily relaxed as Margie gave a weary nod. 'Glad yer back safe, Smudge . . .' she panted, giving him his answer.

'Now when I say push, love, you give it all you've got.' Sally raised her eyes from Margie's nether regions to instruct the expectant mum. 'Baby's on its way. I can see its bum now and you need to be brave cos it might hurt a bit while I'm helping you get the little 'un's legs out. But when I say don't push, then you take a breather.'

'I can't push . . .' Margie gasped. 'I'm done in.'

'Yes, you can. Come on, Margie. I've got yer back.' Smudger gently raised her off the pillow, wedging himself behind her to support her sagging shoulders against his body.

Lily quit her chair at the bedside the moment Sally jerked her head, indicating she needed her.

'Take your friend's leg, love, while I give her a bit of help. Need to hook me fingers over baby's legs in there . . .' she broke off as Margie undulated with another contraction. 'That's what we want,' Sally puffed out in encouragement. 'Mother Nature doing some of the hard work and saving new mum the job.'

Lily swiftly took the weight of one of Margie's legs. Earlier she had helped Sally shift Margie down the bed so her posterior was over the edge. The handywoman had assured her that it would help with a complicated delivery like this. Lily hadn't understood how it would, when it looked so uncomfortable, but she'd done as she'd been told. She and Margie had no option but to put their faith in this woman.

Sally's face was a study of intense concentration as she struggled to dislodge the tiny limbs as gently as she could. 'No pushing yet!' Sally shouted as Margie instinctively bore down.

When seated up the other end, Lily hadn't seen what Sally had been doing. Neither had she wanted to. Now she had no option but to watch. She gawped in fascination as tiny shiny buttocks then legs appeared. Then Margie grunted and yelled as another contraction took hold and the purplish body slid out, leaving only the shoulders and head to be born. Lily gulped in awe. It was a baby girl.

'Don't tell her yet,' Sally snapped below her breath. She had interpreted Lily's muted squeak. 'We ain't there yet. Just make it worse if you tell her and ... you know.'

Margie had no idea how far advanced things were. But Smudger's unblinking stare was on Lily, begging for reassurance. She gave a slight nod and an excited smile before turning her attention back to Sally.

'Shoulders out next, then the head,' Sally rumbled. She was kneeling on the floor close to Margie but she sat back on her heels with a grimace; she'd been stuck in the same position for so long she was in pain herself. 'Hand us one of those nice big bits of linen. Need something to hold baby in. Slippery as an eel, she is.'

Lily grabbed at a folded cloth that was within reach and quickly handed it over.

'Here we are, little 'un,' crooned Sally, wrapping the infant's body in the clean linen that was soon spotted with red. It was barely in time too. Sally slightly rotated the tiny body and the shoulders appeared. 'Right now, Margie. You're almost done, my gel. If you want to hold this baby in your arms real soon, you need to give me a bloody big push when you get another pain.'

'I'm past it ...' Margie panted. 'Can't ...'

Smudger squeezed her hand and bolstered her sagging torso. 'Right, one more go ... come on ... don't give up now. Be holding him any minute now, you will.'

'Her ... be holding *her*,' Lily said, ignoring Sally's warning frown. 'You've got a little girl, Margie. I can see your daughter. She's almost here and she's beautiful. I can see every little finger and toe and they're all perfect.'

Margie pushed.

Lily was crouching against the wall with her face cupped in her shaking hands.

'Bleedin' hell, buck up,' said Sally. 'Anybody'd think it was you been through the mill instead of your friend.'

Lily sniffed a laugh then raised her eyes to the couple huddled together on the bed. They were gazing at the swaddled infant cradled in Margie's arms.

'Only joking, love; you coped very well with that.' Sally patted Lily's shoulder. 'Comes as a bit of a shock, eh, finding out that a gooseberry bush ain't the answer.'

Lily choked an indignant giggle. 'I'm not quite that dumb ... I am a complete wreck, though,' she admitted, shuffling her back against the wall until she'd pushed herself upright. 'Not sure I'll be having any kids after that experience.'

'Oh, you will,' Sally ruefully said. '"Never, no more," we all say after the first. Then the old man gets flirty and a

couple of months later, a gel's up the spout again and knitting bonnets.' She smirked. 'I've got seven and me mother,
God rest her, had twelve kids. Two of 'em was breech birth.
I reckon your friend'll have a brood round her ankles in a
few years. This'll be forgotten in a month's time when she's
knee-deep in dirty nappies and cracked nipples.'

'Thank God it's over, though,' Lily murmured.

'Yeah.' Sally rolled her eyes. 'I wasn't sure we'd be as
happy as we are. Leave it at that.' She glanced proudly at
the perfect consequence of all her hard work. 'That babe's a
smasher, lovely mop of fair hair and ain't wrinkled at all. If
she was premature, it wasn't by much. Mother used to say
her first breech come out looking like a pensioner.' Sally
pulled a screwed-up, gummy face, making Lily chuckle.
'Big handsome brute now, my brother.' Sally resumed stuffing equipment into her bag. 'Anyway, could be the next'll
be a piece o' cake for your friend. She was lucky; not much
damage to her undercarriage, if you get me drift, so she'll
be on her feet pretty quick.'

Lily spontaneously hugged the woman. 'Thank you for
everything you did for her.'

'Only doing me job; though don't mind telling you this
one did give me the shakes.' Sally held out a hand to show
it still quivering. 'Nerves can be a good thing ... keeps
you sharp, see. Don't take nuthin' fer granted.' She gently
elbowed herself free of Lily's embrace. 'Good pals, eh, you
'n' Mrs Green?' Sally was chuffed by that affectionate display of gratitude, but trying not to show it.

'Been like sisters since we was eleven.'

'Can tell you're close like that.' Sally jerked a nod at
Smudger. 'Nice timing, Mr Green turning up when he did,
giving her a boost.'

'He's not Mr Green and she's not really Mrs Green,' Lily informed the handywoman impishly.

'Yeah, I know, love. Seen a few brass curtain rings on gels' fingers in me time. He seems decent, whoever he is.'

'He's Mr Smith ...' Lily said, and suddenly burst out laughing ... letting all the pent-up emotion flow from her in guffaw after guffaw until her eyes were wet with mirth.

Sally joined in, chuckling and rumbling beneath her breath, 'Funny that; most of the unmarried gels I see to *do* seem to be called Mrs Smith.'

'And Margie Blake really will be ... cos Smudger really is Mr Smith and he's asked her to marry him. You heard him, didn't you?'

'Witness here, if she needs one,' said Sally drolly, starting Lily off giggling again.

'That's better; gets it out of your system, having a good laugh or a good cry.'

Lily sighed, a long-drawn-out whistle of contentment and relief. 'Right, time to put that kettle on and have a lovely cup of tea.' She saw Margie was smiling quizzically at her, probably wondering what she'd found so hilarious. 'You ready for your tea now, Margie?'

The new mum nodded, serene as could be.

'You will stay for a cuppa, won't you?'

'Thanks all the same, but I've brought me own refreshment.' Sally drew out a small bottle of gin from her bag and gave a wink. 'Want a livener?'

Lily shook her head. 'I wondered what else you had in there,' she teased.

'All me trade essentials, love. Can't do me job without 'em.' Sally patted her bag then took a glug of gin and smacked her lips. 'Not just for drinking. Spirits are standby disinfectant. Been known to sluice me hands in gin. Not that I like to waste it.' She screwed the lid back on the bottle before slipping it out of sight. 'Right now, me 'usband'll want his tea before long, so I'll get finished up and leave you all in peace.' She turned to Margie, giving her a business-like assessment and her jollity faded. 'She's gonna struggle a bit, fastening nappies with that crippled hand of hers.'

'No, she won't,' Lily differed, sounding proud. 'Margie used to nursemaid our friend's little lad and could change him as fast as I could.'

Sally looked impressed to hear that. 'You need a bit of a freshen-up, missus,' she said to Margie. 'After that we'll have a talk about when baby needs feeding and I'll show you how to hold her to give her a tin bowl bath, too. That all right with proud dad, is it? Unless he'd like to stop and learn about changing dirty nappies and using the breast pump ...'

Smudger shot to his feet. Blushing, he dropped a kiss on Margie's head and sloped off outside the bedroom.

'You staying, Lil?' Margie had watched her friend stacking up the empty water pots before heading for the door with them.

'I'll leave you to it now, Margie, and get that kettle on.' Lily knew Margie had to do the rest by herself. A small gap in their attachment had opened up and it would keep on widening. It was for the best. Margie was now a mother ... soon to be a wife. In the blink of an eye, Lily had lost her place as the most important person in Margie's life. And she was happy about it. 'When I come back though, can I have a cuddle of that little darling?'

Margie nodded. 'Thanks for everything, Lil,' she said softly, her eyes on the sleeping bundle in her arms.

''S'nothing, do it all again ... if I had to,' she finished

wryly. 'Bet you could do with some biscuits to dunk, couldn't you, after all that hard work?'

Margie didn't look up; she was deaf to all but the contented snuffling of her daughter.

Lily found Smudger sitting outside on the steps that led up to the lane, smoking.

She perched on the tread below him, staring at him until he met her eyes. His reluctance to talk or to look up was worrying her. 'You meant what you said, didn't you, about getting married?'

'Yeah ...' He hung his head again, flicking ash. 'If she'd told me sooner about the baby, I'd've asked her sooner.'

'You'll be happy together.'

The smile he gave her was fleeting. He was fidgeting and she could guess what he had on his mind.

'How am I ever going to love *his* kid, Lil?' Smudger sounded tormented. 'Somebody else's ... maybe, but *his*?'

'It's not his kid. Told you that. It's Margie's ... and yours. You're now that little girl's dad and you'll do right by them both, I know you will.' She took his hand, idle on his knee. 'So proud of you for what you did in there. You being with Margie made all the difference. I knew you'd step up and make things right.'

'Things *ain't* right, that's the problem. Not for me.' He pulled his hand free of hers and ground out the stub of his cigarette beneath a boot. He immediately lit another, offering the pack to Lily. She took one, though she rarely smoked. Despite the wonderful outcome, it was taking her a while to unwind; she needed something to calm her and wished she'd taken a swig of Sally's gin.

'You're a good bloke, Smudger,' Lily said carefully; she could tell he was struggling to control his agitation.

'Yeah ... good old Smudger,' he mimicked sourly, and struck a match to light their Woodbines.

'Don't say it like that,' she gently chided. 'Margie's got her pride and if she thinks you've just lied to her about wanting to be a family, she'll not make you go through with it.'

'Said I'll marry her, didn't I?' he said harshly, then shoved a hand across his eyes. 'Sorry ...' He jerked his head to gaze up at the peaceful summer sky. ''Course I want to marry her and do the right thing. This is all my fault, I know that, and I'll do me duty, best I can. Just can't get me head round it all yet.'

'It's bound to have come as a shock.'

'That's an understatement,' he muttered. 'What a bleedin' welcome home this is. Ain't even said hello to me mum yet, and now I've got to start off by telling her these sorts of lies.'

'I've already had to tell her some,' Lily returned bluntly. 'Just before Margie's bump started to show, I had to make up stories about Margie getting wed in Southend after a whirlwind romance. Now I've got to admit it was all baloney.'

'What's happened to this "husband" of hers?'

'Danny Green went off to France to fight and got killed.' Lily exhaled smoke.

''Course he did,' Smudger said.

Lily shrugged at his sarcasm. 'No option but to create a fantasy in the circumstances. Margie would've got spat at and insulted when none of this was her fault. I backed her to the hilt on it. And I'd do it all again if I had to ... lie to anyone I had to.' She sent him a challenging look, daring him to disagree.

'Yeah, I know; you did the right thing.'

Smudger, like most people, was well aware of the abuse unmarried mothers received ... often from their own families. It wasn't unheard of for parents who didn't have the means to hush up a scandal to disown a pregnant daughter rather than bear the shame. Some of the girls got dumped in the workhouse, if the father couldn't be forced to accept his responsibility. A foundling hospital might accept the infant to give a fallen woman a chance to redeem herself – but only if the mother met their criteria of appearing suitably contrite. She might go on to marry and have a family. The innocent children left behind, if not forgotten, would be stigmatised as bastards throughout their lives.

'I s'pose the guv'nor knows about this, does he?'

'Yeah ... he knows. I don't want secrets between us.' Lily allowed herself a thought of Gregory Wilding that softened her strained expression.

'Just muggins 'ere been kept in the dark then, even though it's me who's expected to pick up the pieces.'

Lily could feel her temper rising at his attitude. Now the threat to Margie's life had passed, Smudger seemed to be brooding on his own predicament. 'Margie didn't want you to know about the baby and feel guilty or under any obligation to her. She might have been in the wrong place at the wrong time, but she didn't deserve what that monster did to her.' Lily controlled her rising voice in case Margie heard what was going on. Her friend adored Smudger and had tried to protect him from being hurt, but she was the one entitled to sympathy. 'You haven't got a clue what Margie's been through, have you?' Lily grabbed his chin, making him look at her. 'I'm not just talking about *that*.' She snapped a nod at the flat where Margie had battled to give birth. 'I'm talking about the whole damn lot that she's suffered. If you'd stayed away from a married woman, none of it would have happened.'

Smudger jerked his face free and hung his head. 'I know ... I know,' he muttered between gritted teeth, pressing thumb and forefinger to his watering eyes. 'I'll think of something to tell me mum. It'll be all right.' He sniffed. 'She's always said she'd like grandkids. Well, now she's landed with one she weren't expecting.'

'Eunice told me she would've liked you two to get together.' Lily persevered in trying to ease the bitterness out of him.

'Yeah ... she told me the same thing.' He turned his head away to take a hefty drag on his cigarette and blow smoke.

Lily felt depressed on hearing that. So he'd known his mum would've welcomed Margie Blake as a daughter-in-law. Even that hadn't prompted Smudger to see Margie as a girlfriend rather than a pal. He was fond of her and felt a duty towards her, but he didn't love Margie in the way she loved him. Smudger seemed to be still mooning over a dead woman. Claudette Scully's thug of a husband had found out about her cheating and got revenge on his rival by raping the woman he'd taken for Smudger's girlfriend; a person with a crippled hand who couldn't fight him off. The Scullys were both dead now, but the consequences of Smudger's ill-starred love affair lived on.

'What the hell am I supposed to do if the baby grows up looking like Scully?'

'She won't. She's fair, like Margie. Anyhow, what matters is that she won't have his character because she'll have good people bringing her up. You'll dote on her, you'll see.'

'Maybe ... I don't know.' He shook his head but seemed less angry than before. 'So ... what the hell comes next ...' he sighed.

'First off, start thinking of some girl's names.' Lily took

over before he started wallowing in self-pity again. 'Margie wouldn't choose a name. She said it'd be bad luck to do that too soon, but reckon she'd like it if you made a few suggestions. Second off, buy a wedding ring. Margie'll be back on her feet in about a week. Mrs Ransome said she won't need a lengthy rest, and knowing Margie she'll fidget to get out of bed.' Lily took a final drag on her cigarette then stood up, about to drop the stub and go and make the tea she'd promised Margie. She gazed along the lane and spotted a marching figure; immediately she sank back down so her face was again level with Smudger's. 'Third off … get your story straight. Your mum's on her way. Looks like she's heard from her neighbour that you're back and have been looking for her. She would have guessed you'd head here next.'

Smudger shoved the hair out of his eyes and took a final furious drag on his Woodbine. 'Just my sodding luck!' he exploded. 'I could do without seeing her right now.'

'You could start off by buttering her up … tell her she should give her best dress a brush off, cos next week she's going to a wedding.'

He wasn't in the mood for light-heartedness and continued scowling.

'Might be best to go and meet your mum rather than do your explaining when she gets here,' Lily suggested. 'Margie'll want a bit of notice before Eunice demands to see her granddaughter. With any luck you'll have some breathing space, anyhow.' Lily straightened his red tie, part of a casualty's uniform. 'I reckon the first thing your mother'll want to know is why you've turned up dressed in hospital blues when you've never written to tell her you've been injured. Could be you're in for a tongue-lashing, Smudge.'

With that, Lily hurried down the steps. She had no more advice to give. Smudger had set in motion a tragedy when he made his bed with another man's wife. Now he had to lie on it, hard as he might find it. In Lily's opinion, he was lucky to have Margie in his life, loving him the way she did without rancour or blame. He'd been played for a fool by Claudette Scully. The Belgian woman hadn't loved her spouse or Smudger; she'd given her heart to a fellow refugee who was later accused of murdering her husband. Margie was aware of all of this ... yet she'd not criticised Smudger for making a mess of his life – and hers. She'd dealt with her heartache in a quiet way.

Put in her friend's position, Lily doubted she'd have managed to be so gracious and forgiving. She'd often wondered if more had gone on in that love triangle than she'd been told about. She couldn't complain about Margie keeping secrets, though, when she had her own skeletons locked in the cupboard. Even her brother knew nothing about those. But Gregory Wilding did, and she knew she could trust him with her life just as he could trust her, until their dying days.

Chapter Four

November 1916
Western Front, France

'Who's that fellow over there? The private with fair hair, digging the grave.'

'I believe I heard somebody call him Wilding, sir. Have you an interest in him?'

'I believe so, Barnett. Fetch him. And the stocky man with him ... ginger hair. I'd like to talk to them both.'

'Yes, sir.' Sergeant Barnett gave a stiff salute then marched off wondering what in damnation was wrong with the fool to want to stop a burial party in full swing for a chinwag. In all probability, Major Powley had nothing vital to say. He often patted un-pipped biceps in the belief it made him popular with the rank and file. It didn't; the working class resented being patronised to keep them docile.

Three infantrymen had taken it off their own backs to pitch in and dig a pit. Two British soldiers were in the ditch, an Australian standing on its edge. They all looked gaunt with fatigue following an encounter with the enemy that had been more of an ambush than a battle. The Allied troops had come off worst; like lambs to the slaughter they'd advanced into a barrage of machine-gun fire. The worst of days, and Barnett had encountered some carnage, having served from the start. No official body count was needed to prove this another disaster, especially not to the men who'd obeyed orders and carried on their slow advance while their comrades were cut down all around. By God's grace some had survived to straggle back to survey the cost of scrambling over the top at dawn. These three had soldiered on in their own way, determined to bury as many fallen as they could before the curs fought the rats to get at the corpses. A blood-orange sun was setting on that wretched wasteland where masses of dead would be left. Sergeant Barnett sympathised with the gravediggers; he didn't like the idea of comrades being abandoned where they'd dropped, but there was far too much to be done and lurking peril in the doing of it. Flares would go up at dusk and enemy snipers would be watching for Tommies salvaging pals.

Bantams were nipping to and fro on no man's land collecting dog tags. Barnett stepped over the untidy pile they were building from discs and string. He reached the lip of the pit and, hands on hips, peered in. They kept their heads down and carried on working, though he knew he'd been spotted. Being ignored didn't sit well with Barnett. His weather-veined cheeks took on a purplish tinge.

'You there ... Wilding, is it?' he bawled, beckoning impatiently as finally a muddy-faced private squinted fully up at him. 'Name and outfit? Quickly now.'

'Private Wilding, sir. Middlesex Foot.'

'And you?' Sergeant Barnett eyed the big fellow who'd leaned on his shovel to take a breather and listen.

'Lonegan ... same outfit.'

'Right, Wilding and Lonegan, with me. Officer wants a word.'

'Ought to finish here first. Get some of the poor buggers in the ground at least ...'

'I'm Sergeant Barnett to you. And that sounds like insubordination, Wilding.'

'No, Sergeant; just, this needs doing.'

'Be a blind man not to know that, wouldn't I?' Sergeant Barnett jerked his eyes, savagely sarcastic, to the lined-up cadavers. 'Major Powley, Royal Engineers, begs a word – if that's all right by you. Now!' he roared.

Gregory Wilding threw the shovel to the top of the pit then climbed out after it, wondering what the hell could be so important.

Barnett started off, barely waiting for the two Tommies to roll down their shirtsleeves and retrieve uniform jackets from the ground. They trudged in his wake, doing up buttons. Greg winced as the knotted muscles in his calves gave him gyp. His boots and puttees were heavy with clay, rubbing blisters on top of blisters. He dropped his chin to hide a faint smile in his collar. Of all the things to drive out the madness and put Lily at the forefront of his mind, blisters had, and an image of her in workhouse uniform. On the day he'd removed her from that prison, he'd taken her back to his workplace; along the way she'd stopped to pull the cracked leather boots off and wipe her bleeding heels. He'd never regretted discharging her and giving her a job, though she'd challenged him, disobeyed him and driven him nuts in one way or another ... some of it frustratingly good. Even with tangled hair and dressed in rags he'd found her attractive. She'd not completely trusted him, but she'd sensed from the start that they fitted together, as he had. Uncomplaining and brave, she would have trekked with him to John o' Groats, if that's where he'd said they were heading, though she'd been aching to rest.

As he was now. As some of those who'd made it back were already doing. He couldn't relax until he'd put a soil blanket over the platoon's lieutenant. His commander had been fair and courageous. An officer who'd led from the front and had paid the price for taking the same risks as his men.

'Don't need no lectures off prats been sitting on their arses in dugouts while us lot was target practice.' Lonegan had muttered that beneath his breath to keep it from the ramrod-backed sergeant out in front.

Greg gave him a wink, hoping to calm him down. Lonegan had a short fuse and could grate on a person. He'd been on a charge for losing his rag with a sapper who'd called him ginger-nut. Lonegan wasn't exactly a close pal; just one of two members of the original platoon still going. 'Could be the major's gonna offer us extra rum ration for going above and beyond.' It was a weak joke. It was more likely the officer would bawl them out for ignoring orders. Carting dead men back for burial instead of leaving them to rot slowed troops down, jeopardising a retreat. The top brass wanted enough cannon fodder back in line for tomorrow so they could repeat today.

'No chance of extra booze . . .' Lonegan hawked and was about to spit when the sergeant cast an eye over his shoulder. Lonegan grimaced, holding the slime on his tongue, then expelling it quietly the moment the man faced front. 'I'd sooner have his pass to the officer's mess.' He rumbled a laugh. 'Ain't sure that was dysentery we had. Food poisonin', more like, bleedin' muck they give us.'

'Privates Wilding and Lonegan, sir. Middlesex Foot.' Barnett had come to a halt by a short, weedy-looking officer with a floppy fringe of fawn-coloured hair.

'At ease, men.' Major Powley looked from one to the other of the saluting soldiers. His eyes soared skyward as though he sought inspiration on how to begin. 'I noticed you carried your commanding officer back for burial.'

'Yes, sir.' Greg's back teeth scraped tighter together. No surprises there then.

'Pretty handy with a shovel, Wilding, are you?'

'When I need to be, sir.' Greg skimmed a look to Lonegan. His comrade seemed as blank-faced baffled as he was to where this might be heading.

'You're Londoners by the sound of it. Dug the tube line or sewers, have you? A navvy of some sort in a past life, eh, Wilding?'

'No, sir, costermonger from Poplar.' Greg was aware of the sergeant's narrowed gaze on him. Perhaps he was hoping he'd tell some lies just to keep things sweet.

'How about you, Lonegan?'

'Jack of all trades me, sir. From Peckham Rye.'

The major returned his attention to the blond man's earth-smudged features. 'I reckon you dug out your own vegetables, eh, Wilding? Don't want to split those swedes. Careful as she goes, that sort of thing.' He acted out his remark, employing an imaginary spade. 'I watched your technique, shoring the sides of the grave.'

'Didn't want it caving in on me, sir.' Greg shifted another glance Lonegan's way, wondering if he also suspected the nob was off his rocker.

The major nodded in satisfaction. 'I've seen fools dig themselves into holes they can't get out of. Scramble up in a panic ... bring the whole damn lot down on top of them. There's a knack. Where did you learn your trade?'

'Was taught some skills at an industrial school, sir.'

The officer considered what he'd heard. 'Workhouse educated, were you, Wilding?'

So the major wasn't as barmy as he seemed. He'd pounced on that, no trouble. 'Yes, sir. St Pancras Industrial School.'

'I suppose the Workhouse Union helped start you off in life.'

'They didn't help. I made me own way and run me own business ... sir.' Greg kept his unfocused eyes front, though he was aware of the sergeant glowering at him for not showing sufficient deference.

'A Cockney businessman, eh.' The major stroked his thin clefted chin. 'Well, whatever you were, Wilding, you're in the army now.' Powley clasped his hands behind his back. 'Your platoon is severely depleted ... finished. Tunnellers need infantry riding shotgun. My unit needs to make up numbers after recent ...'

'Disasters ...' Greg supplied after an expectant quiet, earning himself another boiling look from Sergeant Barnett.

'Encounters ...' the major differed in a snap. 'You two fit the bill. I'll speak with the necessary people about a regrouping, and see if I can make it to your benefit—'

'I'd rather stick where I am, thank you, sir,' Greg interrupted.

'And me, sir,' Lonegan echoed, eyes swivelling in alarm. 'Quiet!'

'Let the men speak, Barnett,' said the major. 'Tunnelling is dangerous work ... I'll not hide it.'

'So's that ... sir.' Gregory inclined his head to no man's land, the source of the stench in the air.

'Indeed . . .' The major peered along his aristocratic nose but a smile tugged at a corner of his mouth. 'I think you show promise, Wilding. You'll do, and your pal can come with you. We'll speak more about it tomorrow when you're billeted. For now, dismissed. Finish your pit, then take your rest.' He turned away and strolled off along a duckboard, disappearing into a bunker.

'You heard him: back to those shovels,' Barnett growled; he hadn't liked being overruled by Powley.

'Got an option in this, have we, Sarge?' asked Greg.

'What do you think?' Barnett's mouth disappeared in a mean smile.

Wilding and Lonegan started back the way they'd come, leaving Barnett watching their backs. He was a thickset man, completely bald on top but with an abundance of iron-grey moustache and eyebrows to make up for it. He wiped thumb and forefinger around his mouth, smoothing down the bristles. The infantrymen didn't fancy working alongside tunnellers because the work was unpleasant and perilous. A man had a slightly better chance of a swift clean death above ground than beneath. He'd do what he could to knock them into shape, though he didn't relish their chances. Knowing how to excavate a hole wouldn't save you. These two were replacing dead men who'd not needed a grave dug. They lay unrecovered in the tunnel that had collapsed on them after the enemy detonated a landmine under it.

The Australian was standing where they'd left him on the top of the pit, fag drooping off his bottom lip, tin hat pushed back on its chinstrap as he contemplated the horizon. 'Thanks fer finishing up, mate.' Greg scooped up the shovel and jumped down into the ditch, his sarcasm wasted. The fellow was deaf to everything but the noise in his head. Greg knew how he felt. He was dog-tired but not yet out on his feet and he needed to be to quieten his mind and sleep.

'I ain't clay-kickin' fer nobody.' Lonegan looked down at Greg.

'That right?' Greg took a shovelful of earth and lobbed it to the top, covering Lonegan's boots. 'Seems to me there ain't a lot of choice. Ain't a lot of difference either in doing this or doing that.' He pointed towards the enemy lines. 'Fritz is gunning for us and doing a bleedin' good job of it. If we don't carry on now, none of us will ever get home. If they want a tunnel, I'll help do the fucker. Sooner this war's won, sooner we're all out of here.' He took out his Capstans and lit the last one then set to again with the shovel. 'Steady as she goes, eh?' he muttered past the cigarette clamped between his teeth. He excavated with renewed vigour, and the shovel bit deep into clay that was shot high over his shoulder.

Lonegan dropped down beside him, sullenly digging alongside until the two of them stood breathlessly surveying their work.

'That'll do. Lower the lieutenant down, and careful with it,' Greg called to the Australian. 'Chaplain about? Anybody seen him?'

'One of your lot said he bought it, cobber.' The Aussie had surfaced from his trance. He dropped his dog-end into the pit. Then manoeuvred the first corpse to the edge.

Greg took the weight of Lieutenant Speer and arranged him gently on the ground, settling his cap over his youthful face, unmarked in death. It was the hole in his guts that had done for him. Greg reckoned his commanding officer had been about twenty-three, his own age. 'G'night, guv'nor,' he said, and patted the lieutenant's stiff shoulder. 'Let's have the others.' More bodies were rolled over the side to be steadied in two pairs of filthy hands and laid down, one on top of the other.

'D'you reckon the major would come over to say the Lord's Prayer? Ask him, shall we?' Lonegan suggested when they were back on the top, looking down.

Greg glanced to the dugout where the officer had disappeared. 'Don't need him. We'll say it.'

They left the Aussie to finish filling in the grave. He seemed to think that was his job. They hadn't argued, or asked why he'd helped them. Sometimes strangers passing by stopped and just did. 'Didn't know you was a workhouse kid, Wilding,' Lonegan said as they were tramping away.

'No reason why you should.'

'Got your own business, eh? You never told me that.'

'No reason why I should.'

'Doin' all right as a costermonger, was yer?'

'Yep.' Greg took the half-smoked dog-end from behind his ear and relit it with fingers that had started shaking, and it wasn't from muscle strain after grave-digging. At intervals a rumble of guns in the distance was vibrating earth and atmosphere. Those didn't frighten him now. They might tomorrow, billet or no billet.

The prospect of the time ahead, resting and dwelling on kith and kin, brought the terrors descending like a suffocating fog. He had Lily to love, a family life to plan, yet his future wife and unborn children seemed to be drifting further away from him. He wasn't patriotic like some ... like Major Powley and his sidekick Barnett ... doing it for King and Country. Gregory Wilding was here for himself, to help get this over with and pick up the pieces back home.

He'd fought damn hard for that good life he'd carved out of cruelty and degradation.

The Zeppelins had started coming over, dropping bombs and he'd realised that everything he'd knocked his guts out for was in jeopardy. Out of self-centredness he'd volunteered; this war would soon be won and all would be back to normal if every able Briton helped protect the homeland . . . so ran the official line trotted out at recruiting offices. Now he was here and the lies were easier to spot.

'I did a stint on a market stall with me old man when I was a schoolkid,' said Lonegan. 'Just before he had it on his toes, that was. He never made no money at it, as I recall. Or if he did, he kept it well hid.' He puffed in disgust. 'Me mother, God rest her, used to go out searching for 'im, y'know, after he walked out on us.'

'Find him, did she?' Greg wasn't feeling inclined to talk but neither did he relish the silences, so found something to say.

'Nah . . . I did, though. He'd shacked up with some old gel; must've been a good twenty years older'n 'im. Widow, she was; had a tidy few bob her husband left her. Me old man used to drop me a tanner here 'n' there to keep schtum about where he was. Mum had the last laugh anyhow. Saw the old man out by a good few years. I was a butcher's boy by then, looking after meself.' Lonegan eyed Greg. 'Youngster, was you, when your parents snuffed it? That why you ended up in a spike? Orphan kid was yer, Wilding?'

'Yeah . . .' was the sum of Greg's response to the string of questions. He classed such inquisitiveness as impertinence and didn't talk about his early life to anybody but Lily; and she didn't know all of it. He let it go; he'd not the energy for a ruck with his last remaining comrade. 'Butcher's boy, eh?

Bet you snaffled a few juicy steaks out when the boss wasn't watching.' Greg turned the conversation and their direction, leading the way onto a duckboard. A constant pounding from booted feet had driven it beneath the mud in places. If he'd had the strength, he would have jumped the missing sections. He simply waded through sludge, though he'd lost boots and puttees in the past to the sucking yellow stuff that occasionally gave a Tommy a laugh at a pal's expense. Greg had hooted himself at the sight of a bloke wobbling on one leg before collapsing face first into it.

Having waded through without incident, he reached a dugout and ducked down, entering it. The sun had disappeared but a blush remained on the horizon. It was dimmer inside than out and he slid his fingers along an earthen ledge until they touched a candle stump. He used a foot to locate an upturned crate and drew it closer, then perched on it, just as he would in his office back home. Lily had had the desk chair. He would sit on an upturned orange box in his warehouse crammed with all the costermonger paraphernalia he'd collected over the years. The tools of his trade had made him a relatively wealthy man. Some of the equipment had been used by Wilding's on a daily basis to run street rounds and market stalls; the rest had been hired out to other costermongers. The majority of those young hawkers weren't in Poplar now, and couldn't turn up at the crack of dawn to rent a barrow and a tarpaulin; they'd been conscripted, if they hadn't already volunteered. But they were still colleagues of sorts, if not customers. Greg had spotted familiar faces passing by in marching lines, and he'd get a thumbs up or a shout of recognition from somebody he knew from the good old days.

Lonegan found another candle stump and stuck it into

an empty corned beef tin. Once the two were alight, the gloomy underground room revealed itself to be littered with water bottles and more empty receptacles which had contained treats like ox tongue or beef brisket, sent from home by wives and mothers. The recipients wouldn't be coming back to clatter coins or dice into a sawn-off empty can; they wouldn't burst in to cram the bunks and curse their luck at being in this godforsaken place, while stripping pus-encrusted socks from their feet.

'Nah ... never got no bunce in the butcher's.' Lonegan had decided to answer the question about illicit perks taken at his first job. 'The boss was a Hawkeye and a tight-fist; wouldn't even've let you take the sawdust off his floor, that one.' Lonegan took the lid off a jar of Bovril and peered inside to find it empty. He stuck his finger within, ran it round then licked it before curling up on his side on the hard bunk. 'Bleedin' love Bovril. Got any fags, mate?'

'Just smoked me last. Buy some in the village when we get billeted.'

'I ain't going underground. Don't like small spaces.' Lonegan was fidgeting and grunting, trying to remove his boots without sitting upright again.

'We'll get more pay out of this,' said Greg, ever the businessman. 'Powley mentioned making it to our benefit. That means hard cash, in my book.'

'Yeah?' Lonegan brightened up, turning to pillow his hands beneath his head. His ginger hair refused to be tamed and tufts stuck out at odd angles beneath his clasped palms. 'Don't mind small spaces sometimes.' He grimaced, rubbing his chin. 'Would've preferred staying in the platoon though.'

'What platoon? The major's right. It's gone, mate. Just you, 'n' me 'n' Harris left now, and he's shot up.' They'd helped their corporal back between them and delivered him to the aid post set back behind the line. He'd taken a bad wound to the left leg but would likely get patched up and go home.

'That lucky sod's got a Blighty one,' said Lonegan, reading Greg's thoughts.

Every soldier wanted a Blighty one: damage that was survivable yet severe enough to get them sent home to recover. Some men, desperate to get back to wives and kids struggling to get by, would inflict wounds on themselves and risk the penalty for doing so. If a self-inflicted hadn't done a convincing enough job, he'd end up court-martialled.

'If we hadn't fetched Lieutenant Speer back, we wouldn't have got picked on digging his grave.'

'At least it ain't yours.' Greg was irritated by Lonegan's whining tone. He had a point though. Not looking after number one had backfired on them. Greg would do it again, though; he felt content that Lieutenant Speer and a few of the others were safe from scavengers, human and animal. The enemy, emboldened by victory, could nip over the top later, looking for souvenirs. Greg had the lieutenant's photos and diary in his pocket to be returned to his family. There'd been a letter too, sealed and addressed to a Mrs Speer; either his mother or his wife, Greg reckoned.

He thrust his back against timber struts in the wall and pulled out his own letter from his inside pocket. He tipped his cap over his eyes, wrapping himself in Lily's world; he already knew every word of her news off by heart so didn't need to see the writing clearly. He recited the two pages in his mind, twice through, before putting the letter back close to his heart.

Quietness settled, spoilt after a few seconds by Lonegan

breaking wind. Neither man joked about it as they might have done on another evening, although the sulphurous stink was pretty awful. Greg stared at his hands, clenching and unclenching them on his lap in an effort to stop them trembling. He gave up and pressed his fingertips against his eyelids to block out the images of comrades flopping onto barbed wire or disappearing before his eyes in an explosion of flesh-filled cloth. The screams of men and metal weren't as easy to escape; they whistled about his skull until he felt like ramming it repeatedly against the clay wall.

He loosened his boots but didn't take them off, unsure if he'd walk to the latrines, if only for something to do before turning in. After a while he became aware of Lonegan talking to himself. He was dozing but having nightmares. A long-gone platoon pal used to rib Lonegan about him crying in his sleep. That'd been another occasion when the military police had carted him off to gaol for causing a rumpus. Lonegan suddenly jerked himself conscious with a terrified little shout. He sniffed, pretending he'd rolled too close to the edge of the bunk.

'Nearly come a bleedin' cropper then.'

'I'm off to the bog.' Greg retied his laces and found his gas mask. He stood up, stopping himself laughing. Tumbling out of bed wasn't coming a cropper . . . all things considered.

'That sergeant's a bastard,' Lonegan said out of nowhere, just as Greg was about to duck outside and let his pal fight to fall asleep unwitnessed.

'You reckon?'

'Yeah, I do. Probably cos he's bald and his name's Barnett. Bet he gets some stick . . .' Lonegan turned onto his side, giggling.

Greg hadn't thought of that and it lightened his mood

as he emerged into air that smelled smoky and fetid. He closed his nose to the reek of death and concentrated on the cordite. It reminded him of Bonfire Night at home ... that had come and gone some weeks ago, but he dwelled on it fondly. Scalding hot chestnuts and spuds tonged from braziers burning at roadsides, all washed down with brown ale. Kids haring about getting shouted at by grown-ups for the whizz-bangs they let off, putting the frighteners up the old girls. He chuckled to himself, immersed in happy memories. A dying soldier on no man's land called mournfully for his mother, putting paid to all that. Greg sank down to his haunches, heart pounding and hands clapped over his ears. When he removed them after about a minute only the constant lament remained. He'd cope with that. It was the single voice ... the distinct words that could drive a person mad. He set off again.

You can forget about rest and recreation back home, he told himself. There wasn't a hope in hell of being furloughed now numbers were down and the major had plans for him.

Chapter Five

'I was sure you'd be the first of us three to be married, Lily.' The woman had spoken past the safety pin clamped in her teeth, and while deftly changing her wriggling son's nappy.

'I thought the same thing,' Margie piped up, arranging some cups and saucers for tea. 'Never mind; when Greg gets his leave, you two can tie the knot at last.'

'He could be back tomorrow. Davy turned up at Christmas without any warning at all.' Lily wasn't as untroubled as she sounded but continued to bounce Margie's daughter on her knee. She *was* worried by her fiancé's ongoing absence and silence. She'd been used to having regular, lengthy letters, filled with interesting information about billets and French countryside. The last one of those had been delivered by Smudger on the day little Rosie Smith was born. Margie's baby was almost five months old now.

'Can't see any of our men getting home for Christmas.' Fanny sat her little lad upright now he was clean and dry. 'Last time I heard from Roger, it wasn't even a proper letter,' she said, untangling strands of her fiery red hair from her baby's tugging fingers. 'Roger sent a field service postcard telling me he was all right.' She sighed. 'He's not a scholar at the best of times.'

Lily's brother would utilise the pre-printed forms ... unless he wanted a supply of cigarettes or biscuits sent over. Then she might get a couple of pages from 'her dear brother, Davy' as he would sign off. Any news was welcome, but the cards were impersonal, with phrases for selection or deletion. The recipient couldn't help but fret that something was being withheld. After this length of time, a buff-coloured card from Greg would suffice, though. At least she'd know he was still alive.

'I've not heard from Smudger in ages either.' Margie's heart went out to her best friend, putting on a brave face when she must be worried sick. 'The woman upstairs to me didn't hear from her boy in over six months then in he breezed as though nothing was wrong. She didn't 'arf clip his ear. Whole road heard that commotion. His excuse was that the regiment's post had been left in a dugout and nobody spotted it for ages.'

'Letters do get held up. Sometimes Greg gets several of mine all together.' Lily appreciated Margie trying to buck her up.

'I'll rinse this out before I go, Lil.' Fanny dropped the wet nappy into a bucket by the sink.

'I don't mind doing it; not as though I don't know how to do a bit of laundry.' It was a wry hark back to the years they'd spent sweating over washing coppers and mangles in Whitechapel workhouse.

'Thanks for reminding me of the dump.' Margie's complaint was good-natured.

It had been a miserable time for them all; but at least they'd survived and stayed the best of friends after escaping in their separate ways. Lily had been rescued by Gregory Wilding's offer of employment; Margie by absconding, and Fanny had discharged herself and her infant son, fearing the master would arrange for him to be fostered.

'Can't believe I'm saying this, but I wish I'd got together with a copper. Then me husband would be safe at home with us.' Fanny put her grizzling son to her shoulder, rubbing his back.

'I bet you've *got together* with a copper in your time,' Margie ribbed, exchanging an amused look with Lily.

'Oi, you! I'm a respectable married woman now. Oh all right, a copper did show an interest ... in arresting me for soliciting.' Fanny winked.

'That's enough of that in front of the children.' Lily wagged a mocking finger at Fanny for reminding them of her racy past. Policemen's wives *were* fortunate though. Men in reserved occupations could remain at home with their families. 'You'll wear the bottom out of me teapot, Margie,' she protested as her friend continued stirring the brew, idly gazing into space.

Margie collected herself, and poured out. The trio were having their usual Sunday afternoon get-together at Lily's flat. Once a week they'd catch up with each other's news over gallons of tea and a packet of biscuits. And Lily got to see her friends' babies.

'This'll have to be me last cup. When I've drunk up, I'll get going,' said Fanny. 'A neighbour promised to have Stephen so I can do an evening shift at the munitions factory. It's good money and I promised to send Roger a few treats over when I get paid. He reckons he's lost weight since he enlisted.'

'You might not need to beg favours for much longer.'

Margie arranged some Bourbon creams on a plate then put the tea tray in the centre of the table. 'I heard nurseries are opening up in London so more women can go to work.' Margie took her daughter back so Lily could drink her tea. 'I know we should all help the war effort, but I'd hate leaving her.' She kissed Rosie's pink cheek.

'You're welcome to your old job back.' Lily took the opportunity to bring up something that had been on her mind. 'I'm always being asked to deliver stuff for the Red Cross. Business comes first and somebody should be in the warehouse during the week. If you start doing the accounts again, I'd be able to take a few mornings off to volunteer more often.'

'You should slow down, Lil, you'll knock yourself out doing charity work as well.'

'You *could* do with a day off,' Margie endorsed.

'I don't want a day off,' Lily said simply. Keeping busy tired her out and helped her to sleep instead of fretting about her fiancé and her brother.

Last time he'd had leave, Greg had praised the auxiliaries who worked alongside the regular nurses on the Western Front. It had prompted Lily to volunteer. She'd been welcomed aboard and every Sunday morning would drive to the local Red Cross depot, taking with her any leftover fruit and veg to be donated to the nuns running a homeless hostel. The Zeppelin raids had destroyed housing in the East End, leaving whole families living in shelters.

'What d'you say, Margie? Fit and ready to return to work?'

Margie wrinkled her nose in indecision. 'The money would come in handy, but Rosie's only little; I don't fancy leaving her with strangers.'

'If my mother-in-law lived local and could do a bit of

childminding, I wouldn't let a nursery or a neighbour have Stephen,' declared Fanny. 'You're lucky, Marge, having Eunice on standby.'

'Trouble with that is, she takes over the moment I step inside her place. *And* she keeps going on about me moving in with her, to save rent.' Margie rolled her eyes. 'What she's really after is to take charge of Rosie.'

'Can't blame Eunice, doting on her.' Lily reached across the table to smooth the little girl's downy locks. She was a bonny child with a happy nature. 'She's a real darling and the image of you, Margie.'

'Bleedin' good job she does take after Marge, all things considered!' Fanny said bluntly. She'd gladly assisted with the ruse to protect Margie's reputation, inviting 'the bride' to stay with her for a pretend honeymoon. 'When me and Roger first got back together, I wasn't sure he'd take to Ronny. He did, though, and loved him as though he was his own son.' Fanny's eyes glistened with tears at the memory of her firstborn. The little boy had got sick and died shortly after his first birthday. Since then, things had improved for Fanny: she'd moved in with her childhood sweetheart and they'd been living as man and wife with their son. A few weeks ago, Roger Baker had finally made an honest woman of Fanny Miller at the registry office. Under the influence of a few sherries in the Bow Bells pub afterwards, the younger girls had giggled that it wasn't surprising the bride already had another bun in the oven, considering their surnames. As Sally Ransome would say, Fanny was knitting bonnets again. In fact, they were all knitting most of the time, and not just for the babies; woollies were always wanted for the servicemen preparing for bitter winters. 'Babies deserve to be loved once they're in your arms,' Fanny concluded.

Lily knew Fanny was thinking of her Ronny again. The little boy's father remained unknown; even his mum couldn't be sure who'd been responsible for the deed.

'I'd better get me skates on. See you next Sunday, and thanks for tea.' Fanny stood up and started wrapping Stephen in a shawl taken from the back of a chair. 'Would you give us a hand up the stairs with me stuff, Lil?'

''Course ...'

'Time I made a move, too.' Margie picked up her daughter's bonnet and fastened it under the tot's chin. 'These afternoons are really drawing in; I want to get home and get the fire alight before it's properly dark.'

While the mothers carried their children up the back steps, Lily grabbed hold of her friends' bags, crammed with baby paraphernalia. She'd been surprised at how much stuff a new mother needed for a trip out: bibs and nappies and a spare gown, just in case. Then there was talc and ointment and gripe water; plus a teething ring and a toy or two. Lily deposited the bags at the ends of the respective carriages. The prams were always left at the top of the steps rather than attempting to bump them down to the basement's back door. Now winter was almost upon them, Lily realised the routine would change. She drew her cardigan around herself as the breeze picked up, swirling russet leaves about their feet.

'Have a think about what I said, Margie: if you'd like your job back, you're welcome to it.'

'I know, thanks.' Margie gave Lily a hug. 'It's ... I'm not sure I want to leave her yet awhile.'

'You could bring her to the warehouse, if you want.' Lily would love to have Margie's company more often. She missed her best friend.

'Perhaps I will when she's weaned in a few months' time.'

'Don't want those lads being treated to an eyeful, eh, Marge?' Fanny rumbled a dirty laugh.

'Shut up, you.' Margie blushed. 'I'll see what Smudger thinks.'

Fanny's crude remark was worth consideration. With Eric Skipman and Joey Robley in and out of the warehouse during the day – plus visiting salesmen walking in unannounced – it could be embarrassing for Margie to bring Rosie to work with her until she was bottle-fed.

Margie and Fanny turned to wave over a shoulder before disappearing round a bend in the lane. Lily stood for a while gazing after them, feeling rather bereft. Her friends were young mums now and wrapped up in hectic rounds of feeds and bath times; she felt quite left out of it. She realised she liked having a few wet nappies left behind just so she could dunk them and peg them out and feel part of it all.

Once, they had all lived together in this little flat; single girls with hopes and dreams yet to come true. Margie and Fanny had got what they wanted, and Lily couldn't be happier for them. But she wanted to be married and have a family with the man she loved. She banished twinges of envy, pivoting slowly on the spot while gazing up at the twilight in the sky. She already had a child in her life to dote on, even if they hadn't yet met. Thoughts of her little sister were never far away; she'd no idea where to look for her next. But search she would. She'd no time to feel sorry for herself.

'Glad I bumped into you, Drake. I've been meaning to have a word. How is your daughter faring? She was having problems, as I recall. All better for her now, is it?'

'Yes ... thank you, sir; the family are finding things easier.' Norman Drake hadn't spotted his boss approaching and had given a delayed, rather stilted answer. Many months had passed since the conversation referred to had taken place and he'd believed the episode forgotten.

'That's good then,' said Mr Stone.

Norman shuffled away. He was a little older than his employer, yet the man addressed him as though about to pat him on the head. Norman wished he'd kept at a distance to avoid this conversation. Not that the master often bestowed on him a glance, let alone a word, while sweeping grandly in and out of the workhouse gates.

'Your son-in-law's serving in the navy and your daughter wasn't coping well, that was it, wasn't it?' the master summarised.

'Yes ... that's it, sir. He's a merchant seaman, away most of the time.' It seemed his boss was determined to be bounteous. The sound of St Saviour's bells being rung might've stirred his Christian spirit.

'You're due some time off, Drake. If you'd like a break over the Christmas holiday, I'll see if I can sort out a replacement—'

'I'm fine, sir,' Norman interrupted. 'Right as rain and don't want time off.'

'Good man.' The master beamed, having heard what he wanted to hear. 'Your son-in-law might be lucky and get home for the festive season.'

'That would be nice, but what with the U-boat attacks and so on, keeping those fellows on their toes ...' Norman's voice tailed off.

'The war is putting everything topsy-turvy. Shortages ...' sighed the master. 'We know about shortages, don't we, Mrs

Stone? It's about time our lot saw off those blasted Hun. Our son is caught up in it all on the Western Front. We've not seen him in a while, have we, my dear?'

The woman dressed in finery, hanging on the master's arm, had seemed disinterested in joining the conversation up to now. 'No ... we've not seen him. It would be nice if he visited.'

A flicker of something passed between the couple that Norman didn't understand and was too stressed to give much thought to. But he noticed the mistress abruptly pull away from her husband to adjust a length of fringed silk about her jowls.

He cleared his throat. 'Darned racket those bells are making,' he muttered.

'St Saviour's Advent service, I believe, sir,' explained Norman, who rather liked the sound.

The eagle's head atop the master's cane was put to his hat brim in farewell salute. The ebony stick was then pointed forward, a signal for his wife to precede him through the open gates. The couple were soon on their way along the street into the December twilight. Norman watched them: the master swaggering with his silver-topped stick and the mistress waddling at his side. They were both heavy-built, well-dressed people. The enemy might be attacking British ships, causing food shortages, but those two didn't look deprived of anything. A person who didn't know them might take them for gentry rather than civil servants. Norman had an idea the Stones had benefited far more from the workhouse than all the inmates put together. By eight o'clock they would be back, unsteady on their feet, having wined and dined courtesy of the chairman of the Board of Guardians having opened the purse strings on Whitechapel Union funds.

Through the gloom, Norman could make out the master using his cane to hail a cab. The silver adornment gleamed as gaslight caught it. The vehicle swung about in the road and pulled up beside the couple. Now Norman felt able to relax. He hadn't realised how tense his limbs were until he uncurled his toes in his boots and sank down into them. A wintry draught cooled the sweat on his brow, making him shiver. He took out his handkerchief and wiped it away. His mouth felt dry as sandpaper. He glanced about the road; it was fairly quiet: a fellow warming his chin in his coat collar was approaching. He looked up, realised where he was, and hurried across the road. People often did that rather than walk too close to the workhouse. On the opposite pavement, the lamplighter carried on about his business. The winter solstice had brought ice to the air and to the cobbles. It brought paupers to his door too. Norman hoped he would have a quiet evening though. He rubbed together his clammy palms and went into the lodge.

Chapter Six

The big guns had stopped. Only intermittent cracks of sniper fire and pops from flare-guns broke an uneasy quiet. Fritz would probably send over some shells later, though, to make his presence known.

Greg slithered and sploshed through the trench, edging past a few Tommies loitering by a fire step, smoking pipes. The sentry on duty cast him an indifferent glance but asked where he was going, so he told him he was off to the latrines. The other soldiers were doubtless feeling too agitated to lie down, preferring to let sleep claim them standing up. Grunted greetings were exchanged, other than that nothing was said. A harmonica was being played somewhere and the sound brought Bobby Smith to his mind. Smudger would toot out a foot-tapping tune while bickering between chords with the other lads about who'd cheated at poker. Smudger had been a kid of twelve when he took him on as his first apprentice. He'd employed others later – Lily's brother Davy amongst them; none had measured up to Smudger. He'd been a good friend too, and it'd been a crying shame he'd fallen for the wrong woman. That disaster seemed trifling compared to what they were all facing up to now though. He'd lost touch with Smudger after he'd gone home on convalescence. A few of Lily's letters had caught up with him, so he knew Smudger had married Margie, who was now a mother, and that Smudger had been reposted to France. Wherever he was, Greg hoped he was all right. Most of all he hoped they'd soon all be back where they belonged: in the Poplar warehouse, congratulating themselves on selling out early at Chrisp Street market to the sound of that harmonica.

He reached higher ground and carried on past the latrines and took the valleyed path towards the dressing station, having decided to visit Harris. The corporal had had a snide side, but that didn't seem to matter any more. Greg wouldn't begrudge the man if he managed to get a Blighty one; he'd paid an agonising price for his ticket and had nearly bitten off his tongue during the jolting trek back to the line. At least that lesser injury had taken his mind off the field dressing and string of bootlaces holding his leg together.

The dressing station was about half a mile distant. On his return in about an hour the moonless sky would have lost its faint trace of day. The Verey lights would help him home. They were constantly sketching lime onto the dark heavens, then bursting and turning everything to the colour of new headstones, making Greg feel he was walking in a cemetery.

The track was identifiable anyhow. Deep cart ruts and discarded bits of timber and old petrol cans littered the way, turning it into an obstacle course. He could make out the pinprick lights of a motor ambulance parked up ahead, outside what remained of a farmhouse. The building had been commandeered after the majority of the property was blown to bits, along with some livestock. The bleached bones of cow carcasses winked intermittently in torchlight, giving the jitters to any passing Tommy.

Luckily, the farmer and his family had survived by diving into the cellar. They'd packed up what they could salvage and had gone elsewhere. Dispossessed Belgians never knew where to re-settle with the front lines and the fighting following them around. Greg felt sorry for them: one minute surrounded by Germans and the next by Allied troops. The locals must hate the lot of them and probably didn't give a toss who won so long as they cleared off and left them alone.

Stampeding footsteps caused him to swing about then quickly get out of the way. Two pairs of stretcher-bearers were fast approaching from behind. 'Need an 'and?' He offered his services to the second set. Their panting was almost drowned out by the cries coming from the stretcher. 'Ta, mate,' wheezed the smaller man at the rear. The moment Greg had picked up speed to lope beside him and had got a grip on one pole, his tiring partner concentrated on using two hands on the other.

In a few minutes, they were close enough to their destination for Greg to notice Royal Army Medical Corps orderlies were loading patients into the ambulance van. He was glad he'd made the effort to come back and see Harris to say goodbye and good luck before his corporal started his journey homewards.

Once the invalid was on the ground, Greg left the RAMC boys to it. Inside the ambulance, the stretchers were racked one above the other in sets of two on either side. Walking wounded were hanging around, waiting to squash aboard into the middle space between the rows. He muttered gruff greetings to a few men up on elbows and eager to see what was happening before the doors were shut on them. Others were flat out, controlling their grimaces. Satisfied Harris wasn't amongst them, Greg moved away. He didn't have any cigarettes or tobacco to offer, and they wouldn't want his sympathy. Some of the farmhouse's structure remained, soaring up jaggedly, but the large basement room accessed by some steep steps was perfectly serviceable beneath ground and ran into the cellar of an adjacent dairy.

'Got a light, mate?' The small stretcher-bearer had propped himself against a pile of sandbags protecting the doorway.

Greg pulled matches from a breast pocket and handed over the box.

'Don't you want none?'

'No fags left; you have 'em.'

'Here ...' The fellow shook a Woodbine from his pack and offered it, along with a few matches taken from the box.

'Ta ...'

'Come to see a pal?'

'Corporal Harris ... same platoon as me.' Greg dipped his head to a flame cupped in his new pal's hand and dropped the few matches returned to him in a pocket. The fellow had known he'd eke out the smoke and want a relight later.

'Doc's with him now. Busted leg, ain't he? Just been down there to see where my man is in the queue.' The stretcher-bearer shook his head. 'Ain't a man, really. Nothing more than a kid. Reckon he'll lose his arm.' He chopped on his own limb, indicating the extent of the damage. 'Told his brother I'd report back 'fore I clock off. Twins, them lads; probably ain't seventeen yet. Bedford Light Infantry.'

'Poor sods. Thanks ...' Greg gestured with the cigarette, finding nothing else to say about the boy soldiers. He'd heard similar stories, and was becoming hardened to the tragedy of youths maimed before they'd needed to shave.

Tiredness was creeping up on him now, probably that last spurt with the stretcher had done the trick. He sucked hard on the cigarette to liven himself up with nicotine. Then he pinched it out and put it behind an ear. He went down the winding stairs towards a smell of antiseptic ... and a lovely aroma of home. Burned toast. He inhaled, smiling as he ducked beneath the wonky beam and entered the makeshift surgery.

He spotted the Bedford boy straight away. A nurse was comforting him as he quietly hiccoughed and sobbed. Harris was towards the other end of the room, half hidden behind a white-coated figure. The doctor was crouching down, examining the corporal then making notes on a clipboard. Greg kept to the periphery of the room, trying to keep out of everybody's way. Harris hadn't noticed he'd a visitor. He was settled on a pallet bed, slumped back against the distempered wall with his eyes shut. Greg recognised the nurse with a broad Irish accent from when he'd brought his corporal in. She'd been full of jolly patter last time. She was quieter now, guiding a mug of tea to a patient's mouth. Greg guessed gas was responsible for the covering on his eyes. An orderly, carrying a man on his back, caused Greg to flatten himself against the wall as he barged past, then disappeared into the room that ran beneath the dairy. Kerosene lamps were hanging off black ceiling beams; though the light was poor, Greg could spot a pot of jam on a wall shelf, ready for spreading with a knife stuck upright in it. His lips twitched at the sight of an orderly rotating a toasting fork in each hand towards the stove.

Greg felt the weight of a pair of eyes. The doctor was

gawping over a shoulder at him. The man suddenly straightened up and stood quite still before declaring happily, 'Gregory Wilding!'

Greg pushed away from the wall and strode forward to shake an outstretched hand. 'Bloody hell! Dr Reeve. Didn't expect to see you here. Last time we spoke you was heading to Turkey. That was months ago.'

'Change of plan after the Big Push.' He shrugged. Those who'd been in the thick of it needed no reminder of the disastrous start to the Somme offensive back in the summer. 'How are you, then?' Bumping into Greg had come as a fine surprise and had given Dr Adam Reeve a welcome boost. 'Have you been home recently to see Lily?'

Greg dropped his chin. 'No such luck. Been here, and keeping me head down best I can. Just come to see me corporal.' Greg nodded at Harris, still resting back with his eyes closed. If he'd heard a familiar voice, he wasn't showing it. 'Didn't clock you in here when me and a pal brought him in.'

'I came in the ambulance about an hour ago. I'll stay until relief turns up. Your man will be moved tomorrow. Clearing station, then on towards the coast by ambulance train. Étaples will take him, I expect. Home after that, once he's fit enough to travel.'

Greg gave a nod and a sigh.

'I'm going back as well.' Adam clamped the clipboard beneath his arm.

'You've got leave?'

'A sort of busman's holiday. I'm putting in some shifts at a convalescent home that's opening up in North London. I'll be glad to be back there. I should be able to hang it out over Christmas and New Year.'

'Make the most of it,' said Greg with feeling.

'I intend to. I'll go and see Lily, tell her I've seen you, and spoken to you. I'll reassure her that you're fine.'

'Thanks.' Greg sniffed as a sudden rush of emotion caused his nose to sting. 'Would you take a letter to her for me?' He wriggled a hand inside his jacket and pulled out a crumpled envelope. 'Wrote it a while back but not had a chance to send it,' he said gruffly. 'I was going to put it in the post but I'd sooner you took it.'

'Be happy to.' Adam slipped the letter in a pocket, patting it to indicate it was safe. 'Lily wrote and told me you two got engaged.' He stuck out his hand again. 'Could see that was on the cards,' he chuckled.

'Made it that obvious, did I?'

'The signs were there ...' Adam winked. 'She spoke highly of you from the start, and had a certain look in her eyes when she did.'

'Didn't know that.' Greg dropped his chin, smiling privately at his boots.

'Well, don't tell her I let on.'

A clatter on the stairs heralded a new arrival. Greg groaned, and said beneath his breath, 'Could've done without bumping into him again.'

'You know Major Powley?' Adam sounded surprised.

'He spotted a few of us burying our lieutenant and had a word.' Greg was aware the major had recognised him. Powley didn't approach, though; he went over to the blind fellow who was slowly wobbling his cup to his lips.

'His nephew,' Adam explained in a murmur. 'Powley came in earlier to see him. The lad will be moved down the line tomorrow with your man Harris.'

'Gassed, was he?'

'Not so lucky, I'm afraid. Shrapnel.' Adam gave a long sigh. 'Better go and have a word with the major. Let him know the boy's itinerary.' He patted his pocket again where the letter was. 'I won't forget. Do it first chance I get. Good luck to you.'

'Thanks. Good luck to you, and tell Lily . . .' Greg paused, wishing those last few words unuttered. What he had to say to his fiancée was too precious to be passed on second-hand. 'Just tell her, you know . . . hope to see her soon.'

'Will do.'

Greg gripped Adam's arm in a way that encompassed his gratitude and a farewell. A moment later he'd crouched down to gently prod the corporal's shoulder. 'Hey, all right, mate? See you've had some tea 'n' toast, yer lucky sod.' A plate with crumbs and an empty mug on it were by Harris's hip.

'Got a fag, Wilding?' The casualty opened an eye.

Greg realised then his corporal had been aware of him but had been too dejected to acknowledge him. 'Yeah . . .' Greg took the stub from behind an ear and a match from his pocket, striking it on the wall. Once he'd got the cigarette alight he put it between Harris's bloodless lips. 'Got a Blighty one there, chum. Doc'll see you all right; one of the best, is Dr Reeve. Just come to say good luck, and that's from Lonegan 'n' all.'

'Get Lieutenant Speer buried, did you?' Harris eased his spine to and fro, grimacing with the effort of trying not to disturb his injured leg.

'Yeah . . . he's all right now.' Greg could tell that Harris didn't feel like company. 'Be off then. You get some rest. Be home before you know it, yer will.'

'Bleedin' hope I've still got two legs when I get there.' Harris closed his eyes again, drawing on the cigarette.

'You know that soldier, do you, Reeve?' Powley had observed the interaction between the doctor and Wilding.

Adam glanced over as Greg went up the steps.

'I do. From back home. He's engaged to a friend of mine.'

The major seemed surprised to hear that coming from somebody obviously middle class. 'He's a workhouse boy, you know. Went to industrial school.'

Adam had been in the process of tidying the bandage about Powley Junior's eyes. He stopped and looked up. 'I didn't know that.'

'Workhouse boys make damn good recruits. Used to hardship, you see. Death and disease, empty belly, nothing to them when they've been brought up on it.'

Adam secured the bandage. He couldn't argue with that; still he felt like punching Powley in the mouth. Adam had been employed as a medical officer in Whitechapel workhouse and had met Lily Larkin there. He knew the cruelty and deprivation inmates suffered and considered it an outrage rather than an exploitable asset.

'I'll have him alongside my team, and his pal.'

'He's infantry, sir.' Adam believed the major must be being rhetorical.

'Infantry work alongside tunnellers. That platoon of his is annihilated and our unit needs to boost numbers.'

Adam turned away, keeping himself busy tidying the instrument trolley to keep his tongue still. He wished the major hadn't told him that. When he got home, was he going to tell Lily of the increased dangers her fiancé faced or pretend he didn't know? She'd be sure to demand information about Gregory's whereabouts.

Adam had a great fondness for Lily, and he liked Gregory Wilding. Though they'd only met a handful of times, Wilding reminded him of a person who was dear to him. They were about the same age, both tall and fair and handsome. Ralph Villiers would be fretting about him and wondering when they could be together, just as Lily Larkin would be fretting over the man she loved.

Chapter Seven

'Hello, Mrs Ransome, what can I do you for?' Lily gave the woman a cheeky smile. 'Got some smashing oranges and bananas.' She'd kept her voice down to say that. There wasn't enough exotic fruit to go round every customer who'd want to buy some. Little was left on display; even home-grown apples had almost sold out. She and her foreman had been at Spitalfields before it was light, along with every other costermonger hoping to make a killing on the last big market day before Christmas. She'd been lucky to secure the boxes of imports, and had had to pay handsomely for the privilege. Other foods were in short supply too. The van's headlights had swept across queues already forming outside groceries and butcher's shops at dawn. Margarine and flour and sugar were wanted for last-minute baking. Any rumour that a storekeeper had managed to get hold of some scarce staple would result in housewives scrambling to be first inside when he opened up. Families were struggling, but doing their best to keep up the tradition of putting a feast on the table on Christmas Day.

Lily had put by some oranges and bananas in case Mrs Ransome turned up at her usual time in the afternoon and missed out. Being a handywoman was fitted around Sally's other occupations. Mornings were spent helping her husband run a newsagent's kiosk outside the railway station, sometimes with her grandson in a pram beside her when she was on childminding duties. Sally seemed less rushed than usual though. She crossed her arms as though settling down for a chat.

'*Oranges and bananas?* Blimey, you're lucky, gel. None of them up the other end have got much at all for sale.' She jerked her eyes to the costermongers she'd walked past. 'They was all cursing Fritz, and I won't repeat the language I heard neither. Not that I buy off any of them, o' course. Just browsing down there.'

Lily smiled wryly. She wasn't the cheapest on Chrisp Street market because she chose to sell best-quality stock. Some of her rivals offered second-rate produce and Lily didn't begrudge customers snapping it up if that was all they could afford. She knew what it was to be desperate to fill her empty belly.

'Don't suppose I could afford none of yer oranges anyhow.' Sally mournfully picked one up to fondle. 'I'll just take carrots and onions; pound of each, and better have four . . . make it five, of spuds. That'll see me over Christmas for roasting. Bought me sausages for tonight; the old man likes his bangers 'n' mash swimmin' in onion liquor.'

'You're making my mouth water.' Lily pulled towards her the woman's shopping bag. She weighed out the veg then with practised ease shot it off the scoop into the cavernous opening.

'Oh . . . and some Brussels; can't have Christmas without sprouts. Not that the kids like 'em much. But I do dinner like me mum did. Tradition, see. Leg o' pork and apple sauce and stuffing with roast potatoes and sprouts. The old man's bringing in the meat later.' She tapped her nose. 'His pal works in the butcher's and promised to put by a joint that'll make lots of lovely crackling.'

Lily looked suitably impressed by Sally's luck, having a husband in the know. 'Made your pudding?' she asked while weighing out the sprouts.

'Did that back in October. Glad I did, cos I wouldn't have got the currants for it now. Just needs a good boil up. Could do with custard to go with it. Everywhere I've been they've sold out of Bird's custard powder.'

Lily dumped the shopping bag on the ground and selected three big oranges and a bunch of bananas from the depleted boxes underneath the stall. The fruit was slipped in on top of the vegetables. She didn't want others to see and expect the same generosity. Lily had a business to run and couldn't treat every customer to free stuff. But she liked Sally and owed her a debt of gratitude. Lily didn't think she was being over-dramatic in believing the woman had saved Margie's life and that of her baby during that difficult labour.

Lily needed no reminder of the risks women faced in childbirth. The heartache of her mum's wretched death and her little sister's plight was her constant companion. Even now, on Christmas Eve when everybody was jolly, and the market was cinnamon-scented and prettily lit with naphtha flares, she mourned for the family she'd lost. Her father had been an alcoholic and had drunk himself to death. Lily ached for him too; in his heyday he'd been a good man: funny and popular. She found it hard to stomach that he'd come to such a lonely and sordid end. She jiggled Sally's shopping bag to distribute the fruit and veg evenly within it and try to shake herself out of nostalgia. It was hard to do. Christmas Eve held both sweet and sour memories for her. With her brother and mother she'd entered the workhouse seven years ago on a snowy Christmas Eve, shoeless, starving and frozen. She glanced up at the clear navy-blue sky, where a few palely twinkling stars were visible. Her gaze drifted to the awning on the stall. It was fringed with festive greenery and, on the spur of the moment, she unhooked a bit of mistletoe. 'Here ... you can give your husband a kiss under that, Sally, when he turns up with your lovely bit of Christmas pork.' As she teased the woman, her melancholy fell away.

'Bleedin' hell,' snorted Sally. 'He'd think it was his birthday as well as Christmas if I give him a kiss.' She was grinning as she took the mistletoe to wave over the crown of her hat. She puckered up seductively, giving her frizzy platinum curls a pat.

'Don't do to show 'em too much attention, do it, Sal?' A passing neighbour of Sally's had overheard the joshing and stopped to offer her two penn'orth. 'Sal knows more'n any of us what trouble a kiss leads to, don't yer, gel.'

'Right 'n' all, I do.' Sally wagged a finger. 'Delivered two this week. Can't be knittin' bonnets at my age. Me mother was nearly forty-nine when she had her last, poor cow. "No canoodlin'," I tell him when he gets frisky. Now I've managed to get the last two out from under me feet, don't need no more fillin' that hole.'

'Better give Lily that back.' The woman nodded at the sprig of mistletoe still being swayed about. 'Take that home, and he'll be chasing yer round the kitchenette once he sees it.'

'If it was Mr Wilding give it to me ... I'd've been doing

the chasing.' Sally gave a slow wink and her lips were puckered again.

'Not 'arf ...' Sally's neighbour gave a dirty chuckle. 'I would've pinched me own bit down off that pole and tackled him to the ground.' She gave a saucy shimmy.

Women had clustered about the stall, having got the gist of the merriment. They chipped in some of their own ribald remarks. Suddenly a queue had formed, wanting to buy mistletoe and holly.

'You lot are the bloody limit ...' Lily pressed her lips together on a giggle, rolling her eyes. It hadn't been a ploy to drum up business; nevertheless, giving Sally a gift of mistletoe had worked a treat for sales.

She totted up the cost of the veg and Sally tipped cash into her palm. Lily walked out from behind the stall, lugging the heavy shopping bag, leaving her apprentice to carry on serving.

'Reckon that lot's been at the sherry already.' Sally clucked her tongue in mock disapproval. The gaggle of women were now ribbing young Joey Robley. She wiped away a residue of mirthful tears. 'You're a good girl, Lily. Some women would take offence at their fiancé being spoken of that way.'

'I'm not a jealous sort; I know he loves me,' said Lily with simple innocence.

'Ain't surprised he loves yer; he's a lucky man, having a smashing gel like you waiting for him back home, and keeping his business afloat.'

In fact, Lily felt rather proud that everybody thought her future husband a gorgeous catch. He was handsome; she'd thought that about Gregory Wilding the first time she'd clapped eyes on him. She'd been a tender fifteen and not properly aware of what romantic love was back then, having led a sheltered half-life in the workhouse. With no mother to prepare her for womanhood, she'd felt a confusing mixture of excitement and trepidation on realising she'd attracted the attention of a hound who'd had girlfriends galore.

Sally had taken a peek into the shopping bag and seen the fruit. 'Oh, love, thank you. Those'll go into me grandkids' stockings,' she said gruffly.

'Hope you have a lovely Christmas with your family.'

'You too, Lily ...' Sally belatedly realised that wasn't a clever thing to have said, considering the girl's fiancé and brother were away fighting. She grimaced an apology and received a rueful shrug in response. A burst of raucous female laughter took their attention. 'The lad's all right, is he?'

'Joey?' Lily half-turned to look at him; he was only fifteen but up for a bit of banter even if some of the women were old enough to be his gran. Since brash Eric Skipman had joined the firm, the lads had become pals. Eric, being older, had brought Joey out of his shell; he was no longer the blushing boy he'd been when he'd started as a schoolboy apprentice. 'Don't worry about Joey; he'll give that lot as good as he gets.'

Sally went off with a wave and Lily started neatening the remaining produce on the stall.

The market was getting quieter, the air icier as the shoppers began drifting away. The clang of dismantled poles hitting the ground was drowning out the sole vendor yelling his last-minute lures to stragglers. Joey sat down on an upturned orange box and opened a pouch of tobacco. He glanced at Lily as he rolled a cigarette.

'Shall I start boxing up the odds 'n' ends, miss?'

He always addressed her formally, whereas Eric was more familiar, calling her Lily. Neither of them referred to her as guv'nor. That epithet was reserved for Gregory Wilding. It was the way Lily sometimes still thought of him and she'd use the name to tease him.

'Get some of this stuff shifted, shall I, miss?' Joey repeated past the Rizla he was licking. His legs were stretched out and he was chuckling to himself beneath the lowered brim of his flat cap.

Lily guessed the boys had some mischief planned for later on. 'Yes, let's start clearing away. As soon as Eric turns up, we'll be ready to load.' Her foreman would've finished pushing a barrow, selling door to door, about an hour ago. After dropping off any unsold stock at the warehouse he'd drive the van to Chrisp Street to give them a lift back with the heavy equipment.

Joey got to his feet, roll-up wedged in the corner of his grinning mouth. 'Speak o' the devil, miss ...' He gave a thumbs up to the driver of an approaching van.

Eric was negotiating a slow, steady path towards them to avoid the swinging iron poles being loaded onto beefy shoulders. Bargain hunters wending homewards were also dodging obstacles strewn in their path: folded tarpaulins and boxes were traps for the unwary not watching their step in the gloom. Every so often a ragged figure would dart to snaffle something unwanted rolling towards the gutters.

'Anything goin' spare?' A gruff voice made both Lily and Joey stop stacking empty pallets and glance over their shoulders.

Joey ignored the beggar woman and carried on with what he'd been doing.

Lily found a small cardboard box, empty now of mushrooms, and tipped some potatoes and carrots into it then handed it over. 'Here ... merry Christmas to you.'

'Gawd bless yer, dear. And merry Christmas and a happy New Year to you.' The box secured under her arm, the woman shuffled off to try her luck elsewhere.

When they'd everything neatly stowed in the van, Joey clambered into the back to perch on top of the mound of tarpaulins. Eric slammed shut the doors while Lily settled into the passenger seat.

'All aboard?' Eric called, unnecessarily, as he'd shut his pal in, but it was a lark they had.

Joey gave an answering drum roll on metal, then off they set at a rocking trundle. The beggar was stooped over, fitting some bruised apples into her box as neatly and carefully as if she were handling fruit from the Orient. She stood aside for the van to pass and seeing Lily touched her forehead in respect. They turned out of Chrisp Street and picked up speed. Eric and Lily exchanged an amused look as Joey started warbling 'Silent Night' in the back.

'Put a sock in it, Robley,' the chorister's pal called. 'Sounds like two bleedin' cats havin' a scrap.'

When they arrived at the warehouse, Lily lit the lamps while the lads unloaded and brought everything inside. They were working more speedily than usual and she guessed they were keen to knock off to celebrate Christmas Eve with a few brown ales. Eric was seventeen, though he lacked brawn and looked younger. Her brother Davy was a similar stature: short and wiry. He'd been another one drinking and smoking in his mid-teens. It seemed to be a rite of passage for costermonger apprentices to start those vices early on in life.

Lily finished piling up their cotchels with all the leftover fruit and vegetables for them to take home to their mothers for Yuletide dinners.

'That's about it. All right if we get going?' Eric asked, having put the final folded tarpaulin neatly on the shelf. 'Don't mind hanging on if you want me to.'

Lily would've shaken her head even if his offer hadn't sounded half-hearted. 'No, it's all right. You two get off home.' She gave them both a warm smile, then thought she ought to add something suitably wise as Greg would've done at this special time of the year. He'd had a wry, understated way about him, but had been a hard taskmaster with it. All his apprentices had admired and respected him, minding their Ps and Qs ... Lily included, back when she was a new recruit. 'Enjoy your Christmas holiday, but not too much boozing or you'll end up with sore heads and angry mothers.' She tipped cash from the sales' tin and counted out fourteen shillings in silver. 'A bonus for all your hard work this year,' she said as she handed them half each. 'Merry Christmas to you both. And don't forget your mums' Christmas cotchels or you won't 'arf be in for it.'

The boys grinned delightedly. 'Cor, thanks, Lily,' Eric said, closing his fingers on his Christmas box. 'I'll buy the younger ones a few sweets out of it.'

'I'll treat my brothers too, and me mum.' Joey took his money, looking bashful. 'We got you something between us.' He went to the door where his donkey jacket was hooked up and pulled a small box of chocolates out of the pocket.

Lily was touched by their thoughtfulness and felt a spontaneous lump in her throat. 'Oh, thank you. What a lovely surprise,' she choked out, taking the gift.

The boys grinned at her then at each other. Eric was first to his cotchel. He pulled the top string tight then wound the cord about his palm. Carefully he yanked the bulging sack up to carry over his shoulder. 'Best get this home to me mum. Won't get no tea later if I don't.'

'Yeah ... me 'n' all. Merry Christmas, miss,' Joey said, pulling on his coat then shouldering his own sack.

'And the same to you both and to your families. Don't forget though, back to normal the day after Boxing Day.'

Eric gave her a mock salute and a grin before heading out of the door. Joey gave her a wave. Before they were at the gate she could hear them laughing and murdering 'Good King Wenceslas'.

Lily set about turning off the lamps and locking up. Then within a few minutes she was off home too.

Chapter Eight

'Lily ... got a minute?' Eunice Smith was silhouetted in her doorway by a candle burning on a wall sconce.

Lily raised a hand, pleased that Margie's mother-in-law seemed amiable. Eunice hadn't taken kindly to discovering she'd been told a pack of lies. In an attempt to smooth things over, Smudger had told his mother the girls had been protecting him. It hadn't stopped Eunice being cool and distant with Lily ever since. Margie had been forgiven though; Eunice was canny enough to know she needed to keep on the right side of her son's wife, to see her beloved granddaughter.

Being in no rush to get home, Lily strolled over to meet the older woman by the railings in front of the house even though it was chilly for having a chat.

'Thought it was about time we had a little talk.' Eunice rubbed at her chin, looking diffident. 'I don't like us being at odds. Things have settled down for everybody now. Besides, it's Christmas and time to let bygones be bygones. I thought if you're at a loose end you might like to come over for a drink later; only if you want to, of course. Got a bottle of sherry going begging ...' she added as an inducement.

'Then on Boxing Day Margie's coming over, and I know she'd love it if you came and had a bit of dinner with us.'

'Thank you ... that'd be lovely.' Lily gave her neighbour's proffered hand a firm shake. She wasn't going to apologise again. She'd already done so more than once in an attempt to thaw things between them. 'Wish there'd been another way out of it, but Margie couldn't find one at the time,' was all she said.

'Yeah, I know. Just unfortunate that the gel's letters to Bobby got delayed, and lies got told.' Eunice managed to get in a final dig. 'I still don't see why Margie would've thought he was abandoning her when she knew him the way she did. 'Course something bad could have *happened* to him over there, and I know she wanted to act fast before chins started wagging.' Eunice paused. 'Only wish she'd confided in me. If she'd told me she was expecting me son's baby I would've protected her against all comers. I know how spiteful folk can be. We would've muddled through between us if Bobby hadn't ever come back.'

'Thankfully, it didn't come to that.' Lily patted the croaky-voiced woman's arm.

'Turned up in hospital blues though, didn't he? Can you believe it? Not even telling his own *mother* he was injured. I give him a rocket over that.'

'I expect he didn't want to worry you ...' Lily chipped in before Eunice talked herself back into a temper over it all.

'I know and I'm proud of him, doing the right thing by Margie, first chance he got. Still convalescing at the time, too. What luck I'd kept hold of his father's best suit. I was going to let the totter have it.' Eunice beamed. 'A bride-groom doesn't want to look at his wedding photo and see himself wearing baggy old hospital blues, does he?'

'Made a lovely couple, I thought.' Lily reflected on that July day: Margie looking beautifully serene in her best clothes and Smudger with his bashful expression and slicked-down hair. 'He's a good man.' Lily meant it more than Eunice knew. If the woman ever found out her son was rearing the child of a despicable villain, she'd not be so philosophical about any of it and perhaps might turn her back on the little girl she professed to adore.

'Spotted Margie and Fanny pushing prams down the lane on Sunday. Usually me daughter-in-law calls in to let me say g'night to me granddaughter, after visiting you. She didn't that day though.'

'They wanted to get straight home and get their fires alight,' Lily placated. 'So cold and dark now, isn't it?' She rubbed her chilly arms through her coat sleeves, feeling the breeze stirring the hair at her nape. A scent of mist and chimney smoke was drifting on the air.

'Got me coal delivery the other day. Price has shot up.' Eunice didn't seem in any rush to retreat indoors. She resumed doting on her granddaughter. 'Rosie's getting bonny and she's the image of her dad at that age. Bobby had lovely Goldilocks curls as a baby. He only turned mousy when he was a teenager.'

'I can see Margie in her as well, y'know,' said Lily. 'Same big blue eyes and fair colouring.'

Eunice sniffed. 'Margie was the one wanted them to get their own place. Me son would've taken up the offer of his old room back like a shot.' She crossed her arms. 'Ain't surprising the gel's struggling for money with just Smudger's army pay to live on. She shouldn't be spending beyond her means. That new haircut, for a start. Things like that don't come cheap.'

'I think the short bob style suits her,' Lily said flatly. She had noticed her friend was taking more care with her appearance since she'd got married and thought it a good thing, not something to criticise.

'Suits her or not, ain't worth getting in debt for.'

Lily wondered if there was more to this than Eunice being self-righteous. 'Did Margie tell you she's struggling for money?' Her best friend surely knew she'd only to ask for help if she couldn't make ends meet.

'The totter knows Margie's me daughter-in-law,' Eunice started off, having got the opening she'd been waiting for. 'The bleeder asked me to settle up for shoes she'd had off him when I paid for a blanket I had. Cheek of it! I've not let on. Don't want to embarrass Margie, but something'll need to be said.' Eunice nudged Lily. 'How about you have a word with her? Tell her she'd do better living with me and save rent to pay for her little luxuries. She'll listen to you, Lily.'

Eunice expected something in return for having eaten humble pie then. Lily didn't blame Margie for wanting her own place, and to treat herself to a few nice things. Her reply was non-committal and she followed it up with a valid reason to make a speedy escape. 'I'd better get indoors and get a lamp lit or I'll be taking a tumble down those steps in the dark. Wouldn't be the first time. Reckon a hard frost's on its way.'

'I meant to ask, have you heard from Mr Wilding recently?' called Eunice as they started moving in opposite directions. She always addressed Greg as Mr Wilding, giving him the respect due to her son's employer.

'Not for a while. Post's delayed again, I expect.' Again Lily made to move on and again Eunice stopped her.

'I nearly forgot to say: a fellow walked up the lane on

Friday, asking directions to where you lived. 'Course I told him you'd probably be working at the market stall at that time of the day, but he seemed determined to carry on. I was just off shopping, but pointed him in the right direction.' Eunice looked expectant of receiving some gossip, even though they now stood yards apart. 'Margie told me you do charity work for the Red Cross. I thought he might be one of your colleagues. Catch up with you, did he?'

Lily shook her head, mystified. Nobody from the Red Cross would come looking for her. The only person she was well acquainted with was the secretary who allocated tasks to volunteers. The woman was aware that Lily's services were only available on a Sunday morning. 'Did he give his name? What did he look like?'

'An army officer, judging from his uniform. A bit weedy-looking, I suppose you'd say. Short fellow with brown hair but pleasant and well-spoken. Don't often see that sort round here. I didn't think it was my place to ask questions.'

Lily felt her innards starting to loop into knots. She could think of only one reason an army officer might visit her.

'Probably nothing to worry about, love.' Eunice had cottoned on to Lily's alarm. 'You'd get a notification in the post rather than a visit if, you know . . . bad news was in the offing . . .' Eunice's reassurance tailed off and she gawped into the distance. Suddenly she trotted up to Lily, hissing, 'Bloody hell! I think this could be him, come back again.' She was squinting over Lily's shoulder. 'Is that fellow coming up the lane wearing army uniform? Me eyes aren't so good in this light.'

Lily whipped about, frowning until her vision locked on to a man's figure approaching through the gloom. He wasn't close enough to identify facially and she'd never seen him in khaki uniform, only a white coat, but she'd recognise him anywhere. A couple of years ago she'd watched for him to turn up every single morning. She'd go out of her way to evade the wardens' and skulk under the stairs in a musty corridor, hoping to bump into him. An invitation into his office to work as a clerk for an hour or two had been the highlight of her mean existence. During her tender teenage years she'd believed herself in love with the workhouse's medical officer, the only adult to show her kindness since separation from her mother. Then Gregory Wilding had come along and she'd learned what true love really was. Kindness hadn't always come into it. He'd been brutal at times to teach her necessary lessons about life.

Adam Reeve was important and very dear to her, even though they'd not seen one another or spoken for years. Their letters had grown rather few and far between as well.

'So you do know him.' Eunice had observed Lily's anxiety transforming into a wondrous smile.

'Oh, I do. And what a treat it is to see him.' She gave her neighbour a spontaneous hug before dashing off.

'I'm lucky enough to catch you home today.' He'd halted by a gas lamp and its misty light lent a haziness to his smiling face.

Lily nodded, tempted to fling her arms about him. It wasn't the gap in their acquaintance making her hesitate: a remnant of formality, forged out of a harsh regime intended to keep inmates in their places, kept her still. He was indeed an army officer. She'd addressed her last letter to Lieutenant Reeve, Royal Army Medical Corps. It seemed he'd been promoted to captain, if she'd identified the stripes on his sleeve correctly. She held out a hand. He didn't shake it but gave it an affectionate squeeze.

'It's such a wonderful surprise to see you, Adam.' Lily did hug him then, pressing her warm cheek against his cold shoulder.

'You too, Lily.' He fondly patted at her back. If he was that way inclined, he knew it would be easy to fall for this girl. Even when a skinny little thing, dressed in rags, her thick chestnut-brown locks and deep blue eyes had marked her out as something special. It had been obvious to him that if Lily Larkin managed to escape before the workhouse sapped her spirit, she would be a beautiful woman one day. He held her back and looked her over with several nods of approval. Her plain working clothes couldn't disguise how she'd blossomed. 'Where's that workhouse girl I knew?' he teased.

'Gone forever,' said Lily flatly. 'Thanks to you, and to everything you did to help me while I was stuck in there.' She groaned as a thought struck her. 'If you'd come on Sunday you would have seen Margie Blake and Fanny Miller! They always have tea with me on a Sunday and they'll be so disappointed to have missed you; they'd have loved to see their old medical officer.'

'I'm glad you've all managed to keep in touch. How are those two doing then?'

'They're thriving,' Lily proudly announced. 'Mrs Smith and Mrs Baker are both happily married with babes in arms.'

There was strong and honest contentment on Adam's face at such marvellous news about former inmates. Many carried the stain of the workhouse with them and led stunted lives on the outside. Fanny was a survivor, brash and immoral at times. But he didn't hold it against her or any woman for doing what was needed to get by. Pretty, delicate Margie had been a worry to him with her crippled hand and limited employment prospects. A little younger than Lily, she had relied heavily on her best friend for emotional and physical support. Now she had her own family, and Adam guessed that bond between the girls might ease as they progressed through life.

'Let's go and have some tea and you can tell me all your news.' Lily suspected more than a simple social visit had brought him to her door after such a long time. She slipped her arm through his as they proceeded up the lane. They came abreast of Eunice, who was hanging around. She had conjured up a broom and was pretending to be bothered about sweeping away a few papery leaves eddying on her step. Lily knew her neighbour was really loitering for an introduction, and obliged. When she mentioned that Eunice Smith's son was Margie Blake's husband, Adam became slightly reserved. The change in him wasn't enough to alert Eunice, who was being polite as you like to Captain Reeve. But Lily was attuned to it and said, 'Come on ... let's get that kettle on.'

'See you later fer that sherry then, Lily,' called Eunice.

Lily waved and soon she and Adam were carrying on towards her flat, talking about trivialities and saving all the vital news for when indoors in the warm.

Chapter Nine

Satisfied that the lamps were lit, the kettle on the stove and her guest comfortably settled on a kitchen chair, Lily burst out with a question that wouldn't wait a second longer: 'Have you bumped into Gregory lately?'

Adam arched a playful eyebrow, pulling a letter from his pocket and waving it as though he'd produced a rabbit from a hat. 'Indeed I *have* run into your fiancé, and look what he gave me for you. He wanted me to deliver it personally so I could tell you that he's well and can't wait to see you.'

Lily's joyous gasp preceded her shooting out a greedy hand. She managed to stop herself snatching and took the letter with a thank you. She kissed the envelope before slipping it into her pocket for savouring later. 'I miss him so much. I've not seen him for over a year.' She rubbed at her prickling eyes. 'Hope he's granted leave soon.'

'I hope so too.' Adam didn't know what else to say. There was no point in spouting platitudes with a bright spark like Lily. The Somme offensive had resulted in thousands of Allied troops being lost; able-bodied soldiers weren't likely to be back any time soon.

'You weren't treating him for an injury, were you?' Lily

had joined dots in her head and found a reason why the two men had ended up in the same place. 'You *would* tell me if anything—'

'Of course I would,' interrupted Adam. He got up from the table to emphasise his reassurance, cradling her face and gazing solemnly at her. 'He did come to the dressing station, but only to visit a wounded pal.' She still didn't seem convinced. 'He looked well to me, Lily; tired, of course, but so's every Tommy ready for billeting behind the front line.' He rolled his eyes towards the idle teapot as the kettle started to hiss. 'I'm gasping for a cuppa, you know.' He'd made her laugh and turn away to find some crockery. His smile faded.

He didn't want to be drawn into talking about what was happening over there. Fighting had been savage, often ineffectual. Thousands of men lost in a tug of war over a few kilometres of cratered boggy ground. He would rather not think about, or express, his loathing for his work on the Western Front, battling to repair bits of youthful flesh and bone, rarely worth the saving. Infection would often destroy a surgeon's painstaking work and prolong a patient's agony, only for the mortuary corporal to claim him.

For God's sake, don't ask what I do in a field hospital, he was thinking as he watched her stirring the pot and a homely fragrance steamed forth. Once tea was ready, she might ask about his happiness and what he'd been up to. Events at the place he'd quit less than a fortnight ago were too ghastly to describe. Set close to the line at Albert, multitudes of shattered bodies, sometimes without even a field dressing applied to spurting injuries, arrived in convoys of carts and vehicles. Back and forth the motor ambulances shuttled from front line to clearing station. Those casualties judged able to withstand the ride were sent on down the line to free up space for those destined for the cemetery in a week ... maybe two. Once a Tommy had *ambulance train* written on the docket clipped to his pyjama jacket he would cheer up. The doc thought he could survive an onward journey and hell could wait. Adam wanted to advise every one of them to swing the lead once home or they'd be posted back and Satan would get another crack at them. But he didn't; he kept his upper lip stiff and his comments official.

He didn't want to admit to himself, or to Lily, that he'd sell his soul to be back working in Whitechapel workhouse, treating scabby alcoholics and rickety kids. If he did, it would mean he was a coward as well as a faggot. It would mean his father was right when he said his son was a disgrace and not a man.

He'd return to France; he'd get on a troop ship with all those other servicemen, jovial on the outside while inwardly seething with bewilderment as to how and why it had come to this. In truth there was more to it than acting courageous and noble. His lover had been in England when he arrived but had been reposted. They had spent just a few overlapping days together before Dr Ralph Villiers left for Calais. Already Adam was missing him.

Shortly after seeing Gregory at the dressing station, Adam had been relieved, sent back to Étaples Hospital to await a passage home. He'd not discovered if Gregory's move to Major Powley's outfit had gone ahead, so it was a relief to know he'd be jumping the gun, bringing that up this afternoon.

'When was the last time we saw one another, Lily?' In trying to divert Lily's thoughts from the war, he'd drawn her attention to another disaster. Adam regretted opening his mouth.

A quiet settled between them. Lily carried on rattling cups and saucers and Adam re-seated himself. There was now an elephant in the room that would have to be acknowledged. On the last occasion they had been together, a workhouse officer had died. She refused to think of what happened to Harriet Fox as a murder or a tragedy. The woman had been evil and the act itself, self-defence. Lily poured the tea with an unsteady hand. Usually the incident remained buried in her head; but not today. The man who had caused Harriet's accident had frequently been on Lily's mind; whenever she thought about her sister she'd remembered the Christmas Eve the child had been conceived. 'Have you seen Ben Stone? Do you know how he is?' The men probably avoided one another rather than risk reviving grisly memories.

'Actually, I have had some bad news about him,' Adam began slowly. It was only right she knew about this, in the circumstances. 'He's been killed, Lily. He was working as an orderly at a dressing station when it took a hit. His fiancée was nursing at Étaples, where I was only recently. The poor woman was distraught when she received word.' Adam planted his elbows on Lily's kitchen table then dropped his face into his palms. 'I was going tell you this; I just thought it'd be nice to have our reunion first.'

Lily understood what he meant. The cheerful atmosphere had suffered.

'Despite it all, I rather liked Ben Stone,' he sounded reflective. 'So much nicer than his parents; basically a decent man, I thought.'

'I did too ...' Lily echoed. She let the news sink in but

found no worrying ramifications in the death of her half-sister's sire. There had never been a chance for her to get to know him and she wasn't sure she would have wanted to anyway. But Ben Stone had possibly saved her life. For that alone she felt sorry at his passing. The genie was out of the bottle, pulling her thoughts to the fateful day she'd discovered the truth of her mother's harrowing final hours, spent on a workhouse infirmary bed.

Maude Larkin had died giving birth, but the child Harriet Fox had delivered hadn't been stillborn, as Lily had been led to believe by Miss Fox and the master and mistress. Her sister had survived ... only to be disposed of like rubbish to a baby peddler.

Harriet Fox had been the supervisor in charge of female inmates and had been hated and feared in equal measure by those in her custody. Only later, when free of her clutches, had Lily learned the extent of the wickedness Harriet Fox had directed at the Larkin family. She'd been a cruel, jealous woman, determined to marry Ben Stone and oust his parents to promote herself to running the workhouse with him. Ben had refused to be manipulated and had come to despise his bullying lover.

Lily knew the exact time her widowed mother had started an affair with the master's son: the Christmas Eve they'd entered the workhouse when he'd been guarding the gate. Maude had gone into the lodge to persuade him to allow them entry. Lily and Davy had been left outside, shivering in the snow. By then the family had been homeless for weeks. Lily could still picture the scene, and smell coal smoke, carried on air alive with the sound of carol singers. Church bells had been ringing ... a death knell for Maude Larkin and a clarion call of awful changes for the woman's twins. Lily didn't know how long her mother's liaison with Ben Stone continued. The Larkins had been separated once inside the institution, all three of them taken in different directions. She'd never seen her mother again. But Harriet Fox had, and she'd been enraged to discover her boyfriend had impregnated an inmate, giving Mrs Larkin a child that bore his birthmark. When the master and mistress found out about their son's interest in a widow a decade his senior, he'd been sent away to a job in a northern workhouse. He'd never been told about his baby daughter and only learned the truth of Maude Larkin's death years later, when Lily did.

Harriet Fox had colluded with her employers to keep the child's existence a secret until Ben Stone jilted her. Embittered, she'd then sought revenge in plotting to blackmail them all. She'd had a lot to go on, too. The scandal that had gone on beneath the workhouse roof would have cost the Stone family dear, had the Board of Guardians come to hear of it.

Many years had passed since destiny had lured four people into the master's unoccupied office on a December afternoon. Harriet had sneaked in there first to steal compromising documents. Lily had been next to arrive, hoping to get a receipt from the master for returning Margie's workhouse uniform. Her friend had been accused of theft after absconding wearing the rags. Later, Adam and Ben had barged in, having heard a commotion. Harriet had been swigging from the master's decanter while rifling the filing cabinets, and unhinged by a toxic broth of Scotch and malice, she'd taunted Lily about her mother's death and her sister's fate. The madwoman had lashed out with a paperknife. Ben Stone had defended Lily, causing Harriet to fall. It hadn't been murder. But the law might not have seen it that way had all the acrimony and greed and deceit been uncovered.

The authorities had received a plausible version of an intoxicated workhouse officer fracturing her skull in a mishap. On their return, the master and mistress had been given a full account of Harriet's rampage by their incensed son, including how she'd stabbed him in the arm with his father's letter opener while goading him about the child he'd known nothing about.

Lily had no idea whether Ben had ever had sleepless nights worrying about his daughter's whereabouts. He'd decided not to look for her, and had been spared knowing the infant had ended up in the clutches of a baby farmer named Mrs Jolley.

'Have you had any luck finding your half-sister, Lily?' asked Adam. Clearly their thoughts had collided during the protracted quiet.

She shook her head. 'I'm still searching for her.' She poured the teas, carrying them over on a tray. 'I have made some progress in tracing her though, so have something to tell you.' Her discovery about the baby farmer's involvement had been too horrible to document in a letter to Adam. She sat down opposite him then pushed a plate, piled with a biscuit assortment, towards him. He took one, munching on it while listening to how she'd discovered that Charlotte had been adopted when barely a day old, by a gentleman's mistress. Betsy Finch had been pregnant by Major Beresford but had miscarried quite late on. To keep her lover's pay cheques rolling in ... she'd needed to find a baby to present to him. Mrs Jolley had supplied the answer ... and Maude Larkin's baby had been sold. Lily's knowledge of this hadn't come from Betsy, but from Betsy's housekeeper. Vera Priest had grown very fond of the infant her employer had adopted. When the major died on the Western Front several years later, and Betsy's allowance, and her interest in her 'daughter', dried up, Vera had wanted to keep caring for little Charlotte as she'd been named. But it had been impossible and the child had been handed back to Mrs Jolley. Later, Vera searched for Mrs Jolley to reclaim Charlotte. But the baby farmer had disappeared. Instead, Vera crossed paths with Lily, who'd been hunting for the same little girl. Lily had never been more thankful to make somebody's acquaintance, and had listened greedily to every word the elderly woman told her about her half-sister's start in life. Vera Priest also had information about her father's fall from grace. Back then Vera had worked as a char and cleaned the office where Charles Larkin worked as a solicitor's clerk. He'd been a charming, good-looking man. Lily could understand why a woman might throw herself at him. But she'd never understand the malice behind her father's downfall. He'd been framed for theft then sacked after his jealous boss discovered his wife sniffing around Charles Larkin. And thus had started the whole family's fall into the gutter.

When eventually Lily concluded her tale, Adam gave the table an angry thump. 'I've heard of this Mrs Jolley before, from a colleague who has an interest in women's welfare. I'm surprised the law hasn't caught up with the bloody bitch and put a noose around her neck.'

Lily agreed wholeheartedly with him, though she was taken aback at his language. The Adam she recalled had been more of a moderate fellow before he went to war. 'By all accounts, Mrs Jolley uses aliases and moves house often to avoid interference in her disgusting trade.'

Lily grimaced her disappointment. 'I almost caught up with her, too.' The unfairness of it made her want to scream, instead she drew in a calming breath. 'By the time I had an address in Poplar, Mrs Jolley had done a flit. I banged on neighbours' doors asking where she'd gone, but nobody knew. All I discovered was that her foster daughter appeared very unwell on the day they left the area.'

'Sickly, do you think, or just malnourished?'

'Diphtheria was going round. Eric Skipman who works for me lost his little sister to the disease at about that time.' Lily knew Adam was biting his tongue on reminding her how deadly diphtheria was. 'Charlotte *is* still alive. I won't ever give up believing that until I've proof otherwise.'

He gave a vigorous nod of approval. 'This Betsy Finch must be a callous sort to return the child to a baby farmer after rearing her as her own for years.'

'*She* didn't rear her; Mrs Priest cared for my sister from the start.' She gestured hopelessness. 'After the major died, Betsy couldn't afford a housekeeper. Vera had to quickly find another live-in position, but nobody wanted her encumbered with a small child. So back Charlotte had to go to Mrs Jolley for re-adoption. If she still has her, I pray she has some affection for Charlotte and treats her well.'

'Amen to that,' said Adam. 'Betsy's gentleman friend must have been thoroughly conned to believe the baby his.'

'Apparently so, and I'm glad for Charlotte's sake. My sister benefited from his generosity, though she was little more than a toddler when her luck ran out.' Lily ended on a sigh.

Adam thoughtfully rubbed his chin. The Larkin family's scandal wasn't that unusual on the face of it: a destitute widow sleeping with a man in return for favours for herself and her children. Even had the tale not involved his protégée it would have fascinated Adam, having regressed from the mundane into a tragedy, complete with villainess and a child in jeopardy. It was depressing to learn that Harriet Fox had been replaced by another monstrous woman taking charge of little Charlotte's precarious existence.

'I wonder if Beresford's wife knew about his second family?'

'If he was married, I bet he kept his arrangement with Betsy under wraps.' She paused to reflect on things. 'Lies come easily to some people. The Stones deceived their son for years, yet doted on him and wanted him to step into his father's shoes.'

'That *was* the plan; Ben told me he'd never be workhouse master after what had gone on. He was estranged from his parents. They tried to keep in touch but, according to his fiancée, he refused to speak or write to them. They might not yet know that he's been killed.'

After a few quiet seconds of sipping tea and nibbling biscuits, Lily stood up and shook the kettle to see if there was water in it. 'Another cup?'

'I'd love to stay longer but I'm pushed for time. I have to attend a meeting about work shifts over the Christmas holiday. I've come back from France to oversee the opening of a new convalescent home in Islington.'

'You might bump into Fanny then,' said Lily with a smile. 'That's where she lives now. Margie's still in Poplar.' A mention of her best friend had reminded her of something puzzling. They'd broached more sensitive subjects, so she saw no reason not to bring this up. 'You recognised Margie's husband's name when we spoke to his mum earlier.'

Adam retrieved his cap from the table's edge and rotated it in his hands.

'Did you meet Bobby Smith in France?'

'I believe so; it's a common name though. I might be mistaken. Smudger, is how Gregory introduced him. I bumped into them in a café in Calais ... over a year ago. Gregory called him a work pal from Poplar. It didn't come up that he was married.'

'The wedding was in the summer ... a whirlwind affair.'

'Ah ... a baby was on its way.'

'Should've known it wouldn't take you long to work that one out,' said Lily ruefully.

'I wish Margie every happiness ... and Fanny too.' Adam got to his feet. 'It's been lovely seeing you, but now I have to shake a leg.'

Still Lily felt she was missing something. 'Did you meet Smudger again?'

'I think I caught sight of him at a hospital at St Omer. We didn't have a chance to speak on that occasion.'

'Smudger must've been there recovering after he was injured. He and Margie got married while he was home convalescing.'

Adam sighed. 'I shan't pull the wool over your eyes on this, Lily. He wasn't a patient; he was visiting one of the nurses. A colleague said Private Smith was known as her boyfriend. That would have been ...' He frowned, searching his memory. 'December last year. I recall there were Christmas decorations being put up in the wards. So it was long before his wedding, anyway.'

'I see ...' Lily was taken aback, despite knowing that Smudger had done nothing wrong. In December he'd not had a clue that by the following summer he'd be cornered into taking on a wife and a child. She wished she didn't think of Margie's marriage in that way. But she did.

Smudger had stepped up and done everything expected of him ... yet Lily had sensed that his heart hadn't been in it. She prayed it was now. And that Margie hadn't detected a mournfulness in her bridegroom, as she had, behind his wedding-day smile. 'Did you see them together after that?'

'I didn't go back there. I was reposted on Boxing Day.' Adam tucked his cap under an arm and approached the door. 'As I'm on duty tomorrow, I'll be eating my Christmas dinner with the boys in the ward. I expect you'll celebrate with your friends, won't you?'

'Margie's spending the day at her mum's with her sisters. Mrs Blake heard on the grapevine about her granddaughter and got back in touch. Margie wasn't sure she wanted to see them. Can't say I blame her, considering how she's been treated. She's going for Rosie's sake. She thinks her daughter should get to know them all.' Lily paused, thinking Margie was a good soul to forgive her mother for putting her in the workhouse for being a cripple and a burden. 'As for Fanny: she's been invited to her in-laws. If they don't drive her barmy she said she might stop in Edmonton for Boxing Day as well.' Lily hadn't dwelled on spending Christmas Day on her own; she didn't mind her own company. Neither did she mind that the ties binding them were falling away, to be refastened around other people. Kin exerted a powerful influence and the smaller the person the greater their sway.

'You've got nobody to spend Christmas with?' Adam sounded concerned. 'I might be able to swap a shift with somebody and we could have a roast dinner ...'

'That's kind of you, but it's not necessary. Smudger's mum has asked me to celebrate with her.' It wasn't wholly untruthful and Lily didn't want him feeling sorry for her.

121

'If I'd known you were coming for tea, I'd've put on a decent dress,' she said brightly, twitching her old serge skirt.

'You look just fine,' he said gallantly. 'Anything's better than wearing that bloody old uniform, eh?'

Lily groaned at the memory.

'After the holiday I'll ask my friend if anything has surfaced recently about this Jolley individual, and her disgusting baby-farming business, if you like.'

'Oh, would you? Is he working in a local hospital?'

'*She* is working in a local hospital.' He smiled. 'Evie Osborne is nursing at the new military hospital that opened in Endell Street. Have you heard of it?'

'I read about it!' Lily exclaimed. 'The building was converted from an old workhouse.' The newspaper article had stuck in her mind for that very reason. It had contented her that one of the vile institutions had been put to good use.

'That's the one, in Covent Garden. All the staff are women.' He was only half joking when he complained, 'I doubt they'd employ me.'

'They'd be mad to turn you down,' she stoutly championed, leading the way to the door. 'Sorry I didn't have a little Christmas tipple to offer you. If Fanny had still been bunking here, you would have been in luck.' Lily giggled. 'There was always a bottle of gin or port about the place back then.'

'Sounds like you had a bit of a lark, sharing the place with those two.'

'I did . . . on the whole . . .' Lily rolled her eyes. 'Don't ask.'

'Would you like to come along when I pay a visit to Evie in the New Year?'

Lily gave a vigorous nod then embraced him in thanks and farewell.

'I'll be in touch then.' He patted her back, his voice husky with affection. 'Look after yourself. And don't ever give up looking for your sister.'

'I shan't,' she said simply and kissed his cheek.

After he'd gone, Lily put a hand in her pocket. No matter the friends and family and momentous happenings they'd touched on, she'd always been conscious of the weight of her precious letter against her hip. She sat down again in the kitchen and put the envelope on the table. She studied it, the anticipation of opening it making her heart race. Yet her eyes spitefully prickled with tears. She'd yearned for a letter but not expected one. She'd not confided in anybody that deep down she'd thought no more of Greg's letters would arrive. She'd dreamt he had been buried in foreign earth that she'd knelt on and torn at with her hands until they bled. The dream hadn't receded from her mind as did others at daylight. This particular one had stubbornly clung to her memory, though it had never returned to disturb her sleep. Even weeks later she could vividly relive it if she allowed it the freedom to poison her mind. Its fire and blackness would make her tremble and she'd panic to remember Greg's face and be unable to do so, or to recall the sound of his voice. Then she'd weep, regretting that they'd not gone to have a photo taken together when he was last home. She wanted an image of him to hug to her heart and to kiss. So much had happened during his last leave ... awful things concerning Margie's rape ... that their final days had been filled up with trouble, and had sped by. In no time she'd been embracing him and saying goodbye at Charing Cross station.

In the morning she would write to him. He might be able to get a snap taken in France to send to her. Waiting until he came back would be tempting fate. Just as they'd tempted fate waiting to be married instead of getting on with it when they'd had the chance. He'd be back about springtime, a perfect time for a bride, so their optimistic fantasy had run. Now it was winter, the year almost changing to 1917. Tens of thousands of soldiers would never be coming back and still no end in sight to this bloody, bloody war.

She traced the slopes and angles of her name with a finger, swallowing a sob. She used the heel of her hand on her wet face then dried it on her skirt. She picked up the letter, opening it, laughing as her hungry eyes raced over the words and paragraphs. He'd loved the wafer biscuits she'd sent him and thanked her for the cigarettes. He hadn't seen her brother for a while, or Smudger. He hoped they were both well and when he bumped into Davy he'd remind him to write to her. Most of all he hoped she was well and remembering how much he loved and wanted to marry her, first chance he got. She turned the page, hoping for some more but there was nothing ... no description of village billets, or of the men in the platoon playing practical jokes, or of the prospect of getting any leave. She read it all again, slowly, and noted the date at the top of the page. Lily searched for comfort in the knowledge that he'd written this almost a month ago yet not sent it. He must have been somewhere the post couldn't be trusted. Things had improved for him and he'd reached civilisation and bumped into Adam. Time had passed since the men met up; Greg's relative safety might have gone now. Perversely she realised an injury similar to the one Smudger had suffered might not be too bad. A Blighty one would bring Greg home.

In a short while she was going to Eunice's for a festive drink and she wasn't turning up with her face on her boots.

She jerked herself into action, clearing the used crockery into the bowl, humming a carol to herself. Christmas was a magical time of the year and she'd cheer up if it killed her.

An hour later, Lily was off down the road wearing a cream-frilled blouse and tan skirt. Dainty shoes had replaced her work boots. Her coat was made of chocolate-coloured mohair and her velvet hat matched the shade of her skirt. Her Sunday best had been bought second-hand from Ridley Road market, but when she'd haggled for them they'd looked good as new. She had her box of chocolates in her hand; she'd no bottle of drink to take but was pretty sure Eunice would appreciate the offer of an orange cream.

She glanced up, wondering if Greg was in the open somewhere under a night sky, wishing on a star. 'Merry Christmas,' she whispered. 'Come back soon, my love. I need you to help me find out what's happened to Charlotte.' She imagined the child being happy somewhere, enveloped in a warm atmosphere of ale and spice with a nice family about her. She would be joining in the fun and singing carols with them. Praying for a miracle wouldn't make it come true. If Charlotte had survived her illness it was likely she was still with Mrs Jolley. Christmas Day for Charlotte Finch might be as miserable as any other time of the year.

Chapter Ten

'Merry Christmas, my dear.'

Charlotte looked at the wrapped parcel that had been laid on the tablecloth beside her empty breakfast bowl. The sight of the scarlet paper and the savoury smell in the air had stirred a memory of being with her mother and Mrs Priest. She remembered eating pears and oranges that Vera had peeled for her, while her mother was drinking rum. The gramophone wasn't often used, but on that day it had been wound up. Betsy had whirled about singing in a high sharp voice, her glass slopping rum onto her hand. Usually, she'd overlook her adopted daughter, but on that occasion she had put down her drink to clasp Charlotte's hands and spin them both round and round. The little girl remembered they'd bumped into the prickly tree in the corner and the stars and bells dangling on it had scattered on the floor, making a tune of their own. She'd enjoyed dancing and had wanted to carry on. But Vera had led her to the sofa, telling her to sit down or she'd be sick after eating all that pudding. Charlotte had licked the sticky residue left on her hand by her mother's fingers, curious to know the taste of rum. She'd not liked it and couldn't understand why Betsy did.

With Vera's help, Charlotte had undone the ribbon around her Christmas present. Inside had been a big shiny-faced doll with fair hair and blue eyes and legs and arms that moved.

The Christmas tree had still been in the corner of the room on the day Vera took her away to live with Mrs Jolley. The china doll and all of her other toys had been given to her foster mother and Charlotte had heard Vera saying she must be allowed to play with them. She hadn't seen them again, or Vera. And she still didn't know what she'd done wrong to be sent away.

'It's a Christmas present, dear.' Norman pushed the parcel closer to her. He imagined she'd not received a gift before and might be confused. 'It's something nice ... you'll like it.' He winked and ruffled her flaxen hair. 'Open it then.'

'Have I got to go away?' Charlotte raised her large apprehensive eyes to him. She folded her hands in her lap. She'd rather not have a toy and be allowed to stay with him.

'Go away?' repeated Norman, mystified. 'No, of course not. We've got a roast chicken for dinner. What d'you think of that, Charlie? And figgy pudding for afters.' He would call her Charlie to make her smile. She'd told him she'd sat next to a boy called Charlie in a classroom. She'd also told him she'd rarely been to school; thus it had become clear why she was six yet could hardly read or write.

She could stay. The wonderful news sharpened her awareness of the aroma filling the air, making her feel hungry even though she'd only just had breakfast. She used both her hands to carefully pick at the string fastened around the red tissue. Norman helped her untie the bow then watched as she folded back the paper to reveal a rag doll in a green dress and brown shawl.

'See ... it's got hair like yours,' Norman said, lifting a strand of yellow wool sprouting from the soft squashy head.

Charlotte picked the doll up and embraced it to her chest. It was better than the other one that had felt cold and hard and had been too big to cuddle.

'I knew you'd like it,' he said. 'Now, I'd better get on with our Christmas feast.' He turned back before entering the kitchen to watch the little girl playing with her present. A strong tenderness washed over Norman, the like of which he hadn't felt since his wife and daughter had been by his side. Charlotte looked happy and content ... he wished he were.

The child had told him things about her past life that had confused Norman, making him wonder if she was fantasising. Her father had been a major in the army but had died, she'd said. Her mother was a pretty lady with long brown hair. The woman who had abandoned the children was middle-aged and ugly, according to the tramp who'd been the only one to get a look at her. Norman had sought him out afterwards, mainly to discover how much of what had gone on Jake Pickard remembered when sober. The answer had been: too much for comfort.

Norman mulled all of it over while basting the roast chicken. If those people weren't a figment of her imagination, Norman deduced Charlotte Finch was of good stock. But the family, complete with a servant called Vera, had disintegrated after the father died in the war. It wasn't outlandish: the workhouse was home to every class of unfortunate folk. The widow had surely been desperate rather than negligent when engaging the Jolley woman to foster her children. She might have intended it to be a temporary arrangement while she was forced out to work to keep a roof over her head. Boarded-out children would sometimes be admitted to the workhouse when a foster parent was taken ill or no longer received funds to keep them.

After she'd come out of hospital and was well enough to be questioned, he'd asked Charlotte about Mrs Jolley from Poplar, and produced the addressed envelope he'd found on the baby boy. Charlotte had started to cry when he'd offered to take her back to Poplar for a reunion. The most he'd discovered from her mumbles was that she didn't like the woman who'd abandoned her.

Norman had left it there rather than upset her fragile recovery. Now Charlotte was blooming ... as pretty a child as you'd find anywhere with her large blue eyes and golden hair. Norman felt as proud of her as he had of his own daughter. He felt proud of himself, too, for having wrought that great improvement. She'd been a hollow-eyed bag of bones when he'd brought her home. It was ironic that his own health was failing as hers improved.

He wanted to find her real mother and take her back. But where should he start to look?

Later, when they were seated at the small dining table and eating their Christmas dinner, Norman decided to try again to talk to Charlotte about her parents. 'Mrs Jolley knows where your mother is, I suppose?' he asked casually.

She put down her knife and fork and looked at him with huge unblinking eyes.

'It's all right, dear, I'm not taking you back to your foster mother. But she knows where your real mother is, doesn't she? You'd like to see your mum and Vera, wouldn't you?'

'I'd like to see Vera,' she said.

'Yes ... that's it,' encouraged Norman. 'Mrs Jolley must know where they are.'

'Mother can't keep me and Vera has to go away for now.' Charlotte repeated what she'd been told.

'We could find out if your mum can keep you now ...'

'Have I been naughty?' Charlotte raised tear-filled eyes, pressing her trembling lips tight together.

'No ... of course not.'

'Please may I leave the table?'

'If you want; but you haven't finished eating dinner. And there's pudding to come and custard.' He smiled at her. She was a child with a good appetite and liked a pudding but she had used this tactic in the past to avoid a subject that she found distressing. They'd been doing simple sums one afternoon when he'd suggested going to Poplar to find Mrs Jolley. Charlotte had put down her pencil and gone to lie on her bed, feigning illness as a reason to stay with him at the lodge. Plainly, the little girl was as fond of him as he was of her.

He tapped her plate, urging her to eat. She did pick up her knife and fork but ate with her head lowered, and he saw a tear plop onto her plate. He reached across and stroked her crown of soft fair hair, wanting to say she could stay here for ever. But he couldn't. Too many lies had been told already. She was a sweet, trusting soul who had taken easily to living with him. But this couldn't go on. Charlotte Finch had been well enough to leave here six months ago. As June Gladwell was wont to continually remind him. Norman hadn't seen his girlfriend for a few days. They hadn't spent Christmas Eve together as he'd made it plain he wouldn't leave Charlotte on her own to go for a drink. June had gone off in a huff. They seemed to always be bickering lately. He wondered if she'd put in an appearance on New Year's Eve and try again to coax him to go to the pub with her.

He wouldn't. So it was difficult to decide whether he was looking forward to seeing June or not, though it would have been nice to wish one another a happy New Year.

'You'd better put a stop to this lark. Your guv'nor'll have your hide when he finds out about it. You'll be sorry you didn't listen to me sooner ...'

'Mr Stone knows about Charlotte.' Norman unclenched his teeth to interrupt his girlfriend's sermon. 'I told him my granddaughter was staying with me.'

'She's not your granddaughter. That's a lie for a start.' June sent him an old-fashioned look. 'And the master believes she's long gone. A short visit, you said, until her mother sorted out her problems.'

'If her mother had sorted out her problems she'd have been back to claim her.' His contribution to this conversation had mostly consisted of monosyllabic grunts. June hadn't taken the hint and cleared off, so he'd started answering back.

'You know what I mean, so don't try and be clever with me.' Too het up to settle on a chair, June continued stomping about. 'That woman dumped two sick kids outside, expecting them to be taken into the workhouse infirmary.'

'Well, they weren't. Charlotte ended up in hospital and the boy ...' Norman continued buffing shoe leather, his strokes becoming more forceful as he tried to put from his mind the infant in a pauper's grave.

He was seated at the small square dining table. At present the oak top was protected by a few sheets of week-old newsprint on which rested a burning oil lamp and a pair of boots awaiting attention. The lodge was a compact building: the kitchen that led off the parlour was no bigger than a lobby. There was just space to house a sink and a stove and a pantry cupboard. June was superstitious and didn't like shoes on tables. She used to tell him off for cleaning them here instead of standing at the draining board. She no longer bothered now she'd more important things to carp about.

'After Charlotte came out of hospital, you promised me you'd do what was best for her.'

'And I am.' Norman sounded defensive.

June gave a dry snort. 'You're not doing that girl any favours, and you know it. She should be at school like other kids her age.'

June believed in schooling, though she'd spent little time in a classroom herself after the age of eleven. Whenever her mother had found her with her nose in a book it would be whipped away and she'd be reminded that people like them didn't get above themselves. Doing washing for those better off was good enough to bring in a wage, she'd been told. June had followed the rule for over forty-five years, though it had taken her less than one, sweating over a copper, to suss the con. Charring and laundry had been her working life, as it was for most women expected to bring in a few bob while buckling down to marriage and raising kids in Whitechapel's backstreets. Now she was past sixty and a widow; she was ready for that retirement Norman had said they'd have together. Only he never mentioned it any more, even though her abusive first husband had been buried months ago.

June had spotted evidence that Norman was teaching the girl to read and write. Charlotte Finch had been spelled out in wobbly block capitals on paper torn from his notebook. Spiky sketches of whiskered pets had also featured on the page with *dog* and *cat* written underneath. June had taken heart from the proof he'd listened to her, believing he might come round to her way of thinking. He was brighter than she was, but no schoolmaster. Neither was he Charlotte's legal guardian, though he acted as though he were.

They'd both felt shocked and guilty over what had befallen the children left unattended on a winter's night and had rejoiced when the letter arrived telling them that Charlotte was on the mend.

Then came the headache of what to do next. The hospital staff had swallowed Norman's story about the sick girl being his granddaughter. Back then, June had agreed it would be best to keep up the pretence a while longer. At the lodge the child could build her strength over the summer months and their consciences could also finish healing. Unluckily, Norman had been spotted getting out of a cab with the girl on her first day home, making it impossible to sneak her in. Staff were hard to find with so many men away fighting. Few people wanted to be associated with a workhouse, anyway, and Norman had long years of valuable experience. Grudgingly, the master had given permission after his porter gave assurances that his granddaughter's visit would be brief.

That had been ages ago.

A foster mother might suit, but he'd not see the girl enter the workhouse, Norman had declared on the chilly spring day when he'd carried the little scrap into the lodge, swamped in a warm woollen coat he'd purchased for her. Tomorrow was the start of a new year. But no foster home had been found, or even looked for.

And June had had enough.

'That girl needs a mother and a regular upbringing. By

now she'd have learned how to read properly and do sums. You said she's a bright kid.'

'She is. She knows her letters and her numbers.' Norman rubbed the duster one final time over the shoe on his lap. He placed it on the floor then took its mate off his lap and jabbed the bristle brush into a tin of brown Cherry Blossom.

'Being able to write her name and count up to ten won't get her far in life,' June acidly pointed out.

'She can write other words and read some of this book.' He tapped a copy of *Gulliver's Travels* half hidden beneath a leaf of newsprint. He'd found the book in a box of his late wife's possessions and thought it might be useful. He wasn't one for book reading, though he scanned the *Daily Mail* from front page to back and took the *News of the World* at the weekend.

Charlotte had told him Vera would read her stories after tucking her in at night. Not to be outdone, Norman had read her a page or two of his book at bedtime.

'She can read some of this, can she?' June impatiently tugged at the novel, upsetting Norman's neatly arranged cleaning gear. The rocking lamp filled the air with the smell of kerosene. 'I'd like to hear her try.'

Norman remained calm, although all his brushes and tins were in a muddle. 'When she's older, she'll be able to read all of it.'

'When she's older?' June spluttered, flicking through pages. 'Gawd's sake! You'd better wake up, my friend, and admit you're in this way over your head.'

'Charlotte's mother might yet come back for her.' Norman continued pivoting the shoe on his fist, attacking it with the brush.

'If she was coming back she'd have showed up by now.'

The book was lobbed onto the table, making the lamp flicker and the tin of Cherry Blossom spin.

His feelings for June had weakened since he'd seen this side of her. She'd always been rather selfish. Norman had made allowances for that, considering the life she'd been enduring. Bill Gladwell was now dead, but June hadn't improved. She'd got worse, drinking more and bossing him about as though they were already married. She was a companion for him but sometimes he just wished she'd take the hint and bugger off.

June had no intention of doing that, but she had decided to change tack. 'Let's not argue. You're a sentimental old fool, aren't you? You were worried about Charlotte. And so was I. It's silly to torture yourself over what went on, though, now the girl's blooming.'

Norman gave a hesitant smile, not quite convinced by her old pal's act.

'She needs a foster mother, Norman. I'll advertise for one in the *Gazette* next week. New year and new start for the kid.'

'You will not.'

'Put her where she belongs then: the place her mother intended for her.' June tipped her head towards the workhouse.

'Over my dead body.'

June was determined to persevere. 'Slip on a pair of shoes, love.' She gave his bald pate a tickle. 'It's New Year's Eve. Let's go and celebrate. We can talk about that seaside cottage we're going to have in Clacton. Bill's been buried a decent while; it's high time to get the ball rolling on our retirement. Come on then, shake a leg and get your boots on—'

An exasperated Norman flung the half-polished shoe to

the floor. 'I've already told you I'm not going to the pub,' he hissed, struggling to keep his voice down.

'The girl's asleep ... you saw me check on her,' June reminded him huffily. 'You've gone out for a drink in the past after she's dropped off.'

'I know I have, but I shouldn't have and I wouldn't have if it hadn't been for you driving me nuts with your bloody nagging.' The complaint streamed through his teeth and was accompanied by a resentful glance.

'Nobody'll miss you. You said yourself the poor blighters don't come knocking as often on high days and holidays. Can't blame 'em. I'd choose to spend New Year's Eve in the gutter over that place.' June wouldn't give up. Once Norman was at a distance from Charlotte, with a drink inside him, he usually mellowed. Theirs was no grand love affair but it had endured. She had invested more than five years in this relationship. They'd spoken about growing old together from the start; but she'd always been keener than him to tie the knot. Now he avoided the subject altogether.

She didn't consider Charlotte Finch as family, the way Norman did. As far as June was concerned, she had enough children in her life with her daughter Ginny's kids. She didn't want any more landed on her, at her age. She'd earned a rest and wasn't going into a second marriage with a cuckoo in the nest.

June regretted having drawn Norman's attention to an angelic-looking child this time last year. She wished the kid had run out of the pub and they had carried on enjoying themselves. Jake Pickard had been hanging about and would eventually have raised the alarm about the orphans abandoned in the snow. Norman might have been dismissed for going AWOL; even that might have been preferable to this intolerable situation though. He was still embroiled in misconduct, yet to be uncovered, and in danger of getting the sack.

'It's a lovely evening ... not too cold ... shame to waste it. I've got a right thirst on me, Norm,' June chirped.

It *was* a good winter evening, a waft of crisp dry air came in from outside through the fanlight, pleasantly refreshing. June believed that as it was on the cusp of 1917 there weren't paupers to worry about. She believed that Charlotte had received enough assistance and should be forgotten. She believed the child was no longer his concern and his conscience shouldn't trouble him if she ended up wearing workhouse rags and eating skilly.

Norman knew all this about what June believed because since she'd turned up earlier he'd heard it non-stop. He believed that if she didn't shut up about it he might throttle her.

'I think—' June didn't get any further.

Norman sprang to his feet, banging into the table in a spurt of energy, scattering the boots and brushes and slopping kerosene onto newspaper. 'Get out!' he snarled. 'Get out of here and don't come back until you've got over being jealous of a poor little girl.'

June gawped at him, chin sagging. Then she clacked her teeth together and tilted her chin. 'If I go, I won't be back. And you'll be sorry for all this deceit.' She waited but he made no attempt at conciliation. He busied himself collecting the stuff strewn on the floor.

June turned at the door to look scornfully back at him on his knees. 'She's not your granddaughter ... she's not your business, and you can't change that.'

'Lower your voice. You'll wake her,' Norman growled,

shooting a glance at the box room where Charlotte was. Since she had moved in, Norman bedded down on the sitting-room sofa. And that had been another bone of contention where June was concerned. Their canoodling had dwindled to kissing and fumbling as though they were adolescents. Not going all the way was something of a relief to Norman. Since those aches in his chest had begun troubling him, it wasn't easy to achieve any satisfaction.

'I'll shout if I want to.' June was red with indignation. 'And I'll tell you this fer nothing: me husband might have been a pig but he'd never have put me second best to a stranger's kid. And I ain't putting up with it from you.' The front door was slammed.

Norman used the chair to pull himself to his feet, relieved she'd gone.

Charlotte hadn't been asleep. She'd pretended to be when Mrs Gladwell came in to peer at her. Then when the noise started she had crept from her bed to listen to the voices that stopped and started and hissed and barked. She hadn't been able to make out much of what was said. She'd known they were angry with one another, though, and that Mrs Gladwell blamed her for causing trouble between them all. It had been the same the last time ... and the time before that when Charlotte had crouched behind her bedroom door listening to her name being spoken in a nasty way.

Earlier, before Mrs Gladwell had arrived, her granddad had left his tea and gone to lay down on the settee. He had an ache and didn't feel like food, he'd said. Now he looked sad rather than unwell. Charlotte had wanted to go to him, but Mrs Gladwell wouldn't have liked it. So she had sat behind the door, hugging her knees, with her heart jumping and pattering beneath her nightdress.

She didn't know why she annoyed people when she tried hard to be good. She'd been sent away from her nice home with Vera and her mother. Because she was bad, Mrs Jolley had said, when she'd asked why her real mother didn't come to take her home. Her foster mother would smack her and shout at her and tell her she was a pest. Charlotte knew she had been naughty to take one of Mrs Jolley's pound notes and run away to a neighbour's house. But she'd wanted to live with nice people even though they were poor. Her granddad was as kind to her as Vera had been. In return, Charlotte helped him so he'd always let her stay here. She laid the table at mealtimes and when he was feeling unwell she would drag a chair to the sink to kneel on. She'd wash up the plates then dry them while he rested. When he felt better, he'd get up and stroke her hair and tell her she was a good girl.

She stayed inside, away from the windows, because he said she must. It was wonderful when he opened up the sashes and air blew on her face. She would close her eyes, remembering being in a garden filled with flowers that smelled like her real mother's scent bottles. Vera would sit on the grass with her under a tree and they'd pick daisies to make chains.

Her legs were folded beneath her, and had started to ache, making her fidget. There wasn't a sound coming from behind the door now. She got up and padded back to her bed with her doll under her arm.

'I thought you were asleep. Did we wake you?'

Charlotte had one knee on the bed and she quickly scrambled up onto the mattress and gazed at Granddad before pulling the sheet to her chin.

'Didn't mean to wake you, dear.' He read her anxiety and came fully into the room.

He'd grown to love this child but he was feeling every one of his sixty-three years and was not up to being a single parent. June was an intolerable nag, but she had a point. If she were prepared to join forces with him in bringing up Charlotte then he'd retire. They could move away and make a life between them, hopefully see Charlotte attain an age where she was able to care for herself. But June wouldn't do it graciously; she'd make sure that he and Charlotte suffered every single day for her sacrifice. He supposed he should be grateful June didn't fake affection for the little girl to get husband number two. Deceit, as he'd found out, was a relentless trap.

'How about a cup of warm milk?' he suggested. 'And another little story to lull you back to sleep.' He came closer to tuck the blanket around her.

Charlotte nodded and relaxed with a sigh because he wasn't cross with her. She pulled her doll onto the top of the cover, settling her hands over it.

Norman got the milk pan down off the shelf in the kitchen, and half-filled it. While it was heating up he went into the sitting room and sat down. Charlotte was now about six and a half, he guessed, though she seemed unsure of her birthday. In no time she'd be approaching adolescence and would need a woman's care and guidance. He had a choice to make. It wasn't between June and Charlotte; that was already settled. Charlotte didn't boss him about or chivvy him to spend his money on booze he didn't want. Charlotte was good company and funny in her sweet, youthful way. He'd adore to watch her grow into a lovely, intelligent young woman. But she'd never reach the heights stuck with him, living a half-life in shadows without a proper education and friends. He wanted her to attend school, and get to know other children. For that, he'd need to resign and seek other work and lodgings. If he'd been a decade younger he would have met the challenge, but not now, with his health failing. Nobody would employ him and pay him enough to make that come true.

He got out his notebook and tore a page from it to compose an advert for a foster mother.

Chapter Eleven

'Sorry I can't be of more help. I've no idea what stone that vermin might have crawled under. Mrs Jolley's name's not cropped up for ages. If she's ducked out of sight, maybe she's twigged somebody's on her tail.'

'Never mind,' said Lily. 'I appreciate you sparing the time for a chat. You must be run off your feet.' She extended a hand to Evie Osborne.

'Oh . . . we're just ticking over at the moment.' Evie firmly shook hands. 'When a convoy arrives from Waterloo station, *then* we're run off our feet. I wouldn't be standing around talking to you if an ambulance filled with boys from France needed unloading.'

Lily wasn't offended by a blunt observation that she might soon be in the way. She glanced along the corridor, intersected at stages by other corridors. It looked busy to her: women dressed in uniform, medical and official, were toing and froing, sometimes stopping to exchange papers before purposefully carrying on. There was a constant ring of footfall and the clack-clack of a typewriter being pounded behind one of the office doors. It seemed an impressively spotless and efficient hospital, yet the only man she'd seen about the place was Adam. He'd gone off to visit a patient he'd treated overseas, since transferred back home.

Adam had called round for Lily at two o'clock and they'd hailed a cab in Poplar to take them to Endell Street Military Hospital in Covent Garden. On the way, he'd told her his friend Evie Osborne was a seasoned suffragette who didn't suffer fools gladly, leading Lily to complain she'd have liked better warning of being stranded with a middle-aged dragon. Now she knew why she'd made him guffaw. The young woman he'd introduced her to fifteen minutes ago couldn't have been further from the belligerent harridan she'd anticipated.

Evie Osborne was actually a short, slim blonde and looked no more than five years Lily's senior. Judging by her posh accent, Evie was of good family, but she'd no airs and graces and was startlingly forthright. In looks, she reminded Lily of Margie; in manner, Evie Osborne could give brash Fanny a run for her money. Lily felt comfortable talking about her sister to this young woman, though they'd only just met.

'Now Jolley's name has cropped up, it's brought back some bloody unpleasant memories,' announced Evie. She took Lily's elbow and urged her the short distance along the corridor to the exit. 'I've only ten minutes of my break left and I'm dying for a gasper. Let's natter outside while we wait for Adam. The COs are a pair of sticklers. Doctors Murray and Garrett Anderson don't take kindly to finding ash on the floor.' She smirked. 'I've seen Flora Murray whip a fag out of a visiting RAMC colonel's paw and throw it out of the door – and him after it.' She ferreted in the pocket of her nurse's uniform and produced a packet of Capstans. 'Do you smoke, Lily? It is all right to call you Lily, isn't it?

Don't call me Miss Osborne, whatever you do. I'm just Evie to everyone.'

'I do smoke sometimes, but won't have a cigarette, thanks anyway.' Lily got a word in edgeways as they emerged into January air that was fresh and breezy. 'And I'd like you to call me Lily.' She paused, while Evie exhaled smoke, groaning in ecstasy as though tasting nectar rather than nicotine. 'Those unpleasant memories you said you've got ...' Lily picked up the thread of their conversation. 'Do they involve Mrs Jolley?'

'Not precisely. I was thinking back donkey's years.' Evie led the way round the side of the building to lean back against the brick wall. 'I've heard some dreadful cases of child neglect – and worse – while wending my way through the nursing ranks.' She fumbled under her apron to stow her cigarettes and matches in her pocket. 'I cut my professional teeth assisting a midwife at a home for unmarried mothers in Blackwall. That was an eye-opener.'

The two girls shifted aside to allow a female porter past, wheeling a trolley brimming with cartons. Evie craned her neck to read the labels as her colleague headed towards a building similar to Wilding's costermonger warehouse with large barn-style doors standing open. Inside were others dressed in Women's Hospital Corps uniform: brown skirts and smart military-style belted jackets. They were unloading supplies and making notes on clipboards.

'Those could be the new files and folders, turned up at last.' Evie took another drag, blowing smoke skywards. 'Anyway, what I was saying ... my senior knew her stuff but she was regimental; the sort that believed in being cruel to be kind. If a girl was intending to give away her baby, she'd give her the full treatment.' Evie snorted. 'She wanted to shock them into keeping their kids, you see. The horror stories she came out with weren't lies either. Dead babies had been fished out of the Thames. The poor mites had been murdered by a money-grabbing baby farmer masquerading as a decent foster mother.' Evie tapped ash onto the concrete. 'I don't reckon any of those girls dared uncross their legs again. I got to know a few of them and felt bloody sorry for the mess they were in. Same tale, time after time: a bloke had done the dirty. Promised to marry them then scarpered after he'd had his fun.' Evie frowned. 'One girl managed to hide her belly for almost nine months before her parents chucked her out. She was already in labour when her mother dumped her on our doorstep. We got her onto the ward just in time.'

It was a depressing tale, yet not a surprising one. Lily reckoned a pregnant Margie would have received similar treatment from her mother, had she been allowed to go back home after absconding from the workhouse. Mrs Blake had shunned her disabled daughter then but now welcomed her into the family fold as perfectly respectable Mrs Smith. A son-in-law and a granddaughter to boast about had made all the difference. Smudger had made all the difference. It didn't seem right to Lily that men had all the sway, even when, like Smudger, they didn't want it.

'That midwife might have meant well but she lived in cloud cuckoo land,' Evie concluded her reminiscence about her baptism of fire in South London. 'Most of the girls were working class and an orphanage or a foster home were their options. I doubt if much has changed in the five years since I was a probationer there. The mums will still be wailing when their babies get taken away.'

Evie used her dog-end to light another cigarette, then

held out the Capstans and matches. Lily accepted a smoke this time. She thought of her mum, Margie, Fanny, all of them had broken their hearts with worry over their children.

'When Amelia Dyer was hanged for killing babies, my senior was already middle-aged. She'll be retired now. Others swung for it, but Dyer's the name I remember because that midwife carped on about it. Quite a show trial at the Old Bailey, by all accounts: baying crowds and so on. That's going back about twenty years.'

Lily took a deep drag on her cigarette.

'Sorry ... I've been a bit thoughtless, going on like that. It must be hellish for you, trying to trace your little sister without much of a clue where to look.' Evie straightened up off the brick wall, dusting herself down. 'So that's how I came to know about Jolley and her ilk. It'd drive me barmy to give a baby away. I'd sooner ask dear Papa for a few quid if the worst happened to me and the hot baths and castor oil didn't work.'

Lily grimaced squeamishness. 'I've seen adverts in the newspaper for pills sent through the post.'

'I wouldn't get involved with any of those charlatans selling kill-or-cure potions,' warned Evie. 'Steel and penny-royal?' She snorted. 'Forget it. I'd put my trust in a doctor.'

'One of these?' Lily glanced at the hospital.

'I wouldn't ask a colleague and risk getting them in a fix; but Papa could make discreet enquiries at his club about a Harley Street surgeon. Pretend it was for a mistress, something like that. You know ... all men together. Close ranks, chaps.' Evie had mimicked a gruff pompous voice. 'This isn't the sort of conversation I ordinarily get into with somebody I've just met. Though I do feel I'm already getting to know you, Lily Larkin.' She chuckled. 'Bet you think I'm a right old trollop, talking about such things. Yet I've not even had a kiss in ten months. Boyfriend's overseas at the mo, and no idea when he'll be back.'

'My fiancé's in France. Not seen him for over a year,' sighed Lily.

'Mother keeps asking me when I'm getting engaged. She thinks I'm on the shelf at twenty-three. Bloody hell, give him a chance, I said.' Evie gazed dreamily into space. 'He asked me to be his girl last spring but since then he's been away most of the time. We've been to the flicks twice and to a dance. That's it. He writes a smashing love letter though.' She was studying the bump beneath Lily's glove. 'You're properly engaged, are you? Ring and everything.'

Lily gave a smile and a nod. 'I've known Greg ages ... we got engaged last time he was home on leave.'

'Show off your sparkler then.'

Lily pulled off her glove and wriggled the finger with its sapphire and diamond adornment.

'Phew. That's a corker,' said an impressed Evie. 'Is he in banking? My mother pushed me towards a rich City boy, but I didn't take to him. My Colin's a commissioned officer in the Guards, and not got a bean. Youngest son, you see. We met here when he visited a wounded pal.' She thumbed at the hospital. 'He thought we'd all be man-hating shrews. Didn't take me long to persuade him *I* like men.' She gave a wink.

'Adam told me you're a suffragette.' Lily chuckled. 'You're definitely not what I was expecting though.'

'What were you expecting?' Evie sounded intrigued rather than indignant.

'Somebody older, standing on a soapbox with a

megaphone.' Lily bit her lip to conceal a self-conscious smile. She shrugged an apology but Evie simply hooted in amusement.

'Lily! You have led a sheltered life. How old are you, anyway?'

'Eighteen. Did Adam tell you where we met?' Lily didn't think that Adam would have mentioned the workhouse. Not that it would matter if he had. Lily wasn't ashamed of something she'd had no control over.

'He said you're old friends and you used to do a bit of clerical work for him. He's a good bloke, is Adam. Everybody here likes him. He's not a typical RAMC officer, sneering and telling us girlies to leave it to the chaps and go home and sit still.'

'Adam's been a wonderful friend to me,' said Lily. 'I'd better go and find him in a minute. I've some jobs to do before I'm finished for the day.' Lily had left the boys serving on the stall but the takings needed logging in the accounts book once she got back to the warehouse. And Joey and Eric would want their pay.

'I expect Adam's getting a full report of the Christmas concert. It was a good laugh. Even the boys confined to bed had silly hats on.' Evie crossed her arms. 'Once they get over the shock of finding out they're not going to be patched up by a man, they like it here. Yes, we're suffragettes. We're also bloody good nurses and doctors. We'll get you better, that's all that counts, I tell them.' Done boasting, Evie realised she'd not received an answer to a previous question. 'So what does your fiancé do when he's in civvies?'

Lily smiled, pulling her glove back on. 'Greg's a costermonger.'

'What? He sells fruit and veg and bought you a ring

like that?' Evie spluttered, torn between amusement and disbelief.

'He's got his own business and is brilliant at what he does.' Lily did some boasting of her own.

'He must be. Your Greg got called up then, did he?'

'He volunteered in 1915. I got a letter yesterday. He's been promoted to lance corporal and he reckons he'll get leave soon. He'd better, or I'm going to France to find him.'

A hubbub had started, interrupting the girls' conversation.

Evie groaned. 'If that's what I think it is . . . it'll be good-bye, Lily.' She was already trotting off to peer around the corner of the building. Lily soon joined her. A group of nursing orderlies had congregated on the forecourt to meet a motor ambulance pulling in through the open gates. The nose of another vehicle could be seen waiting behind it.

Evie took a long final drag on her cigarette then dropped the stub and stepped on it. 'Ambulance train must've just got in at one of the stations,' she announced through the smoke curling from her mouth. 'All hands on deck now.' She was briskly on her way to assist her colleagues with the new arrivals. 'Keep in touch, won't you? We could go out one evening . . . flicks or the dance hall, if you like.' She called over her shoulder, then turned around to face Lily, keen to have an answer.

'I will; promise. If you spot Adam, let him know I'm wait-ing outside for him, would you?' Lily received a thumbs up in response.

She remained at the corner and watched. She believed herself to be a robust sort; she'd survived hardship and beatings that no child should endure and stayed defiant. She was unprepared for this though and had started trembling.

Men with pinned-up trouser legs or sleeves were emerging from the back of the ambulance. She could hear groans as they tried to stand up; most were being carried on stretchers. A young fellow with a blood-stained bandage wound about his skull was shuffling forward on his bottom to hang his legs out of the back of the van and gingerly get to his feet. Convalescing servicemen were a common enough sight in London. But she'd not seen this side of things: the damage and suffering that earned the lucky ones a set of hospital blues and pats on the back as they walked down the High Street. Lily wanted to dash forward and stare at every face to reassure herself that neither Greg nor Davy were amongst the casualties. Dread kept her right where she was. She'd fall to pieces if one of those hobbling, bedraggled figures turned out to be somebody she knew and loved.

To her shame, she realised she wished she'd not come and met Evie Osborne and witnessed this. The last invalid to emerge from the bowels of the van was a fair-haired Tommy, pulling his crutches either side of him. They made a scraping sound like fingernails dragging on a blackboard. Lily could tell the fellow was too short to be Greg; but blond hair was what she'd been looking for, fearing to see. She started to cry and sniff and attempted to hide her cowardly face from view by pulling up her coat collar as though the breeze was chilling her. The reality of war was parading before her eyes towards the hospital's entrance. Evie had her arm about one of the blind fellows, guiding him. Female stretcher-bearers were negotiating the entrance steps with care.

The sound of the ambulance driver sweeping out the back of her vacant van eventually became louder than the thud of her own heart. Lily wiped her face with her gloves and stood up straight. She'd spotted Adam hurrying out of the entrance. He gave her a wave and she answered him with a smile, raising a hand, and quickly scrubbed her face again.

'Sorry, Lily ...' He jogged up to her. 'Got talking for longer than expected. It's so nice to see patients looking clean and well cared for and flowers in vases too. Must seem like paradise to them ... Are you all right?' He'd broken off, noticing her pallor.

She nodded. 'It's just ... Evie told me some hairy stories about baby farmers. Oh, I asked her to be honest and not hold back.' Lily couldn't admit to being a weakling. It wasn't how Adam saw her; it wasn't how she saw herself. She put up her chin and smiled. If she came here again and saw a convoy, she'd know what to expect. Next time she'd be absolutely fine.

'Did you two get along? I hoped you would,' Adam said as they strolled towards the gates.

'Like a house on fire. I like Evie. We're going to meet up again. Perhaps go to the flicks or something like that.'

'Good.' He grinned. 'If I wasn't on my way back to France, I'd join you. I could do with a night out.'

'Your busman's holiday is over, is it?' He'd been lucky, being able to extend his time in England by working at the convalescent home.

'I'm afraid it is. All good things, and all that ...' He sighed. 'It's back to France for me. I sail on Friday. I shall miss you.'

She'd miss him too. But Greg was the one she yearned to see more than anyone ... more even than her brother. A few years back she'd never have believed anybody could mean more to her than her beloved twin. Davy was her only remaining blood kin if her half-sister had succumbed to diphtheria.

After listening to Evie's tales of greedy, heartless people preying on desperate mothers unable to keep their babies, Lily was determined to renew her search to find Charlotte Finch. Mrs Jolley held the answers to so many questions and somebody would know where she was. If Charlotte had died, there was no reason Mrs Jolley shouldn't tell the truth about it. She might be a vile individual but couldn't be blamed for her foster daughter's death during a local diphtheria epidemic. There had been numerous cases in Poplar at the time, and several children had died of the disease. In her bones Lily felt sure Charlotte had been luckier and had survived, and so she wouldn't ever stop searching for her to bring her home where she belonged.

Chapter Twelve

'She shouldn't have them kids ... they're better off in the spike, 'n' that's sayin' summat.' Jake Pickard stumbled off the kerb, slopping beer. He licked the back of his wet hand and ambled along in the gutter rather than negotiate a return to the pavement.

Norman had been conscious of the vagrant following him and rambling nonsensically between taking glugs from a bottle. Pickard was his usual noxious self, mantled in a fug of stale alcohol and body odour. Norman was tempted to change course and find a different postbox just so he wasn't downwind of him. Glaring over a shoulder hadn't worked, neither had lengthening his stride to put distance between them. He was soon out of breath and slowed down to steady his heartbeat. When his sleeve received a tug, he jerked it free and crossed the road.

Norman was still twitchy around Pickard and would avoid him. Such tactics hadn't recently been necessary as the local tramp hadn't been about for a while. In bad weather Jake would lob a brick through the police station window to get a few nights' shelter in a cell. He'd disappeared for so long this time that Norman had wondered if he'd perished on the streets in midwinter. To his shame, he'd hoped it might be true. Jake was the only person apart from June who knew the workhouse porter had been carousing on the Christmas Eve he should have been attending to two abandoned waifs.

Local down-and-outs would usually admit defeat at some point and apply to come in. Jake Pickard had shunned the workhouse and looked after himself. And he was still alive, unlike many who'd trudged in and been carried out in a box.

Norman and that tramp had grown old together on the Mile End Road. The men looked of similar age, but Jake was actually a decade younger. Living rough was taking its toll and he'd committed a worse crime than window breaking to overwinter in gaol. Now it was spring, and he'd re-emerged like a hardy weed in stony ground.

Despite his incarceration, or perhaps because of it, Jake appeared fit. Hard labour and enforced sobriety had been unwitting friends. He was making up for the lack of booze but Norman had admiration for any ageing vagrant managing to hold on to his independence on the mean streets of London.

The fingers plucking at his arm were starting to irritate him though. 'What is it you want?' Norman hadn't shaken off his smelly shadow by swapping sides and had been forced to push him away.

Jake regained his balance and came forward in a rolling gait, head lowered, and tangled locks curtaining his face. 'I reckon she's after them kids. Ain't right after wot she did.' He shook open his grey mane to squint at Norman. 'You tell her to clear off. Or I'll tell the master was me found them nippers, not you.'

'What?' Norman had warmed up from his brisk march but now felt a chill come over him. 'What in damnation are you on about, you blathering fool?' Nervously, he glanced around. The street was busy and passers-by were no doubt wondering if he was being badgered for money. Norman pulled his hat brim down, about to rush on, but a sense of foreboding made him hesitate. Jake had never accosted him before to blackmail him. It seemed odd that the man would suddenly make an issue of an event that had taken place over a year ago ... unless something had happened to jog his memory about it.

Pickard's finger aimed jabs at a hollow beneath one of his bleary eyes. 'These peepers doan forget a face.' Having peered into the empty bottle to spot some dregs he upended it to be certain it was all gone before letting it drop.

'Whose face have you seen?' Norman asked hoarsely, though he'd a good idea.

'The bitch wot dumped 'em. I noo she'd be back fer the pretty gel.' Jake sniffed. 'Li'l angel was nice to me. I'll take her home and look after her better'n that cruel ol' cow.'

Norman stopped himself snorting in disbelief. The man had to be utterly blotto to suggest he was able to care for a child. Home to Jake Pickard could be a railway arch or a shop doorway. But Norman was curious about Charlotte having had dealings with the tramp. 'Why do you like her?'

'Sweet, she was ... an' kind to me.' Jake slurred.

Inside Jake's befuddled head could be vital information about Mrs Jolley's whereabouts. That woman was the link to people Charlotte had spoken of with fondness. It was Norman's greatest wish that his adopted granddaughter be happily settled back with her mother and Vera.

Early in the New Year he'd broken his own rule about

leaving Charlotte alone in the evening and visited Poplar in the vain hope of questioning Mrs Jolley. The neighbours there had confirmed she had lived at that address but had added 'and good riddance' when telling him Mrs Jolley had done a flit.

Norman had a letter in his pocket to post to a Mrs Yates. She had answered his advertisement for a foster mother. His notice had been in the *Gazette* for three months yet he had only received half a dozen replies. The majority had contained such ill-spelled sketchy information about the service offered that he had instantly dismissed them. Charlotte deserved a good home and good standards. Mrs Yates had written a nice letter detailing her circumstances. She'd lost her husband in the war, and being childless, would adore to have a dear daughter's company. Her address was Highgate; a salubrious area and close enough for Norman to visit before concluding any deal. Thereafter, he could keep an eye on Charlotte's welfare, from a discreet distance. The woman showed enough promise for Norman to make further enquiries ... anonymously. He'd used an alias in all his correspondence, and a post office box address, to protect himself from tricksters. The only information he'd given about the child to be fostered was her age and sex.

If he believed he could contact Charlotte's real mother, he'd screw up the letter right now. She'd be horrified to learn her children had been neglected by their foster mother and would welcome her daughter back. He'd no moral high ground to claim, given his own failings. Mrs Finch had done what she believed to be best at the time. Charlotte was strong and beautiful, a credit to her mother. As an inducement, Norman could offer Mrs Finch some financial assistance. He had to use his savings in any event, and would sooner they went to Charlotte's family than to a stranger. But he had to find the family and a new lead might come from this tramp.

'Nobody's been back to the lodge for those children.' Norman prodded Jake, who appeared to be dozing on his feet, rocking gently to and fro. 'Are you certain it was the same woman?'

'Not been back?' Jake had slowly processed what he'd heard. 'Thass all right then . . . cos she's no good.' He livened himself up, wagged a finger and stepped off the kerb to wend on his way.

Norman found himself in the odd position of chasing after him now. He grabbed a handful of his filthy donkey jacket, dragging him back to the pavement to talk. 'Where did you see her?'

'These peepers doan forget a face . . .'

'Yes . . . I know.' Norman impatiently cut him off. He ferreted in a pocket for some coppers to use as a bribe. 'D'you know where that woman lives?'

'Might do . . .' Blotto or not, Jake had heard the chink of coins. 'Show yer the house . . . p'raps . . .' He pocketed the pennies offered to him.

'I don't have time. What's the address?' Norman sounded agitated. He wanted to get back to Charlotte. She knew she mustn't answer the door when he wasn't home and there had never been a problem in the past with him briefly slipping out on business.

Jake's disgusted expression indicated he couldn't be expected to recall unnecessary details like addresses. ''S'up there.' He jerked his chin. 'Clocked her by the station then followed her, see.' He grinned, displaying an incomplete set of teeth. 'I know where she went.' He closed one eye and peered calculatingly at Norman with the other. 'Giss two bob and I'll show yer which house.' He pulled on the porter's lapel. 'You ain't letting her near them kids. Swear on it.'

'She won't get her hands on either of those children again, that's a promise.' Norman straightened his coat.

The solemn heartfelt oath was enough to reassure Jake. As was the silver coin that was handed over. He kept it in his fist and set off at a rolling stroll, beckoning Norman over a shoulder with a dirty fingernail.

'Can't you speed up?' Accompanying a tramp along the street wasn't something Norman relished doing at a snail's pace. Every instinct was telling him to head straight home because the drunkard was talking rot.

'Ain't far . . .' Jake ambled around a corner.

Norman was thankful they were off the main thoroughfare now and less likely to arouse interest. June was due to call in about half an hour and if nobody opened the door she'd wonder what was up.

His girlfriend had relented and paid a visit in early January to wish him a happy New Year. The atmosphere had been rather strained, but he'd been pleased to see her. She hadn't said any more about weddings or cottages in Clacton. To his relief, neither had she badgered him to go out to the pub. They'd fallen back into a routine of having a small tipple and perhaps a kiss and cuddle if the sherry had made them particularly harmonious. June was his only adult friend and, thankfully, she had seemed to accept Charlotte was a fixture in his life. He hadn't let on that actually he was trying to settle the child's future in his own way. Better to deal with it then present Charlotte and June with a fait accompli, in due course.

After Christmas, he had made an effort to strengthen blood ties. He had written to his daughter to suggest paying a visit in the summer. Until Charlotte came into his life he had forgotten the pleasure derived from having youngsters around and would like to get to know his grandchildren better. Reading between the scant lines of a tardy reply, he'd concluded his daughter wasn't keen to see him, and would sooner her Cockney father remained at a distance from her and her middle-class family. Though disappointed, he didn't begrudge his daughter moving up in the world, and at least had the comfort of knowing that if she became a war widow her husband would have left her well provided for.

Charlotte and June were really all the family left to him now. Charlotte would always remain beloved. It broke his heart to lose her, but he must, for her sake. Their time left together was precious and he was desperate to get back to the lodge to be with her.

'How much further?' Norman panted out. The tramp was still meandering from garden wall to kerb as he covered the pavement, but had energy to spare whereas Norman was flagging, and falling behind.

Jake veered left into an avenue that curved through a hundred yards or so before opening out onto the main road. Suddenly, he stopped halfway along it. He wobbled a finger to his lips, miming for quiet, then pushed open the front gate. It emitted a long, loud squeak. Undeterred, he proceeded up the path to lean on the windowsill and peer into the gloomy interior.

Norman had skittered to crouch behind the protection of a privet hedge, without knowing why he did so other than to heed the tramp's instruction to beware. He self-consciously straightened up. He'd no reason to hide. If Mrs Jolley lived here, he'd bang on the door and state his business. He'd demand to know where to find Mrs Finch. He might be questioned in turn, but Jolley was guiltier than he was: she had set the tragedy in motion when she'd abandoned the children. He'd no time to go on the attack now, but he could return tomorrow without Jake as an unwelcome accomplice. The man was cannier than his appearance suggested and Norman didn't want him any more involved than he already was. The area was Bethnal Green, close to Victoria Park, and he would easily find this house again.

The stout woman in the sitting room, dressed in a voluminous black coat and hat, was oblivious to the fact she was being spied on as she rooted around in the shopping bag on the table. A stupefied Jake was unaware she'd gone from the room to quit the house until the moment he heard the bolts being drawn. He lurched towards the gate, hissing, 'She's comin' aht . . .'

Norman groaned a curse as the clumsy-footed fellow fell into the flower bed and got entangled in a wild dog-rose. Norman pulled up his collar and hurried down the road, pretending to be minding his own business.

Mrs Jolley suspected the vagrant rolling to his feet had been intending to burgle the house, believing nobody home. To save money, she kept the lamps unlit until it was properly dark, giving the property the appearance of being vacant. It had been a surprise to pull the door shut then turn around to that sight. But fellow criminals didn't faze her; it was the do-gooders she found daunting. She was carrying the large shopping bag and swung it at his head, knocking him back down as he attempted to free himself from thorns and stand up. 'Get off with you or I'll call the police,' she snarled.

When the blows kept coming and Jake had had enough of warding them off, he caught the handle of the bag, yanking it out of her hands. 'You call the police, missus. Go on. I'll tell 'em about you. I know what you did.' He hurled the bag back at her and struggled up, limping out onto the pavement. 'Doan remember me, do yer?' He jabbed a finger close to his eye then pointed at her with it. 'I seen your face, missus. I know you.' He glared at her while her mouth worked as though she chewed on words she'd like to spit at him. She'd rather stab him than bash him with a shopping bag, but daren't, Jake read from that sinister look straining her ugly features. A shiver rippled through him, as though somebody walked on his grave. He shifted further away and glanced about for his companion. He couldn't spot him in the twilight so slunk off alone, shoulders hunched to his ears.

Mrs Jolley's nervous tic started up whenever she feared her business might be scrutinised. Her nose and mouth were madly twitching as she watched the interfering wretch mooching down the street. He was licking his fingers then pawing at bramble scratches on his face like a wounded animal. She found the brown bottle in her pocket and took a comforting nip of laudanum, hesitating at the gate, undecided whether to retreat inside to give him plenty of time to clear off. She'd only moved into this lodging a few days ago; before that she'd not visited the East End since the night she'd left Charlotte Finch and Peter Dove outside Whitechapel workhouse. Her memory had been jogged to the tramp who'd insisted on helping rouse the porter on that Christmas Eve. It had been a filthy winter's night, but she knew it was the same fellow. She had a vivid recollection of him banging on the door with his beer bottle.

Why he'd get a bee in his bonnet over abandoned children that were nothing to do with him was beyond her. He was a lunatic, she concluded, and nobody would take him seriously anyway. Looping the shopping bag over her arm, she set off along the street, peering at intervals from under the wide brim of her hat to make sure he wasn't loitering about. He might be of no consequence, but policemen were another kettle of fish for somebody who earned a living off the backs of vulnerable children. If she'd not got important business to attend to she would have remained indoors and calmed herself down.

She was expecting news of a business opportunity and to get it had to visit a recently sold house in Highgate. Such properties could be useful to a person keen to conceal their whereabouts. Tricking a neighbour into revealing the previous owner's identity was easy. Knowing their name gave credence to her claim to have been their lodger. Then she'd spin a yarn about having rented a room in the house and would ask to collect her post from the new owners. The scam worked nicely, though not for long. The lady had already obligingly handed over letters addressed to Mrs Yates. Before long she would get suspicious, so the matter had to be immediately dealt with. After that, checking estate agents' advertisements would turn up other suitable correspondence drops for baby-farming deals. Some parents insisted on seeing a foster mother in her own home. Depending on their situation, others were willing to hand over a child at a railway station, asking few questions before hurrying away. The business she was chasing concerned a gentleman wanting to settle his motherless granddaughter. He was a stickler for having details, which was a nuisance. Time would tell whether eventually she would secure his twelve guineas and be saddled with the brat. The girl was six. Older children weren't as easy to dispose of as the babies ... Charlotte Finch had been a case in point. She had seemed a valuable asset at one time, but plans to blackmail Major Beresford's family had come to nothing when his supposed bastard got diphtheria. Innocent Charlotte truly believed the major to be her father. She would have been a star witness in compelling the major's widow to cough up hush money. Charlotte had brought disaster down on their heads by running away to neighbours, already infected with diphtheria. Defiant children drew unwanted attention and thus posed a threat. Like baby farmers before her, she'd go to the gallows if caught. With enough notice of impending disaster, she'd pull down the shutters in her own way ...

'Oi ... missus ... you goin' to the workhouse? You won't get them kids, y'know. He won't let you have 'em ... cos I warned him about you.'

The tramp was shouting at her from the opposite pavement, causing passers-by to stop and stare. Her features started jumping and she strode on, averting her face and gripping the small bottle in her pocket. Ignoring him was no deterrent; he continued yelling and loped across the road towards her. Instinctively she broke into a run to escape.

Norman had been loitering about, despite his agitation over Charlotte being on her own at the lodge. The damnable tramp might have scuppered this opportunity to question Jolley now though. The woman probably thought she was about to be mugged in the street. Norman puffed down the road after her, hoping to defuse things and salvage the prospect of a quick conversation. After today there might not be another chance following Pickard putting her on her guard.

Mrs Jolley rushed into the High Street, pushing her hat

out of her eyes as it slipped forward. The tramp was so close now she could smell his sour sweat and hear his grunts. She was more angry than frightened and would have lashed out at him if there weren't so many witnesses about. She barged past people waiting at the bus stop and darted off the pavement to cross the road—

The sound of a horse in distress was followed by a clatter of falling metal. Brakes screeched as a car and an omnibus stopped sharply. Jake Pickard and Norman Drake also came to a halt, many yards apart. The horse-drawn cart that had hit Mrs Jolley had skidded sideways but hadn't shed much of its load. The shovels that had been propped up in the back had scattered on the ground around her prone figure. After a second's silence a commotion started.

Jake had slunk away, wary of getting the blame, as a group of people gathered around the scene of the accident. Nobody was looking at him; they were talking in whispers while gawping at the sprawled figure lying half under the laden coal cart. Norman had momentarily gone rigid with shock before he rushed on to push through the onlookers. Mrs Jolley was the only person who had the information he needed about Mrs Finch. He elbowed his way to the front of the group and strode into the road. A man was crouching down, holding the inert woman's wrist.

'He's a doctor ... jumped off that bus to help ...' somebody murmured.

'Gawd bless him, but reckon she's past help ...' Another hushed voice joined in.

'She jest run straight out into the road in front of me,' the coalman protested while soothing his jumpy nag. 'Didn't get no chance to avoid her. What possessed her?' he continued his defence, holding his sooty cheeks in his hands.

'He's right ... I saw her. She wasn't looking where she was going,' a woman contributed through the hanky she was pressing to her mouth.

'Is it possible to speak to her? Ask her name?' Norman had bent to whisper close to the doctor's ear. The fellow was now stretching beneath the cart to feel for a pulse in Mrs Jolley's neck.

'Nobody'll be able to speak to this woman. She's not breathing,' the doctor said flatly. 'She's taken a whack on the head and her chest's caved in.' He prised an article from her closed fingers. 'Laudanum,' he muttered, having examined the bottle. 'If she's been dosing herself with this, little wonder she was in a daze.' He sighed and stood up. Having retrieved her hat, he returned to cover her bloodied head with it in a mark of respect.

A louder ripple of conversation started up in the crowd. 'A copper's on his way.' The woman who'd backed up the coalman passed on this news to the doctor.

A confirmatory two-tone toot on a whistle was heard. The signal was repeated, and as the constable jogged up, the crowd parted to let him through.

Norman stepped back and kept on retreating. He didn't want to be delayed further by being rounded up for questioning. He couldn't explain why he'd wanted to talk to Mrs Jolley without revealing Charlotte's story. He felt in despair. Just a few things done differently and Charlotte might soon have been going home to her mother.

Norman hobbled up to the shamefaced tramp who was keeping to a safe distance. 'You stupid fool,' he hissed. 'Look what you've done.'

'Ain't my fault. Never touched her.' Shock had sobered Jake up; beneath the dirt and stubble his complexion was white.

Norman knew there was no point in arguing with him. The damage was done. He hurried on towards the Mile End Road, panting and swaying from one side of the pavement to the other, feeling light-headed. A sudden pain in his back made him gasp and hang on to a wall for support.

'Woss up, ol' feller?' Jake had timidly sidled up, unsure if he might get another tongue-lashing.

'Give me your arm, would you? I must hurry up and get home,' wheezed Norman, thankful for any assistance. He'd struggle mustering the energy to make it to the end of the road under his own steam, let alone reach Whitechapel.

Jake clumsily patted the man's arm in comfort. It was obvious the haggard porter was having some sort of bad turn. Jake felt guilty for causing this to happen. He didn't feel sorry about the woman though. He could spot a wrong 'un, having lived amongst so many of them. There'd been something evil about her . . . he'd seen it in her sly eyes.

Norman pressed at his heaving ribs as the pain encircled his chest like a steel band. He cried out in protest against the speed with which he was being hurried along. Jake slowed down but even that snail's pace was too fast for the invalid.

They came to a standstill for a breather, but Norman seemed reluctant to start off again. His frustration at his feebleness filled his eyes with tears. He received another clumsy pat then Jake stooped to manoeuvre the porter up onto his shoulder.

'You'll be right as rain after a rest,' Jake puffed out as he set off with his burden.

Chapter Thirteen

'Where in Gawd's name has he got to?'

June was pacing about outside the lodge, muttering to herself. She banged on the door again but stopped and walked off up the road when she spotted a workhouse officer coming out of the main building. The woman would wonder why she was hanging around outside and ask if something was up. After five years together it was no secret that June Gladwell was the porter's girlfriend. His secret granddaughter would come as a surprise though. If the officer suspected a problem, she'd summon the master. Big trouble would ensue if Norman's grumpy boss barged in on sleeping Goldilocks. June wasn't happy about the Charlotte situation either, but after her last knock-back was carefully considering her next move. Once the officer was at a safe distance, June hurried back to the lodge. She hoped the silly old fool hadn't tried to fix the wall cupboard again. She'd warned him last week about wobbling on a chair, holding a screwdriver. He might have fallen and knocked himself out this time.

There was nothing else for it: she'd go round to the back of the lodge and tap on Charlotte's window. She'd have to wake the child and persuade her to open the door. June was about to negotiate the narrow alley at the side of the lodge when an astonishing sight stopped her dead. She gawped at the unmistakable lumbering figure of Jake Pickard emerging from the gloom. And she recognised the fellow being carried on his shoulder like a sack of spuds. Jerking herself into action, she marched to meet them.

'He ain't well,' Jake announced gruffly before the woman could accuse him of anything. He offloaded the porter and steered him into his girlfriend's arms. With no more ado, Jake scooted off up the road and was soon swallowed up in the darkness.

It took June several seconds to recover. Then she bawled. 'Oi ... come back 'ere. What you done to him, Pickard?'

Norman gave June's arm a feeble shake. 'Shut up,' he panted. 'He's been kind to me.' He thrust his keys at her, jangling in his shaking hand. 'Quickly ... open up now. Let's get inside. I feel dreadful.'

She propped him against the door jamb and fumbled with the keys, trying not to drop them in her haste.

The moment he was over the threshold, Norman tottered towards the settee and collapsed, still in his overcoat. June tried to make him comfortable by lifting his feet up onto the seat and loosening his bootlaces. Then she went to turn up the lamp, thankful he'd left it burning.

'If Pickard did nothing wrong, why did he rush off looking guilty? What happened when you were out? You seemed fine yesterday. Now you look as though you've been through the mill.' She peered closely at his face.

He had been going downhill from the moment those abandoned children had started playing on his mind. Overnight, he'd changed: lost his carefree side and become careworn. In all the years she'd known him, he'd rarely complained of feeling ill, though she'd seen him grimace with bad arthritis or bellyache. They'd joked about being a couple of dodderers when June limped with gout, as she did from time to time. This wasn't a joke though. She'd never seen him suffering like this. He'd curled up on his side, his features contorted in pain.

'I owe that tramp my thanks. I wouldn't have got home without him.' A weary sigh preceded, 'I reckon I'm having a heart attack, June. And there's something important we must discuss . . .' Norman struggled onto his elbows.

'Now, quieten down. You need to rest. You'll be right as rain in a minute.' She encouraged him to settle back on the settee and started easing off his boots.

She'd echoed the tramp's reassurance and Norman wanted to believe they were right. Unfortunately, he knew his own body. Over the past weeks, his chest pains and dizziness had got worse; he could no longer kid himself that old age and indigestion were to blame.

He'd been getting his affairs in order, writing a will and some letters to those he cared about. Not quickly enough though, it seemed. Clinging to a hope that he had plenty of time left had been foolish. If the worst happened, Charlotte must be kept safe. He thanked heaven he and June were back on good terms. He had nobody else to entrust with this most vital of tasks.

'If anything happens to me, I want you to swear you'll never put Charlotte into the workhouse. Please, say it, June, to ease my mind.'

She gave an agitated nod and pushed herself to her feet. 'I'll get you a drink.' She knew he kept a half bottle of brandy for medicinal purposes. Sometimes, he'd pour her a tot if the sherry had run out and he was feeling genial. A good deal more than a stiff drink was needed to get Norman back on his feet, though. June had nursed her late husband and knew a person with a putty-coloured complexion, struggling for breath, was gravely ill.

There was an inch of brandy left and she poured the lot into a glass with shaking hands before crouching down in front of him again. 'What in God's name happened? Why did you go out? Did that tramp attack you then feel guilty and bring you home?' June found the tale of the Good Samaritan difficult to swallow.

'Not at all. He's my saviour.'

June held the brandy to Norman's mouth, insisting he take some though he seemed reluctant.

He sipped then raised a limp hand to wave the glass away. 'Give me your promise, June. You must say it to put my mind at rest.' He worked himself onto his elbows again.

'I swear I won't put Charlotte Finch in the workhouse if anything bad happens to you. But don't ask me to keep her meself. I'm too old and too tired for nursemaiding kids. Same as you are, love,' she added pointedly.

A wry smile tugged at his bluish lips. He didn't need her to tell him that the sad business with the abandoned children had put a final nail in his coffin. 'I so wanted little Charlie to go home to her mother. It seems that won't be.' He sighed. 'I don't expect you to take her on, June. Look in my pocket. There's a letter.' He slowly shifted position to allow her to withdraw the envelope. 'I slipped out to post it and came over funny before I could. I have been trying to find her a new home. I know you were right all along. I've been selfish keeping her. Much as I love her, she has to go, for her own good. Send the letter for me, please. Mrs Yates seems suitable. If I can't make the final decision, I want you to do it.' He clamped his fingers over hers. 'You won't let me down, will you? You'll make sure Charlotte is put with the right person to care for her?'

'I promise I will post the letter and suss the woman out, if it comes to it. But you'll be fine.' She couldn't hold his gaze as she said it and planted a kiss on his cold sweaty forehead. 'You rest now. I'll go and fetch somebody to take you to the infirmary.'

'No!' Panic lent him the energy to lurch upright. 'I'm not going in there any more than Charlotte is,' he gasped out. 'I won't end my days in the workhouse.'

'I'll fetch the doctor then, shall I?' June croaked. 'You must take some medicine or you'll never get well.'

'I don't mind seeing Dr Howes. He's a good fellow.' Norman let his head flop back against the cushions.

June took a livening gulp from his brandy then put the glass in his quivering fingers. 'Drink it all. It'll warm your cockles; you feel frozen, love. I'll only be gone a few minutes.'

'Is Charlotte asleep?'

June opened the bedroom door a crack. 'She is,' she confirmed, having taken a peek at the child beneath the covers. 'I'll be back before you know it.' She returned to the settee to squeeze his hand. 'You'll see the kid safely settled with a new family. I know you will. Then we'll finally be able to retire, eh, love?' She struggled to find something else encouraging to say ... and failed. She resorted to giving his hand a little shake. 'The doctor will give you a sleeping powder ... you'll feel better in the morning.'

'Yes ... I know I will.' He told a lie of his own.

June swallowed her sobs until she was out in the street

and hurrying towards the doctor's house. She was going to beg him to admit Norman to hospital. A lengthy stay on a ward was the only slim chance Norman had of pulling through this.

'Shall I read a story to help you fall off to sleep?'

Norman turned his head to see Charlotte in the bedroom doorway. His pain-creased features softened into a serene smile. Slowly he shifted position so he could put the brandy glass on the floor and hold out his arms, wordlessly imploring her to come closer.

She trotted to the settee to be enfolded in an embrace and receive a kiss on the brow. She sank down to sit beside him with her legs folded beneath her nightdress.

'Your poor old granddad's not well, Charlie. He needs to have a nap. Mrs Gladwell's gone to get the doctor to come here and give me some medicine.' He smoothed the backs of his fingers on her cheek, feeling the silkiness of her hair coat his thin freckled skin.

She nodded to let him know she understood and laid her doll on his chest to comfort him. 'I went to hospital to make me feel better.'

'That's right. That's where I think I shall go quite soon.'

'Not yet though?' she solemnly asked.

'No, not yet. I've plenty of time for that story,' said Norman, trying to sound matter-of-fact. He could feel the weight of her wise blue eyes on him. 'Mrs Gladwell will take you home with her when I've gone. She'll find you a nice new home, Charlie, because I won't be able to look after you now I'm poorly, will I?'

'Not going to Mrs Jolley . . .' Charlotte shot backwards on her bottom and scrambled onto her knees.

'No ... definitely not her, my love.' Norman snatched at her hand to reassure her and stop her leaving him. 'I promise you won't ever have to live with that woman again. Your new foster mother will be nice.'

Charlotte settled down once more. 'Will she read to me?'

'Oh yes, I'm sure she will. And you'll go to school and make friends to play with.'

'I'd like that. I haven't been to school for a long time. When you're better I'll come home again.'

'That would be lovely, dear, but I'm not sure you'll want to come back to this old place once you've made some friends and have your new family. Perhaps you'll have some sisters and brothers ... wouldn't that be grand? Anyway, wherever I am, I'll keep an eye on you,' said Norman, giving her a wink. 'Even if I'm not around I'll know what you're up to. How's that, Charlie?'

'I'd like some sisters and brothers.' Charlotte settled her chin on her knees, looking wistful. She remembered the poor family that had lived near to Mrs Jolley. She'd run away to live with them. Their dirty house had been filled with noise and children. She had loved it there ... had wanted to stay forever.

'Now you said you'd read to me. So off you go and send me to sleep.' Norman raised her small fingers to his lips. 'And don't rush; there's lots of time for you to think about the words.' He curled his hands over the rag doll she had put on his middle and closed his eyes. Then opened one up at her. 'I'll be listening carefully, so no cheating,' he teased, making her giggle. He relaxed as she began to read, skipping over the parts she couldn't work out and reciting a version of the opening passage of *Gulliver's Travels* that she knew off by heart.

He was instantly lulled by her faltering tone, as soft and breathy as wind in leaves. Peacefulness wound about him like a bandage. He didn't regret a thing. He'd gladly do the same again to have this enchanting child ... even for a short while ... in his life. She'd been worth any pain ... every sacrifice ...

Charlotte kept reading even when she heard him snore funnily then fall quiet. She kept repeating over and over again the bit she knew, never stopping or trying to rouse him. Then Mrs Gladwell came in with the doctor.

'He's gone to sleep now,' said Charlotte, and closed the book.

Chapter Fourteen

'Sorry ... the van wouldn't start and the lads were late getting back from the market. By the time everything was unloaded and packed away ... oh, you know how it is. It's been one of those bloomin' days.'

While still on the bus, Lily had spotted Evie Osborne pacing about, smoking. Having quickly alighted, she'd scooted across the road, blurting out an apology.

'Not to worry. You're here now,' Evie said gamely, though she'd been kicking her heels for fifteen minutes and lost her place in the queue of people now filing into the cinema. She dropped her cigarette to give Lily a welcoming hug. 'Didn't mind waiting anyhow. I've been enjoying the attention.' She winked and tipped a nod to a group of smartly uniformed naval officers who were also hanging about. They were eyeing up the two shapely young women decked in summer clothes.

It was a balmy June evening, well suited to the wearing of a pretty lemon blouse trimmed with broderie anglaise. A fawn cotton skirt and a small elegant hat completed Lily's outfit. Evie was sporting a dress of pastel blue lawn with nipped-in waist and a chic straw boater. The girls were glad to be out of their functional daytime attire and were ready for a bit of relaxation.

'I hope your Colin doesn't know what a flirt you are,' Lily teased.

'Oh, he does; I danced with all his pals at the Wood Green Empire. I'd never do more than that though. I'm crazy about him.' Evie squashed underfoot her cigarette butt. 'He knows that too. Perhaps I shouldn't have made it so obvious from the start. Some girls keep a fellow dangling at arm's length when they want to catch him. I couldn't be bothered with being a bitch so went in for the kill and gave him a smacker on our first date. If I really like a chap, I'm a "let's get on with it" sort of gal. I have to be at my age.'

'You're not in your dotage, whatever your mother says.' Lily mockingly patted her friend's arm. 'Did you really kiss him on the lips before he'd made the first move?' She imagined Evie to be joking about being forward with a man she'd just met.

'Oh, yes . . .' Evie growled. 'If he was here, I'd do it again. I'm in desperate need of a good canoodle.'

'I'll introduce you to my friend Fanny. Once upon a time she wouldn't have waited to be asked either.' Lily smiled. 'She's all prim and proper now but has me in stitches . . . or reaching for the smelling salts . . . when she tells one of her stories about her past.'

'She sounds like good fun. I would like to meet your friends,' said Evie, turning serious. 'Ask them along next time and we can make a party of it.'

'It'd be like the old days,' Lily sounded wistful. 'Thing is, Margie and Fanny are mums now. Their little 'uns are just about toddling and Fanny – she's the older one – reckons she needs eyes in the soles of her feet to keep up with

Stephen. He's full of mischief, and she's got another baby due soon. Margie's a few months younger than me but she's been doing her own decorating. She's a proper little home-bird and loves brightening her place up with a lick of paint.' Lily had been seeing less and less of her busy friends as they became more domesticated. She never complained about taking a back seat. At some point it would be her turn to stay home, rocking a crib and soothing a fretful baby.

'The film's probably already started now.' She linked arms with Evie. 'Shall we give it a miss and have a bite to eat instead?' She'd spotted a café on the other side of the road. 'I was in such a rush I skipped having tea.'

'Sounds good to me.' Evie tipped her hat to a jaunty angle on her blonde hair as they passed the ogling sailors.

A long whistle followed them up the street, making them exchange an amused glance. 'He'd be second choice for a canoodle, after Colin,' Evie cackled. 'The muscly one with black hair.'

'Greg'll stop me coming out with you if he finds out what you're like,' Lily joked, urging Evie to trot across the road with her.

'What's *he* like? Oh, I don't mean looks. I remember you said he's tall and fair. I mean, what kind of man is he? Mean and moody? Jealous? He's not a bossy sort, is he?' Evie fired off her questions as they settled into the short stroll to the café.

'He's a bloody wonderful sort,' Lily simply said. And meant it. Without him she'd still be a workhouse inmate. She never took for granted how lucky she was to be free of that place and to be loved by a man she adored … and fancied like mad. Her life now was treasured and she wouldn't let anything – even this damnable war forcing people apart – get her down.

'Have you got a snap of him?' Evie took a photograph from her bag. She handed it over. 'That's Colin. I brought it with me to show you. Gorgeous, eh?'

Lily looked at a serious-faced chap wearing spectacles, dressed in army uniform. He had a hand on a picket fence and a toe stubbed into the ground, setting one knee to a dashing angle. But he didn't resemble the roguish charmer she'd been expecting. 'Can see why you're smitten. He looks like a really lovely chap.' She handed it back and Evie gave her boyfriend's image a kiss before putting it away. 'I haven't got a photo of Greg. But ...' Lily had been saving this news to tell her friend once they were sitting down and could relish it. She couldn't wait, though, and burst out, 'I will have a photo after we've been to a studio in a few days' time. Greg's coming home, Evie. I got a letter yesterday. He's actually got leave at last and his train is due in at two o'clock tomorrow afternoon.'

'You lucky so and so!' exclaimed Evie, stopping and turning to give Lily a hug. 'How long's he got?'

'Ten days, he thinks. Course, won't know for certain until I see him.' She'd waited so long for this that just talking about it brought on the shakes.

'Will you get hitched before he goes back?'

'I expect so,' Lily said, eyes aglow. 'But first ... well ...'

'Well, indeed!' Evie snorted. 'If he's been a good boy over there, he'll want to demonstrate how much he wants you as his wife for a couple of days.'

Lily knew that was true and turned hot anticipating them spending their first night together tomorrow – unless a disaster got in the way as it had last time. 'What d'you mean, "if he's been a good boy"?' Lily pushed open the door to the café and they headed to a window table to sit down.

'French brothels.' Evie came straight out with it while pulling out her chair. 'Officers as well as rank and file go to them. Colin swore he didn't when I quizzed him ... rolling pin in hand.' She smirked. 'He said sometimes you see a queue of men outside a house in a village, waiting their turn. Top brass try to keep it hushed up ... bad for morale back home, don't you know. But being a nurse, I'd heard about it from colleagues who'd returned from Étaples. They'd had Tommies on the ward for treatment for clap, and worse, picked up locally.' She paused. 'I feel sorry for them actually.'

Lily didn't know what clap was but used her imagination, guessing it must be horrible to need treatment. 'You feel sorry for the servicemen?' She wasn't sure she did.

'No, the local women. They probably don't have much choice in the matter if they want to keep their kids fed while their husbands are away fighting. Parts of France are littered with bomb sites and starving refugees are tramping about the countryside. A foreigner with some francs or some food – even if it's only army rations – must seem like a godsend.'

'It's hard to imagine how awful it must be for them,' said Lily, shaking her head. 'We've been lucky over here in comparison.' She crossed two sets of fingers. 'Please God, no more Zeppelins.'

They ordered a pot of tea and cheese-and-chutney sandwiches then settled into their own thoughts while gazing at the street scene and waiting for their meal to be served. It had been an overcast June day, but at eight o'clock it was still bright, a faint glimmer of sun in the west, peeking from behind a ribbon of cloud. Lily put from her mind Evie's talk of brothels and diseases. She trusted Greg when he said she was the only girl for him.

The arrival of the tea tray drew them back into conversation.

'I've also got some news actually,' Evie said, before taking a bite of her sandwich.

'He's proposed!' Lily exclaimed, pouring their teas.

'No such luck ...' Evie spluttered through her fingers. 'I've got a new posting.'

'Oh, you're not leaving London?' Lily cried. They had met up once a month on a Sunday ever since being introduced in January. Evie Osborne had become a close friend and Lily looked forward to their outings. Her workhouse girlfriends would always hold a special place in her heart. Just as she would in theirs; but now they saw less of one another, new relationships had started filling lonely spaces.

'I'm off overseas. Speaking of French refugees jogged my memory to tell you about it.'

'You're nursing on the Western Front?' Lily tucked into her sandwich, trying not to dwell on her disappointment.

'I am, but not in a military hospital. A few of us from Endell Street are joining forces with a Relief Committee providing humanitarian aid. There's bugger all medical care for civilians since local doctors have been mobilised. The French authorities are glad of any outside help they can get.'

'The nuns I delivered fruit and veg to this morning are trying to find bigger premises,' said Lily. 'Sister Louise never turns away people who've been bombed out ... apart from the drunks. She says once the demon drink takes a hold, they're too disruptive.' It saddened Lily to think of those men, like her father, who had no friends left. But the nuns had to protect the vulnerable at the shelter. Charlie Larkin had turned aggressive when under the influence. She and Davy would avoid their father when he'd been drinking, but their mum would scold him, to no useful effect. He'd just shout and throw things before storming out. Often he'd stay out until morning then reappear and make apologies and promises to his wife. But it always happened again. After one such night of arguments and door slamming, a policeman had called the following day to tell them he had been found dead by the canal, an empty spirit bottle at his side.

Evie interrupted Lily's melancholy reminiscence by explaining the background to her new job. 'The Friends War Victims Relief Committee ... to give them their full moniker ... got hold of an old French workhouse and opened up an emergency shelter. Brave souls were behind the lines, too. It was a brilliant success; perhaps ideas were put in heads for commandeering similar buildings in England and putting those to good use.'

'I'm glad the mothers and children aren't being forgotten,' said Lily. 'Must be awful to be stranded in the middle of a battleground.'

'The Friends managed to get a cottage hospital and an orphanage up and running in the region. An Endell Street nurse did a stint out there last year and reported every ward was overflowing. Families tramp for miles to get admitted.' Evie sipped her tea before adding, 'They're still recruiting; the aim is to keep the show on the road for as long as it's needed. Chauffeurs are in short supply, so if you get fed up with being a market-stall girl and fancy driving a van in France ...' Evie hiked a quizzical eyebrow.

'I'll never get fed up of my job,' Lily said. 'I love everything about it. Even the cantankerous old biddies who want something for nothing.' She chuckled. 'I let Joey Robley charm them. He's a good-looking lad with the gift of the gab. A real heartbreaker in the making, is our Joey.'

'I'll come shopping in your market before I ship out.'

'Oh, do come,' enthused Lily. 'I'll show you the warehouse.' She smiled into space. 'My little home from home, that place is.'

Every creaky beam and wonky-wheeled barrow piled with tarpaulins and poles reminded her of Gregory Wilding. And Davy ... Smudger ... Fred Jenkins. All work colleagues back in the day before the war forced them apart. Then Margie and Fanny had joined Wilding's team. They too had moved on. But Lily was there to stay and hold the place together until Greg returned to take over the reins and make it the flourishing business it had once been. She was learning fast to be a saleswoman and an employer, but she couldn't match her fiance's experience, built up over nearly a decade of running his own firm in the East End. Not that he would be able to improve the situation with food shortages any more than she could.

'Well, if you have second thoughts about France, let me know.' Evie crossed her arms. 'One of the boys who's been admitted told me that Dr Adam Reeve saved his arm just before he left France. He praised him to the skies.'

'Adam's a wonderful doctor and a lovely man,' said Lily simply.

'He is, and best of all, he's working at a camp hospital up the road from the refuge. I hope he's still there; I'm bound to bump into him. Adam's good fun; he always plans a smashing entertainment night on the wards he manages.'

'If you do see him, you must say hello for me. I've not had a letter from him in a while.'

'Will do.' Evie looked reflective. 'The lads we nurse at Endell Street are all such dears, but after a few years I'm ready for something new. I want to help the kids. The poor little blighters have no say and no choice but to put up with all the mess adults create.' She paused, leaning her elbows on the table. 'Any news of your sister?'

Lily grimaced her disappointment. 'I ask customers if they know of a foster mother who's moved in locally with a fair-haired girl. I'm enquiring about a friend's child, I say; don't want too many questions.'

'You told me all the ins and outs of it,' said Evie. 'Was I being inquisitive?'

'I didn't mind telling you once I got to know you. We're friends. I'm not ashamed of what happened to our family.' Lily's chin was tilted defiantly. 'It wasn't my mum's fault that her twins ended up as workhouse kids.'

'It's not something you want the whole world and his wife to know.' Evie gave a nod. 'I'd feel the same way, if it were me had that sort of bloody awful luck.'

Lily looked down at her cup. 'You got the silver spoon ... I got skilly. But I'm not complaining and don't want pity, cos me 'n' Davy had some smashing early years when everything was fine at home. We were a happy family.'

'I don't pity you. You were first in line for courage, Lily Larkin. And I'd like some more of that.'

Lily jerked up her head. 'I'm not brave. I cry meself to sleep sometimes, frightened stiff for Greg and Davy.' She hadn't had the fire and blackness dream for weeks and regretted reminding herself of it.

'We all do that, love,' said Evie wryly. 'I've stared at bloodshot eyes in the mirror after tossing and turning all night.' The strain of nursing mangled bodies ... losing men after coming to know and like them ... was getting to Evie. 'Don't think the Almighty's listening to prayers though.'

They fell quiet and Lily's thoughts meandered back to her sister. 'Mrs Jolley has probably left the area and taken Charlotte with her, if she's still alive.'

'You could try the hospitals. If she was admitted with diphtheria they'd have a record of it.'

'I've been to every East End hospital and orphanage and school, and some further afield. A six-year-old was admitted to Whitechapel hospital, but she wasn't my Charlotte. She was fair, but a Mr Drake who was her granddad had come to collect her and take her home the week before.' She paused. 'The lucky little thing got better. My sister might have died.'

Evie leaned to put her forehead against Lily's in comfort. 'Don't say that or you'll give up looking.'

'I won't ... ever,' Lily vowed. 'I'll miss you and our chats.'

'Same goes ...' returned Evie, draining her cup of tea. 'I'll be able to keep an eye on Colin over there. If I find him cosying up to any mademoiselles, there'll be trouble.'

Lily smiled but her memory had been jogged to Smudger's nurse girlfriend. Lily hadn't said anything to Margie in case she rocked a boat sailing in calm water. Smudger was honourable. He wouldn't hurt his wife by carrying on an affair.

'When are you shipping out?'

'Towards the end of July,' informed Evie. 'A summer crossing should be bearable. I've sailed before in winter and it was hellish, blowing a gale that kept us all below decks, throwing up. We used to go to France on holiday when I was a youngster. My mother had a friend who married some count or other. They lived in a huge chateau in Burgundy. That could be a pile of rubble now, like everything else over there . . .' Evie broke off mid-sentence as Lily suddenly gave a squeak, leaping to her feet and craning her neck to get a better view through the window.

'Oh ... what? My God! I think that's *him*. Can't quite see to make sure ...' A second later she had pushed her chair out of the way and was dodging tables to get to the door. 'I'm sure I just spotted Greg amongst those soldiers. He said *tomorrow*. The *thirteenth* of June. I know it was the thirteenth. I thought it'd be unlucky to travel ...' The door swung closed on her, cutting off the rest.

Evie had no intention of staying where she was. She dropped coins on the table for the waitress then dashed after Lily who, holding on to her hat, was flying across the road, dodging traffic. Evie slowed down and grinned, watching her friend launch herself at a lance corporal who'd been talking to some pals outside a pub.

The handsome blond Tommy had crushed her in his arms and was kissing her so thoroughly that her head was forced back against his supporting arm.

'Can see you've got plenty of catching up to do, Lily,' said Evie, strolling up to join them. 'So I'll say toodle-oo for now.'

Lily dragged Greg by the arm to meet her friend, bursting out with an introduction.

He extended a hand. 'Very pleased to meet you, Evie. Lily's told me all about you in her letters.'

'Oh dear,' groaned Evie, theatrically clasping his fingers in all of hers. 'Swear you won't repeat a word of it, sir.'

Greg chuckled, taking straight away to this girl. 'She must've left something out, cos it was all good.'

'I'll come and see you at the hospital first chance I get.' Lily returned Evie's embrace. 'Let's meet up again before you go away.'

'We will. Now don't do anything I wouldn't do ... so plenty of scope there.' Evie winked and sashayed off with a smile and a finger wag for Greg's pals who'd tried to persuade her to join them.

'I'll just tell the lads I'm off. I did say I'd have a jar with them before heading home. But not now,' Greg murmured against Lily's warm cheek. 'That's John Lonegan over there, doffing his cap.'

Lily returned the fellow a smile; Greg had mentioned his ginger-haired friend in letters so she knew they'd served together as fusiliers from the start.

Before he could make a move, she'd flung her arms around his neck again and kissed him full on the lips. She didn't care about the catcalling Tommies, or about acting demure; she needed to touch and taste him. He groaned and his mouth and sinewy body pressed against hers, his hands following the curves of her silhouette.

Finally, her grip loosened. 'Didn't mean to embarrass you in front of your pals, darling. They'll think me a proper hussy.'

'They're jealous as hell, and I don't blame them. Who wouldn't want to be ravished by a girl like you?' He swung her up in his arms and pirouetted around, making her giggle and shriek and draw more whistles from their audience. 'Need to get home, love. You can be a proper hussy with me there. And nobody watching ... so you can take your time.'

While he went to get a ribbing from his pals, Lily tried to combat her daze that owed little to being spun around. She was still in shock from the unexpected gift of his presence.

'You were due home tomorrow.' She slipped her hand through his arm the moment he returned. 'I was going to do you a lovely welcome home dinner, in the warehouse. The sort of feast we used to have back in the good old days.'

'You still can, love ...' He glanced about and hailed a passing cab. 'Or we could head straight to mine with a bottle of something nice to drink.' He helped her into the vehicle that had pulled to the kerb. Once they'd settled back he drew her to him so her head rested on his shoulder.

She snuggled up, content to be quiet and savour this wonderful reunion now her excitement was under control. She tilted her head to glance up at him; his eyes were closed, his expression tranquil. She studied him, unobserved. In Poplar in summer they'd all get a nice colour from the summer sun while working outdoors on the market stall. Greg's foreign tan was a harsher brown and the craters about his mouth and eyes were deeper than when last she'd seen him. He looked older than his twenty-four years, she realised, but still breathtakingly handsome to her.

'I've missed you, Greg.' She moved the bleached tips of his fringe off his lined forehead. 'Missed you so much I thought I might go mad. It's been so long ... waiting all this time to see you. I've been frantically worried ... getting letters is nice, but not the same as this ...' Her voice tailed off and she clung to him.

He lifted his hand from her shoulder to her face, his calloused fingertips tracing soothing circles on her cheek. But he didn't say anything. He couldn't with a huge lump in his throat.

He had a lot to tell her; some he'd rather not say. But she'd ask questions and he wouldn't lie to her. He never had, even when she was a fifteen-year-old innocent and he'd felt confused ... sometimes ashamed ... about feeling horny around her. Not that she'd had a clue he wanted her back then. When awkward questions had arisen, he'd always managed to find an economical version of the truth. She'd been savaged by life as a child – as he had; Lily Larkin was pure courage and loyalty and shouldn't ever have to listen to lies from him. She'd fibbed to him on occasion – on her brother's behalf. Greg hadn't held it against her. Back then, he'd held all the aces and she'd done what she needed to, to protect her family ... what little she had left of it. Now, he shared everything he had with her. He'd never put his faith in anybody in the way he had Lily Larkin.

'Have you seen Davy?' Lily had perked up enough now to ask about the other important man in her life.

Greg smiled and cursed beneath his breath. He wasn't having that conversation now. He turned her face up to his. 'I have seen your brother and I've seen Fred. Remember Jenkins, do you?'

Lily smiled up at him, nodding. She'd not always seen eye to eye with Fred, the first to enlist, back in 1914.

'As for Smudger ...' Greg grimaced and shook his head to indicate they'd not bumped into one another.

'Margie had a letter about a month ago. Smudger's lot was on the move. She did say the French town's name, but I've forgotten it.'

'Right. Well, I reckon that's enough about other people. This is my first night home. Let's just keep it about the two of us and enjoy it, eh? Have you bought your wedding dress?' He lifted her so she was on his lap, half straddling his thighs and wooed her with a sweet kiss.

'I have ...' she murmured when finally his head lifted a fraction. 'It's not a dress, it's a costume and a summer hat and shoes. And that's all I'm telling you. You'll see all on the day.'

'I've got to wait that long? It's not white, is it?' he asked solemnly.

'Close, but not quite,' she teased.

'Sounds perfect.' He growled a chuckle and kissed her again, despite knowing a pair of eyes was watching them over a shoulder. He gestured with a couple of fingers, making the cab driver grin then mind his own business.

Chapter Fifteen

13 June 1917
Poplar

'Hey ... sleepy head. Shall we see if we can get married today?' Greg planted a hand either side of Lily and leaned to tenderly kiss her awake.

She stretched languorously, opening one eye then the other as she surfaced from the most glorious long, deep sleep. Strands of her dark hair, abundant with auburn glints in the early-morning light, were caught on her curly eyelashes. He smoothed them away and the sunbeams gilded her face.

'Do you feel all right?'

She nodded, lazily raising a hand to cup his chin. 'I haven't slept so well in ages. So thank you for that.'

'Anything else?' He nuzzled her cheek, making her wrinkle her nose and giggle.

A pair of deep blue eyes were blinked wide to gaze dreamily at him. Behind his teasing she could tell he longed to know he'd pleased her. He had ... and if she'd stayed awake long enough she might have told him last night. He'd been gentle and patient and sensitive to her need to undress and snuggle into his bed before he stripped off and joined her. At first they'd settled down, wrapped in each other's arms and had talked for a long while about her sister. Lily's tale of disappointment had been punctuated with consoling kisses and caresses from him that he'd lingered over despite his hunger for so much more from her.

When there was nothing left to say she'd felt close to him in body and soul. Not even her twin brother understood her pain of loss the way he did. Nobody made her feel as safe as he did. Just being back together, breathing the same air, moving to the same heartbeat had been blissful. They'd stayed quiet and still for a long, long while to spin out the dream of this heaven lasting forever.

Then she'd entwined their legs, and he'd lifted her atop him, kissing her repeatedly, slow and hard, as though to make up for all the love they'd missed while they'd been apart. The rest had come surprisingly naturally to Lily. On the cab drive home she'd longed to touch and be touched. Lying side by side, her shyly exploring hands, running over his ribbed back and chest, had started him chuckling and groaning. Making love was a weird magic, she'd concluded; exciting pain and a bittersweet ecstasy all wildly spun together. Then a blissful fatigue that had sent her straight to sleep in his arms. She'd want to do it again just to revisit that cocoon, and take him with her this time. He hadn't slept as well as she had. A shade of his restlessness had penetrated to the pit of her oblivion but she had been unable to rouse herself to comfort him.

She was awake now. It was a new day. His first day home. And there were more marvellous days and nights to come. But there was still work to do ... Lily folded upright, blurting, 'Oh no! What time is it, Greg?' She glanced at the window. It was way past the appointed hour for her usual meeting with Eric Skipman at the warehouse. They would drive to Spitalfields to load up with stock while Joey set up the stall in Chrisp Street to the accompaniment of the dawn chorus. 'The lads will wonder where on earth I am. We weren't expecting you to arrive till this afternoon.' She started to scramble out of bed, then remembered she was stark naked.

A twinkle of roguish humour was in his eyes as he watched her dive back beneath the sheet.

She pulled the cotton over her fiery cheeks. It was a bit late for modesty now he'd seen and stroked every bare inch of her.

He was dressed in his costermonger's clothes and loosened his top shirt buttons as he settled down beside her on the mattress. He dropped a kiss onto her covered forehead, smiling at her sweet bashfulness. 'I've just got back from the warehouse. Those two likely lads can cope on their own today. I said we'd be otherwise engaged most of the morning.'

'You didn't!' Lily folded the sheet back from her scandalised face. 'You should have woken me. I would have come too.'

'You were still snoring, I didn't like to.'

'I don't snore . . . do I?' She felt more concerned about that than losing her virginity, unwed. But that didn't matter now they were getting married in a few days' time. In fact the idea of a honeymoon baby was no longer daunting but a secret hope.

'You do snore, love,' he solemnly joked. 'Not enough to put me off you though.' He buried his lips into the crease at her neck, kissing and nipping until she stretched kittenishly and stopped smacking his arm. 'I thought we could try and get married today.' He tipped up her chin. 'Shall we see if we can get a booking at the registry office?'

'It's the thirteenth...' Lily snuggled up, nestling her chin in the hollow of his neck.

'You're not superstitious, are you?'

'No ... just don't like tempting fate,' she said, making him laugh.

'Tomorrow then. We need to get a move on. I've only got eight days. Dates changed, that's why I was shipped home early.'

'We'll make the most of every minute. Tell me all about what you've been doing over there with the engineers,' she said, coiling an arm around his middle.

'Just digging ... stuff like that,' he said, reaching sideways for his donkey jacket on the floor. He found his Woodbines in a pocket and offered her one from the pack.

'What ... digging trenches?' Lily declined a cigarette with a headshake.

'Tunnels ... hush about it.' He struck a match and took a deep drag, exhaling smoke at the ceiling. 'Let's concentrate on lovely old Blighty. That's the only thing any of us Tommies really want to talk about: home and family. How's the business doing? I didn't ask the lads much. They seem to have a routine and know what they're up to, so I left them to it. I'll be glad to get behind a barrow. Be like old times: Spitalfields ... Chrisp Street ... couple of pints with the lads after work ...' Wistfulness had made his voice husky.

'We're making a profit. Nothing like we were, but every costermonger in the market is moaning about the shortages.

As for the boys, they've shaped up well. Eric's the hard-nosed foreman and Joey's the market charmer.'

'Noticed Joey's grown into his looks.' Greg recalled the goofy adolescent of a couple of years back.

'What's happening over there? Tell me what you've had to put up with, then I won't imagine things are worse than they are.'

Greg sucked hard on his cigarette, snorted a stream of smoke. They're worse than you imagine they are, he answered her in his mind. Indescribable. That's why I can't tell you.

Lily rolled over, supporting herself on an elbow. She wasn't a fool. She understood him as well as he did her. From the moment he'd stepped into the master's office and stared at her with his startling tawny eyes she had never stopped thinking about him. She'd counted off the days until he'd return and take her with him. Gregory Wilding had been a stranger whom she'd no reason to trust. Since the age of ten every adult with sway over her life had been mean to her. She'd known he was different, and that he'd be back to give her a better life.

'Is being over there worse than being at St Pancras Industrial School?' she asked quietly.

'Much worse . . .' he said after a few seconds of silence.

'Tell me how it can be.' He had scars on his back from the headmaster's beatings.

'I can't. Wouldn't know where to start. Or to stop.' He got up abruptly. 'I'll make some tea. Fancy some toast?' he sent over a shoulder.

Lily got dressed in yesterday's pretty clothes then followed him into the kitchen.

She laid her head against his broad back, encircling

his waist with her arms. She'd have to be slow in her approach ... treat him, as he had her, with tender patience until the time was right. He was back, safe for now, and questions could wait. 'Wish this bloody rotten war would end.'

'For a while it has ended for us, Lily.' He turned about, lifted her up so their faces were level. 'After we've had breakfast, shall we go shopping for a wedding ring?'

'Do that this afternoon,' she kissed the tip of his nose. 'We should spend the morning in the warehouse. I was late locking up last night and rushed off to meet Evie. There's some catching up to do. The takings need logging, and banking.' She paused. 'I've not seen Margie for a few days. She comes in a couple of times a week to help with the books. She brings Rosie.' She remembered that Greg hadn't yet met the little girl. 'Just wait till you see her. She's a darling ... so like her mum in looks.'

'That's handy.' Greg sounded mordant as he put her back on her feet and poured the tea. 'And how's Fanny doing?'

'She's packed up her factory job now her baby's almost due. She's staying over Edmonton way with her in-laws. Don't see much of her any more.' Lily whipped the toast from beneath the grill before it burned and began buttering it.

This was a bigger flat than hers, in a better area of Poplar, and was appointed with smarter furniture and a well-equipped kitchen boasting a new-fangled gas cooker. He even had a vacuum cleaner, although he rarely used it and Lily told him she didn't reckon they'd catch on, the price of them. A good old dustpan and brush and some elbow grease was best, she'd said. The bedstead she'd just slept in was brass and the mattress thick and comfy. He'd suggested she move in here permanently, but she preferred her basement haven. After they were married they were going to look for somewhere new to live. Their first place together. A family home with a garden; somewhere suitable to raise children, perhaps closer to the countryside.

'When I saw Adam at Christmas he let slip something about Smudger.' She handed Greg the plate of toast, having taken a slice to nibble on.

Greg frowned quizzically, starting to eat.

'Smudger had a girlfriend in France before he and Margie got married.'

'That was ages ago,' said Greg, perching on the table.

Lily sat on the stick-back chair and took another bite of her toast. 'You knew about it?' she said after a thoughtful moment.

'Yeah, I knew. The girl was a nurse.'

'He wouldn't still be seeing her, would he?'

'You asking me if I know Smudger's cheating on his wife?'

'Yes. I am.'

'I don't know, Lily. Haven't seen him in a while. What makes you think he'd do that, anyway? Has Margie said something?'

'No! And I've not mentioned anything to her about it. Smudger married Margie with good grace but ...' She shrugged, remembering his reluctance to take on his enemy's child. 'Margie's my best friend. I don't want to see her hurt any more than she has been. I love her and want her to be as happy as I am.'

Greg put a comforting arm about her. 'Smudger might have told her about his past girlfriends. You know about mine. Anyway, you can't sort out their lives for them, love. Let's leave them to their marriage and plan ours. If we're going to the warehouse to put in a shift, better get cracking or the morning will be gone.' He nuzzled the sensitive spot behind her ear. 'Unless you're feeling sleepy again.'

'I'm wide awake. I might be tired after our wedding-ring shopping trip though.'

'Am I on a promise?'

'Mmm ... might be,' she teased. 'Will you ask your pal John Lonegan to our wedding?'

Greg looked as though that hadn't occurred to him but he wasn't against the idea. 'When the date's set, I'll go over Peckham Rye to see if he'll be my best man.'

'I'll ask Margie to be matron of honour. I doubt Fanny will come. She could go into labour at any minute.' Lily paused. 'What about your Aunt Ruth? We could invite her.'

He appeared taken aback by the suggestion. 'Don't think so.'

'She took you in after your mum left,' Lily reminded him. 'You said you got on with her.'

'I did when I was small. Don't know her any more.'

'All the more reason to go and see her. Shall we?' Lily put her hands on his shoulders to stop him turning away. He never volunteered any information about his childhood.

'Don't even know if she's still alive. She'd be in her late sixties now.'

'Where was she living?'

'Somewhere in Dartford. We lost touch.'

There had been scant opportunity to talk about their pasts since becoming a couple. Just a few months after their first kiss, he'd been on a troop ship. He knew all about her history anyway as Davy had told him the Larkins' tale of woe. Greg had caught her brother stealing after he escaped from his industrial school and fled to London. Instead of turning Davy over to the police, Gregory Wilding, with the reputation of being a villain, had given him a job to keep him out of trouble. He'd then discovered his apprentice's sister was still stuck in Whitechapel workhouse, and why the twins had ended up in there in the first place.

Lily had prised out of her future husband some details of the Wildings' misfortune. Greg's father had been a docker who'd died in a fall from rigging. Mrs Wilding had abandoned her son less than a year afterwards, sailing for America with the new man in her life and their tiny daughter. Six-year-old Gregory had been put in the care of his middle-aged aunt. That meagre comfort had come to an end for him far too soon when that family also disintegrated. Lily was curious to know why it had.

'Do you blame your aunt for taking you to the workhouse?'

He shook his head. 'She did what she could for me, for as long as she could.'

'Wouldn't you like to see her? She was your foster mum for two years.'

'I know, and I'm grateful she took me in.'

Lily could tell he was getting fed up with her questions, but she wanted to learn about what had shaped Gregory Wilding into the man she loved. 'You liked your cousin. Catherine was a bit older than you, wasn't she?'

He thrust his fingers through his hair. 'I thought we were going to concentrate on us, Lily.'

'We are; your past is part of you, just as mine is part of me. And there's nothing you don't already know about the Larkins' skeletons.' She started to wash up the breakfast crockery in the bowl. 'What happened to your poor aunt? She must have been in a desperate situation to have admitted you and her own daughter to St Pancras work-house.' She was teasing rather than nagging when adding, 'I reckon it's time you told me all about how you ended up as a workhouse kid. We're getting married and husbands and wives do talk about such things, you know . . .' She flicked water off her fingers, glancing over a shoulder at him. He seemed in two minds whether to comply so she found the tea towel and started drying cups, and waited.

What was he scared of? His future wife had the most beautiful, generous soul. She'd comfort him. But he didn't want to be diminished in her eyes. She believed him popular and invincible: the man able to put everything right with his money or his fists. He'd need to shatter that illusion in telling her that once nobody had wanted him and he'd been a snivelling waif, needing rescuing himself.

The silence lengthened. Lily continued wiping teaspoons, slowly and carefully.

'I got taken there in the winter. It was a long walk. I remember me fingers felt frozen from hanging on to the pram handle and being dragged along in the snow. I didn't know Mum's sister; we'd not visited her since I was a baby in a pram meself. That was something to do with me real dad not getting on with her husband. Wise man, me dad.' Greg sounded sardonic. 'Anyway, after Dad died, Mum built bridges. The day we went there, Cousin Catherine came over and held my hand while the adults were talking about me.' He paused, uncertain whether to continue but too much had been said not to carry on. 'Aunt Ruth said she couldn't have me and we got shown the door. Obviously, her and me mum weren't back on the good terms me step-father had hoped for. They argued on the way home; I got a wallop off him because he had to carry me suitcase back.'

He gave a sour laugh. 'Couldn't have been heavy ... wasn't much in it. Just a few clothes and a book about horses that used to belong to me real dad.' Greg lit another cigarette, smoked for a bit before speaking again. 'I was skidding about on the ice so Mum lifted me up to sit on the pram. He wouldn't have that. Made me get off and walk.' A bitter laugh conveyed his opinion on that sort of meanness. His stepfather had been the first person Greg had hated. 'Next time they took me there some money changed hands. That did the trick. Suitcase got taken upstairs that day.' Greg smiled acidly at the memory. 'I kept out of me aunt and uncle's way. Catherine became a friend though; we'd walk to school together.'

Lily wanted to put her arms around him in comfort. But he hadn't finished yet, his eyes were on her but he was look-ing inward. A string of memories was being fished from his mind. If she broke the thread, it'd be snapped for good. He'd not return to this again. She concentrated on wiping a china plate, long since dry, while tears gathered in her eyes and her throat thickened.

'Things went downhill. Aunt Ruth lost her job. There was a fire in the big house where she worked in the kitchen. The cook was to blame but me aunt was the scapegoat. Uncle Bert didn't want his wife out of work. He didn't want me. I was a jinx, he said.' Greg propped an elbow on the wall, and smoked the cigarette down to the stub. 'She used to bring home fancy leftovers from big dinners in Mayfair. Lovely grub it was. Reckon that's where I got me taste for custard tarts.' Greg smiled, properly amused. 'He didn't 'arf moan when that stopped. So ... couple of weeks later, I suppose it was, he took me to the workhouse while she was out. She came and fetched me home that time and the arguments went on for weeks.' He shrugged. 'Might as well have left me there; wasn't long before she took me back. None of it was her fault though. Bert was to blame. Catherine and me watched him clearing out the wardrobe one day on the sly. Ruth was out looking for work. I was glad to see the back of him. But Catherine followed her dad up the street, crying. He told her to clear off and got in a cab. Me aunt came in and went nuts. She tipped out every drawer. All gone. Even the rent money.' Greg pinched the dying glow out of the cigarette stub. 'Weren't long after that she took us both to St Pancras workhouse. And that was that.' The tale was brought to an abrupt end and he lobbed the butt into the ashtray on the table.

'I didn't know you had an uncle living there at the time,' said Lily with heartbroken softness. 'You've never spoken about him before; I assumed it was just you and Catherine and your aunt.'

'Wasn't worth speaking about. Lazy bugger, he was. Left her to do everything. He was only a casual worker so would be at home a lot of the time.' He crossed his arms, leaning back against the wall, and staring up at the ceiling. He'd seen the sparkle in Lily's eyes. He couldn't bear the thought that he'd upset her enough to start her crying. When he spoke again he sounded dispassionate, as though relating somebody else's hard-luck story. 'I found out Ruth did go back for Catherine, but she was too ill to be discharged. I ended up at industrial school in Watford. Ran away a few times, trying to get to London to see Catherine. Never got far; was taken back to solitary confinement and a caning.' He chuckled in real amusement. 'The headmaster was over the moon to get rid of me. That old git wouldn't have been so pleased with himself if he'd known he'd done me a huge favour, discharging me to a costermonger wanting an apprentice. Stepped out of that dump and never looked back . . .'

'Bit like me . . . when I stepped out of South Grove . . . with you.'

'We're out of the same mould, me 'n' you, Lily,' he said.

'Lenny Todd was your boss.' Greg had told her before about his first and only employer. At sixteen he'd been his own boss, and still was – leaving aside the War Office.

Greg was happier to be on more familiar ground, talking about business. 'Old Lenny, God rest him, was renting the warehouse back then. He let me take over the lease when he got sick. He warned me I was getting in over my head, taking on a premises when I was still a kid wet behind the ears. He came back to see me about a month before he died. Shook my hand and wished me all the best. He could see I was struggling but he didn't say: I told you so. Good bloke, was old Lenny.'

'You proved them all wrong, didn't you, though?' She knew he didn't want her sympathy about his early torment; she'd never wanted his either. They'd been soulmates before they became lovers, united by their hatred of the institutions that had deprived them of a decent childhood. She'd fared better than he had; she had cherished memories of her early years at home with Davy and her parents. He had been six . . . so young when his father died and his birth family crumbled. Lily refused to be resentful; she didn't want him to let bitterness fester either. The boil had been lanced. They were talking about it, diluting the poison with every chuckle and shared memory.

'Lenny sold off all his stock and equipment. Didn't blame him for doing that. He knew he was dying of cancer and he had a wife to think of. Back then I couldn't afford to pay him what the stuff was worth. Just started off with a home-made barrow. Got most of the wood off the banks of the Thames, down by the docks, where it had washed up. Found a wheelbarrow before it got lost and used the wheels. Too small really, to do the job, but they got me up and running. Poached a street round. And slept in the warehouse to save rent.'

'I didn't know you bunked down in there,' she exclaimed, half-laughing.

He chuckled too, happy to dredge up fond memories now. 'Better than a school dormitory any day. Straw bed. Water on tap for washing and a hot drink boiled up on the primus. Handsome. Had to fight every day back then though. The other bloke gave up in the end when he realised I wasn't gonna.' His mouth quirked in a half smile. But within a moment it had gone and he looked meditative.

'You don't blame yourself, do you, over Catherine?' she asked.

'If Aunt Ruth had left me at St Pancras first time round, things might have been different. Her husband might have stuck around. Catherine was too delicate for work-house living.'

'Your mum should never have abandoned you in the first place!' Lily cried and launched herself at him to hug him. 'I'm glad you stayed in England though, or I wouldn't even know you.'

He closed his eyes and planted a kiss on her fragrant, chestnut hair. 'Talk about something else now, eh? I'm home on leave, Lily, and want to relax and forget about bad times. And I want to get married.'

'And so do I. I just thought your Aunt Ruth might like an

invite to the wedding; she'll be happy to know you're doing all right for yourself.'

'Yeah ... I thought that,' he sounded sarcastic. 'She's not interested in me.' He sighed. 'I paid her a visit years ago when I was turning eighteen and on the up. Took some flowers. She was on her own in a dump of a room, surrounded by boxes. Looked like she was doing piece-work from home,' he explained. 'I tried to make conversation. She didn't want to talk. Didn't want to see me or me flowers. She was bitter about things and didn't bother hiding it. She told me to stay away. So that's what I do.'

'That's her loss then,' Lily declared, eyes sparking in indignation. 'You don't need her anyway. You've got me now to love you.' Lily hugged him as tight as she could, burrowing her face into him.

'And you're all I need,' he said gruffly.

'You rescued me from the workhouse because you couldn't rescue Catherine, didn't you?'

'I rescued you, Lily Larkin, cos once I'd clapped eyes on you ... that was it. Reckon it was love at first sight for me.' There was a contentment and a glint of wolfishness in his golden gaze as he looked at her. 'That's enough now. Come on, let's get going to the warehouse, or wedding ring or no wedding ring I'm taking you back to bed.'

Chapter Sixteen

Greg pulled the van onto the warehouse forecourt. While he and Lily were getting out of the vehicle the unmistakable sound of people arguing drifted to their ears. Margie's voice was identifiable but whoever she'd been shouting at had fallen quiet.

'Margie must have turned up early and one of the lads let her in.' Lily frowned. 'Perhaps Eric came back for some reason and is in there with her.'

'Sounds like unrest in the camp,' said Greg. 'They like a ding-dong, do they?'

Lily shook her head, baffled. 'Margie gets on well with the lads.'

The couple exchanged a dubious glance as they approached the sturdy wooden barn-like building that easily spanned seventy feet in length. There were windows inset along the flank but nothing much could be glimpsed within. A skeleton framework of market poles and stacked pallets obscured the view.

Inside, Margie was pacing about, rocking her whimpering daughter in her arms. Her husband was perched on the orange box that was utilised as a stool, his head lowered into his hands.

'What a lovely surprise!' Lily exclaimed into a leaden atmosphere. 'Didn't know you'd got leave as well, Smudge!'

He jerked to his feet with a surprised hoot of welcome but strain was apparent on his face and Margie's too.

'Sorry to be late for work this morning, love.' Lily acted normally to save the couple any embarrassment. She hadn't seen Margie in nearly a week and gave her a hug and little Rosie a peck on the cheek. The child was a friendly little thing and brightened up now her parents had stopped yelling at one another. Rosie held out her arms and Lily took her, bouncing her on a forearm.

'Wasn't expecting you in today; thought you'd be getting ready to welcome Greg home this afternoon.' Margie had turned away to discreetly wipe her eyes with the hanky discarded on the desk. It looked sodden.

Lily maintained a breezy demeanour though her friend's bloodshot eyes and thick-throated voice told their own unhappy story. 'Greg's dates changed and he turned up early.'

'When did you get back, Smudger?' Greg extended a hand, following Lily's lead in ignoring the elephant in the room.

'Arrived at Dover on Wednesday on a ten-day pass.' Smudger shook hands then jangled the warehouse keys in his fingers. 'I still had these so thought I'd pull on me work clothes and put in a shift this morning.' He smiled wryly and ran a hand through his cropped hair. 'Had a lie-in first, though.'

'Stroke of luck, this is,' said Greg. 'I've a couple of favours need doing and you're just the man for them. The motor's playing up, so if you'd take a dekko under the bonnet, that'd be handy. You've always understood what makes the old gel tick better'n me.'

'What's the good news?' Smudger asked ironically. He was relaxing into the spirit of being back with his pals in Wilding's warehouse.

'Ah ... now that really is good news. We're getting married before I go back, and I want you to be my best man.'

Smudger grinned and clasped his boss's shoulder. 'Be honoured, I would, and if I may be so bold, 'bout bloody time too.'

'That's what I said, Smudger.' Lily still had an eye on Margie. She hadn't joined in the banter though she'd looked up when the wedding was mentioned and she'd murmured a welcome to her guvnor.

'Catching up on Davy then, Lily? Twins do similar things, even when far apart, I heard.' Smudger's grin faded.

'How d'you mean? What's Davy done?' Lily looked puzzled and a tad troubled.

'Ain't put me foot in it, have I?'

'I was going to tell you later, love.' Greg frowned at Smudger and received an apologetic look. 'Davy got married, Lily. Last time he was on leave.'

'He's having you on,' she spluttered, half-laughing. 'He's my brother. He would've told me first. Anyway, he's not had leave ...'

'He took his leave in Ireland about a month ago,' Greg explained. 'He married Keegan's stepdaughter there.'

'After all the trouble he had with her ...' Lily sounded more bewildered than angry. Keegan was a local café proprietor. He was also a thug who in the past had tried to get Wilding's to deliver produce on account, then had withheld payment. After that they'd refused his custom. It had been bad news when Davy Larkin took up with the crook's stepdaughter. Angie Clark had pretended to be pregnant to swindle money from Davy, on her stepfather's say so. Unsurprisingly, a bust-up had followed when Davy found out. He had enlisted and that had seemed to be that with Angie, or so Lily had believed.

She gave a philosophical shrug. Davy was old enough now to make his own decisions and take a wife if he wanted to. 'Perhaps this time Angie really is expecting,' she said. 'Well, thanks for telling me. I'll write and tear him off a strip. And congratulate him. Hope they'll both be happy.' She meant it too. Whatever he got up to, Davy would always mean the world to her. He was the link to her mum and dad and to those sunlit garden days, long, long ago when the Larkins had been a happy family. 'He could at least have let me know.' She finished on a grumble and gave Greg a speaking look. She knew why he'd delayed telling her though, and was glad he had. That news would have spoiled their wonderful first night together.

'I told him to write to you and put you in the picture. You know Davy . . .' Greg gestured his frustration with his future brother-in-law.

'I do indeed know Davy.' Lily was well aware her twin brother could be self-centred and inconsiderate. He'd dodged telling her he was enlisting, aged just fifteen, and had never been as interested in looking for their half-sister as she had. Or as keen for them to keep closely in touch after he went overseas. Perhaps his loosening of the ties that bound them had been the right thing to do. Better that than they be severed.

Relieved she'd taken the news so well, Greg deemed it time to bow out. 'Let's get that engine looked at then.' He headed for the door and Smudger followed, having first given his wife a sheepish look.

Lily knew there was nothing up with the van. Greg had understood her need to speak to her friend alone.

As the door swung closed, Margie took her daughter from Lily and put the child back in the pram. 'Bloody men! Davy should've told you, the wretch.' She snorted. 'Smudger thought you knew. I said you'd've told me about something like that.'

'You didn't row about it, did you?' Lily hoped that wasn't the case.

'No ... not about that.' Margie didn't bother putting up a brave front. She slumped down in her chair behind the desk, holding her head in her hands.

'Oh, what's up, Marge?' Lily crouched down beside her dejected friend.

'Everything. His bloody mother don't help either ...' Margie had replied quickly and bitterly, as though wanting this off her chest.

Lily felt a tinge of relief. Mother-in-law woes were solvable. Just last week Margie had been on better terms with Eunice and had sought her advice on whether her daughter's rash was measles or whether cutting teeth was making Rosie spotty and miserable. The little girl couldn't have had a serious ailment. She was full of beans now, bouncing in the pram to gain attention. 'What's Eunice done?' Lily prompted.

'Told her son I've run up debts.'

'Have you?' Lily hadn't brought this up before. Eunice might believe her daughter-in-law a spendthrift in need of a talking-to, but Lily reckoned Margie was sensible enough to do her own budgeting without a lecture from anybody.

'I owe money to the totter for a few things,' Margie owned up.

'Do you need a sub on your wages to pay it off?'

'I was going to ask for one, but Smudger won't let me,' she sighed. 'He said he'd deal with it and shouted at me to act like a responsible wife. So I told him to practise what he preaches and be a good husband.'

'What's that mean, Marge?'

This time Margie took her time in answering. 'Just after we got married I found a snap of a nurse in his wallet. Didn't bring it up back then. He asked *me* to be his wife and I didn't want to rub it in that he'd need to throw over his girl in France.' Margie curled her finger stumps into her palm. 'Could see why he'd fallen for her. Pretty face and black hair, like Claudette's.' Margie scowled at the memory of the married woman Smudger had got involved with. 'I know I'm no catch with me crippled hand and me illegitimate baby.' She remained quiet for a while. 'I thought if I bought a few nice clothes on tick and visited the hairdressers once in a while, Smudger might notice *I* look pretty sometimes. He was pushed into being a husband and a father, but I want him to be proud of me and Rosie. I want him to be glad we're a family. Why can't he love us back?' Margie wept quietly into her palms.

'Oh, he *does* love you, Marge.' Lily cuddled her heartbroken friend. 'Anybody can see he adores you and little Rosie.'

Margie shook her head, cuffing away tears. 'I emptied his pockets to wash his clothes. He's still got that photo. Men who love their wives don't keep other women's photos in their wallet, do they? I reckon he's still seeing her ...'

Lily sat down on the orange box, wanting to deny those suspicions. But there was only one person who could put Margie's fears to rest. 'Have you asked Smudger about her?'

'Not yet. I've been too scared ... in case he chooses her and leaves us.'

'He wouldn't do that!' Lily believed Smudger too decent to abandon his wife and child.

'I thought he wouldn't chase after another man's wife, or keep a nurse's photograph in his wallet after he got married himself, but he's done both those things. Not sure I even really know him, Lily.'

'Perhaps if Greg has a word ...' Lily gave Margie's hands a squeeze.

'No!' Margie pulled free. 'Smudger don't like any interference.' She pushed herself to her feet as Rosie wailed and held out her arms to be picked up.

'You should say something to him, love, you'll drive yourself mad.'

'I was building up to it when you and Greg turned up. Could tell Smudger was relieved you'd interrupted us. He'd guessed what was coming.'

'Well, we're off in a minute, so no excuse for him not to listen then. We're going to a studio to have photos taken. After that we're buying a wedding ring.'

'Hope you'll be happier than I am,' said Margie with sweet sincerity.

Lily embraced her, rubbing her back in comfort. 'You were happy when you got married, Marge. It's your first wedding anniversary soon. By then you'll be happy again. Know you will, love.'

Greg shook a cigarette from the pack he'd just bought. He struck a match, slanting Lily a smile. 'Shall we have a bite to eat before looking in jewellers' windows? It's almost midday and I'm feeling peckish.'

'And me ...' Lily took his arm as they started to stroll away from the shop.

They'd just visited the photographer's studio. It was a simple room above the tobacconists, accessed by some rickety stairs situated at the back of the premises. They'd forgone a rustic bench or a gate to pose against and had stood before a plain backdrop. Lily had smiled on cue though she couldn't stop thinking about Margie, desperate for an explanation from her husband. What innocent excuse could there be, though, for him keeping that nurse's picture?

Greg glanced at Lily's solemn profile. He found her loyalty and affection for her friends touching, but she was making herself blue brooding on this. 'We should go back in our wedding outfits and get a few more photos done,' he said lightly. 'If the weather's fine we could get one taken over there.' He jerked a nod to a patch of greenery close to the studio. A large lime tree dominated a shady space that would provide an ideal setting for a summery shot.

'A group photo with the four of us would be nice. And Margie could get a snap done with little Rosie. Smudger can put it in his wallet to replace the one he'll have got rid of.'

'Enough about them now. How about we go to Hatton Garden to look for a ring?' He raised an eyebrow at her. 'D'you fancy a trip further afield?'

'Poplar High Street's fine by me. I'd sooner go to the place where you got my engagement ring ... what's that?'

Lily had lifted her smiling face to allow the sun's warmth beneath the brim of her hat. On opening her eyes she'd found herself squinting at a glinting silver cloud in the sky. The mass was approaching at speed and was close enough now for individual aircraft to be identified. She turned to Greg but he'd spotted the German squadron and horrified shock had immobilised his features. He knew what a Gotha looked like from aerial bombardment over France and had dreaded hearing news they'd headed over the Channel and reached the city of London.

'Aren't they our planes?' she cried in alarm, shaking his arm.

He furiously shook his head, dropping his cigarette. Snapping into action he propelled her along the pavement, causing her to hop and skip to keep up. A few passers-by still seemed oblivious to the peril and Greg roared at them to take cover. Most people had by now heard the thrum of engines though and recognised the oncoming foe. Merchants had dashed out from behind their counters to find out what the fuss was about. There were shrieks from women, bellows from men. Parents instinctively lifted small children into their arms and bolted while overhead the moth-shaped aircraft droned ever closer and the atmosphere vibrated. Panicking people sought to hide in shop doorways then thought better of sheltering close to large windowpanes destined to be shattered.

Greg let go of an exhausted Lily's hand to allow her to catch her breath. 'We need to get back to the warehouse ... warn Smudger and Margie,' he yelled over the pandemonium. Filled with impotent rage, he watched the leading aeroplane release bombs lodged under its fuselage. They fell like a grotesque insect's excrement. Within seconds there was an explosion. It shook the ground and drove them at a cowering crouch to the nearest wall to protect themselves against falling masonry and flying glass.

Silence ensued for seconds then a hysterical woman began shouting at her husband to get up, slapping his face to rouse him. Greg helped her manoeuvre the elderly fellow to a seated position with his back resting against a garden gate. He appeared to have collapsed from fright rather than injury. Others milled about in shock with bleeding faces. Some remained prone amid debris littering the pavement. Blast followed blast and Greg and Lily gave up tracking the position of the hits, or assisting the casualties. Either they sought shelter or risked joining their number.

The smell of burning wood began swirling around on a hot wind. Greg grabbed Lily's hand and they set off again at a run. They ducked down once more as a building across the road took a direct hit; the roof caved in with a crash, sending up a dust smog.

Lily jerked a hate-filled look up at the alien contraption circling overhead, marked with a cross of black. These were smaller, but noisier and far more deadly craft than those others that had glided over like bloated silverfish seeking a hunting ground. The foe in those Zeppelins had been hidden from view. This attack had come during daylight and the Germans were visible. Overhead, the same Gotha passed, picking a target. The outline of the pilot's head and shoulders rising from the cockpit was so distinct she could see the wool collar of his coat; his features were indistinguishable beneath goggles and helmet. Lily threw back her head to spurt at him a stream of abuse, shaking a fist. She knew he couldn't hear her but he could see, and was maddened when he saluted. She could imagine him grinning in beastly amusement.

Greg lifted Lily to her feet, calming her with a cuddle. Grabbing her hand, off they went in the direction of the warehouse. She was sobbing for breath but kept up with him from sheer determination, converting her rage to energy.

Flames were shooting up above the rooflines, indicating

a bombsite some streets away. Greg gave a shout of denial and let go of her hand, to sprint to the corner.

Lily knew why he repeatedly, despairingly, bashed his fist against brick, staring into the distance. The warehouse had been hit. Though spent, she dragged herself on, pressing the stitch in her side. Wordlessly she held out her hand for him to grip to pull her along. She ignored the burn in her muscles that owed little to the fires. Her throat was sandpaper dry and her lungs scalding. Grit drifting around them had blurred her vision and was mixed with tears that rolled a clean stripe through smuts on her skin. Blindly she kept going, until she was following him onto the forecourt where they'd left the van earlier. The vehicle was intact, the pram outside, but the building was ablaze and no sign of their friends or Rosie.

Greg barred her way with his forearm as she headed straight for the warehouse.

'Stay there!' He pointed a finger at her, his eyes savage with pain. 'Stay there. Don't you dare come inside.'

She lunged for his arm to stop him, but he slipped free and disappeared, swallowed by orange smoke.

Lily stumbled on her weakened legs, giving a prayer of thanksgiving as Margie emerged. She grabbed her friend's arm, ushering the wheezing girl away from the heat towards the road.

'Where's Smudger and Rosie?' Lily gasped out, jerking up Margie's drooping chin.

'He's got Rosie . . . a beam fell down . . .' Margie started to swoon, her mouth agape in a silent shriek.

Lily caught Margie around the middle as she sagged, lowering her to the concrete forecourt. She scrambled off her knees, heading for the warehouse. Flames were snaking from the windows that had lost glass. One pane remained intact and she peered in, rubbing furiously at it to try and improve her view. Nothing was visible other than fire and blackness. Lily rushed to the door. He'd ordered her to stay outside. But she had to help. Greg might not be able to get Smudger and Rosie out in time. She could grab the child. There was no happiness without him anyway ... she'd sooner go in there than carry on alone ...

Two hacking figures burst out of the thick smoke, making Lily totter back to avoid them and the roasting temperature. Greg had Smudger's arm over his shoulder to support him as he limped along dragging his right leg. Lily glimpsed Rosie tucked beneath Greg's jacket and he twisted his body to allow her to get to the silent child. Lily put Rosie on the ground beside her mother then fumbled beneath the child's knitted jacket, pushing her hand to and fro to detect a heartbeat. She sighed in relief at a faint pulse in her palm.

Smudger was yelping in pain, coughing and gulping in air. Lily hurried to help settle him against the fence. Within a second Greg had sprinted to the water standpipe and filled a bucket. He came back, emptying it on Smudger's charred trouser leg. The invalid grimaced and shuddered. Greg repeated the process, patting Smudger's shoulder as his friend gritted his teeth and groaned.

'Reckon his leg's broken as well as burned,' he rattled off. 'Trapped under timber.' Greg let the bucket fall to the ground and thrust his shaking fingers through his hair, powdered with ash. 'No point waiting for help or even trying to find it. Chaos everywhere, I expect.' He'd decided on a course of action and set off for the van. 'I'll start the motor and take them to hospital.'

'Where's Margie?' Smudger had drawn enough strength to call out. 'Where's me wife and baby? All right, ain't they?'

'Margie passed out ... she'll wake soon though.' Lily crouched down by him, talking soothingly. 'Rosie's right by her ... see.' She gently manoeuvred his chin, so his red-rimmed eyes could focus on mother and child, side by side.

'Bring me daughter to me ... please ... I want to hold her,' Smudger held out a palsied arm.

Lily went to get the child. She rubbed one of Rosie's cheeks to try and rouse her and thrust a hand to and fro on her chest, rubbing the place where the pulse had been. Convinced she'd felt a quiver she settled the little girl in her father's arms before going to help Greg empty out the back of the van.

'Be easier to take Smudger to hospital lying flat than try to get him in the front.' Greg carried on throwing tarpaulins and ropes to one side on the concrete.

'Rosie won't wake up. I think she's breathing though.' Lily slanted an anxious look at the family, while clumsily stacking pallets.

'Couldn't see much at all in there,' explained Greg bleakly. 'Smudger took the brunt of the fall on his back and his leg to protect Rosie but something could have caught the little 'un. I'll take her to hospital with us.'

Lily gave a vigorous thankful nod. 'Will the fire brigade come soon?'

Greg had watched her swing a glance from the bucket to the standpipe as though weighing up the chances of putting out the inferno and saving the warehouse. 'It's too late,' he sounded resigned. 'The warehouse has had it, Lily, so's everything in it. Forget it and take Margie home while I'm gone.'

She saw him wince and gasped out, 'Are *you* hurt?'

'Just burned me fingers ... nothing a bit of ointment won't put right,' he said when she tried to examine the blisters. 'I'm all right, love.' He hugged her then started the van's engine.

Before Lily could insist on looking at his hand a sound of pounding feet and a yelling voice diverted them to the gate.

Eric Skipman plunged into view, red in the face, his eyes popping with the urgency of his mission. He bent over at the waist, swinging gangling arms in front of him. 'Upper North Street School's been hit,' he panted. 'Joey's brothers are in there. All the mums are in hysterics, trying to find their kids under the rubble.' Eric gazed at the burning warehouse, noticing the casualties. 'Fuckin' 'ell . . .' he said on an elongated groan. 'Not this place too. Smudger'll be all right, won't he? What's up with Marge?' The boy made to dive her way, but Greg stopped him.

'She's fainted. Just the shock. Give me a hand to get Smudger into the van. He's in a bad way and needs to get to hospital. His wife don't. After that, help Lily get Margie home safe.'

Between them the men got the casualty into the back of the vehicle, handling him as carefully as they could, while Lily cradled the child in her arms.

She kissed Rosie's cheek before handing her back to her father. 'Take Rosie with you. Doctors can check her out.'

'Is she bad?' Smudger gabbled, bending his face close to the tot to try and hear or feel her breath. The roar of the fire and distant clamour of bells and alarms made even holding a conversation at normal volume difficult.

'Doctors'll soon see to her.' Lily forced confidence into her voice.

'Margie come to yet, has she?' Smudger's face was running with sweat from trying to control his agonising pain. 'I gotta say something to her.' He attempted to shuffle out of the vehicle to go to her. Greg eased him back, urging him to lay down.

'I'll look after Margie.' Lily gripped his arm in comfort. I'll tell her you're all right. You will be, Smudger. And Rosie.'

He nodded, lying down with Rosie clamped to his chest, tears dripping into the hair at his temples. 'Tell her I love her. Tell her we'll both be home soon.' He stroked his daughter's face.

'I'll tell her,' vowed Lily.

'Would you make sure me mum's all right? And tell her I am too. Just getting patched up and nothing to worry about. Don't want her fretting.'

'I'll tell her, Smudger ... promise.'

Greg shut the back doors of the van, turning to Lily. 'The basement flat will be the safest place to stay. Those bastards might come back with another load of bombs.'

Lily returned his hard kiss with equal ferocity. Greg put her away from him and got in the van, reversing in a screech out into the road.

Lily and Eric watched the vehicle disappear behind a fog of dust and smoke layering the atmosphere. 'Where's Joey?' she asked.

'At the school ... I left him helping the others. Teachers and mums are all digging into the rubble, looking for kids.' Eric cuffed wet from his face. 'Bomb fell through the roof and went right down into the infant's class.' He paced about in an aimless daze, clenching his fingers in his hair. 'Shouldn't have come to this. Ain't fair, murdering kids.'

'I know ...' Numb with shock and disbelief, Lily was unable to properly express her despair.

'Going back there now to help.' He sniffed back a sob and squared his shoulders.

Lily hugged him in comfort. Eric Skipman had always been a cheeky blighter – a fatherless lad who came from a notorious family, headed by an alcoholic mother. Yet he had battled on, keeping a cheerful outlook. Lily had never imagined seeing him as distraught as this.

'Where's Rosie? Where's me daughter and Smudger?' Margie had revived and pushed herself up to sway on her feet. She whipped a glance to the disintegrating warehouse. A section of roof had fallen, sending up a shower of sparks. 'Smudger!' she screamed.

Lily dodged to catch her friend in her arms as Margie shot towards the smouldering building.

'Rosie's with her dad. Greg's taken Smudger to Poplar hospital. He's got a broken leg.' Lily burst out with some facts, rocking her trembling friend in her arms.

Margie's hysteria subsided as she digested that. She elbowed free of Lily's embrace. 'I'm going there then.' She brushed herself down and shook her head to liven herself up.

'Will you be all right getting to the hospital on your own?' Lily wasn't going to shelter in her basement. She couldn't. Every pair of hands would be needed at the school.

Margie gave a single emphatic nod, eyes agleam and focused on something distant, like a tigress scenting a lost cub.

The trio walked to the gate then halted and exchanged unblinking stares, unwilling to voice an awful possibility. They might be parting for the last time now the war had been brought to them. Lily hugged Margie. And Margie hugged Eric. She was the first to go. Without another word she rushed off in one direction and seconds later Lily and Eric took the opposite, towards Upper North Street School.

While breathlessly trying to keep up with Eric's speed, Lily remembered her promise to speak to Eunice. The woman, in common with them all, wouldn't yet know the extent of the damage and devastation the bombardment had caused. Word would quickly spread though once the initial panic was over. Lily shouted at Eric that she would soon catch him up, then diverted towards the lane where Eunice lived.

Chapter Seventeen

It was June, the days useably long, but twilight had now fallen and hurricane lamps had been strung up to enable the rescuers to continue working. The frenzied scramble of eight hours ago had since flattened into a grim, determined dig. Dirty-faced adults on all fours churned bitterness behind vacant expressions while tugging at chunks of wall and ceiling that once had formed Upper North Street School. It had been the place the working-class mothers and fathers of Poplar had trusted would give their kids learning, and a better life than they'd had.

It was quiet, nothing much being said. Failing energy was reserved for scraping shovels over fallen masonry, or to work raw, bloodied fingers into shattered plaster and glass in the hope of finding a small hand that moved. But hope was fading as minutes ticked by.

Mothers who had been shocked into hysteria had gone, taken their grief – or their relief, as a child was found alive and rushed to hospital – back to hearth and family.

'You need to go home now, Lily.' Greg caught her under the armpits and hauled her off her knees to her feet.

Lily shook herself awake. She hadn't realised she had

keeled forward, her forehead resting on a hump of concrete. 'I'm fine. Not going home.' She sounded drunk, her speech slurring from fatigue. She pulled away from him and sank down to begin pawing at the wreckage again. Her arms felt leaden but she threw several bits behind her to join the pile already shifted.

Greg crouched down, taking her gaunt face in his hands. 'Eric can take you back. Go and get some rest, then return in the morning if you want. I'll still be here, I expect.'

Lily rubbed her filthy face. She knew he was right. She could barely keep her eyes open to look at him. But these were her people, housewives she'd filled shopping bags for. Women who loyally came week in week out to buy at her stall, and to have a laugh with the lads. Women who juggled in their arms a tired little 'un and cabbages while counting coppers from their purses to pay her. Some of those children would have been making paper lanterns with their friends in the infants' class. Right where the bomb had exploded. Those stoic women who'd lost a boy or girl today would never know real happiness again. And neither would Joey or his family.

Greg lifted her again. Hugged her, kissing the side of her head where her hair was gritty and pale from lime blown on the breeze to thicken chestnut tangles. 'Go on ... home now. You've done enough. Eric will come back for another shift. Know he will.' Greg picked up the shovel he'd put down and leaned on it, whistling to attract Eric's attention. The youth was stationed on a clump of rubble thirty yards or so away and was also taking a breather. He had a short, wiry build and surprising strength for a man of his size. He'd been a coalman's apprentice from the age of twelve and was fast and efficient with a loaded shovel.

'Has Joey gone home now?' asked Lily as the youth mounted the last precarious hillock then stood beside them. The swinging hurricane lamps passed a yellow light over the three figures.

'Yeah ... taken his mum back. Staying with her.'

'Good ...' Lily nodded. There was nothing else to say to express her profound sorrow. Joey Robley's five-year-old brother had been found a couple of hours ago and had been removed to the mortuary. The two older boys had been taken to hospital with injuries not thought to be fatal. The bomb had passed through three floors; the older boys and girls had been above the infants' class where the bomb had done its cruellest work. With her husband away at sea for long periods, Mrs Robley relied on her eldest son to be man of the house. And God only knew she would need his support now.

The bell of an approaching ambulance drew little attention from the people who wouldn't give up.

'See Lily home in the van. She's out on her feet.' Greg held out his flat keys but Lily shook her head.

'Going back to the basement. Margie'll come there. She'll need me.'

Greg nodded acceptance of that and pocketed the keys. He knew but couldn't say that Margie was going to need Lily as never before. His throat was thick with dust and bottled-up rage and sadness. But it wasn't that keeping him quiet. 'Get off now,' he gruffly said. 'Eric, if you're up to it, come back and give us a hand. Need to keep going ... still time ...'

In France tunnellers had been hauled out alive after being buried beneath exploded clay. An air pocket ... a beam fortuitously fallen and providing shelter, could make the difference between surviving ten minutes or ten hours. As long as the rescue teams were able to carry on the search for those comrades praying in suffocating darkness. Every soldier accepted he was a target from the moment he dressed in khaki, but beneath this ruin were innocent little victims. Rules had been broken.

'I'll be back, don't you worry about that,' said Eric. He'd worked through his distress into exhaustion and needed a break. So did everybody else keeping going from sheer bloody-minded determination with one thought in their heads: weak voices might be calling ... small hands scrabbling. And if the Boche thought killing kids had them on the run, they could think again. Eric knew he was out of work. There was nothing left of his guvnor's business. But there was somewhere else Eric could go, and he reckoned he'd be joining a queue of like-minded lads. Tomorrow, if he wasn't needed here, he'd be down the recruiting office claiming to be nineteen. Eric had a younger brother and sister. Annie was old enough to be working. George had played truant today ... as he often did. He hadn't got a clipped ear. He'd got a hug from his mother that had gone on for ever. Eric's little sister, Clare, had died in the diphtheria epidemic. Had she not, she would have been here and might by now have lain alongside Joey's littlest brother on a cold slab.

Eric took Lily's arm and guided her down the shifting rocks to the van. She glanced wearily over a shoulder. Greg was employing the shovel again, a hunched clockwork silhouette against a menacing sky. He didn't wave goodbye but the handkerchief he'd wound about his burned hand flapped.

*

Her back was stiff and sore and her hands and knees scraped, but Lily had slept for eight hours and not stirred. She'd not had the fire and blackness dream.

She hadn't washed last night and her face and limbs were grimy. She'd taken off her shoes then fallen straight into bed in her good clothes, now reduced to rags. She sat on the edge of her bed and unbuttoned the once pretty blouse that had ripped sleeves and the tan-coloured skirt that had holes where she'd knelt on it for hours on end, abrading the cotton to threads. The remnants would make dusters. She padded through to the kitchen in her underclothes and filled the kettle at the chipped china sink. Hot water was needed for tea to revive her and for washing. Then she'd go back to the school, do whatever she could that might help, even if it was only making hot drinks for the workers. It would be a recovery rather than rescue operation now.

She had drained her cup and was seated at the table, flannelling her skinned knees of crusted blood when somebody started hammering on the door.

She rushed to yank it open, hoping it would be Greg. Just one more survivor would be wonderful news ... Or perhaps it was Margie to tell her how Smudger and Rosie were doing ...

'Eunice!' Lily hadn't been expecting to see this woman at six o'clock in the morning. She'd found Smudger's mum at home yesterday and had quickly told her the bare bones of the catastrophe at the warehouse, leading to her son's injury. Lily had known the woman would rush to the hospital to see for herself how her boy was doing. He might be a married man with his wife at his bedside, but Smudger was still the most important person in Eunice's life.

'Come in, can I?' Eunice had been weeping; her

complexion was pale beneath the blotches and her eyes bloodshot. But she was composed now.

'Is it Smudger?' Lily ushered the woman in.

'He's still at hospital. Doing as well as is to be expected with his leg mangled to bits. He's comfortable now he's had some morphine.' She snorted back a sob. 'It's Rosie ... me little granddaughter is ...'

'No!' Lily swung away before the woman could utter the dreaded word. 'No! She wouldn't wake up. She's in shock, like Margie was when she fainted. She's only tiny ...' Lily started to howl, folding over at the waist in utter despair. The warmth she'd felt on the little girl had been lent by the fiery atmosphere and the pulse in that fragile chest had been an echo of her own pounding veins. She'd refused to accept it then or to allow the child's parents to have any hint of such unspeakable fears.

Eunice put her face in her hands. 'Doctors can't be sure yet what it was,' she whispered. 'Could be she breathed in smoke, or might be the heat was too much for her little body to cope with.'

'Where's Margie?' Lily used the heel of her hand on her wet face.

'At mine. That's why I come to get you. Last night I brought her back from hospital cos she was upsetting me son. Bobby's groggy from the drugs but he knows about Rosie. He wanted to discharge himself and be with Margie, but he can't hardly stand up on that damaged leg,' Eunice sobbed. 'Margie's mad with grief, been shouting out all sorts of nonsense about Bobby never wanting his daughter. I just can't deal with her no more.' Eunice rubbed her eyes. 'She wants you, anyhow. She come here to find you after we got back from the hospital. She stayed at mine, but neither of us slept.' Eunice shook her head. 'That poor girl was hollering so much me neighbour come in at three o'clock in the morning to see if she could help. Old Mary always has a bottle of laudanum about the place. We managed to get a dose down Margie to knock her out for a few hours.'

'I'll come ... 'course I'll come.' Lily had been listening, feeling anguished, but she immediately made for the door, sniffing and brushing away fresh tears with shaking fingers. She was reaching for the latch when it hit her that she was shoeless and still in her underclothes. 'I'll get meself dressed, Eunice, and be straight down.' Lily opened the door to let Eunice out.

The woman seemed to want to stay, preferring Lily's company to that of her inconsolable daughter-in-law. 'Was you out at the school, helping the rescue?' She followed Lily back to the bedroom and watched the girl pulling on her clothes with clumsy haste.

Lily nodded, bending to thrust her feet into her work boots.

'How many lost, do you think?' whispered Eunice.

'Don't know,' Lily said hoarsely. 'Won't know till the men have finished there.'

'Heard that the school caretaker found his own little boy ...' Eunice's voice tailed off.

'Joey Robley's youngest brother is dead.' Lily heard Eunice's in-drawn groan. There was no kindness in being mealy-mouthed to protect feelings. Crying wouldn't help either. Grieving together, and sharing strength and money, might. A collection for the heartbroken families would be needed, though Lily prayed the final toll of coffins wouldn't be more than could be counted on her hands.

'If I was a man, I'd be on me way to France and killing Hun with these.' Eunice showed two shaking fists, her lined face screwed up in hatred.

Lily stood up and dragged a brush through the knots in her hair. So much had happened in the space of twenty-four hours that her mind was crammed with memories. One that stood out was seeing that German pilot gloating at what he'd done. She knew how Eunice felt. Yet revenge was a false friend.

Lily found her door keys. 'Let's go,' she said, then followed the older woman up the steps to the street.

'Gawd ... what now?' Eunice groaned. 'I closed that, know I did.'

They'd entered the tenement and hurried along the dim passageway to find the woman's door ajar.

Eunice burst into her lodging, calling out to her daughter-in-law. There was no answer from Margie and no sign of her either. Eunice had only a bedsitting room cum kitchen and a smaller room that had once been where Smudger slept on an iron bedstead. Eunice now made use of it, although at times when money was tight, she'd take in a lodger for extra income and return to sleep on the saggy settee. Eunice opened the bedroom door to make sure Margie hadn't flaked out in there. She turned to Lily with a hopeless shrug. 'I left her dozing in the chair. I told her I was off to look for you and it seemed to settle her down. Only been out for a matter of fifteen minutes or so ...'

'Perhaps she's gone to the hospital to see Smudger. Or she might be back at home.' Lily was equally worried, though determined not to panic. Eunice looked close to the end of her tether and one of them needed to remain calm and logical if they were to find Margie. 'I'll go and look for her. She can't have got very far.'

Eunice seemed grateful to be released from the burden of caring for her traumatised daughter-in-law. 'Would you, love? I'll stop behind then just in case you miss her and she comes back here.'

Within minutes Lily had set off towards Margie's road with a rising sun in her eyes. After a hundred yards she realised she wasn't optimistic about finding her friend at home. That place would be filled with sad reminders of beloved little Rosie. It was more likely that Margie would seek her husband's company.

Lily changed direction and started to trot towards the hospital, her pumping lungs heaving with the smoky residue of yesterday's blitz. She could see evidence of the devastation as well as smell and taste it. There were dumps of fallen concrete overflowing on the opposite pavement where homes had been hit. A wallpapered parlour sliced open to the world before the family realised what was happening. The wreckage petered out as she came abreast of shops that had suffered blast damage rather than bombs through the roof. A bundle of garments was on the step of one. Lily hurried on past then halted so sharply she almost tripped herself up.

She retraced her steps and darted across the road. Her hunch had paid off: the clothing was hiding a slight fair-haired woman lying curled up on her side.

'Been looking for you, Margie,' Lily said quietly.

'Was looking for you. Couldn't find you though.'

'Eunice told me. Sorry, was at the school ... helping out. I would've come home sooner if I'd known you was back from the hospital.' Lily paused. 'Where you off to?'

'Dunno ... forget. Just resting. Bad there, is it, at the school?' Margie was still on her side, cheek resting on her clasped hands and her knees drawn into her chest.

'It is, Margie. It is bad.' Lily sank down to sit next to Margie, careless of the glass and wood splinters littering the enclosed space. Margie also seemed little bothered about cutting herself.

'Eunice told you about Rosie.'

'Yes ...' Lily rested her scalp back against the wall and held out a hand into her friend's line of vision. Several minutes later Margie pushed herself up and clasped Lily's patiently waiting fingers.

Lily kissed those small stumps before letting them go so she could put both her arms around her friend. She eased Margie's head down onto her shoulder, staying silent when Margie's volcanic sobs transformed into screams of rage and vile rants directed first at the pitiless foe, then at her husband.

'Smudger'll be pleased she's gone,' Margie's voice rasped in pain. 'He never wanted her or me. He'll be relieved he don't have to say he's her dad no more.'

'Don't say that, Marge,' Lily spoke up. 'I saw with me own eyes yesterday how much he loved you both. He wanted more than anything to hold you both and talk to you. He wanted you to wake up so he could talk to you before he went off to hospital.'

'Why you sticking up for him?' Margie hissed, struggling to break free of Lily's embrace. 'You're just lying to make me feel better.'

'We've been through too much, love, to tell lies to one another now. But say it all, everything that's in there eating at you. Don't bottle it up and let it fester.'

Margie shoved her straggling fair hair off her wet face. 'Did he kiss Rosie before she died?' Her gleaming eyes bored into Lily's. 'Did you see him cuddling her as though he loved her? She would've known she was with her daddy. She was starting to say Daddy ...'

'He kissed and held her tight like he'd never let her go,' said Lily with simple honesty. 'Greg said Smudger would have died for his little girl; he begged to be left behind in the fire to make sure Rosie was taken to safety. In the end they all came out of the warehouse together. Thank God.'

That had also been a fact. After taking Smudger to hospital, Greg had sped to the school to join the rescue party, realising that's where he'd find Lily. The damage to Smudger's leg would have been less severe if he'd not battled for Rosie to be rescued first.

'She's with her real father now. D'you think Scully will be kind to her? He's so nasty, and Rosie's only little ...' Margie shuddered and sobbed.

'That little angel's in heaven and I don't reckon that monster is,' Lily soothed. 'She's watching over you both. Rosie wants her mum and dad to be happy.'

'Something I never told you about the business with Scully.' Margie's forehead had dropped to rest on her raised knees, muffling her words. 'The Belgian didn't kill him.' Margie had gone back in time to when Rosie was conceived. 'That day Claudette did herself in I went over to comfort Smudger. He loved her and I reckoned he'd be in a state, and he was. After we'd talked for a bit he said he'd see me home. It was a filthy night ...' Margie's voice trembled. 'We was walking down a back alley, trying to keep out of everybody's way and Scully just jumped out of the fog and started on us. He was going loony, saying it was Smudger's fault Claudette threw herself down the stairs. He was winding Smudger up, saying she never wanted him anyhow cos she was in love with a Belgian.' Margie jerked up her chin. 'Scully threatened to rape me again to get his own back. He pulled out a knife and a fight started.'

Lily halted the confession, putting a finger to her friend's lips. The Belgian fellow who had been blamed for Scully's murder had fled back to his homeland. The can of worms had been sealed for a long while and if the lid was prised off there could be dreadful consequences. 'That swine Scully had it coming to him. So let's leave it as a secret ... even between us, Margie, cos what I don't know, I can't tell even if a judge tries to make me.'

Margie grasped Lily's arm. 'You mustn't tell! Smudger told me never to say anything. Even to you.'

'You haven't told me all of it. Scully had fights with everybody. He pulled a knife on Greg and they fought.'

'Rosie's paid for our sins. Scully's got back at us in that way, by taking me daughter ...'

'Hush ...' Lily rocked Margie in her arms, remembering Evie Osborne's comment about children suffering for the mess adults made. Only days had passed since she and Evie had drunk tea in a café and been given the eye by sailors. It felt as though a decade lay between that carefree time and now. 'Hush ...' she crooned as Margie sobbed louder. 'Scully hasn't got that sort of power, dead or alive. He's nothing.'

Lily had long since worked out what had really happened, and why Smudger had suddenly enlisted in the army and gone overseas. She'd kept her suspicions to herself though she knew Greg had come to the same conclusion as she had.

Rory Scully hadn't been a murder victim; he'd been out

to *commit* murder. The blade had ended up in his chest but it could quite as easily have been Smudger's ... perhaps Margie's too; the vile beast wouldn't have wanted a witness to his crime, or for Margie to accuse him of rape.

Nobody had mourned Scully's death. It'd been a relief. Lily did feel guilty that she'd once hoped Margie might miscarry her rapist's baby. Rosie had been the loveliest child. She'd deserved a full life. Yet her months on this earth had overflowed with the greatest love and care. Margie had adored her daughter; and Rosie had been *all* hers. No trace of Scully in looks or temperament had damaged her or her mother. Awkward questions had been avoided after Smudger married Margie and claimed his enemy's offspring as his own. Rosie had been a fortunate child. Her parents, not so lucky.

Margie's weeping for her lost baby was different now: a lament that carried a long way. Concerned people on their way to work in the dawn sunlight hesitantly approached to offer sympathy, believing them to have been bombed out. They'd be all right, Lily told them to make them move on. And they would be. Heartache was par for the course for two workhouse girls. They'd come through it before and would again, and be stronger for it.

Lily stayed still and quiet. When first learning of her father's death she hadn't wanted to be smothered or talked at. She hadn't known what she'd wanted. Sometimes just a light touch from family was enough. And they were as close as sisters.

Finally Margie struggled to her feet and Lily followed on stiff legs.

'Want to go back to my place?' Lily brushed debris off her skirt, Margie's too when the girl seemed uncaring of the scraps clinging to her.

'Go to Eunice's. If Smudger gets out of hospital, he'll think I'm with his mum.'

Lily murmured an agreement, though, from what she knew of Smudger's injuries, he wouldn't be coming home for a long while.

'He'd be better off with a nurse for a wife now.' Margie sounded oddly matter-of-fact as they walked along, arm in arm. 'If he wants to go, I won't stop him. That's if she'll have him now. Doctor said Smudger's likely to lose that leg. He'll be a cripple, on sticks.'

'Won't come to that.' Lily tilted her head to Margie's in comfort.

'That's what he said. He might have to let them take it though, if it gets infected. I'd sooner have him alive than dead from stupid pride. Wouldn't make no difference to how I feel about him. Smudger'll always be the only man for me, with one or two legs. But it's up to him what he does.'

Chapter Eighteen

'Got anything to spare for the children?' Sally Ransome shook the collection bowl she was holding. She'd been going house to house, knocking on doors, but seeing a familiar face she'd given a shout and a wave and crossed the road. Sally liked Lily Larkin and knew she was a generous soul.

Lily immediately trotted to meet Sally.

'Whip-round for the families of those poor little kiddies,' Sally explained, jiggling the pudding basin again.

'Oh ... of course. I'm glad a collection's started.' Lily pulled her purse from her bag, dropping a handful of coins into the receptacle. 'You've done well.' It was barely eight in the morning yet the big basin was filled almost to the top with copper and silver.

'People are digging deep.' Sally glanced up at the tranquil sky. 'And I pray to God those wicked swine don't come back and send me out doing this again.' Sally's words were as heavy as her eyelids. Between consoling people and watching for another attack, few locals, apart from spent rescuers, had managed a wink of sleep. Everybody was dazed; housewives were still conscious, though, of making ends meet. And funerals cost money. Other Poplar streets would have women like Sally Ransome pounding the pavements, banging on neighbours' doors and rattling a tin for bereaved families.

Sally fished a gold pendant from beneath Lily's florins. 'Look at that. Widower put in his late wife's jewellery.' She blinked back tears. 'Somebody else told me it's going round that most of the dead are five- or six-year-olds. Couldn't bring meself to go down to the school. I'm too old to be of use and people staring just get in the way.' She noticed Lily's grazed hands. 'You went digging, didn't you?'

Lily nodded and bit her lower lip to stop it wobbling. She'd known that appalling fact from having watched small bodies being unearthed and wrapped in blankets. Six-year-olds ... children the same age as her little sister. Charlotte Finch might have attended that school had Mrs Jolley not done a flit from Poplar. Lily couldn't be sure her sister had survived diphtheria but at least she'd not perished beneath the rubble of her classroom.

'Not seen much of you lately,' said Sally, casting around for something cheerful to say. 'How's your friend doing? I was only thinking the other day that Margie Smith's little girl's coming up to her first birthday. Crikey, won't ever forget that breech delivery and don't suppose you will either. Or poor Margie. We all fought hard for that baby and what a beauty she is ...'

Lily's tortured expression wiped away Sally's smile. 'Margie's all right, ain't she?'

Lily frowned into the distance, trying to control her voice enough to answer. Sally wasn't to know this was an excruciating thing to have brought up. 'The warehouse was hit ... Margie had taken Rosie to work with her.'

'They got out in time though?' Sally gabbled.

'Margie did. Her husband was injured. But Rosie . . .' Lily shook her head, her eyes prickling.

Sally emitted a wail and wedged the pudding basin under an arm to hug Lily with the other. 'No! Can't believe it.' She was groaning, her quivering body rattling together the coins. 'Said to me husband last night . . . I hope none of the lost children was ones I'd brought into the world. Some of 'em must be, though, cos I've been in most of the houses round here. Didn't expect to hear bad news about that little sweetheart. She nearly didn't make it in the first place. Might've been kinder if . . .' Sally couldn't finish that sentence. 'Oh, tell Margie I'm so sorry, won't you?' She pulled out her hanky, scrubbing at her eyes. Wearily she retrieved the basin and held it in two hands, staring into it as though it were a crystal ball. 'I was for this war when it started. Believed what we was told, you see, about it all being over by that first Christmas. Said to me grandkids it was the right thing to do.' Sally grimaced, shaking her head. 'Could cut me tongue out.'

'No chance of an end in sight after this,' Lily sighed, but wishing for a magic clock to turn back or to wind forward to the day when it was over, wouldn't help. 'Best be off. Work to do.' Lily patted the woman's arm in farewell.

The wonder of seeing a newborn take its first breath had stayed with Lily. As had the memory of the serenity on Margie's face as she counted fingers and toes the moment her perfect baby was put into her arms. Nothing would persuade Lily that the battle for Rosie to be born had been in vain, but the midwife thought that, and that Margie had suffered unnecessarily by getting to know and love her daughter for those brief months.

Earlier, Lily had accompanied Margie back to Eunice's

and stayed for a while. Eunice had made tea and the three women had sat in a close huddle, sipping and murmuring about those other families who'd started this day with a loved one missing from the breakfast table. Knowing she wasn't the only mother grieving for a child provided Margie with scant solace but she'd settled down and slept.

With a promise to return later, Lily had set off towards what had once been her workplace and now she'd reached her goal.

The van was parked up at the kerb. Lily had known Greg would come to sift through the wreckage of his citadel. The warehouse had been the making of him, and his refuge. Lily could also claim those things from it. Within those planked walls had passed some historic moments in her life after the workhouse.

She had told her twin brother about their half-sister's existence in there, shocking him into shouting and swearing in disbelief. A sweeter memory was that of playing piggy in the middle with sprouting potatoes with her colleagues, and of the barrow race that had taken place around its sturdy perimeter. Back then she'd been a girl having fun with the lads, and Mr Wilding had been her disapproving guvnor, not her lover. The theft of money from the desk had been the worst time; suspicion and resentment had driven them all apart. Davy had eventually owned up to having been duped into stealing by his girlfriend. Plots and plans and jealousies had all been brewed up in Wilding's warehouse along with the tea.

The rough-beamed edifice that had once seemed enormous to her fifteen-year-old eyes was now reduced to stumps of charcoal and discoloured steel. The barn doors had gone but a metal frame remained and from habit rather than necessity she stepped through the portal, holding her skirt away from the muck that crunched underfoot.

A remnant of shelving hung in mid-air where some brass bolts had refused to part from the charred timber they'd been married to. The iron pedestal of her swivel chair was also quite recognisable and sprouted some coiled springs that yesterday had formed the hide-covered seat. The pine desk had collapsed but the keys its drawers had protected had fallen to the floor, where they lay beneath a blanket of ash. The ledgers and files were unidentifiable as such, now just soot that puffed up at her approach. She picked a path further through and saw the brass scoops that in their time had weighed tons of fruit and vegetables. The heavy pound weights had dropped and the brass ounces had scattered in all directions, their edges molten and misshapen. Metal eyelets winking in sunbeams clung on to canvas tarpaulins, reduced to a parchment-like ebony wedge. The market barrows had gone; axles and spokes remained, tilting at odd angles. Lily had been fond of the carts, to such a degree that she'd named some after the people they reminded her of.

One had been called Lily. Greg had loaned it to her to start her street round, back in the days before she'd known she loved him and had sold soap and soda door to door with her friends. Like a homing pigeon she'd come back to him. Then there was another, smaller handcart that Fanny had borrowed to move her stuff from Poplar to Islington to start her new life as a wife and mother. The barrow Davy had favoured as being easier to manoeuvre on his patch around Bethnal Green had been last in line. One handle remained, identifying it as he'd branded it with a penknife.

The market poles had been neatly stacked on racking but now littered the ground, half hidden beneath debris.

Lily took care to avoid stepping on them, knowing they'd roll and cause her to fall. She continued into the black bowels and emerged from the far end into a mockingly fine June day.

'Knew I'd find you here.' Greg was by the iron filing cabinet that had held the valuables. He'd dragged it outside and was cooling off the money tins in a bucket of water drawn from the standpipe. She'd not bothered looking for him at his flat, knowing he'd come straight here, as she had, to rummage for bits to assist Wilding's costermongers to rise from the ashes. They would make a success of things again, once the men were back from the war and life returned to something resembling normal. For now, salvaging stuff to sell, and dreaming up ideas for those better days to come, would do.

She hunkered down beside him, coiling her arms around his neck and hugging him in love and comfort. She had a lot to say but couldn't find the words in the aftermath of a catastrophe that made the loss of this cherished place and their livelihoods seem insignificant. Their future together had been cemented here. German bombs couldn't destroy that.

'See if we can open them up, shall we?' He'd welcomed her with a smile and lightness in his tone, drawing her to her feet with him and kissing her with gritty lips.

His appearance told the truth. He was hollowed out with fatigue and still wearing mucky clothes. His unshaven face and blond hair were covered in dirt, testament to the fact he'd not been home after coming away from the school. He'd toiled until after dawn broke when the fellow coordinating the rescue had called a halt. Not all the missing had been accounted for and it was likely some remains would never be identified. Greg was used to seeing carnage but not like this.

After he'd left Upper North Street he'd driven here then had slouched in the van, able to rest if not sleep. He'd assessed the smouldering mess for an hour through the windscreen, and had found the energy to punch the steering wheel before filling some buckets and throwing water around in an attempt to cool things down to make a start. He prised open one tin filled with copper and silver; the other would be more difficult to get into as the lid had melted into the base. Greg let that one drop with a clatter. 'Always meant to get one of those fireproof safes. The Milners salesman came in one day. I thought he was asking too much.' He grunted in ruefulness. 'That'll teach me ...'

'We can build a new warehouse.' She looked around. The size of the plot could be more easily appreciated now the structure wasn't blocking the view.

'Yeah ... we can. It's an acreage and I own the freehold.' He sounded proud. 'We'll put the bugger back up. Start next time I'm on leave. I'll clear the site while I'm home so it'll be ready to start building on straight away.'

'Go down to the banks of the Thames, shall we, and collect the wood we need ...' It was dark humour he appreciated.

He started to chuckle, quietly at first then, when Lily joined in, they clung together, roaring until they had wet eyes. The warehouse's rebirth was forgotten; the schoolchildren had their tears. As did baby Rosie and Smudger and Margie.

'You knew Rosie had died, didn't you?' Lily found her hanky and wiped her face, then his.

'Wasn't sure until I was at the hospital. I held her while

the nurses saw to Smudger. I guessed then but never said.' He closed his red-rimmed eyes and sighed. 'Have you seen Margie?'

'Yes ... she's ...' Lily paused and considered. 'I'm not sure how she is really. When I left her she was quiet, but I expect she'll be up and down for a long while yet. Things might be better for her once she knows what's happening to Smudger.' Lily sighed. 'The doctor told her his leg might need to be amputated.'

'I heard. So did Smudger. He'll do his damnedest to get stronger and keep that leg.'

'I pray he does ... but Margie'll love him no matter what.'

'I know. But they can't live on fresh air, and he'll never be passed fit to fight even with two legs.' Greg pulled his wallet from his pocket. 'He might not be able to work either for months. Not that I've got a job to offer him now.'

'I should go and see Joey. And Eric. Pay them their wages and ask them if they want references. I'll write those today, if necessary.'

'Eric won't want one; he's enlisting.' Greg emptied his wallet of banknotes, handing the money to Lily to put in her pocket. 'Give them bonuses ... whatever you think we can afford. I'm going to visit Smudger in hospital later. I'll promise to help in any way I can. The van can be sold, and there's still some money in the bank account. I've posted a note through the insurance company's door, asking the agent to call. There could be a claim for losses.' He cupped her face in his hands. 'We can still be married, Lily ... later in the week ... if you want ... before I go back.'

She smiled sadly, knowing he didn't really believe it. And neither did she, or want it. They deserved a happy wedding day with their best friends in attendance, and memories to celebrate. That couldn't possibly be now; their best man and matron of honour were planning their baby's funeral. June 1917 would be remembered by Poplar folk for its mourning, so grievous a time in East End history that descendants would commemorate the date in centuries to come. 'After I left last night, were any more children found?'

'Some ... they were taken to the mortuary.' He searched in his pockets for cigarettes and found a crushed, dirt-smudged pack, offering it to Lily. 'After I've finished here, I'll go back to the school and help clear up.'

She took a cigarette and they stood smoking quietly.

'You'll need money to live on once I'm gone. I'll send my army pay, but lance corporals don't get much.' Greg voiced what had been on his mind.

'I can get a job.' Lily had been thinking along the same lines, mentally investigating avenues of earning her keep. 'Munitions workers are needed. I'll try the factory in Islington. Fanny said they always want staff and the pay's good with overtime. Bet they'd start me straight away.' She frowned. 'Fanny's going to be dreadfully upset when she finds out what's happened to Rosie and Smudger. She's probably just had her baby. Perhaps it's a girl this time ...' Lily took a deep drag on her cigarette, wondering how poor Margie would cope with finding that out.

'Smudger and Margie will have other kids,' Greg said, reading her thoughts.

'Please God ...' Lily murmured, leaning her forehead against his shoulder and nestling into his embrace.

'Oh ... mmm ... I wasn't sure anybody was here. Heavens ... you've taken a bad hit.' A smartly suited fellow had walked out from behind the van that was parked block-ing the view of the open gates.

'That was quick. Didn't expect the insurance people to come and talk to me today.' Greg had spoken to Lily, but the newcomer had heard the comment.

'I'm not insurance, sir. And I'm not here to see you.' He extended a hand. 'I'm a solicitor. Mr Beane, from Beane and Groves. I imagine you are Mr Wilding.' The two men shook hands. 'I've come to speak to Miss Larkin.' He turned to Lily. 'Are you Miss Larkin?'

'I am,' Lily said, and shook the pudgy fingers held out to her.

'If I'd known you were in such a pickle I would have called you into my office to deal with this. But Hertford is a trip for you, and I was coming to London on other affairs.' He glanced about at the charred remains. 'What a dreadful shame this has happened.' He sorrowfully shook his head.

Lily was confounded as to what a solicitor might want with her. Then her mind darted back a couple of hours, to Margie's confession, and her own comment that she'd not be able to bear witness to a judge . . .

'What's your business, Mr Beane?' Greg asked mildly. He had sensed Lily's hand tighten on his.

'Mmm, it's confidential.'

'You can talk to me in front of my fiancé,' Lily blurted. 'I'd prefer that.'

'Ah ... good. And very sensible; it's always best for a young lady to have a father or husband in attendance when money matters crop up.'

Lily barely heard his chauvinism, so relieved was she to know she wasn't about to receive a summons. 'Can't offer you a chair or a cup of tea. Sorry.' She'd seen him glance about as though seeking somewhere to perch.

'Quite. Well, no more ado. I can see you've plenty to get

on with. And I'm pleased to bring you good news. Mrs Priest advised me your address was Wilding's business premises, Miss Larkin. So here I am.'

Lily relaxed, and a wondrous smile curved her mouth. 'Mrs Priest? Has she sent me some news?'

The fellow beamed, obviously glad to have cheered her up.

Lily's hopes soared. The woman must have news of Charlotte but had been too frail to deliver it personally. 'How is Vera? I hope she is well.'

Mr Beane's smile faded. 'Ah ... I see you didn't know that she had passed away. About a month ago. She was frail but attained her three score years and ten.' Lily's little cry of dismay prompted him to hastily produce a letter from his briefcase. 'There. Mrs Priest wanted you to have that.' He handed Lily a business card as well. 'Now if you require my services for anything else or advice on investing the money ... that's where you'll find me. And with that I'll bid you both a good day.' He glanced about at the wreckage, cleared his throat. 'And the best of luck, too, for the future.' With a bow he turned and was soon marching along the street.

Lily held the envelope. It was a bittersweet moment. Though she knew Vera Priest had given up her search for Charlotte, it was another precious link to her sister broken. Vera had loved Charlotte enough to want to find her and care for her herself, even though she was ready for retirement.

'Aren't you going to open it?' Greg asked gently.

Lily nodded and unpicked the flap to take out the contents. There was a cheque for ten guineas and a letter. She frowned while reading it.

'Vera wanted me to have a bequest to help in the search

for Charlotte.' Lily tilted her head back with a muted groan. There was no news of Charlotte's possible whereabouts, just Vera's heartfelt best wishes for Lily's eventual success. 'Vera Priest was a lovely lady,' she said simply. 'I was going to visit her as soon as I found a spare minute to travel to Hertford. I knew she had retired as a domestic ... she wrote and told me. I shouldn't have waited so long. I should have made the time.'

'She didn't forget you, Lily, any more than you forgot her.'

Lily looked at the cheque. 'This'll help us rebuild the business.'

'You should save it for Charlotte.'

'You really believe, don't you, that she is out there and I will find her.'

'Don't you?'

Lily nodded, tears blurring her eyes. 'Vera told me that we're all in the lap of the gods but Charlotte would battle through her bad luck and be waiting for me.' She put the cheque and the letter back into the envelope. 'But she doesn't need money. She needs a family. She needs me.'

Chapter Nineteen

'I told you, me hands are full with me own kids and I've got no husband around to help out.'

'Well, you ain't alone there,' June retorted. 'No woman your age has got her husband about since conscription. But at least you've *got* a husband, so be thankful.'

Ginny rolled her eyes. Her mother was still bitter that Norman Drake had popped his clogs before marrying her. Considering how unhappy June had been during her first marriage, it was amazing to Ginny that she'd wanted to go there again. 'There's not an inch of spare space in my place, Mum. We're packed in like sardines as it is.'

'All I've done for you over the years, my gel. And you can't even do this one thing fer me so I can keep me promise to Norman.' June gave her daughter a disappointed look. 'Well, I'll make it five bob a week then, but that's it, so don't waste time trying to hang out for more.'

'It's not about money.' Ginny gestured in exasperation. 'I've already got four kids driving me bonkers, and don't want no more.'

'Charlotte's a good kid, she won't misbehave. The extra

cash for fostering her means you'll be able to pack up work. Everything won't be such a mad rush for you—'

'Pack up work?' Ginny barked in disbelief. 'Ain't doing that! I like me job and me work pals. Best of all, I like me wages,' she announced flatly. 'So that's that.'

June had another go at persuasion, but her daughter cut her off.

'After the school bombing at Poplar I don't want a foster kid. Got enough worry with me own. And I don't want to be taking on another mouth to feed. It's a big responsibility.'

'Don't I know it,' muttered June. 'Well, please yerself. I'm not stopping around here though. I'm off to Clacton at the end of the month. I promised meself that was where I'd retire and I will do it if it kills me.' June was also conscious that the East End was a target. Many a Londoner was talking of upping sticks to somewhere safer since the air raid had caused such devastation.

'What'll you do with Charlotte then? Take her with you?' Ginny ventured.

'No fear!' snorted June. 'I'm too long in the tooth for rearing kids. Somebody'll bite at the fostering fee.'

'I'd better get off now,' Ginny said quickly before her mother started on her again to be that somebody. 'The kids need picking up from school.'

Once her daughter had gone June opened the back door and watched Charlotte sitting in the sun, quiet and content, playing with next door's cat. The little girl liked to be outside in the air, feeling the warmth on her. June reckoned that was because she'd spent so long cooped up in the lodge. The child had seemed to accept that her granddad had gone and wasn't coming back, though June had heard her talking to him, as though she believed he could still hear her.

She *was* a good kid, and it wasn't that June disliked her; although, being honest, she had felt jealous of the time and attention Norman had given her. But that was all in the past now and June wasn't one for bearing grudges. She just wasn't good with children and she needed to be to have the girl permanently around. The money Norman had left for Charlotte's care couldn't compensate for the carefree retirement that would be lost to conscientiously rearing a child. June had her own standards and wouldn't do half a job or pretend to have feelings that didn't exist. So she and Charlotte would be parting company soon. June had friends in Clacton and wanted to spend a jolly time with them until it was her turn to push up daisies.

Norman's funeral had taken place months ago. True to her word, June had taken Charlotte home to live with her temporarily and had posted the letter to Mrs Yates. She'd waited for a reply from the foster mother but none had arrived. So she'd sent another ... and waited and waited in vain for a response. June thought the woman rude not to reply, even if it was to say she'd had a change of heart. At first June hadn't been too bothered about the delay in settling Charlotte as twelve guineas could be saved if Mrs Yates wasn't needed. She'd been confident that Ginny could be tempted to let Charlotte grow up amongst her brood. The cash could have stayed within the family and Norman would have been pleased to think the little girl had been kept close. She'd told Ginny that the foster mother must have changed her mind about taking Charlotte on. But no offer to step up and fill the gap had been forthcoming.

Not only had Norman misread this Mrs Yates's character,

June had misread her own daughter. Ginny had changed since starting work in a munitions factory. Having her own wages and independence suited her. She'd been taking on more shifts and gained a promotion to charge-hand. The weekly fostering fee of five bob hadn't been enough of an inducement. Paying more was impossible; Norman had only left twelve guineas to see Charlotte through to an age where she could earn her own keep.

When clearing out his possessions from the lodge June had been surprised to find he had written a will. He'd left his few household items to her, together with a small amount of cash. The lion's share of his savings had been put into another envelope marked, 'For Charlotte's foster mother'.

June reckoned there was nothing for it but to visit the woman in Highgate and see if persuasion might work. Letting her see what a pretty little thing Charlotte was might do the trick. June didn't have the time or patience to go through the lengthy process of advertising in the *Gazette*. She wanted to leave London in weeks, not spend more months exchanging correspondence that might run into more dead ends. If no joy with Mrs Yates, an orphanage was a last resort. The girls' Barnardo's home in Essex was reputed to be better than most. First June would have one last go at carrying out Norman's wishes: she'd go to Highgate and knock on Mrs Yates's door.

'Hello, stranger.' Sally Ransome had been coming out of the baker's and turned around to come face to face with somebody she'd not seen in a while.

June gave the chubby blonde a smile, though she wasn't really in the mood for a chat. 'Hello, yourself. Still working with the old man then?' She jerked a nod to the news vendor, lounging behind his counter. He was using a lull in business to prise the lid off a tobacco tin.

'I keep an eye on the old sod, in between doing a hundred and one other things.' Sally rolled her eyes. 'Always thinking about his belly, he is. Look at him: thin as a rake. I only need to sniff an iced bun and me skirt buttons pop.' She swung the paper bag she was carrying. 'Hard to resist though when we're so close and the smell of baking is in the air.' Sally tutted. 'Hark at me rabbiting on. You look browned off, June. Can guess why that is.' She gave the older woman's shoulder a pat. 'Very sorry to hear Norman had passed away, I was.'

June smiled. 'Yeah ... he was a good man. But ...' She expelled a sigh. 'Life kicks you in the teeth when you least expect it, eh, love?' Despite all their ups and downs, June had never lost hope that they would end up retiring to Clacton together.

'I heard you'd got a granddaughter living with you. Your Ginny struggling, is she?' Sally reached out to the quiet child holding June's hand and chucked her under the chin. 'She's a smashing-looking gel. Heartbreaker she'll be in a few years.'

June ruffled Charlotte's fair hair. 'She's not me granddaughter, she's just staying with me for a while.'

'Oh ... must've got it wrong. I heard you'd taken in family.'

'Well, you heard wrong.' June didn't like people discussing her business behind her back.

'No offence meant ...' Sally raised an eyebrow at June's sharp tone. 'Just with all the men off fighting, I know plenty of women who are having a tough time of it.'

'Didn't mean to jump down yer throat, Sal. Bit on edge today.' Sally Ransome had been trusted in the past to keep

252

June's secrets. June had only one child: Ginny. But she had been pregnant several times. With a workshy bully for a husband, she'd made sure no more children arrived. Sally's mother had been the handywoman when June had her first abortion at twenty-two. She had been forty-three when she had her last, performed by Sally, who'd taken over the trade on her mother's death.

June wasn't browned off because of thoughts of Norman; she'd been on her way back home from Highgate with depressing news. Mrs Yates was no longer where June had thought she'd find her, and the new occupier of that house didn't have her forwarding address. June was conscious that bumping into Sally could be a blessing.

'I'm looking after Charlotte because her foster mother can't keep her. Norman knew the family and liked this little one.' June clucked her tongue. 'He was a sentimental old stick, and wanted to see her settled again with a new mum. Trouble is, he got sick before he could see that through. I promised to make the arrangements, if he couldn't.'

'I bet you like having her around. She must be good company for you.' Sally tickled the child's cheek again.

'Oh, I can't keep her.' June hastily made her position clear. 'I'm retiring; off to live with friends in Clacton before I fall off me perch as well.' She'd made Sally chuckle. 'Already bought me bucket 'n' spade and I'll be off in a few weeks, making the most of the summer down there.'

'Can't say I blame you, upping sticks. After that dreadful business in Poplar, who wants to stick around London?' Sally looked up at the sky. 'Was about this time o' day they turned up; me 'n' the old man are getting cricked necks, watching for German planes all the while.' She glanced at Charlotte. 'Don't do to frighten the kids so I'll mind me tongue.'

June gave a distracted nod of agreement, swiftly bringing the conversation back to the matter preying on her
mind. 'Anyway, Charlotte's a good kid – no bother, are
you, dear?' She playfully swung the child's hand and
received a shy smile. For all her dumb obedience, Charlotte
was taking it all in; she was a bright kid and June didn't
feel comfortable discussing this further while she was
listening. 'See those cakes in the window, Charlie?' June
pointed and handed over a few coppers. 'There. Go and
choose a nice treat for being a good girl. I'll be right here,
where you can see me.' The moment Charlotte had entered
the shop, June burst out, 'I thought she was settled with
a permanent foster mother, Sal. Would you believe it, the
woman's moved house without having the courtesy to let
me know the deal's off. I need to quickly find somebody
else to take her.' She paused. 'Know of any foster mothers,
do you?' She used her trump card when Sal looked about
to say that regretfully she didn't. 'Norman left something
in his will for her care. It's enough to pay Charlotte's keep
until she's quit school. You can see for yourself, she's not
a bother.'

'Crikey! That was good of him, being as she's not his
family,' exclaimed Sally.

'Like I said: sentimental old fool, he was. Treated
Charlotte like a grandkid. He never saw much of the real
ones, you see, being as his daughter lived so far away and
reckoned she'd gone up in the world.'

'Shame for all concerned.' Sally gazed at Charlotte inside
the shop waiting patiently to be served. 'Can't really help
with a foster mother off the top of me head, but I'll ask
around, see if anybody bites.' She didn't sound too hopeful
of success. 'Trouble is, there's plenty of work around lately;

women want to earn a few bob and get out of the house more, don't they?'

June nodded glumly. 'Appreciate your help, anyway.'

'Charlotte's an orphan then?' Sally gesticulated at her husband to pipe down. He was beckoning her, looking hot and bothered in the July sun, now a queue of customers had formed.

'Her father was killed early on in the war and her mother's disappeared off the scene. If I knew where Betsy Finch was, I'd take her daughter back to her.'

'Betsy Finch?' Sally echoed, frowning. 'I know somebody by that name.'

Having recovered from her surprise, June gave a delighted smile. 'Is she local?'

'Last I heard, she was still in the East End, but ...' Sally chewed her lip.

'What?' June prompted.

'Well, the Betsy Finch I knew wasn't a motherly sort. She made sure of it ... came to see me a few years back, if you get my drift.'

June did. She was that sort, too. But she had one daughter and perhaps this Betsy Finch did too and the child's name was Charlotte. June was determined to follow this lead up and find out.

'Last I heard, Betsy had got in with bad company.' Sally was being diplomatic. She knew the girl was living with her pimp of a boyfriend.

'Norman really wanted Charlotte to return to her real mother. The kid spoke fondly of her mum and another woman. Vera! That was her name. Charlotte's father was a major somebody or other. Norman told me that much about it all.'

Sally clapped the palm of a hand against her open mouth for a second. 'Blimey! Betsy *was* in clover at one time and had a housekeeper called Mrs Priest. I think she *was* a Vera and Betsy's sugar daddy *was* in the army. She was proud of having hooked him ... then it all went wrong for her. There was a rumour she'd had his child, but I reckoned it was just talk. Never saw her out with a pram. Betsy kept to herself back then though ... quite hoity-toity, she was.'

A wondrous smile lit June's face. 'Right ... that's enough to be going on with. Where is this Betsy? I'm paying her a visit.' A polite fellow in the baker's queue had opened the shop door to let Charlotte out.

'You could try the house next door to the ironmongers on East India Dock Road. She was living there with her bloke ...' Sally clammed up; June had put a finger to her lips to warn her the child was approaching.

'What've you got there then?' June bent to look in the paper bag in Charlotte's hand. 'Cor ... that looks nice. Marzipan.' She glanced up at Sally. 'Thanks ...' she said quietly. 'Stand you a drink if this comes right.'

'Good luck, June.' Sally sounded solemn and gave the child a pitying look over a shoulder as she headed off.

June was excited at this turn of events. Rather than carrying on home she headed to a low brick wall fronting an office building.

'There, have a little rest and enjoy your food,' she said, settling the child on the parapet then standing beside her to give her some shade from the hot sun.

The break was more for her own benefit than Charlotte's. June needed a moment to mull things over. There was no time like the present to sort this out, she inwardly argued. She should go and find the Finch woman. Charlotte could be reunited with her mother today. Norman would've been delighted about that, and what a lovely ending it would be for the little girl. Using a hanky, she wiped crumbs from Charlotte's mouth and sticky fingers then helped her down. Hand in hand they set off for the bus stop.

A moment later, June's contented smile had drooped. She cursed beneath her breath, having caught sight of a couple heading towards her. They were acquaintances but the master and mistress of Whitechapel workhouse deigned only occasionally to acknowledge her. Bertha Stone hadn't shown up to pay her last respects at Norman's funeral, but the master had been there and had said a few words about his much-missed, conscientious employee. The couple were staring at her as though they might be preparing to stop and speak.

'Hello, and how are you, Mrs Gladwell?' asked Bertha.

'Very well, thank you, and hope you are too.' June rattled off with a dip of her head, edging past. She wanted to catch that bus to the East India Dock Road.

'I expect this little one must be your granddaughter. And what's your name and age?' Bertha inclined towards the child being dragged behind June.

'She's called Charlotte ... she's six.' The older woman's friendliness seemed odd and June wanted to escape. 'Well, nice to see you, but I'm in a bit of a rush.' She was conscious that if the lodge were mentioned, the girl might say something she shouldn't about her lengthy stay there with her 'granddad'.

June hurried up the road with the child trotting to keep up. Bertha watched them, resisting her husband's tugs on her arm. 'Our granddaughter would be about that age. She might be as pretty as that girl with her fair hair and blue eyes ...'

'For goodness' sake, Bertha,' he cut across her. 'Give the matter a rest.'

'I will not. Our only child is dead and we don't even have Benjamin's daughter as a comfort,' she cried, oblivious to the fact she'd just spoken to her.

'And whose fault is that?' he hissed. 'You told Harriet Fox to dispose of the brat.' William used more force to pull her with him.

'That was to protect our son's reputation. He made a slip-up, but he deserved better than to be trapped by that Larkin woman. She was older, and already had children. Benjamin was only a boy at the time.'

'He was twenty-four and old enough to shoulder his responsibility. He would have done so . . . if you would have allowed him to by telling him about it.'

Bertha gave her husband's arm a vicious pinch so he'd let go of her. '*I* didn't tell Benjamin he had a bastard for his own good. You kept quiet because you didn't want the Board of Guardians investigating your cooked books.'

The veins on William's cheeks became engorged and ruddy. 'As I recall, madam,' he enunciated through his teeth, 'you didn't complain at the time about receiving the benefit of those irregularities.'

Bertha retreated into sullenness, unable to deny it. 'It's time to find our granddaughter and bring her to live with us.'

'Don't be so foolish!' he snarled. 'She was premature and sickly. I doubt she survived to her first birthday.'

'We don't know that,' said Bertha stubbornly.

William was out of patience with his wife. Since learning of their son's death at the Somme she had become worry-ingly depressed. Before then she'd been a robust character.

Her melancholy and fixation on their son's bastard was exasperating, especially as it had been Bertha's idea to keep Benjamin ignorant of the fact he'd impregnated a female inmate. He hadn't discovered he was a father until years after the event, when Harriet Fox taunted him over it while attacking him with a knife. Benjamin had defended himself against the girlfriend he'd spurned. The drunken harpy had caused her own fatal accident, but the matter had been hushed up to protect Benjamin's future and to prevent investigation into the Stone family's management of the Whitechapel workhouse.

The whole episode had been long buried, if not forgotten. William didn't want to resurrect something so sensitive. But his wife's increasingly bizarre behaviour was putting everything at risk, even the good name of the dead son she still adored.

William had persuaded Bertha to visit a physician for a tonic to boost her mood, but it hadn't helped. She needed something stronger than medicine. He had found toy rattles and baby dresses that she'd bought recently, hidden in boxes in the wardrobe. Bertha had obviously forgotten that almost seven years had passed since their grandchild had been an infant in need of such things. He didn't dare suggest another doctor's appointment in case her demented state became apparent and the fellow recommended treatment in an asylum.

'Harriet Fox knows our granddaughter's whereabouts.' Bertha fiddled with her handbag, avoiding her husband's outstretched hand. 'I'll demand she give it to us.'

'Miss Fox is dead, Bertha, as you know.' The effort of not shouting at her was forcing his speech to emerge in a slow, laboured way. 'We won't find the child because Harriet never revealed where she took her ... and now she's dead and buried.'

'Our granddaughter is alive. I know she is,' Bertha wailed.

'*Harriet* is dead.' He removed his hat, ran a handkerchief over his perspiring brow. It had been his idea to come out for a walk in the sunshine, believing a constitutional in the fresh air would buck his wife up. It seemed to have been working, too, until they bumped into the dratted Gladwell woman and the blonde child. 'Listen to me, Bertha. Shut up about this or you'll stir up trouble and smear Benjamin's memory. Then you'll regret it, won't you? A scandal. Your precious son disgraced. Is that what you want for our war hero?'

She grasped the truth in it and it shook her, as did the fact they'd drawn an audience. People had started to dawdle past just to gawp at the spectacle of a smartly dressed elderly couple snapping and snarling at one another.

'Well ... you've made a laughing stock of us both, haven't you, Bertha?' he hissed, thrusting his nose upwards and an elbow her way.

She didn't reply but took his arm and they proceeded in silence back the way they'd come.

Chapter Twenty

The moment the bus pulled in at the stop June alighted from it then turned and lifted Charlotte down from the platform. They had sailed past the ironmongers shop while still on the vehicle. Taking the girl's hand, June set off briskly back towards it. She was anxious to get this business over with, but Charlotte was flagging after having been out for so long. The heat of the summer sun had put a rosy glow in her cheeks and she wriggled her fingers free of captivity to drag her feet. June stopped and inclined towards Charlotte to warn her of what might happen next. She wasn't a child prone to showing her emotions. In fact, June thought her composed for one so young. But this was a big moment for her after being separated from her real family for a long time.

'Now, you remember your mum, Betsy, don't you?' Having received a nod, June continued, 'I think she might be in that house just there. You'd like to see her again, wouldn't you, Charlie?' She took the child's hands to give them a squeeze. 'You'd like to live with her again, I bet.'

'That's not my mother's house.' Charlotte remembered where she'd lived with Betsy and Vera. The house had been bigger and there had been a high hedge at the front. This was more like the dirty street that she'd lived in with Mrs Jolley. Charlotte pulled her hands free and backed away.

'Yes, I know it's not the same house.' June hurried after her. 'That's because your mum moved from that place to here, you see.' She drew Charlotte to her side, preventing her running off.

'Is Vera inside there as well?' Charlotte's eyes had widened and she brightened up.

'I'm not sure, Charlie. Won't find out, will we, until we knock on the door and see what's what.' June sounded matter-of-fact.

That seemed reasonable to Charlotte, so she trotted up the path and banged on splintery wood with her small fist.

'Well ... end of discussion.' June sounded rueful but needed no further proof that the little girl wanted to be with her mother and Vera. She added her weight to Charlotte's, giving two sharp raps with the knocker.

The terraced house where June lived was rundown, but it wasn't a mess because she had certain standards. She polished the step and kept her few rooms clean and tidy, even if there was paint and plaster missing from the walls, and the neighbours lived like pigs. Whoever lived here didn't give a monkey's about cleanliness.

Behind a cracked window pane, a scrap of greying net curtain obscured the view of the front room. Looking upwards, she could see the bedroom sash was half open. She stepped back a few paces in case somebody had heard her knock and was peering down. There was no sign of life and the house was silent. June's elation began to wilt. She'd not considered this to be a fool's errand, even though Sally had given no guarantees that Betsy Finch would be found on East India

Dock Road. June looked speculatively at the ironmongers. No doubt they'd know who their neighbours were. Though she wanted to find Betsy Finch, she was praying Charlotte's mother wasn't living in this pigsty. If she'd moved, the shop-keeper might have her forwarding address . . .

'What you after then?'

Out of the blue had come a raucous shout to make June start. She looked up to see a woman's face draped in strag-gling brunette hair. She appeared to be dressed only in her underclothes and her indolent fingers drooped over the sill, holding a smouldering cigarette. Her other hand clasped a tumbler containing something treacle-dark. Rum, guessed June, who didn't mind a nip of Lamb's herself. The glass was emptied in a gulp, then the younger woman leaned further out of the open window, displaying an ample cleav-age framed by lace.

'You Betsy Finch?' June sounded defensive, not only from being startled but from realising that, if this was indeed Charlotte's mother, she didn't look fit to care for a dog. It was late afternoon, yet the slut was smoking and drinking in her petticoat. June knew she shouldn't leave Charlotte with somebody like that but should take her straight home. In fact, she regretted ever having come here.

June beckoned the child perching on the step to rest her legs. 'This isn't the right house, Charlotte.' The sound of the bolts being drawn prompted her to quickly lift the girl onto her feet.

A dark-haired fellow in a vest tucked into belted trousers propped an elbow on the half-open door, displaying a hor-ribly hairy armpit. 'Who wants Betsy Finch?'

'Who are you?' June countered, instinctively pulling Charlotte close to her side.

'I asked first, love.'

He'd smirked, but June wasn't fooled by him. Or by what was going on in this house. Betsy Finch was a trollop and this was either a client or a pimp.

'Where's Vera?' Charlotte suddenly piped up. 'Is she in there?' The child wasn't talking to him, but to the face that had appeared over his muscly shoulder.

'Oh, my good Gawd,' Betsy breathed out. 'It's Charlotte.' When peering out of the upstairs window, she'd not spotted the child sheltering beneath the porch.

He pivoted about to frown at her. 'What? Who is it?'

Betsy put a hand on his shoulder and garbled in his ear in a voice too low for June to catch more than sibilant hisses. But she could tell Betsy wasn't pleased by the turn of events. He, on the other hand, appeared more thoughtful than annoyed. His black-bristled chin had dropped towards his thick neck and his lashes were over his eyes.

'Is Vera here?' Charlotte piped up again.

'No, she bleedin' ain't,' retorted Betsy. 'And neither should you be.' She turned a hostile look on June. 'Who told you where I was, whoever you are? And why've you brought the kid here? If you think I'm taking her back . . .'

'No need to be hasty on it, Betsy, love,' the man cut across her, jerking up his smiling face. 'How rude of me, should've asked you in, Mrs . . .'

'Gladwell,' June supplied in a snap. 'And you are?'

'I'm Mr Vincent. Michael, me friends call me.'

'Well, Mr Vincent,' said June with a sniff, 'I won't waste any more of your time or mine. Come on, Charlotte . . .'

'Hold on a minute.' He came from behind the door like a striking snake. 'I think we need to have a talk, Mrs Gladwell. Overdoo reunion of mum 'n' daughter ain't something to discuss on the step, is it now?' He corralled her towards the open doorway, elbowing Betsy out of the way.

'No point coming in, cos there's nothing *to* discuss.' June had got a glimpse and a whiff of the decay within the house and had dodged free of his stocky body. She wasn't letting him block her escape and force her and Charlotte inside. 'Mrs Finch doesn't want her daughter, so she's off home with me.' June attempted to lead Charlotte away, but he'd imprisoned the child's other hand in some stubby fingers and started patting the back of it.

'You've given Betsy a shock, turning up without warning. She didn't mean to be offhand. 'Course she wants her kid. She talks about missing Charlotte all the time.' He gave a sulky Betsy a glare from beneath a pair of dark, hooded eyelids. 'Make yerself presentable for visitors. I'll make a pot of tea.' He turned back to June. 'Apologies for how we look. So hot today, ain't it? We was upstairs changing into something cooler.'

'Yeah ... that's what I thought.' June's sarcasm was accompanied by a contemptuous stare, flitting from one to the other of them.

'You come here to see Mummy and old Vera, is that it, nipper?' he cooed to Charlotte. 'In yer come then and we'll have a nice time.' He gave June a sly smile as the child nodded and let go of her hand to allow him to usher her over the threshold.

June felt a curdling in her guts. A protective instinct had prompted her to follow the little girl, but he'd barged her back onto the step, pulling the door to behind him.

'So, Mrs Gladwell, how did you get your hands on Betsy's daughter?'

'Didn't get me *hands* on her,' June snorted, not liking his tone. 'I put meself out to take care of her when nobody else would. Her foster mother's off the scene now. Charlotte's a good kid. Deserves to be well looked after. I thought her mother was the best person for that, so I brought her here. More fool me.'

'How d'you know where to come after Betsy?'

June didn't like being interrogated and obstinately crossed her arms. 'That's my business.'

He smiled his wily smile, displaying a hint of gold at the back of his mouth. 'Not to worry. Little Charlotte's back where she belongs now. Thanks for looking after her, but I'll take it from here.'

'You let me say goodbye to her.' June tried to push past, into the dank hallway, but he stopped her.

'You're not seeing her again. You'll just upset her with long goodbyes. She's with her mum . . . her *real* mum . . . and I'll make sure everything's fine 'n' dandy.'

'She needs her things: clothes 'n' toys and so on.' June sounded alarmed.

'Well, you tell me where to come, and I'll fetch 'em. But don't go coming back here.'

He was still smiling at her, but June could read a violent man like a book. She'd been married to one for nigh on forty years.

'Charlotte!' June yelled. 'Come here, love! Let's go home. It's teatime. We'll stop at the baker's and get some more cakes for later.' June was desperate to get past Vincent without touching him, but his beefy body left little room for manoeuvre. She shot a hand over his shoulder to shove against the door and was immediately and lazily pushed away by his knuckles on her solar plexus. June tottered on her heels then went down, arms flailing.

'You silly old dodderer. You want to be more careful,' he said, pretending she'd tripped herself up. He rolled his eyes at a passer-by who'd noticed June fall. 'Don't mind her ...' Vincent called. 'She's getting on a bit, eh, Ma?' He grabbed June's arm and yanked her to her feet. Inclining his head close to her ear he purred, 'Get going while you still can. I don't like interfering old cows, perhaps I didn't make that plain before.'

June was breathing hard from shock and pain. She'd landed heavily on her backside and though he'd not punched her she could feel where his knuckles had been rammed against her ribs. 'Big man, aren't you, pushing women around,' she panted out. 'Brave young feller like you should be in uniform, fighting the Hun. Why ain't you?'

'Only wish I could. But the doc says me chest ain't up to it.' He rubbed his breast bone. 'Asthma ... plays me up something chronic.' He flexed his pectorals beneath his thin vest and gave June a taunting wink.

'Your chest, eh? I reckon it's your yeller belly you need looked at.' June shook his hand off her arm in disgust. She gave him a filthy look, then turned and walked away. At the end of the street she halted to stare back at the house, her mind agitated. Despite knowing he'd go for her again, she felt tempted to return and cause a scene. But what right did she have to do that? Betsy Finch was Charlotte's mother and Norman had wanted more than anything that they be reunited. Charlotte had fond memories of her early years and hadn't seemed upset by her mother's unkindness, or by seeing the woman drunk and half dressed. It was as though it were nothing new for her.

June set her shoulders and trudged on. With any luck Michael Vincent might be a similar sort of bully to June's late husband: Bill Gladwell had regularly set about his wife but had never laid a finger on his only child. The further away from the house June got, the more she reminded herself that she'd fulfilled her promise to Norman Drake and should be satisfied with that. In the end, Charlotte Finch wasn't her family. She wasn't really any of her business. And June had her own future to think about. The heaviness in her heart made her oblivious to the ache in her hip where it had hit the ground. She was past it, she realised as she limped on towards the bus stop to catch her ride home. Had she been ten years younger, she'd have gladly done battle for Charlotte. But she knew if she tried taking on a vicious character like Vincent at her age she couldn't win. She might just make things worse for Charlotte and get herself killed in the process.

Inside the house, the atmosphere between the adults was tense but Charlotte had settled onto a battered armchair and was looking expectantly at her mother. 'Is Vera upstairs?'

Betsy didn't answer. She glared at her boyfriend. 'Very clever of you to get me landed with her like that. How am I supposed to work now?'

'Mind yer tongue in front of her.' Michael had made some tea and poured the girl a cup from the pot. 'Bet you'd like a biscuit, wouldn't you, nipper?' He held the cup out to her.

Charlotte nodded, taking the drink in two hands.

'Well, she's out of luck, cos there ain't none,' Betsy snapped.

'So get off your backside and get dressed, then go to the shop,' he said. 'Bourbons. I like those,' he called after her as she left the parlour, grumbling.

'Can we go and see Vera soon?' Charlotte asked, giving him a shy smile.

'Reckon so, nipper ...' He sat down on the sofa, arms

stretched out either side of him along the chintz cushions, and stout legs akimbo. He contemplated the pretty little girl from beneath his lashes. Years ago, Betsy had told him all about how she'd bought an orphan off a baby peddler to scam a rich gent into believing he'd had a daughter with her. Major Beresford ... the name popped into Michael's head. After the major dumped Betsy, he'd carried on keeping her and their 'daughter' right up until he died in the war. Michael had thought him a prize punter and regretted there weren't more like him.

When the money dried up, Betsy had come back looking for her first boyfriend. Michael and Betsy went back a long way. He'd not begrudged her feathering her nest at the major's expense; Michael knew she'd be back, and he always played the long game.

As he was now. He studied a pair of deep blue eyes and hair that was wheaten yellow. Betsy's 'daughter' would develop into a beauty; he liked to think he was a bit of a connoisseur when it came to the fairer sex. It was his job after all to latch on to profitable faces and figures. And he reckoned in seven or eight years he'd have a goldmine on his hands in the sweet shape of Charlotte Finch.

As the kid had been brought up in a household of women, it'd be a good idea to get her used to being around men. And it was never too soon to start; the years would fly by and she'd be fourteen in a trice. He shifted position, making space and patted the seat. 'Come and sit here beside me then, Charlotte, so we can get to know one another.' He thumped the seat again when she hesitated. 'Come on then ... no need to be shy. Come and say a proper hello to your uncle Mikey.'

*

'My little sister's seven soon.'

Greg turned to Lily, seated next to him in the van. 'Not a baby any more, is she?'

'No . . . she's a girl growing up fast. Where is she though?' she sighed, planting her elbows on the steering wheel.

'Not long to wait and I reckon that riddle will be solved, love.' Greg drew an affectionate finger down her cheek.

She turned to him, looking wistful. 'I hope with all my heart you're right.'

His arm around her shoulders, he urged her closer. 'I am right. The two of you are destined to meet, same as we're destined to grow old together. Just got to be patient for a little while longer and everything'll come good.' He'd seen the sparkle of tears in her eyes and changed the subject. 'Now don't forget that the fellow is coming on Sunday to pick up the van. He'll give you a cheque for it.'

'Hadn't forgotten. I'll miss the old girl . . .' She leaned her head against his, patting the cracked leather seat by her hip. The van had been sold to a builder who claimed to be arranging a bank loan to pay for it and would come at the weekend to drive it away.

'Soon as we can, we'll get another, newer model,' Greg said. 'Have it properly sign-written.' He theatrically cleared his throat. 'Wilding's Costermongers. Proprietors: Mr and Mrs Gregory Wilding.'

She smiled. 'We could put a bunch of bananas underneath the name.'

'And some carrots.'

'Something bigger and better: a wooden pallet over-flowing with a selection of fruit and veg,' Lily announced. 'And the company name arching over the top of it.' She drew a curve in the air in front of them. 'Then beneath:

Finest costermongers in the land.' Her hand swept through another arc.

'Yeah ... sounds just the job.'

They were talking about anything and everything to put off the inevitable parting. The van was parked outside Waterloo station and Greg's train was due in about fifteen minutes' time. It would take him onwards to the troopship bound for Calais. Neither of them had wanted to get out and go inside to the platform, preferring to stay right here until the last minute, cocooned in their own familiar little world. The back of the van was empty and had been thoroughly cleaned for its new owner, but a redolence of earthy potatoes and ripe fruit still scented the interior.

'That's your friend John Lonegan, isn't it?' Lily's eyes had focused on a jaunty Tommy bowling across the road, kitbag over his shoulder. He hadn't spotted them and Greg slid down a bit in his seat, pulling Lily with him. 'He'll come over if he sees me, and I want you all to myself for a bit longer.'

She gulped and the sob she'd been holding in burst from her. No more pretending now. They had only a matter of minutes left together. She flung her arms about his neck. 'I don't want you to go away again. Can't you stay for a few more days? You were supposed to have ten days at home, not eight. Just stay a few more days ...'

'Doesn't work like that, Lily.' He dried her tears with his thumbs, resting his forehead on hers. 'It won't be such a long wait for my next leave. With any luck, I'll be back Christmastime.'

She used her sleeve on her eyes and nodded. Neither of them believed what he'd said. She felt guilty, breaking down when she'd promised herself, and him, she'd be brave.

It was four o'clock in the afternoon. They had spent a

lovely morning together; the only one in the aftermath of the bombing that hadn't been taken up with shovelling up debris or visiting bank or insurance officials to discuss finances. With some help from Eric, who fitted it in between his army affairs, they'd cleared the Wilding's site, ironically by building a pyre of charred timbers. Those bonfires had gone on for several days and drawn solemn spectators to watch the end of Wilding's. Then nothing remained of the barrows or the warehouse and the site was empty of all but neatly stacked metals, and the water standpipe standing up lonely and proud. The heavy iron gates had been locked yesterday evening before they came away for the final time. They'd stood behind the bars watching grey ash billowing in the breeze before getting into the van and driving off.

This morning they had gone shopping. Greg had wanted to visit the jeweller's on the High Street so he could buy her wedding ring, for next time he was home. Lily had gone along with it, swallowing her misgivings about tempting fate. The plain gold band, engraved inside with their initials, was in his breast pocket. A talisman. They'd also visited the photographer's studio to collect their prints. The snap of her was also in that pocket close to his heart.

Lily's eyes darted to the station clock. It was almost time for him to get out. She wouldn't go in with him; she'd break down on the platform. He was turning towards her, about to ask the question. Before he got a word out, she blurted, 'Can't. I'll stay here.' She blinked, giving him a tremulous smile.

'It's all right, darling,' he sighed, cupping her face. 'Not sure I can stand much more of this either . . .'

He kissed her properly, no pecks or teasing nips. It was a hard, hungry kiss for all they had planned to do but hadn't. And for the future they'd almost grasped but felt slipping away.

'Let me have that photo in your pocket. I want to write on it.' She held out a hand, aware of the seconds ticking down. Everything had suddenly become an urgent rush.

'Will I get it back?'

'Of course, just a few words to remind you of me.'

She got a pencil from the notebook on the dashboard and wrote quickly. She flipped the snap over, gazing at a stranger's smiling confidence. That girl had believed she'd be a bride by now, saying goodbye to her husband. But just minutes after that happy second, captured in time, everything had crashed down around them. 'Off you go, Lance Corporal Wilding, or you'll miss your train.' She handed the print back and he quickly tucked it away.

He swiftly kissed her again then got out, pulling the kitbag to his shoulder and striding off. He stopped to turn around at the station's entrance, dodging aside so she could still see him when a crowd of youthful Tommies dashed past, having heard the guards' whistles. Lily waved frantically, beaming at him as though he were properly visible instead of a kaleidoscope of glassy fragments. Then all the men had gone and it was quiet. She hung her head, huge sobs rattling beneath her ribs before being choked out.

Chapter Twenty-One

As soon as Margie discovered the date her husband was due out of hospital, she'd started planning his welcome home. After they were married, the couple had set up home on the ground floor of a terraced house in a turning off the High Street. The lodging consisted of two rooms: the one at the front was utilised as a bedroom and the back parlour was fitted with a fireplace cooking range. The sink was located in a rear lobby that opened onto the coal shed, set against the fence in a small square yard. At present, the shed was also home to Rosie's lonely pram. Eunice knew somebody who was looking to buy a second-hand pram so had offered to shift it out of the way. Margie had refused to part with it, despite the generous cash offer, and had carefully cleaned it then shrouded it in an oilcloth. Eunice, and Lily, too, had believed such care and attention to be a good sign. Margie wasn't making a shrine; rather she was being practical, thinking of future babies being tucked up in it. She was beginning to heal.

All morning, Eunice had been helping her daughter-in-law to prepare for her son's party. Lily had offered her services but had bowed out after Eunice made a comment about too many cooks spoiling the broth. The older woman seemed to believe this to be a job reserved for the two most important people in Smudger's life. Lily couldn't disagree and was happy to be a guest at this longed-for occasion. Fanny had turned up to it without her husband as Roger was serving in the army. Joey and Eric and some neighbours had also popped in to wish Smudger well in his continued recovery.

He did look better than most people had expected, and had an air of determination, as though he'd not let this setback defeat him. But the sturdy young man he'd once been was nowhere to be seen. He had lost weight and at just twenty years old his light brown hair had started to turn grey. He'd wanted to attend his daughter's funeral, but it had gone ahead without him as he had been flat on his back in hospital, fighting infection at the time. It had been a quiet affair. Margie had wanted only her best friends and her mother-in-law with her when laying her baby to rest. She had remained calm and dry-eyed throughout as though her tears had all been used up. The others had battled to equal the bereaved mother's composure. Later this afternoon, after their guests had gone, and before the cemetery closed the gates at dusk, Smudger and Margie planned to take a slow walk to put flowers on Rosie's grave.

'It's so good to see you, Smudger.' Lily gave his arm a gentle squeeze so as not to overbalance him. His leg had been saved but he was on two sticks. He refused to sit down, joking he wanted to keep on his feet in case he never hauled himself off a chair again. Lily guessed he wanted to exercise those withered muscles as he was constantly on the move, testing himself.

'Got you something ...' Lily put down her cup and

saucer and pulled from her pocket a small silver horseshoe. Smudger had given her the charm as a good luck token when she started her street round with her friends. It had been years ago, before he'd even met Lily's best friend, destined to be his wife.

Smudger leaned a hip against the wall and put his stick against it too to take the charm, displaying it on his palm with a faint smile. 'I'd forgot about that ...'

'I hadn't. I remember you said your granddad gave it to you just before he passed on. He'd want you to have it back.'

Smudger slipped it into a pocket. 'Something else I've got to say thanks for ...' He paused. 'Margie told me Wilding's paid for the funeral. I'll be able to settle up for it soon. I'm going to the labour exchange tomorrow. I can sit at a bench, making munitions. Don't need no strong legs to do that.'

'Any factory boss'd snap you up,' said Lily robustly. 'But you don't owe a penny. You earned that money.' Lily looked him straight in the eye to impress on him this wasn't charity. 'You used to turn up earlier than the rest of us, and you'd stay later and fix the carts that needed fixing ... sometimes on a Sunday when the rest of us were having a lie-in. You were due a bonus. What with everything going on, though, we never got round to sorting it out for you. But it wasn't forgotten. So, that's that.'

'Thanks ...' he said gruffly. 'And for looking after Margie while I've been in hospital. She's been such a brave gel, but I know it's you helped her cope with the pain of losing Rosie.'

'Do anything for Margie. She's me best friend.'

'Miss me daughter so much ... that's the honest truth,' Smudger burst out in a suffocated voice. 'I loved her and wish I could have saved her.'

'I know.' Lily gave his arm a comforting rub. He'd hung his head, positioning his sticks carefully on the rug.

'When's Greg next got leave?' Smudger changed the subject to stop the flow of tears.

'He said perhaps Christmas when I saw him off at the station.' Lily picked up her tea, sipping at it to soften the lump in her throat. She'd already received a letter from him, full of concern for her welfare; he'd asked how she was managing financially. There had been no mention of when he might be home again. She'd longed for him to stay, but he'd been ready to go back. He'd suffered a bitter blow, losing his business. But the tragedy with Rosie and the schoolchildren had hardened the resolve in him. And others. A common sentiment had united the community like an iron bolt shot through it: this was now a fight to the last man standing. It was the only way.

'Never thanked the guvnor for saving me life, either,' said Smudger.

'He knows you'd've done the same for him.'

'I would.' Smudger gave an emphatic nod. 'Once he dragged me outside though, he could have tried to put out the fire. He might've still had the barrows and tarpaulins then. The lads could've carried on with those, on a smaller scale.' Smudger had obviously been giving it all a lot of thought and was agitated by the enormity of his boss's losses.

'Wouldn't have crossed Greg's mind not to get you straight to hospital.' Lily bucked him up with, 'It's not the end of Wilding's anyhow, Smudge. Before Greg went back over there we talked about replacing the warehouse. With bricks this time, if he can get to grips with a builder's trowel.' She'd made him chuckle, and it was a lovely sound.

'Greg's got big plans to make it better than ever, after the war,' she added. 'He wants you back as foreman. Keep those two in line.' Lily tipped her head at the approaching lads.

'Blimey . . . here comes trouble.' Smudger grinned at his younger colleagues. 'When you shipping out then, Eric?'

'Next week; finished me training,' said Eric, munching a fishpaste sandwich. 'How about you?' he ribbed.

'Give us another week . . .' Smudger shifted his weight on his sticks. 'Be playing football 'n' all.'

'Bloody shirker. Reckon you're swinging the lead,' said Eric.

Lily left the two of them batting good-natured insults to and fro and turned to talk to a quiet and thoughtful Joey. 'How's your mum now?'

'She's better than she was, miss,' he replied politely and took a bite of biscuit. 'She said thanks very much for the money you sent.'

'I'd like to pop round and see her. Would that be all right?'

'Kind of you, but she's not really up to having visitors. She still cries a lot.'

''Course . . . I understand.'

A mass funeral had taken place of Upper North Street School victims. Eighteen children had died, sixteen of them infants. And more than thirty had been injured, Joey's other siblings amongst them. Lily had heard those boys had already been discharged from hospital. 'Are Kenny and Sam still on the mend?'

'Oh, they are, miss, thanks.' Joey perked up. 'Getting on me nerves as usual, 'specially Kenny.' He shook his head in disgust.

'I've got a brother like that,' said Lily wryly. She had received a letter from her twin. He'd been shocked into getting in touch once the news of the Poplar atrocity reached the servicemen in France. Davy had informed her feeling was running very high over there amongst all the Tommies, but especially the Londoners. In a final paragraph he'd apologised for not letting her know he'd got married. It'd been a spur-of-the-moment decision, was his excuse. Lily thankfully hadn't got any indication from that footnote that it had been a drunken spur of the moment, or that he'd had second thoughts about marrying Angie Clark, so she'd written back to congratulate him.

'That's a cracking little 'un. She's the spit of her mum.' Joey was admiring an infant with a mop of red hair. Fanny was talking to Eunice on the settee and the baby's tiny, nodding face was peering over her mother's shoulder at them.

'Gorgeous, isn't she?' Lily glanced at Margie, darting to and fro with teas and plates of sandwiches. She had given Fanny's new arrival a kiss and a cuddle earlier. It couldn't have been easy for her to be so gracious after everything she'd been through.

'Handed me notice in at Mason's,' Joey said.

Joey's old boss at Mason's department store had offered the boy a job as soon as he learned of the Robley family's misfortune. Joey was months younger than Eric, nevertheless he too was an underage army recruit. Lily guessed she was about to hear that Joey was heading to a military training ground. 'Have you told your mum?' she sounded a caution.

'I have, miss. After what happened at the school, she could see I'd made me mind up, and no point arguing. Kenny's her blue-eyed boy, anyhow. He's been larking about with his pals since he had his stitches out. If he can do that, he can look after Mum and Sam while me and Dad give Fritz what for.'

'He likes the idea of being man of the house, does he?'

'Ain't told him about it yet,' was Joey's blunt reply. 'Like it or not, he'll have to just get on with it, same as I had to at his age.'

'Who's for a sausage roll?' Margie had slid a plate of food under their noses.

'Ooh, ta.' Joey took one and Eric, having got a whiff of the warm savoury aroma, stopped talking to Smudger and dived in.

'I'll give you a hand with the teas, Marge.' Lily finished her tasty sausage roll in two mouthfuls, licking pastry flakes off her fingers.

'You've done a smashing spread, love. And you look ever so elegant in that new outfit.' Lily had filled the kettle and was lugging it into the parlour just as Margie placed an empty plate on the table. Lily was admiring Margie's silver-grey dress with pearl-buttoned bodice. With her fair hair prettily bobbed she looked as stylish as a fashion plate in a magazine.

'Wanted to make a special effort to welcome him home.' Margie glanced at Smudger. 'He said I look beautiful and the colour suits me. I chose grey for Rosie. I've worn enough black.'

'Grey does suit you.' Lily left it at that. This was Smudger's special day, a celebration of him defying all the odds to arrive home, under his own steam, in a taxi cab. The driver's offer of an arm to lean on had been politely declined. Smudger had walked up his garden path with the aid of his walking sticks, and let himself in, Margie had proudly declared to one and all.

'Those sausage rolls didn't hang about,' observed a rueful Lily. 'Was hoping to help meself to another.'

'Eunice made them, and the sandwiches. I did the cakes; the big sponge flopped in the middle cos the oven lost heat.' Margie grimaced at the concave cake, oozing plum jam, in the centre of the table.

'Looks fine and bet it tastes all right too.' Lily gave Margie a spontaneous hug, whispering, 'Smudger seems very happy and this is the best party. Wish Greg could've been here.'

'Smudger feels lucky to be alive, and says so all the time.' Margie gave her husband an affectionate glance. 'He's already talking about looking for work.'

'He told me.' Lily sounded full of admiration.

'And he's had a word with his mother to stop going on about us moving in with her. I know Eunice means well – she's worried about us affording the rent – but we want our own place and some privacy.' Margie's eyes strayed in her mother-in-law's direction. 'She's a dear when she don't interfere too much. And we will manage, if we're both working.' She moved her deformed hand. 'Just hope somebody'll take me on after they spot this. I don't mind charring. Do anything to pull in a wage.'

''Course you'll get a job! Look at you: you can cook, and you keep this place spotless. You can do bookkeeping and have got the best handwriting of any of us,' declared Lily.

Margie darted a scouting look around for eavesdroppers before hissing, 'He's given me that photo he had in his wallet. Told me to tear it up, if I wanted to, cos it wasn't important. Said he wasn't sure why he'd kept it.'

'*Have* you torn it up?' Lily busily stirred the teapot, banging the spoon about on china to conceal the fact they were whispering together.

Margie shook her head. 'Took me by surprise when he

just come out with it. But I've had a think now. I'll tell him to send it back to her. That way she'll get the message.' Smudger had sensed his wife's observation and looked over, giving her a wink that made her blush. 'Now he's crippled himself he thinks he's let me down, being as I got there first. Way I see it, though: between us we've got everything we need. Apart from Rosie.' Margie blinked back tears. 'Miss my little love. But we'll pull through it together now he's back home for good.'

Fanny's baby let out a mewling cry, drawing their attention.

'Fanny's lucky.' Margie's tone was wistful rather than envious. 'Son and daughter.' Stephen was a boisterous toddler. Today he was good as gold, seated on the floor with a toy train, at his mother's feet.

Fanny rocked the tot, but baby Victoria continued to whimper. Fanny stood up and came over to her friends, rubbing her daughter's back. 'Reckon she's got colic ... was farting like a good 'un just now. Nearly gassed Eunice.'

'Give her here ...' Margie beckoned. 'Show you how it's done.'

She crooned a soft lullaby to the tiny bundle in her arms and gave Fanny a triumphant beam. The baby had stopped wriggling and seemed to be listening, dark blue eyes wide open and staring up into Margie's face. 'You two can stop looking so scared.' Margie mockingly clucked her tongue. 'I know she's not mine. I'll give her back. Won't stop me dreaming that someday I'll be rocking another baby of me own, though.'

'Way Smudger's been looking at you all afternoon, won't be daydreaming in yer glad rags fer much longer, will yer?' Fanny rumbled a dirty chuckle. 'Don't need no crystal ball to see you in a pinny, dunking nappies in nine months' time.'

'Fanny!' Lily hissed a warning, compressing her scandalised smile. She'd noticed Eunice and her friend on the sofa were trying to listen to their conversation.

'What?' Fanny looked a picture of innocence. 'Just saying he was a long time convalescing with only nurses for company. Reckon Smudger's waiting for us lot to leave so he can have a lie-down and let his wife attend to him.'

'She already has ... if you must know ...' Margie poked her tongue into her cheek, and with a saucy smile, sashayed off holding the teapot to refill empty cups.

Lily and Fanny exchanged a look then in unison burst out laughing. Margie giggled, too, giving them a private smile over a shoulder.

They were workhouse girls again, huddling together in a nook beneath the huge dark stairway where, away from eagle-eyed Mr and Mrs Stone, they could comfort one another and share secret dreams of the futures they longed for outside. A sausage roll, a sponge cake – even one sunk in the middle – had seemed as far from their reach as the moon back then, when an extra dollop of potato given by a distracted officer had been cause for furtive celebration.

'Is Mr William Stone the master of this establishment?'

'He is.'

'Is he within? I need to speak to him.'

The porter studied the policeman, wondering what his business was at a workhouse. Being an inquisitive fellow, he jumped in and asked.

'It is a matter of no concern to you. Open the gate.' To impress on the upstart the importance of his mission and his authority, the constable withdrew his notebook and pencil as though preparing to log this conversation.

The sullen porter did as he was told and watched the constable march on towards the institution's entrance. The porter hadn't been in the job long and he wasn't sure he wanted to stay in it either. He'd been told at his interview that the previous occupant of the post had been a conscientious, long-standing employee, and the late Norman Drake's shoes would be difficult to fill. It was hard to fathom what Drake had liked about the job when day in day out whining paupers turned up, wanting to take up your time. And the hours were long with little free time. The lodging was a bonus, but a good factory job might make paying rent on a room a more favourable option now the alternative had been tried.

'Where's the other bloke gawn? Where's Norman Drake what used to be 'ere, doin' the job?'

The porter swung about in time to see the local tramp stumble off the pavement. Jake Pickard was always making a nuisance of himself, spouting rubbish. 'Told you. He's dead. How many times do I have to say it? Why d'you keep asking about him, anyhow? Did you know him?'

Jake stepped up onto the kerb and wobbled his head in an affirmative. 'Did he help her 'fore he went?'

'What? Who the hell are you talking about now?' The porter waved the tramp back. He'd come too close and a stench of body odour was assaulting his nostrils.

'The li'l kiddie. I know he wanted to help that sweet li'l angel. If she's still stuck in there, I'll take her. If I had some money, you'd let me ...'

The porter made an exasperated noise. 'Clear off, you mad fool.'

Jake continued mumbling to himself as he traipsed off along the pavement, swigging from his beer bottle.

'And don't come back,' the porter snarled, and for good measure, found the apple core in his pocket and chucked it at Jake's head. He smirked when it found its target, making the vagrant lose his balance and stumble back into the gutter. With a swipe together of his palms, the porter disappeared into the lodge to make a cup of tea. He'd take the weight off his feet and watch out of the window for the copper to leave.

'Is Mrs Bertha Stone your wife, sir?'

William pushed himself up from his chair. The policeman had barged in without a by your leave, having seen the name plate on the door.

'She is,' William announced sternly, wiping his lips. He'd been having a crafty afternoon snifter from the whisky decanter.

'Ah ... well, I have some bad news, I'm afraid, sir.' The constable secured his helmet beneath an arm, adopting a suitably solemn air.

William's florid complexion drained of blood. He sank down into the seat, clasping his heavy jowls. He had worried for a long while that his wife's demented state might make her harm herself in some way. She had been getting steadily worse, and going out more, too, against his advice.

'Where is she?' he croaked. 'She said she was off shopping ... a new hat.' He reached for the decanter to refill his glass and brace himself for what was to come. He replaced the stopper without pouring and stoically levered himself upright with the aid of the desk's edge. 'Come tell me the worst. Is she dead?'

'Dead?' The policeman looked and sounded shocked. 'No ... she's at the police station, sir. She has been arrested for hoisting from Gamages. Why would you think she was dead?'

'Arrested!' William barked. He steadied himself with the chair-back as the full force of that sank in. He would sooner have heard she'd thrown herself under a bus. The shame of it! The repercussions! It was bound to get out. 'You say she's been *shoplifting*? There must be some mistake,' he blustered. 'My wife is an upstanding woman, she heads several charities and is mistress of this establishment.'

'Your partner in crime, here, eh?' The policeman's attempt to lighten the mood and calm the man fell flat. Unbeknown to him, the joke had touched a raw nerve and the master continued blushing and blanching as though he might either explode or collapse. 'Yes, well, admirable as your lady wife's work might be, Mr Stone, she was arrested by the store walker in Gamages. In her bag were found several toys and some items of girls' clothing. No lady's hat.' He raised an ironic eyebrow and took out his notebook. He familiarised himself with the facts of the case, anticipating another angry outburst from the loyal spouse. Mr Stone's mouth was working like that of a beached fish, but it seemed he was stumped as to what else to say in mitigation. 'I came to inform you of her whereabouts. The sergeant thought you might want to pop down to the station and have a word with him about this ... umm ... delicate business.'

William was already on his way to the coat stand in the corner of his office. He slapped on his Homberg. 'Indeed, I will accompany you there. This is an outrage.'

*

'Where did you get this, Bertha?' William Stone threw the baby gown onto the bed.

As he'd expected, when he'd got to the station the police sergeant had been prepared to cover up Bertha's peccadillo for a small consideration. The items recovered from her bag had never left the store but had been retained in the manager's office. The matter was to be shelved; explained away as a misunderstanding. Mrs Stone, upright citizen that she was, had been preparing to pay for the items when she was apprehended. Theft had never been her intention. So after having endured a pompous lecture about being more careful in the future, Bertha had been allowed to leave the police station accompanied by her simmering husband.

'Where did you get this, Bertha?' William retrieved the small lacy garment from the eiderdown and shook it in his wife's face. His patience was at an end. As was his gullibility. He'd truly believed she'd bought the stack of children's stuff she'd accumulated and hidden in the wardrobe. Now he realised all of it had been stolen. Had the policeman made a search of their quarters, he would have uncovered the lot, price tags and all. And, worst of all, he might have accused William of being an accomplice.

Bertha picked up the scrap of material that had been hurled to the floor this time and carefully folded it.

'I bought it. I can buy things if I want.'

He shook her violently, making her head wobble. 'Don't you lie to me, you stupid woman. You've been caught stealing this afternoon and you're damned lucky it's the first time, or you'd not receive leniency. You'd go to gaol. Where did all this come from? Not Gamages, I'll wager, as the detective there knows what he's about. You would have already tasted porridge if you'd been regularly filching from that place. And it's worse muck than the gruel we dish up here, I'll vouch.'

William went to the wardrobe and started pulling out the boxes and packages that contained his wife's booty. 'This can all be destroyed. I'll cut it into pieces myself if need be and put it on the fire.' Dresses and bonnets and shawls were soon littering the rug.

Bertha clung to his arm. 'Those are for our granddaughter! She's coming home soon to live with us.'

William shook her off, raising his hand as though he would strike her. He lowered it again. Bertha was pathetic, a quivering fat grey-haired woman who appeared older than her sixty-one years. He realised that over a short period of time his exasperation with his wife had turned to disgust. He'd sooner remember her as she had been in her heyday, matching him for grit and shrewdness. She'd taken no nonsense. The inmates and the staff had respected and obeyed her. The other day he'd caught a female officer mimicking his wife behind her back as she dithered making a decision on a rota. He had stepped in and dismissed the mocker before insubordination spread. When they'd been alone later that day he'd snapped at Bertha to buck herself up and stop making a fool of herself.

William was a selfish man and determined to protect himself and the nest egg he'd built to see him through his twilight years. Prescribed tonics to calm his wife's nerves hadn't worked. He hadn't brought her depression up with the workhouse's medical officer. Bertha's doctor wasn't so close to home. He had a Harley Street practice and was an arrogant fellow. He would defend his treatment. He'd ask Bertha questions then pass her too truthful answers on to mutual acquaintances sitting on the Board of Guardians.

William didn't want those fellows getting wind that his wife was a shoplifter, living in a fantasy world with a non-existent granddaughter. If inspectors came sniffing around, Bertha's mental state wouldn't be all that was uncovered.

William came to a decision; he'd have to quietly commit her to an asylum in the shires. Her absence could be explained by a plausible tale about her elderly widowed sister requiring assistance. It was the norm for a married couple to run the workhouse as master and mistress. For now, a female officer could act as proxy. If Bertha got better, she could return to her post, in time. If not, he would retire himself. But he could drag the matter out for a while yet.

Chapter Twenty-Two

'What a friend you must think me. I'm so sorry you've had such rotten bad luck. I would've come over sooner to see how you were coping, but it wasn't possible. I've been in Kent, you see.' Evie Osborne was on Lily's doorstep, making her apologies while shaking her umbrella.

'Oh, what a smashing surprise!' Lily gave a delighted smile. 'Come in out of the rain. I've been thinking about you and was going to pop over to Endell Street to see if you'd gone off early to France without telling me. I didn't think you'd do that though.'

In the wake of the bombing raid, Lily hadn't received a note from Evie asking if they were all right. The devastation in Poplar had been widely reported, as had the schoolchildren's mass funeral a week later. The service had been held at the parish church, and the burial carried out at the East London cemetery. It had been one of the biggest London funerals ever seen, with more than six hundred wreaths being laid.

'What a disastrous thing to have happened.' Evie sounded solemn and sympathetic. 'And you've been caught right in the middle of it. I did write from Kent the moment we got the news. I sent the letter to your warehouse, but it was returned to Deal, undelivered. I guessed then that you hadn't escaped unscathed.'

'We didn't,' confirmed Lily on a sigh. 'The warehouse was hit. Is that where you've just come from?'

Evie nodded. 'I found the site easily enough as Wilding's name is on the gates. I peered in at the salvage then dashed over the road to ask the woman in the baker's if she knew what had happened to you.' Evie gave a phew. 'Can't tell you how relieved I was to hear that you were all right, and luckily she knew you lived in this lane. I've been up and down twice without much idea where to find you. A woman came out of her house and I nabbed her to ask for directions.' While talking, Evie was slipping out of her damp jacket. She fanned her face. 'It might be drizzling but, crikey, it's warm.'

'Come into the kitchen and I'll put the kettle on and tell you all about it. It's not at all a happy tale, I'm afraid.' Lily led the way. She pulled out a chair for Evie to sit at the table. 'You're in luck. I went to the shop earlier and bought some biscuits.'

While busying herself making the tea, Lily reported what had happened on the day the Gothas came. She started at the beginning, with the enjoyable trip to the photographer's studio and kept going to the very bitter end. By the time she was putting the tea tray on the table Evie was wiping her eyes. Lily sat down opposite. Going over the tale had made her feel emotional too. 'It's hard to believe it's really happened, isn't it?' she said croakily.

Evie nodded. 'As I came into the East End I saw the damaged buildings but ... how do people cope with burying their children? If I'd had to deal with half of what your friend Margie, or any of the other mothers have suffered, I'd be an utter wreck.'

'Margie was in a terrible way for a while. She's better now her husband is home from hospital.' Lily poured the tea. 'I expect you must get hardened to nursing men with those sorts of injuries every day.'

'We get to know the chaps and to like most of them, although you get the occasional horror. But even the nicest aren't proper friends or family. If my brother was brought in to Endell Street ... or Colin ... I expect I'd fall to pieces.' Evie took a sip of tea. 'Margie must have thought it was the end of the world, losing her baby and not knowing if her husband would be crippled.'

'Margie's made of tough stuff. And Smudger's making marvellous progress.' Praising her friends had bucked Lily up. 'I saw Margie recently and she said he's already getting about with one stick instead of two. He's been taken on at a munitions factory and starts Monday. She's applied for an office job in a biscuit factory. She's an excellent clerk. I hope she gets it. I've done her a reference and didn't need to use any exaggeration in it.'

Evie helped herself to a digestive biscuit. 'Her Smudger sounds like the right sort of chap. At Endell Street the men who grit their teeth and get out of bed seem to recover earlier than the wallowers. Can't blame any of them for being fed up after what they've been through, though.'

They drank tea and dunked biscuits for a moment, then Lily said, 'I suppose you've been in Kent spending time with your family before being posted.' It had come up in a past conversation that Evie's parents had a farmhouse in Deal where Evie and her brother and sister had grown up.

'Yes and no. I would've gone back to say toodle-oo to

them, but after I left you with Gregory that day I received a telegram from Mum. I packed a bag and caught a train that evening. I was too late though to say goodbye to Dad.'

'He's passed away?' Lily put down her cup.

'It was rather a bolt from the blue. He'd had a riding accident. Nothing could've prepared Mum or any of us for losing him like that.' Evie sighed. 'She got quite clingy with me, so I agreed to stop with her for longer than I anticipated I would. They were understanding at Endell Street, thankfully. My younger brother's serving in the Air Corps. My sister ... well, Sonia's absolutely useless. Middle-class twit ... pretending to be a bohemian poet.' Evie rolled her eyes and took a gulp of tea. 'Living in a garret somewhere with her conscientious objector lover, probably doped up to the eyeballs. Mother expects me to scour Soho looking for the silly mare to tell her about our father. If I did unearth her, I doubt it would make a blind bit of difference. Sonia wouldn't stir herself to go home to help. Unless her allowance was cut off, that is. I did suggest that to Mum as a way of reeling her youngest in.' Evie rubbed her forehead, looking weary. 'To be honest, I think having her around would just depress Mum. Anyway, I haven't the time to kick Sonia up the backside before I leave for France.'

'Oh, Evie ...' Lily squeezed her friend's hands, in rueful commiseration.

'*C'est la vie* ...' Evie smiled. 'Practising my French ...'

'*C'est la vie* ...' Lily mimicked. 'What's that mean?'

'It means ...' Evie sought a loose translation. 'I suppose it means when life gets you down, better just get up again. Or something to that effect.' Evie finished her tea and looked around at her surroundings. 'This is a nice place you've got. Cosy.'

'I like it.' Lily had always adored her little basement sanctuary. It didn't receive a lot of light and could do with the plasterwork being freshly distempered. But it was clean and equipped with everything she needed. The kitchen had a simple gas stove and a china sink and a brass tap. The larder was always stocked with a few groceries and shiny pots and pans. And the pine table and chairs were serviceable and smelled of beeswax polish.

'I can see why you feel at home here,' Evie said. And she truly could, though she had a far superior London apartment, paid for out of a family allowance. This little place felt like home, not a rented lodging. 'Can I see the rest of the flat?'

''Course.' Lily was pleased to be asked. 'I don't have a sitting room. I live in the kitchen or the bedroom. Let's start there.' She led the way to the big bedroom. 'Margie and my other friend Fanny used to share this room before they both became old married ladies. I had the smaller one that started life as a coal bunker. We had some larks, the three of us.'

'I bet . . .' Evie sounded envious. The bed was covered in pristine white linen and there was a vase of lavender cut from the back-yard bush on the bedside table. Evie picked up the framed photograph of Greg placed next to it. 'He is gorgeous, your lance corporal.'

'I know.' Lily took the photo and gave Greg's handsome face a kiss before replacing it. 'We were hoping to be married before he went back. That all got put on hold after the bombing. Have you heard from Colin recently?'

Evie sadly shook her head. 'I wrote and told him about my father and that I would be in Kent for at least a month. The funeral went off well. A good attendance. Dad was well liked in the village.'

Lily led the way to the smaller second bedroom, opening the hallway cupboard to display the ample storage as they went past it.

'This used to be my room. It was the first place I slept after leaving the workhouse. I thought it was heaven.'

Evie looked around the dim interior that smelled faintly of soot. 'Bit spooky ...' She walked to the small window and looked up at the street. 'Have you got another job, now the warehouse has gone?'

'Not yet ... I've been selling off the equipment we salvaged. The van's gone and the poles and weighing scales that were still serviceable. The business had banked a bit of cash. So I'm all right for money for a while.' Lily sighed. 'To be truthful, I don't really know what I want to do. I like being a costermonger: working out in the air and dealing with people in the market. It's good fun and it suits me. But I couldn't join a rival firm, it wouldn't seem right.'

'How about joining my firm?'

'Nursing wouldn't suit me.'

'Driving would, though. And we need chauffeurs. You'd be welcome to come with us to France. You're just the sort of person we need: capable and strong. You're not too precious to do a bit of demolition, so you'd fit right in.' Evie teased, 'We're always in need of a handywoman with a toolkit.' Lily had drawn an admiring look from Evie when telling her she'd pitched in with the men, dismantling the remains of the warehouse, using crowbars and wrenches and getting filthy dirty in the process.

Taken aback by what was being suggested, Lily was about to decline. For some reason, she didn't.

'And you know what it's like to fret about a child's safety and wellbeing,' Evie continued. 'Don't mean just feeling sympathy. You know what being a mother feels like, even if you're not yet one yourself.' Evie paused. 'Don't suppose you've had much time to look for Charlotte lately, with what's been going on.'

'She's been on my mind a lot, though.'

'It'd be smashing to have you along, Lily. You'd get a wage, though I can't promise you a fortune. You probably earned well in your business.'

'It's not the money. I'm not sure I'd be any good at it over there. I don't speak French, for a start.'

'Find me a Tommy who did when he first docked at Calais,' returned Evie bluntly. 'They all know a few words by the time they come back on leave ... not all repeatable either.' She chuckled. 'You'd be dealing with French house-wives and their families, in a refuge rather than a market. It'd be more or less the same as you were doing in Poplar, without the Cockney and fruit and veg. And you'd be driv-ing a van, of course, to pick up supplies or ferry people about from place to place.'

'I'd be in trouble with Greg if I went.' Lily spoke her thoughts aloud. 'Wouldn't be the first time though.' When she'd first found out her little sister was alive, she'd been in a state of euphoria, wildly claiming she'd go to France and comb the battlefields for her twin brother to bring him home. Together they'd find the lost girl, she'd boasted. Greg had been the voice of reason then, banning her from attempting any such thing. But Lily wasn't an impetuous sixteen-year-old now. She was almost nineteen and a woman who wanted to be of serious use. She also wanted to be with the man she loved. And Greg was in France.

'I know it's a big challenge, so I don't expect you to

make a snap decision. Why don't you think about it and let me know.'

Lily nodded and led the way into the corridor, mulling things over. She wasn't comfortable with being idle. She'd not rushed to get other work as Margie had greatly needed her support and that had been more important than earning a wage. But Margie now had her beloved Smudger by her side. She was doing well. And Lily was feeling restless. She'd planned to go to Islington on Monday and apply to the munitions factory. That would be the sensible way to proceed after the loss of her livelihood. The work wouldn't be much of a challenge. Sitting at a bench for hours on end in a room heavy with stale, solder-laden air would be. She closed the door of the bunk bedroom. 'Fancy another cup of tea?'

'I'd better get going. I'm on night shift at Endell Street. And now I know you're all right, I can relax. I'd been worried stiff about you ever since I heard what'd gone on in Poplar. I only went back to my flat to dump my suitcase, then came straight here.'

'You won't get rid of me that easily.'

The girls hugged at the front door. 'Thanks for coming over, Evie. It's been smashing to see you. Such a dreadful shame about your dad, though.'

'I do miss him, but he'd had a good long life, and he would have preferred to go this way. He loved riding and being in the open air.' After a reflective pause, Evie added, 'Just in case it might persuade you to join the expedition: don't forget Adam Reeve is stationed a mile or so up the road from the refuge in a camp hospital. You'll be able to have a reunion with him.'

'I'll think about it, promise.'

'Right, well, I'm off. Onwards and upwards.' With that, Evie climbed the stairs to the street.

'Is Evie Osborne on duty today?'

'Evie?' The nurse shrugged that she couldn't say. 'Hold on, though. One of that lot might know.' She tilted her white cap at a trio of her colleagues proceeding towards the hospital's entrance with a patient. Two were carrying the stretcher while another nurse walked at the restless boy's side, holding his hand in reassurance. The forecourt was noisy; a wheelchair was being bumped down some steps to receive a casualty with bandaged eyes, and between groans some men were bravely attempting to banter with the nurses. Before Lily could repeat her shout that it wasn't urgent, the nurse had trotted off to bother the stretcher-bearers. Lily hadn't wanted to get in the way so had stopped by the open gate; it seemed she'd made a nuisance of herself after all.

Two ambulances had been in the driveway of Endell Street Military Hospital when Lily turned up. Her friend wasn't amongst the half a dozen nurses surrounding the vehicles. Last time she'd been here she had wanted to hide from witnessing this. Today she'd sooner help than be a bystander. This didn't frighten her now she'd withstood the sights and sounds of maimed children.

The nurse called out to Lily, 'Evie's assisting in the operating theatre. She can't be disturbed. Shall I say you called to see her?'

Lily approached the nurse rather than shout her reply. 'Would you give her a message, please? If you'd just say Lily Larkin's had a think . . . and has bought herself a French dictionary from Foyles.' Lily flicked the pages of a small book taken from a pocket. 'She'll know what I mean.'

Soon she was on her way to the bus stop. She couldn't be absolutely sure that she'd made the right decision, but she wasn't going back on it so must ignore those niggling doubts. If she found being in France an ordeal she'd come back. She was still, just about, a woman of independent means and could finance her trip. She hadn't yet told her friends about her plans, though she must. She hadn't written to inform Greg either. She'd do that this evening, even though it was bound to dismay him. She wanted no deceit between them. He would probably dash off a letter back telling her to stay where she was. Despite what had happened to Poplar, England was still safer than France.

There were French refugees praying for a place of safety. Her conscience would be easier if she helped them rather than made munitions to orphan German children. Worthy reasons aside, there was a selfishness in going: in France she might bump into the brother she'd not seen for over a year and ached to hug. They'd been two peas in a pod when young, looking, talking and thinking alike. Her twin had almost been a part of her until the workhouse cruelly separated them. After the briefest of reunions, the war had then driven a wedge between them. Lily accepted that the chance of crossing paths with her brother was remote. But it would be lovely to see Adam Reeve, and from what Evie had said, there was a likelihood she would.

There was another person she'd met through the Whitechapel workhouse. Through him she'd gained a future and re-found happiness. She'd snatch at any chance, and travel any distance, if there was a prospect of seeing Gregory Wilding: the man she loved and the father of her unborn child.

She knew she was pregnant even though barely six weeks had passed since the first time they'd made love. Back then a wedding had seemed assured, and the possibility of a honeymoon baby, a blessing.

They had shared a bed and slept in one another's arms again in the final days of his leave. He'd used a Johnny because by then the bombing chaos had receded and realism was back with a passion.

Lily didn't look or feel different and a late monthly was all that she was going on. But she knew. And she wasn't as terrified as she thought she'd be, given the circumstances. Her friends had both braved the experience of giving birth unwed. Margie's and Fanny's lives had had ups and downs but seemed to be working out for them and Lily clung to the hope that hers would too.

France had churches and civic centres for ceremonies. Once Greg knew she was in France, he'd leave his billet and come and find her. She'd return home a married woman in good time for Sally Ransome to deliver her baby.

She felt confident fate would be kind this time, and allow her plans and dreams to come true. Soon she'd be a wife and mother.

A child of her own wouldn't stop her searching for her sister. She'd never give up on that.

Chapter Twenty-Three

'What the bloody hell are *you* doing up? You're supposed to be in bed.'

Betsy had struggled up off the sofa but Charlotte had already ducked back outside the door. She'd been thirsty so had crept downstairs to get a cup of water. Before reaching the kitchen she'd heard people laughing in the front parlour. She knew it wasn't Uncle Michael in there as she'd watched him go out from her bedroom window.

Charlotte had been living with her mother for months now and had often heard laughing and gramophone music coming from downstairs after she was put to bed. Sometimes she heard men's raised voices, as though people were arguing, and the doors slamming.

Usually she would burrow further beneath the covers and try to block out the noise. This time, curiosity and thirst had overcome her fear of getting into trouble. She'd poked her head around the parlour door and seen her mother and a stranger on the sofa. They'd not spotted her, and Charlotte had watched as rum was poured and swallowed. Then they'd no longer been sitting side by side but lying down and her mother was half hidden beneath him, dressed only in her petticoat.

Charlotte knew she had to quickly get her water because her mother would come after her now she'd been naughty. She fled into the kitchen. Borrowed light from the hallway gas mantle outlined some cups on the draining board. She grabbed one. It wouldn't have mattered which she picked; they were all unwashed and stained brown. After two goes at twisting the stiff tap she moved it and water dribbled out. The cup was almost half full when she was startled into dropping it into the china sink.

'You little bugger! I've warned you to stay upstairs after your bedtime,' spat Betsy. She had come up behind Charlotte with her hand raised. 'Why can't you do as you're bleedin' told?'

'Sorry ... was thirsty,' Charlotte whispered, flinching, but the blow didn't come. She'd not been smacked by her mother before, but she could remember the sting of Mrs Jolley's hand.

The frustration went out of Betsy as she looked at a pale, bowed head. Charlotte was slump-shouldered in her nightie, clutching her rag doll. It was hard not to feel sorry for the poor kid. Betsy had had a bad start herself, brought up by her grandmother after her mother died and her father scarpered. Her grandmother had done her best for her, and Betsy knew she'd only herself to blame for the way she'd turned out. If she'd not let Michael Vincent turn her head when they were both kids at school ... perhaps things might have been different. But he'd wormed too far into her now.

She bent down so she could read the girl's hidden expression.

'Nobody's child, that's you, Charlotte,' she said softly. 'No proper mum or dad … no family. Just me – and I don't mind telling you, love, I'm bloody useless, so no point pinning your hopes there.'

'Is Vera coming soon?' Charlotte timidly asked as her mother stood up. She'd asked every day about Vera. Every day she was told to shut up going on about it. Still she asked. Today her mother finally told her the truth.

'Vera ain't coming back. She's dead, so best forget about her.' Betsy retrieved the smashed crockery from the sink and put it on the draining board. Since Charlotte had turned up out of the blue, Betsy had tried to track Vera down, hoping her old housekeeper would take the girl off her hands. She'd been prepared to offer some money to help pay for Charlotte's keep. Vera Priest had loved this orphan as though she were her kin. But the woman had been getting on in years. Betsy had guessed she might have retired and no longer have the means to feed another mouth. She had written, anyway, to Vera's boss in Hertfordshire, and had received a letter back informing her that Mrs Priest had retired as a domestic and had subsequently passed away. The Hertfordshire housekeeper had stayed in touch with her old colleague, unlike Betsy, who cut ties quickly and easily with people of no further use to her.

Charlotte felt sad about Vera; she'd guessed though that after all this time she wouldn't see her again. But there was somebody else who might yet rescue her. Somebody who'd recently been kind to her. 'Will Mrs Gladwell come back to get me?' Charlotte knew her mother didn't want to keep her. It didn't bother her as she hated it here with Betsy and Uncle Michael.

'Don't reckon so. Best forget about her as well.' Betsy sounded glum. Mrs Gladwell had been back, but not to fight for Charlotte. After banging on the door the woman had skedaddled before it was opened. A bag of Charlotte's things had been left on the step and all Betsy had seen of Mrs Gladwell was her crossing the road, in the distance.

'Here ...' Betsy held out a cup she'd filled. 'Take that upstairs. And stay there. Go on.' She crossed her bare arms, jerking her head at the door.

Charlotte mumbled a thank you and slipped past her mother's silky, petticoated figure into the shadowy hallway. The fellow was waiting in the parlour doorway, silhouetted by the glow of a lamp. He tried to chuck her under the chin before she reached the stairs but Charlotte shrank away from his outstretched fingers.

Betsy grumbled at him, bundling him back into the room and hurriedly closing the door behind them.

Charlotte had reached the top of the stairs without spilling a drop of water when she heard the sound of the key in the lock. She swiftly sank down, wetting the front of her nightdress, and peeked through the banisters. Uncle Michael came in with another fellow, dressed in a dark overcoat and a hat. He was shown into the back parlour. The cool night air that'd been let in wafted upwards making the gaslight, and Charlotte, shiver. She wanted her bed now but the man who'd tried to touch her came out of the front parlour so she stayed still and silent. He handed over some money and was about to leave when Uncle Michael suddenly barged after him and grabbed his shoulder. Charlotte heard them arguing before Uncle Michael pushed him outside and shut the door, having received more coins. Then the man in the coat and hat went into the front parlour and Charlotte heard him laughing with Betsy.

'Interested in seeing what goes on, eh?' Charlotte saw cigarette smoke curling up the stairs. 'You'll get your turn in the front room, nipper, don't you worry about that. Just need to wait a few years.' Charlotte had thought she was safely out of sight. But he'd spotted her, crouching up there in the dark.

Charlotte's stomach lurched as he tilted his dark head so she could see him, down there in the hallway. He took the cigarette from his mouth to smile at her with a glint of gold. She jumped up, holding her cup of water in two hands, and ran into her room.

'How many times do I have to tell you to leave the girl alone?'

Betsy had come into the sitting room to find Michael tickling Charlotte's ribs, making her squirm on the sofa to try to escape him. She yanked on Charlotte's arm, pulling her to her feet.

'She likes me playing with her. Don't you, kid?'

She didn't answer but retreated quickly to the seat by the window, gazing through the half-open sash. Some brown leaves had drifted to settle on the outside sill and Charlotte crunched one in her hand and let the bits fall to the ground.

When she had lived with Mrs Jolley, she would sit by the window in her locked bedroom, hoping her friend Annie would go by so she could wave to her and feel part of the outside world. Now Charlotte stared out longing to see Mrs Gladwell. She was clinging to a hope that her mother was wrong and Mrs Gladwell would reappear and ask to take her home. Mrs Gladwell hadn't always been kind, but Charlotte had preferred being with her than with these two. At this hour in the afternoon children passed by on their way home from school. Charlotte would watch them and remember her granddad saying that when she couldn't live with him any more she'd have a nice family and have school friends. Vera had promised her something similar. None of it had happened.

Raised voices in the background made her blink but she continued watching boys kicking a football in the road. Betsy and Michael argued all the time, and when they got really het up he would hit her mother. Charlotte had tried to stop him once and he'd knocked her away, making her fall down and bang her head. He pretended to be nice but he wasn't. She didn't like his rough hands tickling her or grabbing her and swinging her round so her feet left the floor and she felt giddy.

'Wouldn't hurt you to show the kid some attention. She's yer daughter, after all.' Michael picked up his cigarettes and took one, throwing the pack down without offering it to Betsy.

'No, she ain't, not really, and you know it. So don't try that angle to make me fall in with keeping her around.'

She helped herself to a cigarette and they stood smoking, glaring at one another while the noise of children playing outside drifted into the room. 'It's about time she went to school,' he said. 'She's been here months. It'd get her out of the house and give you more time to yerself.'

Betsy knew he meant she could earn more money by taking clients during the day. But she wasn't about to approach a school and register Charlotte as her daughter. She'd no intention of the girl being a permanent fixture in her life, or Michael's. For the first time Betsy's conscience was pricking at her where Charlotte was concerned. She'd guessed Michael saw her adopted daughter as his nest egg. Betsy wasn't having that. Charlotte wasn't her flesh and blood and she had no strong bond to her, but the girl was an innocent and deserved better than having a life of vice chosen for her when she was only a kid. The time had come to put a stop to this.

'If you reckon she needs some time spent on her, I'll take her to the park. Could do with some air meself.' Betsy stubbed out her cigarette. 'How about you – coming along?' She was banking on him turning the offer down.

'Can't, love ...' He feigned regret. 'Should get going up to Wardour Street. See how the land lies.' Michael started rolling down his cuffs and buttoning them.

Betsy had regular clients who would travel from the West End to visit her. She knew Michael also had a fancy piece up there. He thought she knew nothing about his other women. She knew him a sight better than he knew her.

Once he'd gone out, Betsy reached across Charlotte and pulled down the sash.

'Right, young lady, it's time to get your things together.'

'Are we going to the park?' Charlotte had only been taken there once and had loved to run on the springy green grass and sit on a bench, watching people go by. It had been just after Mrs Gladwell left her here. When she'd asked to go again, she'd been ignored.

'S'pose we could take a detour and go that way. Yeah, if you want, Charlotte, I'll take you back through the park,' Betsy said, putting on her shoes. The least she owed this girl before dumping her was a trip to the park.

'Am I going to Mrs Gladwell?' Charlotte smiled, sensing something momentous was about to happen.

'She don't want you, love,' Betsy said flatly, ushering Charlotte into the passage. 'Come on, let's get your bag packed. I'm taking you back where you belong.'

Chapter Twenty-Four

Western Front, France

'She doesn't belong here with us. Send her away, mam'selle,' a French woman had called out in heavily accented English while shooing somebody off with a flapping hand.

Lily had been taking boxes of bandages and lint dressings from the back of the ambulance parked on the shingle drive. More voices joined in, babbling in French. She went through the open doorway to discover why the refugees queuing inside for a midday meal were more excitable than usual. A small auburn-haired child standing at the back of the line seemed to have drawn their rancour. The girl wasn't a regular, but in the multitude of thin bedraggled children Lily had encountered on her travels, she could recall having seen her once before.

The girl had turned up for food that day but had been shunned then as well. The head-scarved mothers with dark frowning brows had pulled their offspring to their sides, as though this child might infect them. An older boy had spat at her, yet she couldn't be more than five years old. Lily had been driving off in the ambulance at the time and could only bang on the windscreen in rebuke.

'Why are the others horrible to her?'

'Poor lass is the daughter of an alleged collaborator,' explained Adam Reeve, who knew what went on in the local communities. 'The villagers can't take it out on her parents, so are spiteful to her instead. This lot lost their homes and relatives during the German bombing in the spring. The survivors ended up camping here.'

'Where are her parents?' The child had a sweet but solemn face, partially obscured by a covering of matted hair. Two huge dark eyes were peeping out at Lily, pleading for an ally.

'Dead, as far as I know; perhaps they weren't very good collaborators,' he remarked dryly. 'The girl's illegitimate; cared for by an ancient grandmother.' Adam had spotted the crone outside her cottage once with the child by her side. 'This waif will eventually be rounded up and taken to an orphanage.' He gave the girl a pitying look. 'I expect she'd rather stick with her grandmother while she can.'

The child had been shoved away again to stand in solitary confinement in the shadows, making Lily's blood boil. If they did it again, she'd intervene. She knew they were all on edge, alert for the bombers to return. Fearful also of missing out on food or clothing that was handed out: she'd seen the women fighting over who got the last blanket. These refugees had all suffered, but Lily wasn't about to stand by and watch them take it out on a child.

'Mob rule and her parents' sins … it's a lot to be up against at that age.' Adam shook his head, wishing it was possible to put this right. But he was an army doctor helping civilians in his spare time, and he still had other places to visit before heading back to St Omer hospital to do a regular night shift on a ward overflowing with injured servicemen. There was just too much to do. Besides, the little girl and her grandmother wouldn't thank him for poking his nose in and perhaps landing one, or both, of them in an institution.

He strode towards the dispensary with his arms full of medical supplies that had been collected from the depot. They had already distributed some to the maternity hospital a few kilometres away that had been converted from a workhouse. Lily had entered that building quite dispassionately, though it was even uglier than its Whitechapel equivalent. She'd amused Adam, pointing that out. The various blocks resembled matchboxes set on end. But like Endell Street Military Hospital, it had been turned from a miserable institution into something good.

Lily had waited in the ambulance while Adam assisted in a complicated birth. After a happy outcome, she'd continued to drive him on his rounds. He helped the refugees from the goodness of his heart, but it also gave them a chance to spend some time together. Adam was a novice driver who underplayed his limited skills, thus it seemed Lily was a necessity if he were to get around as speedily as possible. She found it poignantly like old times, working alongside him. Neither of them had brought up the secret they shared from those days. Though they had talked about Lily's half-sister and the man who'd sired her. Ben Stone had perished in this area of France, Adam had said, in enemy shelling when he was acting as a stretcher-bearer. In this dangerous world they now inhabited, Harriet Fox's accident seemed rather insignificant. Lily supposed that the persecuted girl's plight might seem so too. Babes in arms had been brought into the refuge without a family member left to them. At least this child had her grandmother.

The shelter had been a fine chateau once; it had been abandoned following bomb damage to one wing. In the dining hall a local woman stood behind a counter, dishing up soup from a vast metal tureen. Once the children's bowls had been filled, they seated themselves around a pine trestle table and tucked in. As the orphan edged forward to be served the kitchen maid turned her back on her, pretending not to have noticed her waiting.

The wickedness of it made rage bubble up in Lily. She stopped counting boxes of Eusol. She marched over and ladled out soup, right to the top of the bowl, glaring at the woman who'd tried to elbow her away, having guessed her intention. Lily added a chunk of bread to the plate the bowl stood on. Then took another for good measure, and with a blazing blue stare, dared the woman to deny her. She carried it to the table and sat down, beckoning the girl. She was aware of a hateful silence, broken only by the clatter of the children's cutlery as they ate. The unwanted girl nervously perched on the bench. Her unblinking black eyes were darting from the food to Lily's face. Used to being tormented, she wasn't sure if this was a trick ... if this wasn't a friend after all. The soup might be snatched away or tipped on her. Lily read her anxiety and could have cried. She'd seen some dreadful things during the course of this war, but cruelty to an innocent child was equally hard to witness. Enduring malice had been part and parcel of life as a workhouse girl. She knew how it felt to have a belly rolling with hunger and to feel alone in the world.

'*Manger* ...' Lily whispered, mimicking eating. She had

learned some French phrases during her few months in France.

'*Merci* ...' The child grabbed the spoon and scooped frantically, eyes jumping around the table at hostile faces while her small teeth tore off chunks of bread.

Lily was aware of the angry murmurings starting up. The mothers watching their children eating didn't like Lily going against them. This pretty young woman who helped the doctor had ferried some of them in the ambulance to the maternity hospital up the road. But siding with an enemy's daughter was making them see her differently. They knew they'd get their turn at the table. Depending on what remained in the pot they might have to wait until more soup was prepared and brought from the kitchen. The children were served first. None of them minded that. But feeding traitor's spawn was a waste of food in their eyes.

'What's your name?' Belatedly Lily realised the girl probably hadn't understood her. She'd no need to test her limited French though.

'Danielle Fontaine ...'

'You speak English?' Lily sounded surprised.

The girl gave a slow nod.

'You learned at school?'

'At home. Grandmother lived in London.'

Lily liked listening to the child's soft, accented English. 'I come from London. Is that for your grandmother?' Danielle had slipped the second chunk of bread into her pocket.

Danielle nodded. 'I might not come back here tomorrow.' She wiped the crust of bread around the soup bowl to get every last drop.

Adam had returned to point at his watch then thumb at the exit, demonstrating he was running late and must get going. Lily knew he'd been delayed at the maternity hospital. She got up, hurrying toward him. When she turned to give the girl a farewell smile only an empty bowl and plate marked where Danielle had sat. Lily hadn't seen her slip away. Many pairs of unfriendly eyes were on Lily; she put up her chin to let them all know she didn't regret what she'd done.

'Don't worry about that lot,' Adam said, and gave her arm a pat. 'Well done for sticking up for the poor kid. Ready for the off?'

She nodded and followed him out onto the forecourt. About to climb up into the driver's seat, she spotted Danielle scampering over the green to escape a boy chasing her. He was pelting her with rotting windfall apples gathered from around the base of a tree. It looked like the same lad who'd spat at Danielle last week. Lily shouted but it made no difference. The missiles continued to be thrown and one hit its target, making her stumble. Lily turned to Adam. 'You go on. I'm going to take Danielle safely home to her grandmother. I can walk back to camp. It's not far and the exercise will do me good.'

'Is she hurt?' Adam frowned.

'No, I'm sure she's all right.' The child was still on her feet.

Lily pulled her serge skirt away from her boots and dashed to catch up with the little girl.

Now his prey had backup, the bully abandoned his pursuit. He swaggered over to the tree and leaned against it, looking sullen. He shouted something in French at Lily. She didn't understand it but guessed it was abuse from the sneer that accompanied it. He looked at least thirteen and had the greasy hair and skin of an adolescent. She restricted her disgust to giving him a filthy look as she

314

passed. Danielle was weeping and she crouched down to comfort her.

'Come on, I'll walk home with you.' Lily took the child's hand. 'You'll have to show me the way, though.'

The girl trustingly slipped her fingers into Lily's.

'I don't have tea to offer you.' The elderly woman attempted to struggle up. 'I have a little beer left. You must have something for looking after my granddaughter.'

Lily quickly gestured that she didn't need refreshment.

The woman sank back into her chair. 'It is good of you to bring Danielle home.'

She spoke in a wheezy English accent. It was hard to establish just how old she was; she could have been sixty or ninety. In either case she didn't look long for this world.

Lily was curious about the family, and how one of her countrywomen came to be living with her granddaughter in what remained of a French village. This tiny cottage was one of a terrace of three still standing. They had passed many ruins as Danielle led the way off the main track and into a lane that opened onto an area of tumbled white-washed masonry, the church and houses all destroyed. Danielle's grandmother looked unhealthily gaunt; the hand that lay on the arm of the chair resembled foxed parchment stretched over long sticks. Her colourless hair was so sparse that her scalp was visible in places.

'Would you like a glass of beer?' Lily blurted. The woman seemed about to nod off and Lily wanted to talk to her.

The grandmother declined with a grimace. 'She has eaten?' She inclined her forehead at the child who had settled at her feet.

'Danielle's had bread and soup.'

The elderly woman reached for one of Lily's hands, clasping it in her ice-cold grip and bringing it to dry lips in wordless gratitude.

'They don't always feed her. They're mean to her.'

'I know,' said Lily in an apologetic way.

'They say she's a whore's spawn. My house remains standing in the village. So they blame my daughter now she's dead and can't defend herself.'

Lily hadn't been offered a seat, but she took one anyway: a three-legged stool close to the unlit fire. The cottage was cluttered with mismatched furniture, some of it quite elegant and other bits, like the stool, fit to be housed in a barn. Lily glanced at Danielle, leaning her head against her grandmother's bony knee and sucking her thumb. Lily felt a surge of pity for them both. If those villagers believed this pair fortunate, they were wide of the mark. 'Why do they blame your daughter?'

'Suzanne caught a German officer's eye.'

Lily remained quiet, mulling that over. The child was too old to have been conceived after the war started.

'You now think the same as they do. Suzanne was an unmarried mother, but she wasn't a whore or a collaborator. My daughter was pretty and caught a man's eye. That's all. But these ignorant peasants wanted a scapegoat for what happened to the village. They picked on us even though Suzanne perished too.'

'I wasn't thinking badly of your daughter, madame,' said Lily earnestly. 'I was wondering about Danielle's father.'

'Oh, him.' The woman sighed. 'Suzanne met a fellow in London while visiting her English cousins before the war. She came home unaware she was pregnant. She wouldn't write and tell him. We argued about that. She should have sent Danielle to him when the war started. To keep her safe.' She pulled her shawl about her shoulders. 'Suzanne had a point though: he'll deny she's his. And he won't be in London, anyway. He'll be away fighting. That's what my daughter said. She wouldn't reveal his name.' Madame Fontaine rattled out a dry cough. 'I wish now I had settled in England,' she said on regaining her breath. 'My late husband was French. He said we must stay in his homeland. That chateau where the refuge is was once our home, you know.' She sounded proud and her lips quivered in a smile. 'He was a successful man, once upon a time. We were a respected family. Now look at us ... humbled.' She suddenly inclined towards Lily. 'How old do you think I am?'

Caught off guard, Lily cleared her throat. 'Mmm ... not sure ...'

'Seventy-two,' the woman supplied. 'I look older, I know. And feel it.' She patted her flat chest. 'This old ticker has been broken too many times.' She stroked her granddaughter's abundant auburn hair. 'I had hair like this once. We were all good lookers, you know.'

Danielle took the bread from her pocket and broke off bits to offer to her grandmother. After two mouthfuls, the woman waved away the rest and flopped back into the battered upholstery of her armchair, closing her eyes. Danielle finished the bread and then curled up against her grandmother's knees.

Lily stood up, ready to take her leave before they both fell asleep.

'Will you take Danielle to England for me?' The grandmother had heard movement and her eyelids had flown open.

'What?'

'You're going back home soon. Take Danielle . . . please.' The woman eased forward on her seat. She had the same dark brown gaze as her granddaughter and Lily felt the full force of it.

'My sister will look after her. She's younger than me. I'll write a letter for you to take to her. And a note permitting you to be my granddaughter's guardian on the journey.' She fiddled down the side of her armchair to fish out a brooch. 'There. That should be enough for her passage.' She was animated and bared a few teeth in a hoarse chuckle. 'It is gold. I was saving it for Danielle when she was older.'

'I'm not going back soon.' Lily avoided the issue and didn't take the jewellery.

'You won't have your baby in France. You'd be a fool if you did.'

Lily sank down onto the stool, astonished. 'How did you know that?'

The woman gave her a wink. 'You're slim and pretty, like Suzanne. She didn't show until the end either. But I knew her condition when she came back from London.' She sighed. 'Where is he? Not fighting, I hope. You've no ring, yet. Don't suffer like Suzanne. They'll call you names. What *is* your name?'

'Lily Larkin.' She smiled. 'I do have his ring.' She did her own fiddling for jewellery, producing her engagement ring, on a silver chain, from beneath her bodice. It lay warm and heavy against the palm of her hand.

'Ooh . . . look at that, Danielle.' The child's grandmother nudged her awake. 'I once had emeralds. All gone now. He is a rich fellow, your fiancé?'

'No . . . not any more. But we've all we need.' Compared to these French folk, they were rich.

'You will take Danielle for me? If you don't, what will happen to her after I'm gone?' The woman's eyes glittered but she wouldn't let Lily see her tears and turned her head.

'I don't think that's possible. I have to go now,' Lily said, putting her ring back between her buttons. She felt rotten not giving the woman the answer she wanted. But once that promise was made she couldn't renege on it. 'I'll come back tomorrow.'

'You won't come back.' There was no blame, just sadness in Madame Fontaine's tone.

'I will. I'll bring food. I promise.'

Her declaration was met with silence, so Lily murmured a goodbye and went outside. She picked her way through the ruins to the road that led to St Omer.

She set off, avoiding the potholes that could rick an ankle and played havoc with the ambulance tyres. She hoped that Adam might be on his way home and pass her on the road. She'd get a lift back to the camp then. She didn't mind a walk but she felt weary from the burden now placed on her by Danielle's grandmother. Would it be too much to take on the task of delivering an orphan girl to an aunt in England? Lily wouldn't like to see any child spend years in an institution as she had. Madame Fontaine didn't look as though she had many months left in her. Winter was coming. And Danielle would have to live on her wits or submit to bureaucrats dictating her life. With no locals willing to help her, she wouldn't last long on her own, free to run about the lanes and meadows. Lily didn't know the family ... yet oddly felt as though she did after that brief meeting with Danielle and her grandmother. An echo of her own life was there in their sadness.

She'd value Adam's opinion on whether she was being

daft to consider acting as the girl's escort. He'd probably say she was ... and she'd do it anyway. How utterly thankful she would be if somebody turned up on her doorstep with Charlotte, believing it the right thing to do. Nevertheless, she would like another chance to talk to Adam today. She sighed and looked around as she marched along. The countryside was a tawny brown ... the colour of autumn reminded her of Greg. The first thing she'd noticed about him as a fifteen-year-old girl hadn't been his blond hair but his striking hazel eyes.

She heard an approaching vehicle and glanced over a shoulder, hoping to see the ambulance with Adam at the wheel. An army truck was lumbering towards her, and judging by the faint strains of 'Mademoiselle of Armentières' reaching her ears, she guessed a load of Tommies were on the move. She got out of the way to allow it to pass.

She received a toot from the driver as the vehicle passed, then whistles and shouts of appreciation from the men in khaki seated in the back. She waved and smiled at the laughing faces.

'Lily!'

She almost lost her footing and fell into the ditch at the side of the road on hearing her name roared out. Then one of the soldiers tumbled out of the back and was running towards her, arms outstretched.

'Davy!' Lily would recognise that voice anywhere. But this meeting seemed too wonderful to be true, and she doubted herself. When he was close enough for her to see his dear familiar features and bright blue eyes, she sobbed and held out her arms. They embraced so tightly she could feel his belt buckle digging painfully into her ribs.

'When you wrote and said you was in France I wondered

if I'd bump into you,' he garbled. 'What you doing? Where you going?'

'Back to camp. Been helping Dr Reeve on his rounds.' She cupped his face in her hands, brought it forward to place her lips on his stubbly cheek. 'Oh, I've missed you, Davy.'

'Likewise ...' he said simply, and gestured rudely to his pals who were catcalling from the back of the lorry. The vehicle had stopped some thirty yards along the road, waiting for him.

Lily knew they wouldn't have long together and there was so much to say. 'Are you happy now you're married?' She started with the most important thing to know about him.

He beamed. 'Yeah ... me 'n' Angie are doing all right. When we're all back home, we'll get together again ... be a big family.'

She nodded fiercely. 'We will. And have a party. Have you seen Greg? We were going to be married before he came back, but it didn't happen. The Poplar bombing ...'

'Must've been dreadful,' Davy said. 'Was thinking of you, Lil; worrying all the time, I was. 'Specially when I heard about the warehouse getting hammered. Now every time I see a Gotha I take a potshot with me rifle.' He aimed some fingers at the sky. 'Ain't seen Greg. But then he spends most of his time ...' He pointed at the ground. When his sister looked puzzled he added, 'He told you he's a clay kicker, didn't he? Tunnelling. Sooner him than me down there.'

Lily felt her guts tighten. 'Yes ... 'course ... he told me he's digging and so on.'

Davy tried to back-pedal, realising he'd been too direct and worried his sister in a way Greg hadn't wanted. 'Greg'll be all right. Knows how to look after himself, does Greg.'

He gestured again at the hecklers, now encouraging him to hurry up. 'Better get going, Lil. We're being moved up to the line.' He hugged her, kissed her forehead. 'You take care of yourself. Say hello to all of 'em when you get back. How's Smudger doing?' he called, remembering to ask about his lame pal. He'd got Lily's letter informing him about the tragedy that resulted in Smudger being badly injured trying to save his baby.

He was glancing over a shoulder at her as he loped back to the vehicle, waiting for a reply. She stuck up both thumbs to let him know Smudger was on the mend, then blew kisses he didn't see. His chums were manhandling him onto the back of the truck to sit amongst them.

She continued waving and didn't move from the spot until the truck had disappeared into the distance.

Chapter Twenty-Five

A camp of Nissen huts set up on the edge of town was home to Lily and her volunteer colleagues. It was far from luxurious accommodation. In fact, the hard bunks in regimented cubicles reminded Lily somewhat of the Whitechapel workhouse's spartan facilities. Shortly after they had arrived, Lily and Evie had visited the local market to purchase some material to brighten the place up. The red, yellow and blue cloth was strung across the windows as makeshift curtains. Lily had had every intention of hemming them to stop the fabric fraying, but there had always been something more important to do in a spare moment, like letter-writing to friends and family. As a result, the curtains had an added detail: a fringe of rainbow threads. There was a stove on which they could brew up hot drinks and a bedside cabinet on which photos could be placed. Lily had Greg's photograph facing the bed. Evie had Colin's on her table. Her roommate had arranged it with her bosses that she would share a hut with Lily. They didn't see an awful lot of one another though. Evie was an experienced theatre nurse. She went frequently and without hesitation to an army hospital to assist the Royal Army Medical Corps surgeons. Lily had soon learned that a willingness to pitch in and jump from pillar to post was a necessary part of a medical team's role on the Western Front. She thought it was a wonderful way to be. She missed Evie's company when her friend stayed in the nurse's quarters at the hospital. They got together as often as they could when their shifts allowed, going to restaurants and enjoying coffee and eclairs eaten off tables covered in the same colourful check that dressed their windows.

Being billeted on her own didn't get her down. Lily was independent and content to have her own company. She'd not told anybody she was pregnant even though she'd known for a while that she definitely was. She'd felt queasy some mornings. She remembered Margie and Fanny throwing up, and felt lucky not to be suffering as badly as that.

At first, she had kept quiet in case Evie advised her against going to France after all. Lily had hardly gained weight and remained slender. She'd been confident that only she could see and feel the small bump that strained her serge skirt buttons. Yet Madame Fontaine hadn't been fooled by her shapeless brown uniform.

Her buoyant mood after meeting Davy soared higher as she entered the hut. Evie was already back, sitting cross-legged on her bed, in her petticoat.

'Hello, stranger ... you'll never guess who I've just seen...' Lily's cheerful welcome petered off. Evie was reading a letter and it had become obvious that her friend was upset. 'What is it? What's happened?'

Evie let the letter drift from her fingers to the eiderdown and she hung her head. 'That stupid cow,' she choked out. 'I'll bloody kill her for this.'

Lily hurried to sit down on Evie's mattress and put an arm round her. Thankfully, it seemed this wasn't bad news concerning Colin, so that was a relief. In his last letter he'd proposed and Evie had been overjoyed.

'Read that . . . go on.' Evie poked a finger at the letter then found a hanky to use on her wet eyes.

Before Lily could retrieve the paper, Evie was paraphrasing its contents. 'My bloody sister has only gone and overdosed. The boyfriend must've got the wind up and scarpered when she took too much stuff and he couldn't wake her. She was found in some scummy bedsit in a backstreet off Soho Square by a debt collector. They got her to hospital but Sonia's in a coma.'

Lily's mouth dropped open in shock. 'Oh, no! I'm so sorry, Evie.'

'So am I. I'll have to go home.' She sniffed, composing herself. 'No choice in the matter now. That letter's from my brother, who's stationed in Malta. The doctor wrote to him to give him the gist of it and say Mum's had to be sedated. A woman in the village is calling in to see her, and the doctor visits every day. But something permanent needs to be done now. She was already in a bad way after Dad died.' Evie shrugged. 'My brother can't drop everything and go back so I'll have to.' She clasped her face in her hands. 'If the worst happens, I suppose I'll have to arrange the funeral as well. The silly, stupid, bloody girl.' She sounded tortured with guilt when adding, 'I should have made the effort to go and find Sonia before I came out here. I should have made her go home to Mum. It wouldn't have come to this.'

'It's not your fault!'

Evie got up and pulled on her dressing gown. 'Well, that's it then. I'll let my commandant know I'm off home as soon as I can get a passage. I don't regret coming. I doubt I'll be back though.'

Lily hadn't made any conscious decision over her future plans when entering the hut. She knew what she'd do now. Perhaps Evie's confession had prompted her to finally admit to her own mistake. It hadn't been sensible to come to France in her condition. She was glad she'd done it, even for a short time. She had taken a leap of faith and crossed the Channel to help the refugees. And she'd seen and spoken to Davy. She'd only been in a foreign land a matter of months, yet had bumped into her twin brother. They'd not shared a hug in London for over a year. The chance to reunite with Adam had been an added delightful bonus. But she'd failed to spend any time with Greg. And that had been her prime reason for coming.

He'd written to her before she left England. He'd not banned her from going, as she'd anticipated. He'd told her to take care and to write the moment she knew her postal address. She'd received one letter from him while in France, filled with love and wishes for them to get leave together so they could go home and be married at last. She touched her breast pocket where the letter stayed until taken out to be reread at every bedtime. From it she knew he was somewhere around Passchendaele. She hadn't appreciated how big a country France was until she turned up in it. Greg was a distance from her, not an afternoon's jaunt away. He was proud of her and would come to visit her camp as soon as he could get away, he said. The way she'd coped with the aftermath of the Poplar bombing had proved to him she was capable of doing this, she realised. She loved him the more for the strong belief he had in her and yearned for him. She wanted his voice, his touch, the scent of him until she physically ached. Lily supposed most separated couples felt that pain, then bucked themselves up and carried on. Finishing this was the only way to make a fresh start back home. She'd not told Greg she was pregnant. She'd not wanted to worry him. Now she was worried that it might have been best to bring it up straight away.

'I'm going home too, Evie,' Lily blurted. 'We can go together.'

Evie stopped morosely yanking a brush through her fair hair and turned around. 'You're going *back*? Why? I thought you were settling in, and Adam says you're a marvel to have around.'

'I'll miss Adam; it's been smashing working with him. But I am going back. Got to, really.' She took the brush from Evie, dropping it onto the mattress, then clasped her friend's hands. 'I've some news, actually. Couple of eye-openers, too. I'll start by letting you know I'm pregnant. Sorry. I should've told you sooner.'

'You should've!' Evie goggled at Lily's waistline. 'I'm not surprised I didn't notice. Not much to see, is there?' She suddenly grinned, whispering, 'Are you pleased? I think I might be, in your shoes.'

'Well, I am, though it's not ideal timing, is it?'

'You definitely need to go back. You are going to be able to cope until Greg gets home, aren't you?'

'I'll have to,' Lily said flatly.

'So what else do you have to tell me? It has to be an anti-climax after that bombshell.' A few minutes later, having heard about Lily's encounter with the Fontaines, Evie spluttered, 'Crikey! It wasn't that much of an also-ran.' She patted Lily's arm. 'Good for you, helping them. I would've done the same if the old lady had approached me. Now let's scrape out what's left in the cocoa tin, and make a hot drink.' Evie put the kettle on the stove and said over a shoulder, 'Then

I'm starting to pack before I change my mind and let Sonia stew in her own juice. She really is the limit. Oh, and by the way, you got a letter as well when the post turned up earlier. I put it on your cabinet.'

Lily dashed to get it. She felt mean being disappointed to receive a letter from Margie. She'd hoped to hear from Greg.

She'd heard colleagues talking about the tunnellers who burrowed beneath enemy lines to blow up their trenches . . . and often suffered the same treatment by their German counterparts. Clay kicking, Davy had called that treacherous job. Lily understood now why Greg had wanted to skim over telling her what he did. He'd not wanted to worry her; just as she'd not wanted to distract him with news of their baby.

There was no point driving herself mad with anxiety for his safety. It wouldn't change anything. Praying for luck and God to be with him was all she ever did, anyway.

But last night in this hut, she'd woken up in a sweat with a thumping heart. She'd had the fire and blackness dream again. Yet she'd thought that over and done with after hell in Poplar had come to pass.

November 1917
Passchendaele, France

They'd left their billets less than three hours ago. Before filing out into the dismal grey atmosphere, Greg had given a letter to the mess corporal and received a promise that it would go into the mail sack. The other men had received identical promises as one by one they trudged by, letting go of their sealed dreams of home. When they'd all gone, the cook had collected up the envelopes and cards, cussing them getting in the way of his saucepans. He'd stacked them into a neat pile, making it easier for them to be picked up later.

In every letter she sent, Lily asked about what he was doing. But Greg couldn't tell her. Better to fill paragraphs with reminiscences about the good life they'd had and his hopes and ideas for the one they planned to build together. The present was best avoided. He thought about Lily constantly, especially when on the way towards the front. He'd lock her image in his mind, praying he'd get another chance to look at her photo and her letters, and that he'd not seen those poor substitutes for the last time. It had been bad in Poplar … a harrowing, shocking time. But at least they'd been together then, able to touch and talk and breathe the same summer air. If he closed his eyes, he could smell the scent of blossom and hear a blackbird's song as they walked to the photographer's studio on the morning after he got home. The reek that came afterwards was banned from that memory. The smell of burning was something he associated with here, not home.

The drizzle had started up again. Sergeant Barnett was trudging in front, his greatcoat pearled with water trapped on sodden wool. At Greg's side, John Lonegan's grizzled face was half hidden beneath a muffler and a cap topped by a tin hat. Rain had long since extinguished his cigarette. Still, he sucked on it, lips moving forward and back like a kid with a dummy.

They'd passed the support trench and were nearing the front line. Slimy mud was up over their puttees and the stench of the latrines was beckoning them on. None of them wanted to go on, yet they knew they couldn't halt, or turn back.

Greg had once believed that being unarmed and meeting a thug with a knife outside an East End pub showed courage. He'd do that all day long compared to digging a tunnel into the earth's innards with a troop of nervous engineers and a canary in a cage. A clay kicker never knew if he'd seen his last daylight, or whether Fritz might burst through from his warren into yours. The not knowing was the worst of it. The element of surprise gave the attacker an advantage. In the last bout of close combat, by sheer fluke a half-shored-up ceiling had tumbled down to flatten the Hun invaders, allowing their lot to scramble into an adjacent tunnel and lick wounds. All noise – loud, soft – was a torment. As was the lack of it. If the canary went quiet, panic spread that he was dead from noxious gas rather than feeling disinclined to chirp.

'That bleedin' bird gets more grub than we do. Fatten it up and we'd have a meal,' said Lonegan, who would hide his terror with banter that got sillier the closer they got to the head of the tunnel. They had seen some of the men they were relieving. Bearded, and squinting in the unfamiliar natural light, they shuffled along, still slightly stooped after being cooped in low narrow spaces. Lonegan was directly behind a fellow Tommy who was whistling and swinging a birdcage in one hand and a bag of seed in the other. At intervals he'd tip some through the bars for the canary.

'Poor little blighter'll drown in this downpour.' Greg pulled his collar up against the rain driving against his nape. The canary had been flapping about to dry its feathers.

'Treat it like a pet since the dog went AWOL, don't yer?' Lonegan bawled at his whistling comrade, who feigned deafness. The cur that had hung about the village billet had disappeared as though it knew to look for other company now this one was on the move.

Sergeant Barnett swung about as they approached their destination. 'Bunk where you can. Get some shut-eye,' he told nobody in particular.

'Sing us a lullaby then, Sarge,' came a disembodied voice.

Greg had saved his rum ration to help him sleep. Every time he nodded off with his back against lumpy mud, he'd jerk awake with the smell of soot not earth in his nostrils and his hands clammy with sweat. He'd never told anybody – even Lily – that being in a tunnel reminded him of being punished in his uncle's black cellar when he was a boy. He wasn't about to start now. Not that it'd make a blind bit of difference if he did. There was no compassionate leave here for childhood demons. They'd see him differently though if he showed weakness. Even Lonegan thought him a cold bastard. He swallowed the last of his rum ration.

'Lance Corporal, get the men to shake a leg. Fall in.' Sergeant Barnett had come into the dugout and in the dim light made eye contact with Greg. It was then he realised he must have dozed off again because a breaking dawn was visible as a pink halo about Barnett's capped head.

'Tell this lot they can thank their lucky stars we moved yesterday,' Barnett said as he was ducking out. 'Fritz gave the place a pounding last night.'

'Woss he say?' a sleepy voice mumbled.

'Post we left behind won't get delivered,' Greg said, fumbling for a cigarette and levering himself off the earthen ledge.

He blinked a look around. Men were slumped in corners, chins resting on chests or pointing at the ceiling, mouths sagging open. Those that weren't asleep stared vacantly at fingers fiddling with tobacco tins. A few attempted a nervous smirk, acknowledging what lay ahead. Lonegan was stretched out on the ground on a tarpaulin. Greg gave his boots a kick to rouse him.

'Time to go, mate,' said Greg.

Chapter Twenty-Six

North London

'I'm going to knock on the door now. I bet you'll like it here once you go inside, won't you?' Lily had bent down to whisper an encouragement. Danielle was blinking rapidly as though about to cry.

'Will you stay?' The girl's small fingers clung more tightly to Lily's.

'I can't, sweetheart,' Lily told her. 'These are your people ... your family. Your aunt and your cousins are inside this house.' She cupped the child's solemn face, gently rubbing colour into her pale cheeks with her thumbs. The letter she had received from Danielle's great-aunt had expressed surprise at the turn of events, as was only to be expected. The communication had also stated that the little orphan would be welcomed into her extended family. 'You'll go to school and have friends to play with. You'll do well here.' It wasn't a platitude; Lily believed that Danielle had found a home and would learn to be happy in it.

A promise of friends was a temptation for a child who'd

been mocked and shunned for most of her life. Finally a glimmer of a smile lightened her expression.

Lily neatened Danielle's shiny auburn hair and straightened her coat. She had been bathed and had on her best set of clothes, freshly laundered and pressed for the occasion. Her white socks were pristine and her shoes polished to a high shine. She was still thin, though steadily gaining weight with better nourishment. In all, the waif had gone; Danielle looked adorably pretty and a credit to any family.

After they'd returned from France, she had stayed with Lily in the flat while arrangements were made for the transfer of guardianship to take place the following week. Lily had realised that simply turning up with the little girl could cause bad feeling that the child might suffer for. Lily had sent a letter ahead to Mrs Bloom, enclosing Madame Fontaine's letter and Danielle's heirloom brooch. Mrs Bloom had deserved fair warning that a stranger had been asked to deliver her great-niece into her care. Lily had got a speedy and heartening response.

And so here they were on a scrubbed doorstep in Muswell Hill on a bright December morning. It was a neat house situated on a modest tree-lined avenue. Lily put down the small valise that contained Danielle's few possessions and then rapped on the door. She kept the child's hand firmly in hers, giving it a playful shake. When Danielle squinted up through cold sunbeams, Lily boosted her with a bright smile.

A woman of about thirty opened the door promptly as though she'd been awaiting their arrival. 'Hello ... I'm Mrs Bloom's daughter. We've been expecting you. Come in.' She ushered them into a hallway where they were met by a cosy aroma of baking.

'Thank you for getting in touch, Miss Larkin. And for

bringing Danielle to us. I'm pleased to meet you.' Mrs Bloom got up from her chair. She had a firm handshake and looked to be in her mid-sixties. She was far sturdier than her elder sister. But the facial likeness between them was remarkable and it seemed Danielle had noticed it too. She appeared confused, staring at the lady who had her grandmother's face, if not her white hair. Mrs Bloom still had waves of brown in the silver tresses looped into a chignon. 'My daughter will fetch some tea while we have a talk. We've baked a cake to welcome Danielle.'

'That's lovely. Thank you.' Lily put a comforting hand on Danielle's shoulder as the child pressed against her side.

There were two children sitting at a round games table. The boy looked about eight and younger than the girl, who might have been a year older. He seemed bored and was swinging his legs, but he grinned at Danielle. His sister had her hands neatly folded and looked more reserved.

'Sit down by me, Miss Larkin.' Mrs Bloom indicated the other chair close to logs burning in the grate. She launched into, 'We would have offered to help sooner if we'd known how badly things had gone for my sister.'

'She didn't write and tell you?' Lily allowed Danielle to perch on her lap.

'My sister is a stubborn woman. Proud and inclined to be private.' Mrs Bloom sighed. 'We've only just found out that my niece has perished. Suzanne was a dear. She came to stay before the war but her mother declined our invitation. My brother-in-law had passed away, but still she stayed at home.' Mrs Bloom paused, choosing her words carefully. 'There was a rift in the family after she married Fontaine and moved to France. All those years wasted.' She sorrowfully shook her head. 'Suzanne let us know she'd had a daughter. We wouldn't have known Danielle existed otherwise.' Mrs Bloom pulled her sister's letter from her pocket, adding, 'This is the first communication I've had from her in a very long time. I wondered if she blamed us for Suzanne's seduction. I know it happened while she was in England as our guest.' Mrs Bloom put the envelope aside. 'I've written back. I hope she gets my letter in time. She informs me she is declining rapidly and that's why urgent arrangements had to be made for her granddaughter.' Mrs Bloom glanced at Danielle, unwilling to say something that might upset the child. There was a question in her eyes when she looked at Lily.

'Madame Fontaine appears to be very frail and poorly.' Lily moved her hand from Danielle's shoulder as the child made a tentative move to get off her lap. The boy had got down from the table and had held out a box containing a selection of magic tricks to show her. He put it on the floor and crouched down, taking various pieces out of the box and arranging them on the rug in front of the fire. After a few seconds Danielle took a step closer to him.

By the time the children's mother came in with the tea tray, brother and sister were sitting together on the rug. The girl beckoned Danielle, who hesitated only briefly before kneeling by them.

'Well, I never,' said the mother. 'Now they're grouped together, I can see the likeness between them all.'

'Actually, so can I,' declared Mrs Bloom. 'Danielle definitely takes after our side of the family. The auburn hair, and that finely shaped chin. She's a good-looking girl. She speaks English very well, my sister tells me.'

'Oh, she's fluent in English and French.' Lily sounded like a proud parent.

'It would be good if the children picked up some French. A head start at school ...' remarked their grandmother. 'Perhaps she would like to take her coat off. She looks quite warm by the fire.'

Danielle's coat was unbuttoned and Lily helped her slip out of it, laying it over the arm of her chair.

She accepted her tea, and a slice of freshly baked cherry cake and watched the children. It seemed the boy had mastered the trick of making cards disappear.

Lily took her leave after about forty-five minutes, with thanks for the tea and a promise to keep in touch. Danielle came in from the garden to hug her goodbye, dressed again in her coat to ward off the winter air. She asked Lily to come back to see her and received a firm assurance that she would. There were no tears at their parting, though the child looked solemn. But Danielle was easily persuaded to re-join her cousins on the swing secured to the apple tree bough.

Lily got off the bus in Poplar High Street and was heading towards her lane when she spotted Sally Ransome talking to another woman.

Sally immediately hailed her. 'I heard you was back from France, Lily.'

'Got back last week.' Lily didn't want to seem standoffish so stopped for a chat. She was always happy to make time for Sally.

'I also heard you'd got a kiddie living with you. Spill the beans then.' Sally loved a gossip.

'I was minding her for a short while, that's all. She's back where she belongs now, with her family.'

Sally nudged her friend. 'Your mum got into a spot like that, didn't she? She asked me if I knew of a foster mother, but I didn't have nobody to recommend for the job. June wanted to find the kiddie's real mum.'

'Oh, that all sorted itself out,' said Ginny. 'Mum got her wish and Charlie did go back home. It was the best thing for all concerned.'

'Sorry ... should've introduced myself.' Lily extended a hand. 'I'm Lily Larkin.'

'Ginny Gould.' The woman shook hands. 'Me mum's bloke didn't mind having a kid around all the time,' she explained for Lily's benefit. 'He died though, and that life didn't suit her. She said she was too old for that sort of responsibility.'

'Can't say I blame her,' Sally chipped in. 'How's June liking retirement in Clacton, Ginny?'

'She loves it, being with her friends. Would've been better for her though with him by her side.' Ginny looked rueful. 'Norman Drake was the love of June Gladwell's life, even though they never married.'

'Didn't know him well meself, but I found him decent,' declared Sally. 'And how's your fiancé, Lily?'

'He's well, as far as I know.' Lily crossed both sets of fingers. 'By now Greg should know I'm home. I wrote and told him. But sometimes the post takes ages to arrive if they're on the move.'

'I like me munition's job, but I'd sooner have my husband home safe than have money in me pocket.' Ginny clucked her tongue. 'It's time this war was won.'

'Think we all feel that way, gel.' Sally patted Ginny's arm. ''Specially when another Christmas will soon be here.'

The trio of women stood contemplating the horizon.

'S'pose I'd better be off,' Lily said. She smiled a farewell, edging away. She felt oddly bereft without little Danielle.

She had been a sweet-natured child and Lily was already missing her company. But things had turned out for the best for her, if not for her grandmother.

'How's your friend Margie?' Sally had trotted after Lily while Ginny headed off in the opposite direction.

'Oh, she's doing fine!' Lily beamed. The letter she'd received in France, from Margie, had borne the best news. Her friend was expecting again. Sally looked delighted to hear that.

'And I suppose you was going to tell me your news, was yer?' She cast her eyes down at Lily's waistline.

Lily had believed her winter coat concealed her bump. She'd not wanted Mrs Bloom to think her niece had been entrusted to a person of low morals. She'd worried unnecessarily about meeting a holier-than-thou type. Mrs Bloom was down to earth and it seemed a shame that Madame Fontaine had missed out on her support and friendship for all those years.

'Nothing gets past you, Sally Ransome,' said Lily wryly.

'Nature of me work.' Sally smirked. 'Ginny don't often come to see me unless she needs some such advice.'

'Is she in the family way?' Ginny hadn't looked pregnant.

'One of her factory pals is ... but I don't do that sort of sorting out no more. Told her I couldn't help.'

Lily wanted to get off that subject. 'Speaking of work, I need to look for a job. I might apply to a factory.'

'Ginny's making munitions in a local factory. Good money it is, too, by all accounts.'

'I'll bear that in mind then,' said Lily.

They parted at the mouth of the lane and Lily headed on towards her basement home. She'd put the kettle on the stove before even taking off her coat, feeling in need of some warm comfort. Restlessly she paced about from sink to stove while faces of people she knew circled in her head. Evie, Adam, Davy and Greg, always Greg, the love of her life. As Norman Drake had been June Gladwell's. Those people were strangers to her, but loneliness was common enough. Easy to understand.

Evie had gone home to Kent to sort out her problems. In a week's time, when her friend had had a chance to get a grip on her situation, Lily would write to her. Adam had come to their Nissen hut to say goodbye before they left for Calais to journey home. He'd told Lily he would try to get Madame Fontaine a place in an old people's home, if she'd agree to go. It would be for the best. But she was stubborn and proud, as her sister had said.

Adam had looked strained and unhappy that day. Lily had been worried and asked what was up. His best friend had been moved down the line to a casualty clearing station. Reports had come in that enemy shelling had destroyed some medical posts in that area. The man was Adam's soulmate, yet the taboo subject meant not much could be spoken about it. She'd hugged him in comfort and had said she'd pray for him getting good news. Evie might by now know her sister's prognosis. Lily hoped that would be good news. She wanted some good news. Just a letter from Greg or a word about Charlotte would give her cause for celebration ...

Something was in the back of her mind, niggling at Lily. She sat down at the table and sipped her tea. Somebody had said something that could be significant, yet trying to fit together bits of information to come up with an answer seemed impossible with her head crammed with a million things.

She turned her attention to practicalities. A munitions job would pay good money. The ten pounds that Mrs Priest left her had gone, swallowed up by her French adventure and the cost of passage home for her and Danielle. She'd not sold Madame Fontaine's brooch. The heirloom should be kept safe for Danielle, as a reminder of her grandmother. Lily didn't think Mrs Priest would begrudge the bequest being spent that way. Lily would resume the search. But where next? So many places had been dead ends: orphanages, schools, even hospitals to ask about a child with diphtheria . . .

Lily got to her feet, frowning. An elderly fellow had discharged his granddaughter from Whitechapel hospital, the matron there had told her, when checking records for her sister. The girl's name had been Charlotte Drake and she had recovered from diphtheria. Lily had just heard Ginny Gould mention a fellow called Norman Drake who'd fostered a child named Charlie. Lily had imagined it to be a boy but . . .

She grabbed up her coat and left her tea virtually untouched on the kitchen table. In minutes she was dashing back down the lane.

'Well, I do know where Ginny lives, but what's the big hurry, love?' Sally tried to calm Lily down. The girl's thick brown hair, usually so prettily styled, was in disarray around her shoulders and her lovely face was sweaty and pink. 'You can't be that desperate to get a job in a factory. Come inside and have a cup of tea. You'll do yerself a mischief, charging around like that.'

Lily did step over the threshold as far as the hallway but shook her head at the offer of a seat or a cup of tea. 'It's so important, Sally,' she panted. 'I've been looking for my little sister, you see. And what you and Ginny were saying about the child Mr Drake was fostering has rung a bell.' She paced wildly to the door and back again. 'I *might* be wrong, but I have to know. Was Charlie a little girl, aged about seven?'

'About six, I'd say. But you're barking up the wrong tree, love,' Sally said kindly. 'I saw her once with June Gladwell, out walking. Little blonde angel she was. Her name was Charlotte Finch, not Larkin. She wasn't your sister, she was Betsy Finch's daughter.'

Lily laughed, screamed in delight, making Sally jump back in alarm. 'Do you know where Betsy lives?' Lily caught Sally's arms in a way that made the woman hunch her shoulders, believing she was about to be shaken.

'East India Dock Road. Next to the ironmongers,' Sally gabbled. 'That's what I told June when she asked. She must've found Betsy if the girl's back with her family ...'

'*I'm* her family,' Lily breathed, eyes spitting blue fire. She darted back through the door and was running towards the High Street to find a cab. Sally whipped outside to lean on her front railings and goggle after her.

Chapter Twenty-Seven

Michael Vincent had been mooching along, opening a new packet of Weights he'd just bought at the tobacconists. He glanced up the road, and seeing something odd, his thick black brows drew together over a pair of shrewd eyes. He took the unlit cigarette from between his lips and stuck it back in the pack. A woman was standing by his front door. Men he expected to see there. Some huddled furtively behind turned-up collars and pulled-down hat brims, others strolled up, bold as you like, and said good day to the nosy neighbours to wind them up.

But a woman ... a pretty, young one at that. No. Something was wrong. He watched her banging repeatedly with her fists then the knocker, her luxuriant chestnut-coloured hair swaying about her shoulders with the effort she was putting in. He was a distance away but could hear the row she was making. He'd left Betsy inside getting herself ready for work. She was probably hiding. Only bailiffs gave a street door that amount of stick.

Michael had sensed something bad looming since the day Charlotte had gone missing. Betsy had told him the girl had run off while her back was turned in the park.

She'd blamed him. Said he shouldn't have been so rough with the child, making her frightened of him. Betsy had threatened to report her missing at the police station. That had convinced him that she was lying. Betsy Finch had been around Michael Vincent for long enough to know he had nothing to do with coppers. He'd asked where Charlotte's things were and had hurried Betsy's answer with his fist. She'd admitted then to taking the child to the nuns in the hope Charlotte would end up at the girls' Barnardo's home. Michael reckoned that could be a lie as well. But he'd more important things on his mind now a rival was trying to put his girls on Michael's West End patch. Whatever she'd done with the kid, Betsy would pay for stealing his nest egg.

Betsy had opened the door, and was peeping around the edge of it. Michael strode up the path and knocked it wide open so he could push the visitor inside. He slammed it behind them.

'Where's Charlotte Finch?' Lily didn't like being man-handled. And she wasn't bothering with niceties. Straight off, she could tell these two weren't the sort of people any adult, let alone a child, should associate with. She'd come from Sally's in a cab, so joyous and excited that she'd almost run off without paying the driver. She felt light-headed. Her eyes were darting about, searching for a sign of a fair-haired girl peeping from a doorway to see what the fuss was about. There were no small coats or shoes in evidence, though two overcoats and an umbrella were hooked up. Impatiently, she slipped past Betsy and went into the front parlour.

'Oi! Who the bleedin' hell d'you think you are, barging in like this!' Betsy was in her dressing gown. She'd been upstairs, styling her hair, when somebody came hammering on the door. One side of her brunette hair was still in curling rags while the other bounced to her shoulders. She was getting over the shock of nearly jumping out of her skin after the door took a hammering. She marched after the intruder and grabbed her arm, swinging Lily to face her. 'I said, who are you?'

'I'm Charlotte's sister,' Lily announced, a warning glitter in her bright blue eyes. 'And you'd better tell me where she is. I know you've got her and I'm taking her home with me.'

Michael had been doing his usual trick of staying quiet and listening while rope uncoiled for somebody to hang themselves with. So this pretty lady believed he had something she wanted. There was a profit in that. 'Seems like a chinwag's in order,' he said smoothly, darting a warning look at Betsy.

'There's nothing much needs to be said. Other than Charlotte's my blood and she's going home with me. Where is she? Upstairs?' Lily guessed that was the place to start searching but her path was blocked by the stocky man. He gave her a false smile and held out a hand.

'Intradoos meself, shall I? Michael Vincent.' He withdrew his fingers, inspecting his nails when Lily avoided touching him. 'And you are?'

'I'm Lily Larkin. I was in Whitechapel workhouse when my mother gave birth to my sister.'

Betsy's gasp was heard by the room's other two occupants. She whispered into Michael's ear when it was inclined her way. 'Vera Priest recognised the name Larkin. Ma Jolley come out with it, the night she turned up with the orphan.'

Lily heard every sibilant word. She closed her eyes in sheer thankfulness. She knew for certain now that she was within touching distance of her sister. 'You're Betsy Finch and you bought my mum's baby to trick Major Beresford. Before she passed away, Mrs Priest visited me to tell me all about it. I'd already started searching for my sister, that's how our paths crossed.' Lily realised she was wasting time, going over old ground for the benefit of these two. She was impatient to have Charlotte safely in her arms. She made for the door. Again, he got in her way.

'Now you just hold on a minute,' Michael snarled. He was no longer bothering to be polite. 'If you know all that, you know that kid cost money from the start. Recently, she's been another mouth to feed. You want Charlotte, you can shell out for her like we had to.'

Lily shifted away from him, not liking his smell or anything else about him. She glanced at Betsy, who'd blanched at this shocking turn of events. She was licking her lips, frantically attempting to guess what might happen next. She'd never anticipated any comeback from tricking the major, other than from *his* family. If the kid had still been around, she would have willingly handed her over to her real relatives. But Michael had that dangerous look about him. Lily Larkin was pretty and he saw profit in her. As he had in her little sister. He wouldn't let this young woman go until he'd struck a deal.

'Charlotte ain't here,' Betsy blurted. 'I never wanted her to turn up again like a bad penny. The kid knew she wasn't wanted and buggered off one day when I took her to the park.' She dragged Lily by the arm towards the door. 'Go on, you do the same ... and you can tell that bloody Mrs Gladwell I know it was her sent you.'

Lily wrenched herself free. 'Never spoken to Mrs Gladwell. But Sally Ransome has, and she's a good friend of mine.' Lily had had enough of being fobbed off. While

Vincent was distracted in giving his girlfriend a threatening look, Lily darted past him. She didn't leave the house, she dashed up the stairs, hoping to find Charlotte in a bedroom. She frantically flung open a door. Then the next, her frustration building as she peered into another uninhabited space.

'Believe me now, do you? Kid ain't here, is she?' Michael had nudged Lily inside the bedroom and closed the door. He stroked his shady chin and assessed her from head to toe.

Lily wasn't frightened of him. She cocked her head and looked him over equally thoroughly. 'Where is she then? You know, don't you?'

He nodded his head, slowly and mockingly. 'I know all right. Like I said, you pay for what you want.'

Lily delved into her pocket for cash. She'd give this evil wretch every penny she had with her ... but not until he'd told her where Charlotte was. It suddenly dawned on her that she might be somewhere as innocuous as a classroom. Her fingers tightened on the coins. 'Is she at school?'

He snorted. 'Kid's never been to school more'n a couple of times in her life. She said so.'

Lily held out her handful of silver and copper. 'Take it. It's all I have.'

He threw back his head and guffawed. 'That wouldn't buy me another gold filling, love.' He approached to get a better look at her body, saying with genuine disappointment, 'That's a bloody shame. He's away fighting, is he, your fiancé? Is it his? Or have you been a naughty gel?'

Lily was furious that he'd detected that much about her. She felt that her precious private loves had been defiled. 'You don't know what you're talking about.'

'My professional eye says I do.' He tapped a temple then

suddenly grabbed her left hand and lifted it. 'You're a good looker but no use to me pregnant. This might make amends though. The ring for your sister. Call it quits, eh?'

Lily wrenched herself free, clasping her hands together to hide her beautiful sapphire engagement ring from his greedy eyes. She suddenly felt stifled by him looming over her, shadowing her every step. She reckoned she'd get more information from Betsy Finch than from him. She managed to dodge past by giving him a hefty shove and ran out onto the landing. His hot heavy hand was on her nape, to stop her as she reached the head of the stairs. She jerked free and, losing her footing, pitched forward and tumbled to the bottom.

Lily stirred herself when she heard the knocking at the door. She tried to move to the edge of the mattress, but her bones ached down to their marrows and the effort was too great. She settled her cheek into the pillow beneath it, wet with tears.

The noise came again and through the thump in her skull Lily heard a woman's voice. Whoever it was seemed to be whispering, to keep the neighbours from hearing.

Lily struggled to a seated position then, wincing, got up and pulled on her dressing gown. She walked carefully along the passage and opened the door, expecting to see Sally Ransome checking up on her.

She stared at Betsy Finch, who stared back, eyes wide and darting about in agitation. 'Come to talk to you. Sorry about your accident.'

Lily stood aside to let her in. Betsy's sheepishness didn't last. 'It's your own fault it happened. I told you to clear off. You shouldn't have bloody trespassed in the first place.'

She shoved a shaking hand through her hair. 'Least you're all right. You could've broken yer bloody neck. Thought you had. Or at least a leg or something.' Having given Lily the once-over and seen no obvious damage, she blew out a relieved sigh.

Lily waited, expecting Betsy to go now she'd eased her conscience by seeing her still standing on her two feet. The silence lengthened. 'What do you want?' Lily had been gazing into space. 'Is he outside? If Vincent's sent you in for money or jewellery, you're wasting your time.'

'Michael doesn't know I'm here. He can't ever know I come to see you. If he finds out ...' Her boyfriend's arrogance had disappeared the moment he saw Lily Larkin lying sprawled at the bottom of the stairs. He'd thought he had a body on his hands and a murder charge to answer, and he'd appeared more worried than Betsy had ever known him to be. Then Lily had started to stir and pull herself up. He'd dragged her to her feet and bundled her outside as fast as he could.

'Just go away, Betsy. I need to rest.' Lily reached for the doorknob. She felt giddy and swayed against the wall.

'You should lie down. Reckon you've got concussion.' Betsy seemed as though she had something else to say as well, but couldn't spit it out while Lily was in this state.

Lily trudged back to her bedroom, steadying herself with a hand trailing the whitewashed wall. She sat down on her mattress.

Betsy followed her into the room.

'Not up to offering you tea if that's what you're after,' Lily said.

But she'd lost Betsy's attention. The woman was staring into the open drawer of the dressing chest at the minute face of a swaddled infant. Then she noticed a heap of sheets on the floor, red with blood.

'Is it ... ?' Betsy whispered, though she could guess at it. She'd miscarried babies in the past about that size, three months early. Often, she'd helped it happen. She'd never wrapped them, so they appeared to be sleeping on a soft blanket. They'd been disposed of as soon as possible by a madam or a pimp and Betsy had never asked how. The only time she'd wanted a child was when the major knocked her up. And that one had decided to go of its own accord. Hence her need for a substitute to keep him hooked.

'Stillborn.' Lily dropped her head to her chest. She'd not grieved properly yet. She'd not had time. The bleeding had started before she got home, soaking her skirt and her coat. She'd wanted Sally or Margie or anybody ... but there'd not been time to find a friend to help her through this. She'd been at Margie's labour and remembered more or less what to do afterwards with the mess that followed. And how to cut the cord that bound them together.

Betsy came over and kneeled on the floor in front of Lily. 'Don't know what to say.' She put her hands over her face. 'You wanted it, did you? Ain't done you a favour, has it, falling down the stairs, what with you not being married?'

Lily closed her eyes and her throat against a howl of bitter laughter. 'Didn't do me a favour.'

'Sally Ransome told me where you lived. Shall I go and fetch her for you?'

'I'm all right on me own now. It's all done. Just want to be on me own.'

'Can get rid of that for you ... if you want ... if it's upsetting you.'

Lily glared fiercely at her. But she could tell from Betsy's earnest expression that the woman honestly thought she was helping by offering to dump her son like rubbish. 'I'll keep him with me. Lay him to rest,' she said.

Betsy hung her head. Tentatively, one at a time, as though she expected to be flung off, she took Lily's freezing cold hands in hers.

'Something to say and you mustn't never let on I told you. If he ever found out ... well, I'd be for it.' She waited a second then said, 'Charlotte wasn't safe with him, so I took her back where I thought her family might find her. I thought if anybody was looking for her they'd go back where it all started.' Slowly Betsy got to her feet. 'Charlotte didn't run off. I told him I took her to a convent. That's another lie, to throw him off the scent. Your sister is in Whitechapel workhouse.'

Lily's head jerked up.

'Good luck in getting her. I know she'll be all right with you. And just so's you know, she had a good start with us. I was useless ... still am, and can't deny it. But Vera loved her ... really cared for her as though she were her own. Charlotte had a good start. I tell lies, but that's the truth.'

Lily heard the door click shut. She got up and went to the drawer where her baby lay in his makeshift crib. She picked him up and kissed his stone-cold cheek. Then touched his downy fair hair, like his father's. She carried him back to the bed and lay down with him beside her.

Chapter Twenty-Eight

The porter in attendance years ago had gone. The new fellow was younger, but seemed surly and discontent with his work. After stating that her business with the master was urgent, he'd allowed her through into the compound.

Lily now stood at the top of a deserted corridor in which the offices were located: the master's and mistress's and the medical officer's, where she and Adam had once worked together, he writing his patients' notes and she copying dockets for supplies. At this time of the morning, the inmates and the wardens would be busy with their routines: the laundry room at the back of the building would be heaving with steamy activity. The medical officer would be attending to the sick in the infirmary upstairs. It was close to Christmas, but the festive season was no different to any other for the poor wretches within these walls.

She'd vowed never to enter this building again but crossed over the threshold and started a determined march along the stone-flagged floor, passing the chunky black stairway. She tilted her head to see the recess underneath where long ago she and Margie and Fanny would dream their dreams.

And look at her friends now: women with husbands and families and decent homes to go to. Her chest swelled with pride at the thought of their success. On she went, glancing about. The gas mantles were unlit. It was a bright but cold winter morning. The smell of sickliness and skilly overlaid with disinfectant curdled her belly as did a long low moan emerging from the bowels of the place. Her nape prickled at the despairing lament. Her pace didn't falter, but she prayed none of the others would join in. One howler often set off many in an eerie choir.

She'd reached her destination and stopped. She rapped smartly on the master's door, head up, heart pounding.

She heard her permission to enter and didn't hesitate.

'Miss Larkin,' the master said after a full half a minute struggling with his surprise. He got to his feet to stare at his visitor. He'd have recognised her anywhere from her blue eyes, as vividly direct as ever they had been. She was no thin waif now but a beautiful well-dressed young woman. She had a quiet sadness about her. No smile, even to mock him, but fierce determination radiated from her, setting him on edge.

'What can I do for you, Miss Larkin?' he said officiously while cleaning a pen on his blotter.

'I've come here to discharge a girl.'

'Oh ... you want an apprentice.' He had heard on the grapevine that she was still with the costermonger who had bought her freedom.

'I don't. I want a child. I know her family.'

'I see. What name?'

'Charlotte Finch.'

'I will look into it for you.'

'I will take her with me today.'

'You can't do that, I'm afraid.' He sounded patronising. 'Permission has to be sought from the Board of Guardians.'

'Not always. I walked out of here on the day Mr Wilding paid you to free me.'

Mr Stone slid a finger between his jowls and his collar. He remembered that day. And the humiliation of being bested by a barrow boy dictating terms.

Lily drew out a pound note and dropped it on his desk. 'That's for her uniform. Please ask matron to bring Charlotte Finch here.'

'My wife isn't available. She's ... indisposed. In any case, she would tell you no different.' He flicked the cash away as though it were an insult. 'If you wish for a meeting with the child, you can see her; but you can't take her until procedures have been followed.'

Lily inclined her head as though in agreement to that and went to stare out of the window. She heard him leave the room but she didn't move from her spot. The fire was crackling, casting a warm glow but she didn't seek it. Her cold, white-knuckled hands gripped the window ledge until she heard the door open again.

The master entered alone; he'd obviously read her fury from her expression. 'An officer is fetching the Finch girl. I've just been told she missed school for disobedience. She was in the punishment room.' He was annoyed that he felt the need to explain himself. Since Bertha had been admitted to an asylum he took even less interest in the female inmates, or anything at all, really. He felt lost without his wife at his side. They'd been a good team. She would have known how to handle this upstart. Bertha had regularly updated him on female troublemakers and how she quelled unrest. Disobedient children had always been beneath his notice, though he recalled Lily Larkin had been one of the worst offenders.

The door opened again and a warden and a child entered. It would have been hard to tell if it were a boy or a girl but for the dress she wore. She'd recently been shorn, but a wispy fair halo of hair about an inch long covered her scalp. Her eyes were deepest blue and lively. Charlotte looked at Lily and a smile of wonder crossed her face as though she recognised her. Or perhaps the officer had told her somebody had come to take her away and she'd not believed her luck until now.

Lily steadily approached Charlotte without a trace of emotion betraying her. She drew her sister in front of her, holding her with two secretly loving hands. 'Send the officer away. You'll regret it if you don't,' she added when the master looked outraged by her high-handed behaviour.

He jerked a nod and the woman closed the door behind her.

'I'm taking Charlotte Finch with me now.'

He stomped out from behind the desk, his face turning florid with more than anger. He was unsettled. There was something he hadn't grasped about this odd situation. Why had Lily Larkin returned to a place she'd openly loathed? As a child she'd been bright but far too bold, and she'd often been in trouble for it. 'The girl goes back to her punishment. And you can return to your market stall. How dare you come in here and try to bend the rules.'

'Oh, I dare,' said Lily. 'How much do you want?' She removed one hand from her sister's shoulders to dig it into a pocket and pull out the money ready for this purpose.

She'd received fifty pounds for pawning her engagement ring. She dropped ten pounds on his desk to join the smaller banknote.

She read in his face his suspicion and that he was dismissing it as absurd. Lily knew eventually he'd accept the possibility. He'd deduce that no other reason would have brought her back here for a seven-year-old girl.

'I've paid for her uniform and for the inconvenience of you sending the necessary paperwork on. There' – she handed him the card Mrs Priest's solicitor had given to her – 'send it all to that fellow. I'm not waiting. We're leaving now.' Lily sounded cool and quite calm.

He made to snatch the child, but she put Charlotte behind her, out of his reach. She wouldn't let him touch her sister's clothing. 'You don't need to look to see if she has a birthmark on her chest. And neither do I. You didn't expect to have your granddaughter under this roof again, did you? When she was born, you had a chance to give her a good life.' Lily's voice was tremulous with suffocated rage. 'You knew who she was, but you turned her out. You and your wife didn't care then if your granddaughter lived or died. Now my sister is coming home with me.'

'I don't think so, Larkin. Give me the girl.' He beckoned wildly. His face had turned pallid in shock and disbelief. The child that his poor wife pined for had been beneath his nose. If Bertha ever found out about that it would finish her off.

He lunged forward but still Lily nimbly evaded him, keeping Charlotte protected behind her. 'Do you remember what Harriet Fox did with this?' She'd picked up his letter opener from the desk. The silver gleamed as it caught the firelight. From experience she knew it was sharp. 'I know you do. You were told the whole story by your son and Adam Reeve. I didn't need to be told. I was here with them and saw and heard when Harriet Fox met her end. She'd been drinking your whisky and looking in there for evidence of your corruption.' Lily pointed the knife at the filing cabinet. 'She found what she was looking for.'

That fluent threat had stopped William Stone in his tracks. He licked his bloodless lips and blinked at her. He recognised blackmail when he heard it.

'I'm taking my sister with me. She'll be safe and loved, I promise. That might not matter to you, but I think your son would have liked to know it.'

Lily let the knife fall to the blotter and walked calmly to the door with Charlotte's hand in hers. She hurried them along the corridor, listening for pursuit or a bellow to halt. She couldn't be sure he wouldn't call her bluff and try to stop them.

They emerged into crisp cold air and Lily drew in a huge shuddering breath of relief. She wouldn't feel completely at ease until they were out of the gate. She scooped her sister up into her arms and ran, ignoring the niggling pain in her healing womb. Charlotte felt as light as a feather and Lily hugged her bony little body, kissing her soft cheek repeatedly, until the child screwed up her eyes and nose and squeaked a giggle. Past the bored porter they went and then they were out and free on the Mile End Road. Lily put her sister down, her chest heaving. She felt like whooping in glee and thankfulness.

'I knew you'd come,' said Charlotte. 'She told me.'

'Who told you, darling? Your mum, Betsy?' Lily drew the girl to shelter against the wall of the workhouse to talk to her. She crouched down so their faces were level.

'Not Betsy or Vera. The other lady who comes at night. She looks like you a bit . . . but older.'

'Oh . . . I see . . . a dream, you mean.'

'Are we going home?'

'We are. We're going to ride in a cab to get there quickly. There are so many people who want to meet you. You've got lots of friends. And you'll have even more when you go to school.' Lily saw her sister's expression change. 'Don't you like school?'

'I do, but I'm a dunce. I can't do spelling or sums.'

'Who told you that?' Lily stroked her sister's small sad face.

'The schoolmistress and some of the other children in the class. I hadn't been to school much until I came here. I want to learn to be clever.'

'You will be. You wait and see. You'll be the cleverest of them all.'

Lily had been aware of a tramp crossing the road, drinking from a bottle of beer. He had stopped to stare at them. A smile creased his bristly cheeks as he watched Lily hugging a little girl with cropped hair, wearing a workhouse uniform.

Something about him and this place, seen together, seemed familiar to Lily.

'Is the li'l angel going home with you?' He'd ambled closer but kept to a respectful distance.

'Yes . . . she is.' Lily smiled at him, though he looked the sort of individual a sensible person would avoid. 'Do you know her?'

'These peepers doan forget faces.' He tapped beneath an eye that glittered with emotion. 'An' I know you 'n' all.'

'He helped me bang on the door when it was snowing, so we could go inside,' Charlotte said, smiling at him.

He wobbled his unkempt head. 'I did do that, li'l one. An' you helped me when I fell over. So we was quits, wasn't we?'

Lily wasn't sure what had happened between them, but she could see Charlotte trusted this rough fellow to laugh with him, and that was enough.

He tilted his head. 'It was a long time ago you climbed that wall. Jest a kid then, you was.' Jake was speaking to Lily now. 'Climbed it like a lad. Over you went. Bet you landed on yer backside.' He shook his head ruefully.

Lily remembered him then. 'You gave me the leg-up to get over it.'

'That's it. You said you was after yer brother. You both got out of the workhouse then?'

'We did ... thank you.'

He sniffed, said croakily, 'Glad it's worked out nicely for you, miss. Good luck and merry Christmas to you both.'

'Here ... wait.' Lily pulled some coins from her pocket and held them out. 'I don't even know your name, but thank you for what you did for me and my sister ... and a merry Christmas to you.'

'Jake Pickard, that's me.' He was looking at the heaped silver. More than a dozen brown ales' worth. Plus a week bunking in a doss house instead of sleeping on the ground. 'God bless you, miss, but don't need it. Ol' Jake's all right 'n' all.' He turned away before his watering eyes betrayed him.

Lily hailed a cab and helped her sister into it. She immediately snuggled the child into her side. Charlotte seemed content to be quiet and Lily left her alone to gaze at passing scenery. A flow of emotions was flitting over Charlotte's small features as she took everything in with wide-eyed wonder.

Lily swallowed the lump in her throat. She'd waited so

long for this, yet her happiness was incomplete. It had taken her a while after the miscarriage to feel strong enough in body and mind to face the next challenge of bringing her sister home from the workhouse. Even the loss of her beautiful little boy had briefly been forgotten when a few days later a letter had turned up. A Major Powley had written personally to inform her that Lance Corporal Gregory Wilding was missing in action. As his next of kin, and future wife, he believed she should know. She'd already started planning a joyous Christmas for when Charlotte came home. Then fate had cruelly turned against her, whipping away her happiness and leaving her to smile fraudulently.

She'd come anyway to do battle for her sister's freedom, though her heart was breaking. She couldn't bear the thought of Charlotte having a workhouse Christmas.

'This is the best Christmas Eve ever, Lil. Even better than when we was kids at home. Seems like so long ago when Mum 'n' Dad was alive and we'd decorate the tree and have mince pies for supper then go to bed all excited.' Davy sniffed the air. 'Reckon there's something tasty warming in that oven.'

'Sausage rolls and mince pies are almost ready,' Lily chuckled. 'I made sure I got plenty from the baker's when I knew you were coming.'

Lily gave him a spontaneous hug, overjoyed to see him. 'Mum would be so happy to know that we're all together like this.'

'She would at that. Can hardly believe it myself. It's like a miracle.'

'I'm so glad you managed to come home for Christmas this year, Davy.'

'Me sergeant put a word in for me when I told him I had a special family occasion to get to. He thinks it's about Angie having the baby any minute. But this is just as important to me. I couldn't wait to come back.' He looked at the little sister he'd met for the first time today. Charlotte, dressed in pretty clothes, was seated at the kitchen table with paper and pencils. At every opportunity she would practise her writing or read one of the books Lily had bought for her. The child had been delighted to be introduced to her brother half an hour ago. She had answered his questions about where she'd been and what she'd done, as far as she could remember. While she'd chattered away he'd sat opposite her at the table, holding her hands and gazing at her with a mix of adoration and wonder. She didn't mind talking about the hardships she'd been through but had clammed up when asked about Mrs Jolley. Lily had warned Davy not to press Charlotte, knowing from previous gentle probing for clues that memories of the evil woman upset the child. In the months and years ahead of her, Charlotte would exorcise that demon in her own time.

Today, they'd concentrated on the people who'd been kind to her: Norman Drake and Vera Priest, even Jake Pickard. They'd also talked about the woman who had ultimately done Charlotte the biggest favour of all. Betsy Finch had bought a newborn infant for selfish reasons, but in removing Charlotte from a baby farmer's clutches she'd saved the little girl's life. Recently, Betsy had again protected Charlotte, this time from a pimp's influence. It was hard to like Betsy Finch, but it was harder to hate her.

'I'm so proud of you, Lily, carrying on looking for our

sister. I should have helped you do it. I thought you was wasting your time. I never imagined you'd manage to track her down after all this time.' Davy's voice was gravelly with shame.

'I thought it might be a lost cause, as well,' Lily said honestly. 'When it seemed hopeless and all I was coming up against were brick walls, I just reminded myself that I'm a stubborn so and so.' She put a hand on his shoulder and pecked his cheek to cheer him up.

A bang on the door broke them apart. Then some noise filtered through from the street that made them both chuckle. 'We Wish You a Merry Christmas' was being sung at the tops of some lusty voices on Lily's front step.

'Reckon I know who that is.' Davy was grinning as he went to open the door of the basement flat.

'Sooner hear you tooting that harmonica than singing, mate, and that's saying summat,' Davy ribbed his old pal. 'What's the password?'

'Booze . . .' said Smudger.

'In you come then, all of yers.'

Smudger, using a walking stick, Margie and Eunice trooped into the hallway, carrying bottles of drink and presents.

'These are for Charlotte. Put them in the bedroom for tomorrow, shall I, Lil?' Margie indicated the gaily wrapped parcels in her arms.

'Oh, thanks, Margie.'

'And how are you doin', young lady?' Smudger had ruffled Charlotte's short fair hair with his free hand and received a grin and a polite request for a glass of lemonade. Whenever she saw Uncle Smudger he always poured her a drink of fizzy. He showed her the bottle of pop he'd put on the draining board, giving her a wink as though it were their secret.

'Want these sausage rolls and mince pies taken out before they're charcoal?' called Eunice, peering into the oven and busying herself with the tea cloth.

'Oh, thanks,' said Lily.

Smudger and Davy were busy cracking open some brown ales. And Charlotte was sipping her lemonade in between drawing a picture of a snowman. Lily opened the bedroom door for Margie to deposit the presents under the bed. They were stacked on top of others already there, from Lily and Davy, ready for opening on Christmas morning.

'Crikey, she's got a pile to keep her busy,' Margie said.

'It's such a special Christmas. I've spoiled her.'

'Don't blame you, Lil. Still can't quite believe it, you know, that she's home at last. Bet you can't either, can you? God only knows you deserve this; something good happening at last.'

Tears sprang to Lily's eyes. She cleared her throat, said brightly, 'Come and have a bite to eat and a glass of port.'

'Just you hang on,' Margie said softly. 'You don't get away that easily. Not from me.' Margie put her hands on her friend's shoulders. 'No need to put up a front, Lily Larkin. I know you don't want this Christmas, or any other. I know all you want is to hear that Greg's all right.'

Lily folded over at the waist as though in sudden agony.

'Don't talk about it this evening, please, Marge,' she gasped. 'Davy doesn't know he's missing, and I'm not bringing it up. I'm not ruining it for everybody. There'll be an atmosphere. It's Charlotte's first proper Christmas with her family.'

'I know,' Margie said flatly. 'And Smudger knows to keep

it buttoned. We won't say a word. But when I lost Rosie, you told me not to bottle up the pain and let it fester. Was wise advice that I'm giving back to you, love.' She drew Lily into a hug, comforting her best friend in the way she'd been comforted by Lily so many times in the past when life had seemed too horribly bleak to bear. 'You can talk to me without any of them knowing. Let it out.' She cradled Lily in her arms, rocking her gently as her friend's body jerked with sobs. 'Charlotte's gonna love her Christmas,' Margie crooned. 'She's got all of us round her now. We're all her family too, even if we ain't blood. You can step back a bit, if you want to, have some time to think about other things that have happened. Things that need grieving over.' Margie got out her handkerchief and wiped Lily's streaming eyes.

Margie knew about Lily's stillborn son. So did Smudger. But nobody else did. Lily had been in France in the early months of her pregnancy and her best friend was the only one she'd confided in before she went. Davy hadn't been told she was expecting, neither had Fanny. In light of the tragedy that had followed, Lily was glad she'd kept it to herself. Only Margie, and Betsy Finch, knew that Lily Larkin had given birth to a tiny stillborn son, alone, in this basement room. Only Margie had been with her when she laid her baby to rest on a dull rainy day.

'Have you had any further news from France?' Margie wiped tear smudges from Lily's pale cheeks.

Lily shook her head, sniffing. 'I don't think I can go in the kitchen and join them yet. Need a minute, Margie. I'll be all right then.'

'Know you will,' said Margie. 'And if you're not all right in a minute, take a bit longer. Take as long as you like. Me 'n'

Smudger are here to hold the fort for you.' Margie smoothed a lock of chestnut hair off Lily's brow. 'This is gonna be a lovely Christmas for Charlotte. It'll soon be New Year's Day, love. A time to make wishes. And you've proved to all of us doubters that wishes *can* come true.'

Chapter Twenty-Nine

A Year Later

'I don't expect you to give me an answer straight away, Lily. I know you must think carefully about it. I do love you, though you might find that rather odd and difficult to believe. And I will always take care of you and your sister. It's wonderful that you've found her. Quite astonishing. Now the war has ended at last, we could move away from here if you like, and be a family. I expect Poplar must hold bitter memories for you.'

Lily had been pouring tea. As she'd got the gist of what Adam was building up to, she'd put down the pot to sink into a chair. He'd turned up a short while ago, back from the war for good. She'd been delighted to see him and had questions to ask about Mrs Fontaine. From Adam's letters she knew the woman had held off entering the geriatric home, but had succumbed to the inevitable in the end. Two weeks ago she had passed away. When Adam broke the news, Lily had brought him up to date with how well the woman's grand-daughter was doing. She had visited Danielle several times during the year and found her happy and eager to meet

Charlotte. Mrs Bloom had suggested they take the children somewhere nice after Christmas, perhaps to a pantomime in the school holiday. Lily had rattled all of this off quite chattily, as normal, but she had noticed Adam seemed to be acting out of character. Usually he would relax and take a seat at the kitchen table. But he'd paced restlessly, as though preoccupied. The news that she'd brought her sister home at last had been saved until they met face to face, as she'd not wanted to write something so important in a letter.

It had stopped him in his tracks and had seemed a catalyst to him spitting out his proposal.

'I've shocked you,' he sounded regretful.

'Yes, you have, Adam,' Lily said bluntly.

'Don't turn me down straight away, please. Just think about it for a while.' He cradled his forehead in his hand. 'We've both lost the people we loved. I know Gregory can't be replaced in your heart and I'll be a poor substitute. I understand those feelings ... because of Ralph.' It was one of the rare times he mentioned his late lover by name. 'Would it be so bad if we became man and wife? I've loved you for a long time. Not as Gregory loved you. But it's love, nonetheless. I'd never do anything to hurt you or Charlotte, I swear. We can give her a good life.'

Lily had shaken off her daze and placed a hand on his arm to make him stop talking. 'It's lovely of you to ask me to marry you, but I don't think I'm ready for anything like that ...'

'It doesn't have to be yet,' he interrupted. He took her hands in his. 'I've never had such deep feelings for any other woman. We have always been a good team ... good friends. Will you think about it?'

At one time – and even after she'd met her new boss Gregory Wilding – hearing this would have been music to her ears. As a girl of fifteen, Adam Reeve had been her hero. She'd dreamt of him asking her to be his wife. Now she was a woman and knew what real love was. A platonic version might never be enough for either of them. And lies and deceit might follow and rot the little they had.

'I'll come back next week for an answer, shall I?' He sounded like an eager boy.

'Yes. All right.'

He visibly relaxed. 'Where is Charlotte? I'd love to meet her. Is she like you?'

'She's at school. And yes, I think she is like me and Davy . . . but with fair hair. We've all got the same blue eyes.'

'Are you still working at the baker's?'

She nodded. She'd not taken a job in munitions after all – not that factories were making any now the war was won. She'd wanted a job with shifts to fit around caring for her sister. Something that allowed her to pick Charlotte up from school. Margie had offered to childmind when she could, so she could find better paid full-time work; so had Eunice. But those women had new family in their lives. Eunice doted on her twin grandchildren, a boy and a girl. And Margie was the happiest that Lily had ever known her to be. Besides, Lily still had some money put by from pawning her engagement ring.

'You're too good a clerk to settle for selling buns. I have to pick up the pieces of my career. I hope to open a children's clinic with some money my late father left to me.' Adam hadn't expected a penny. He'd received thousands of pounds despite his late father having aired his disgust over his son's lover from the moment he found out about him. 'I'd like you to work with me, Lily. We can be a husband-and-wife team. You're a boon to have around in an office. I intend to try to lure Evie Osborne back from Kent to join the staff.'

'That's a great idea,' Lily enthused. She and Evie wrote regularly and Evie knew Lily had miscarried her baby. They hadn't seen anything of one another since they'd left France. Lily's wonderful news about her sister had been met with sad news on Evie's side. Her sister had died after months in a coma and their mother needed caring for now her nerves had got the better of her. But Colin was a darling, Evie had written, and prepared to wait patiently for the right time for them to be married.

'Please don't think I'm telling you this to bribe you,' Adam said. 'Whether you marry me or not, the job would be yours. You could pick the hours that suit you.'

'I'll think about it.' Lily walked him to the door. Usually she'd peck his cheek; she didn't this time.

He cupped her face with two hands. 'I know you're still hurting. So am I. But it's been a year now and we can't look back. We have to try to make a life for ourselves from the ashes. We're luckier than some. We've come through this more or less whole. And I think the people we've lost would want us to be happy.'

After he'd gone, Lily went back into the kitchen and sat down, staring wistfully into a cup of cold tea. She lifted her gaze to a blackbird bobbing on a bare branch outside the window. But there was no answer for her there. The lure of working in a children's clinic with Evie and Adam was great indeed. And she could pick her hours. Adam would be a kind and loving husband and a father figure for Charlotte. How many men would welcome a cuckoo into the nest when starting married life? What Adam had proposed sounded like her ideal life. But it wasn't. Couldn't be, without Gregory Wilding in it.

Armistice Day had come and gone. Lily and Charlotte had joined in with the celebrations. The children had formed a procession in the lane, tooting whistles and banging saucepans with spoons as they marched up and down. Everybody had been laughing and singing; she had too. Inside, her heart had been breaking. She'd hated resenting other people's joy that she felt obliged to fall in with.

Eleven months had passed since Gregory Wilding had gone missing after a tunnel had been breached by the enemy during a skirmish. She'd received another, more informative letter from Major Powley a month ago. At that time the war had almost been won and he regretfully informed her that no new information about the lost tunnellers had come to light. He had wished her well. In utter desolation she'd ripped the letter to bits. She'd never had the fire and blackness dream again. It had been Gregory's hell she'd foreseen. And now it was over for him and she prayed he was at peace.

The two demobbed Tommies who'd been chatting on the platform moved along to make room for others, still in uniform. There wasn't much space to stand, let alone find a bench to sit down to wait for the trains heading inland from Dover.

'You all right, mate?' one demobbee said as his pal got jostled.

'Bleedin' rude buggers,' muttered the older fellow,

straightening his hat that had been knocked askew as men crowded past.

'Can't blame that lot having the hump ... what they've been through.' His companion shook his head. 'Me pal over there told me that bunch come from behind the lines. Look like skeletons some of 'em.'

The older man didn't have any sympathy to express. He curled his lip and brushed down his crumpled sleeve then struck up their conversation again. 'So Dr Reeve is setting up a free kids' clinic, is he?'

'Getting married as well. I heard some nurses talking at Calais. One of 'em had just come over from London to help with the influenza patients. She wants to have a job at Dr Reeve's clinic when she goes back. It's opening in the East End and Reeve is running it with his wife. I hope it's Stepney way. If it is, I'll tell the missus to take our kids there.'

'Wife? Him?' The older fellow snorted in disbelief. 'I heard he was ... you know ... a faggot.'

The younger fellow frowned at him. 'Keep yer bleedin' voice down! You'll get him in trouble saying things like that. He was all right, whatever he was,' he added stoutly. 'Weren't for Dr Reeve I wouldn't still have me two legs.'

'Perhaps she's an understanding sort,' smirked the older fellow.

'She's a smashing sort,' the younger fellow said loudly, glad to be on safer ground. 'Good looker, and friendly. She was a volunteer with the Women's Hospital Corps out in France for a while. Miss Larkin, that's what her name was. She was a chauffeur working alongside Dr Reeve at the refugee camps. He used to go there in his spare time, y'know, after he'd put in a shift with us lot in hospital.'

The older fellow turned around in a huff. ''Ere, woss your game, that's the second time you've barged past me, chum.'

His younger pal shook his arm to calm him down. 'Give 'im a break. I reckon some of them are prisoners of war.'

Chapter Thirty

December 1918

Lily heard the letter box clatter and stopped sorting out Charlotte's clothes for washing. It seemed late for the second post. But then it was nearly Christmas and the postmen were busier than usual. Especially this year. A long-awaited Christmas with the world at peace had finally arrived. Everybody was rejoicing and sending lots of cards and parcels to kith and kin.

She picked up the unaddressed envelope and turned it over. There was no indication who it was for. She opened the flap and took out a creased and smudged photograph. It was the one she'd given to Greg. Her heart started to pound and her fingers scrabbled inside but there was no accompanying letter. She leaned back against the wall, a suffocating lump of emotion jammed in her throat. If it had been retrieved with Greg's things from a trench dugout, the envelope would bear her name and address and a postmark. A few words of consolation would have been included by a sympathetic officer. She turned the photograph over and read:

. . . I'll be waiting.

Tears burned her eyes, blurring her vision. One plopped onto the inscription. She blotted it carefully to preserve words that seemed now a relic of a time long ago when she'd been whole, not hollowed out by grief. The snap must have been found by a Tommy who recognised her likeness and thought to kindly return it to her. It seemed a weird coincidence that somebody from round here would be in the right spot in a foreign land. She was searching for a miracle and mustn't. She'd bring all the agony crashing down again just as it was settling into a more manageable ache. Why would he put it through the letter box and disappear? Hope was making her foolish . . .

She stared at her writing, barely legible now. She knew how he'd read it, if he were alive, and knew about her and Adam. Sarcastically.

She yanked open the door and dashed up the steps and down the lane until finally she spotted a boy in front of her. He'd trotted into a patch of light shed by a gas lamp. Then the gloom swallowed him up again. It was five o'clock and completely dark. She could rick her ankle in a pothole. She slowed down, holding the stitch in her side. She was pathetically clutching at straws, she told herself. A well-wisher had sent one of their kids with it.

She returned to the flat and descended the steps to her front door. Charlotte was in the middle of the passage, waiting for her. Lily had left her sister finishing up her tea of macaroni cheese at the kitchen table. The homely smell welcomed her in, eclipsing the fresh scent of frost that clung to her clothes.

'I wondered where you'd gone.' The child looked anxious.

'Sorry, darling.' Lily felt guilty. She quickly closed the

door and cuddled her. 'Just thought there was somebody outside that I knew. I was wrong though. If you've finished eating, it's time for your wash. It's bedtime for you now. School in the morning. It's the carol concert, don't forget. And I reckon after you've got your nightie on, you'd like a Christmas story, wouldn't you?'

After Charlotte had been tucked up, Lily cleared away the tea things then took the envelope from her pocket. She gazed at the photograph and smoothed a finger over fissures in her face, remembering how happy they'd been that day before the German planes came. Her insides rolled. She'd felt this nervy just before fitting together the final piece of the puzzle to trace Charlotte.

It wouldn't take her long ... only minutes ... to find out if her mind was playing wicked tricks on her. She could ask Eunice to come and sit in the kitchen while she was gone, rather than leave Charlotte alone. Begging a favour would beg an explanation for her absence, though. She'd lied to Eunice before and regretted it.

Margie would understand. But Lily wasn't about to knock her friend up at eight o'clock on a dark night, on a whim. Margie had her hands full with babies.

Lily opened the bedroom door, listening to her sister's quiet breathing. She withdrew and urgently put on her shoes and coat. She felt tortured by uncertainty and couldn't endure it. Soundlessly, she let herself out and hastened down the dark lane. The area was poorly served by streetlamps, so Lily watched her step until she was on the main road. Then she sped over ground she'd covered a thousand times in the past when late for work. The entrance was in sight. One second she was certain she'd glimpsed a flare, the next she'd told herself it was moonlight reflected on stacked metal.

She saw a van parked. A smaller one than Wilding's had previously had.

Anybody could have left that there, she told herself as her heart leapt to her throat.

She went in through the gates ... left ajar as though he knew she'd come.

A single naphtha beacon was burning, outlining a figure crouched over an upturned cart. Tools were strewn around as he worked on it. He was smoking, but he was aware of her; he couldn't miss her shadow overlaying his.

Aged sixteen she'd come upon him just like this, mending a cart by lamplight, inside the warehouse, not out under the stars. She'd had tea with Adam Reeve on that afternoon and had returned to Poplar to find Gregory Wilding drunk and jealous. It had been the first time he'd let slip how he felt about her. She could sense those raw emotions at play, though he'd not even acknowledged her, and he looked sober.

The moment he stood up and turned around, she launched herself at him, hugging him with crushing strength. 'I've missed you ... I've missed you so much. I've been worried sick ... thinking you were dead ... all this time. Why didn't you write? I've had no word ...' She looked up at him through a veil of tears and straggling hair. His arms had remained at his sides. 'Why d'you do that? Why d'you send a kid to put that photo through the letter box? Why didn't you just bang on the door and ask me if I was getting married to somebody else?'

'I didn't want to see you.' He moved away. 'Clean break's best.'

'You liar! You knew I'd come here.' She tried to hug him again, but he avoided her outstretched hands. 'That's it, then, is it?' Lily ran at him and pushed him. 'You let me think you're dead then come back and carry on without me? You want me out of your life, is that it?'

'I'm sorry you thought I was dead. Wasn't far off the mark for a while, anyway. There wasn't much I could do to let you know different, camped out in a forest.'

'Were Germans there? Were you captured?' Lily whispered.

'Doesn't matter now. It's over.' He hunkered down by the cart again and closed his eyes as a thunder of guns rolled in his head, mocking him.

The Allied tunnel had been scuppered by the enemy. The resulting close combat had been disgustingly chaotic. Noble savages nowhere to be seen as desperate men had gouged and battered one another with any grabbed makeshift weapon. Pointing and firing a rifle or using a bayonet was a dignity removed for soldiers fighting in a cavity crammed with clay and broken timbers. Greg had been wounded, as had Lonegan, but they had escaped with a couple of comrades through a maze of abandoned tunnels. Greg and his pal had stuck together while the others took a different route. They had emerged into enemy territory and been captured. The night sentry had imagined his prisoners too badly mangled to make an escape. While he was spewing up, drunk on Russian vodka, they'd scrambled out of the ditch and crawled into the woodland behind. The sentry had given up the chase. It wouldn't have been worth the embarrassment of calling in assistance to recapture two injured Englanders. Along the way Greg and Lonegan had got separated. Greg had no idea if his pal had survived, living off the land, or strangers' kindness, as he had. But he knew they'd turned the right way out of the tunnel:

boarding the troop ship at Calais he'd found out from some old muckers that those colleagues had been shot, not taken prisoner.

The underground blast had given him wounds in the face and thigh, and he'd feared infection setting in. He'd become delirious though he couldn't be sure for how long, or how he came to be holed up in a derelict barn. A local had probably taken pity on him and dragged him into the shelter before abandoning him to luck and his army rations. When those ran out he'd eaten anything edible growing in the fields or forest, unearthed by hand, and any creature he was capable of snaring.

He'd had no weapon for months but after his wounds had closed he'd ventured further afield to look for one. Eventually he came across a German corpse that hadn't already been relieved of rifle and bullets. In June he'd reached an outpost of American soldiers pushing towards the Hindenburg Line who told him an Allied victory was hopeful. Their commanding officer had promised to send a message through channels to the Brits to let them know Lance Corporal Wilding had turned up more or less alive. By that time Greg had dysentery and was close to being a corpse himself. He'd been admitted to an American camp hospital and by August was fit enough to be discharged and join the fight for Amiens. By September a marathon Allied attack on the Hindenburg Line had the Hun on the run. Greg had been attached to a British rifles battalion by then, but the Australian and Americans were out the front in the thick of it. He suffered a shrapnel wound that put him back into hospital at Bellicourt. It seemed a scratch and a minor inconvenience compared to what he'd already been through. The non-stop echo in his head from the noise of the bombardment was what had troubled him. News of the armistice came while he was playing cards with a fellow patient. They'd all sung 'Rule Britannia'. Then he came home. And wished he'd turned the wrong way out of the tunnel.

When he'd overheard the demobbed soldiers' conversation at Dover, he'd just settled down on a bench to write to Lily. He'd wanted to post the letter ahead of his arrival in London, rather than turn up out of the blue. He'd hoped that Powley had received word from the Americans that he had survived and had passed a message to his next of kin. Otherwise Lily would think he'd perished after so long a silence, missing in action. He'd believed she would wait ... until the war was over and the troops all back ... to see if he was still standing. He'd not counted on her first love putting in an appearance with a wedding ring.

'I heard you're getting married to the doctor.' Greg forgot about France, and about messages not getting through. He'd got the message. 'Thought you might already be married, as it happens. I'm pleased for you.' He lit another cigarette from the burning stub and collected the parts he'd been using. 'Reeve must've liked women more than he let on.' He'd heard her furious snort. 'It was always him you wanted, wasn't it? Right from the start, you told me you loved him. You went to France to be with him, didn't you? I'm not blaming you for giving up on me.' He stood up, hurled a handful of parts and a hammer towards an empty crate. 'Never could tell if it was real love, or if you were paying me back for getting you out of the spike.'

Lily hadn't expected that; he wasn't just saying it to wound. 'If that's what you think, then you don't know me. I *was* grateful. But I don't pay debts that way. And I went to France to be closer to you. So we could be married. Everything you told me about loving me and wanting to marry me.' She paused, unwilling to accept what she was about to say could be true. 'You didn't mean any of it then.'

'I'm bowing out, Lily, like a decent fellow would. I can't give you what he can. You'll have a good job and a nice house. I can't match that now.'

'Well ... who'd've thought it?' She barked a harsh laugh. 'Gregory Wilding is a bloody snob! What's worse ... he thinks I am, too!' She pushed him, then did it again, aching to provoke him into touching her back. He was trying not to ... circling away from her to keep control.

'Go home, Lily. I've work to do.'

'You always had work to do ... money to make.'

'Yeah ... and now it's harder than it ever was.'

'The van's yours, is it?' She jerked her head at the kerb.

'Insurance money came through at last. Got just about enough to start off again.'

'Not enough to want the burden of a wife round your neck though.'

'Go home, Lily,' he said again, hoarsely.

'I will. Got something else to say first. You've checked up on me but missed a few points. I'll fill you in.' She knew he was hurting but so was she. 'Adam asked me to marry him; I said I'd let him know. Now I have. I sent him a letter yesterday telling him I couldn't because of you. Even though I thought you were dead, I couldn't stop loving you, and living a pretence wouldn't be fair on anybody.' She paused before crying, 'If you'd given me a chance, I would have told you all about it.' She marched away a few steps towards the gate, throwing over a shoulder: 'And I found my sister. Charlotte's been home a year, if you're interested.' She swung back, her voice ragged with emotion when adding, 'I've left her alone to come and find you, and I swore I never in my life would do that. And there's something else.' She was quiet for so long he started to walk towards her, frowning at her distress. Her chest was pumping as though what she wanted to tell him was choking her. 'I miscarried our baby.' The words were ejected and she gathered up her skirt in her fists and pelted towards home.

The flat was quiet, her sister still asleep. Lily crept in and sank down by Charlotte's bedside, whispering sorry to the sister she'd betrayed.

Her face was cold and wet from the tears that hadn't dried in the wind. Sobs were welling up again and she left the bedroom to muffle the sound in two trembling hands. They usually slept together. Charlotte loved to cuddle, and Lily hadn't wanted to let the child out of her sight at first. But it was time for more independence now a year had passed and she was eight.

She undressed and lay down on the lumpy mattress in the small room; it had been her bed on her first night outside the workhouse and innumerable times since.

She dozed for a while, then opened her eyes in darkness to the shape of somebody beside her. She knew it wasn't Charlotte, she could smell his musky tobaccoey scent. He was sitting on the edge of the mattress with his back against the sooty wall. He'd let himself in with his key and had come here to comfort her on the night she'd discovered her sister hadn't been stillborn but had been smuggled away to God only knew where.

And on that night had begun that long search. And their love affair.

'What's happened to us?' she sounded bewildered.

'It's not your fault. I'm different now.'

She levered herself up to sit beside him, studying his profile. He wasn't the same: a line of puckered skin from jaw to ear looked silver in the light leaking in through the small window. The cheek above was concave and his narrow lips thinner. As was his frame. He was malnourished. She'd seen all these changes in him earlier but none of them had mattered enough to mention. They mattered to him. He turned to enquire for her opinion with a sardonic look sent from beneath long lashes. He was still heartbreakingly handsome to her. The one she wanted. She wouldn't lie.

'I can see you're not the same.' She lightly traced the scar until he removed her caressing finger. He tried to withdraw but she coupled their fingers, moving them in a slow dance to rest on the mattress. Lily had heard women in the baker's talking of the change in their men. Worry and disappointment had come fast on the heels of the joyous relief of peace and husbands home. The armistice celebrations were over now and reality had set in. Jobs to find, rent to pay. A stranger back to get to know his children.

'Why d'you stay here in this basement? You could have got yourself something better by now.'

'I like it here. You gave me my first kiss right here, in this room.' She sensed the increased tension in his fingers and brushed her thumb on them, remembering the glorious feel of them on her body. 'I got rid of your flat to save the rent.'

'I know. I barged in on someone.'

'Where are you staying?'

'Got a room.'

'This is a room. I sold my engagement ring. I had to, to pay the master to let Charlotte go. She was in Whitechapel workhouse. She'd been taken back there.'

That news had made him look at her in disbelief. She caught his face in her hands before he turned away. 'You can have the money for the business. I've got thirty pounds left.'

'I don't want it. I swapped your wedding ring for food in France.'

'Good. I'm glad,' she said fervently and placed her lips on his scar.

'Tell me about the baby.'

Her hands dropped away from him. 'A stillborn son ... about three months early. Fair hair like yours.'

He put his arms around her, burying his face against her neck to shield the water in his eyes. 'Were you still in France then?'

She shook her head and told him what had happened.

'This Michael Vincent pushed you down the stairs?'

'No ... I don't know. He tried to grab me. I banged my head and don't remember much. I just wanted to get home.' She leaned towards him and kissed his damaged cheek again, sweeping her lips to and fro in a caress. 'I'm different now too. Almost a mother. None of us are the same, Greg. We can't go back to who we were. Smudger and Margie are getting on with it. They're happy. Why can't we be?'

'I'll disappoint you, Lily.' He raised a hand to the mark on his face. 'It's not only this ... on the outside.'

She was quiet for a long time, trying to find the courage to say what she had to. It was festering inside and had been for over a year because there was nobody but him she could tell this to. 'When I lost our baby I thought I'd disappoint you. I thought you'd think I'd paid too high a price for my sister.' A sob exploded in her chest and this time when he reached for her she held him away. 'I think so too. I think if I could go back, I wouldn't risk our child's life for hers. I don't want to think that way ...' She tapped her forehead with a closed fist. 'It won't go away though.'

She dropped her head to her chest to stifle her sobs in case Charlotte heard and came to investigate.

Greg pulled her against him, cradling her in his arms. 'I'm glad you found her, and brought her home safe. I want to meet her.'

'You can ... if you stay till morning. Do you love me?'

'Yes.'

'I love you. It's only ever been you.' Lily lay down.

He stood up and she thought he might leave but she heard his shoes then his clothes being discarded.

Without waiting he came down over her, settling himself immediately between her thighs. His hands went to her nightdress lifting it to her waist.

Lily entwined their legs, shuddering and sighing at the feel of his rough skin abrading hers. Familiar even after their long time apart.

He kissed her without preliminaries, hard and plunging, tasting every part of her mouth and feeding on its heat, then her breasts. He entered her with little finesse and a groan that made Lily fold up to press her hand over his mouth to stifle the sound. Moments later he was quietening her with a kiss that went on and on until their frantic movements settled into a rock. And then they stilled and lay in congress and slept.

'Time to get up. Do you remember what day it is?'

'Carol concert.'

'Here, slip into this.' Lily did the buttons up on her sister's dressing gown. Then she smoothed down Charlotte's shoulder-length blonde locks. She looked her over. She was a beautiful child; strong and healthy. 'Ready for breakfast?'

Charlotte nodded. 'I'm hungry.'

'Somebody's here to have breakfast with us, love. He's making the tea and wants to say hello to you before he goes off to work.'

'All right. Poppy asked if she can come to play after the concert. I said you wouldn't mind.'

'I don't mind ... if her mum doesn't. Has she asked her?' Poppy and Charlotte sat next to one another at school.

'Think so. Who is it in there?' A faint rattle of crockery could be heard coming from the kitchen. 'Is he somebody nice? Will I like him?'

'I think so, Charlotte. I think you'll love him almost as much as I do.'

Epilogue

Spring 1919
Poplar

'Hello. Do you remember me?'

'I do, miss. Won't ever forget you.'

Jake Pickard tapped an eye socket but was too astonished to spout his favourite phrase about his peepers.

The lovely young woman had walked up to him then settled down on the grass beside him. Jake's ankles were dangling over the bank, his holey boots almost skimming the water of Mile End Lock. He fidgeted backwards into a neater position, pulling his gangling legs in their grimy clothing up to his body and hooking them there with his arms. Nobody ever stopped and spoke to him, let alone sought his companionship. During daylight, on a fine spring day such as this, couples might promenade along this tow-path or working men might take this short cut to the factory beyond. They all kept their distance and turned up their noses on passing. After dark the area was populated by prostitutes plying their trade and by other vagrants. Even some of those preferred to keep themselves to themselves.

A fellow cycling on the opposite side of the canal was slowing down to gawp at the bizarre sight of the tramp and the lady looking ready for a picnic. Jake elevated his bristly chin, feeling proud and lucky that this lovely girl had sat by his side, unashamed to be seen with him. She'd been special even as a kid in rags; he'd admired her pluck a decade ago. She'd not lost any of it. Young as she'd been back then, she'd demanded better than the workhouse for herself and her family. Jake felt as content as any father might to know she'd done all right.

'How's that li'l sister of your'n?' Jake pushed away the two empty brown ale bottles as though they were somebody else's rubbish.

'She's very well, thank you,' Lily said. 'Charlotte's at school. She loves to learn.'

'Ah ... a sensible li'l angel.' Jake wobbled his grey head approvingly.

'The porter at the workhouse told me you'd probably be here, by the lock, so I came to see you. It's a nice spot.'

''Tis now, miss, on a fine day such as this. Don't you come at night though. 'T'aint a place for such as you.' He shook his head. 'Very rough by night.'

'I won't be back,' Lily said, and stared along the glittering ribbon of water, towards Hackney. It was further along the Regent's Canal in that direction that her father would have hunkered down to drink himself insensible. Until one night when he took so much that he couldn't wake up again. Lily had long wondered if that had been his intention or whether it had just been an accident. Visiting the place of his death had seemed a morbid thing to do. So Lily hadn't. Today she had come not for Charles Larkin but for Jake Pickard. He'd refused her money, but she still wanted to help him.

Nobody had offered to help her father, even those that should have: the people who'd wronged him. His boss had resented his wife flirting with handsome Charles Larkin so had ruined his reputation and his life. His employee had a wife and a young family but that had counted for nothing in the eyes of a jealous man. A hand of friendship offered to her father in those early dark days might have made all the difference.

'I got married recently, Mr Pickard.'

Jake gave her a gap-toothed congratulatory beam and clumsily patted her arm.

'I'm moving into a new house soon with my husband and my sister. It's got a big garden with apple and plum trees.' Things were on the up for Wilding's. The firm was trading again, and doing well. The warehouse had been rebuilt in brick and iron and stood proudly behind its name-plated gates once more. All thanks to Gregory's determination and non-stop hard work. Hers too ... but he had been the driving force, as he always had been. The rebirth of Wilding's costermongers was its founder's success.

'God bless you all and your home. I hope you'll be very happy in it.' Jake sniffed and used a dirty thumb on his eyes.

'We will be,' said Lily, settling her chin on her drawn-up knees and smiling. 'I shall miss my old home. But it's time to let go of it now.' She took the flat key from her pocket and put it on the grass between them. 'I've been living in a little basement since I left the workhouse. It was heaven to me to stay there when I was young. Just what I needed. I always felt that was where I belonged. But I'm a wife now. Time to start afresh.' She put a piece of paper on top of the key. 'That's the address and the rent's paid for a year. It's your home for as long as you need it. If you want it.'

She could see she'd shocked him into disbelief. Then when it fully sunk in that it wasn't a joke, he started to softly weep, hiding his face behind two black-fingernailed hands. Lily clasped his arm in friendship then pushed herself to her feet. 'Thank you for what you did for us. I'd better be going now. But when you get a chance, Mr Pickard, why don't you come to Chrisp Street market and say hello.' She noticed the key remained untouched. 'If you don't think it'll suit you living there, you can give me that back another day.'

In answer, Jake picked up the key and held it in a fist tucked beneath his chin.

'I hope you'll come and see us in the market anyway. You can't miss us lot,' she boasted. 'My husband, Gregory . . . he's tall and blond and shouts the loudest of any of the traders. And we've got a double pitch with lots of staff. I'll introduce you to my brother. The one who was on the other side of the wall.' She paused. 'Wilding's . . . that's us,' Lily said proudly. 'Best fruit and veg merchants you'll find anywhere.'

September 1931
Poplar

'Do you want a cocktail, Lil?'

'Better not. It'll set my head spinning and I might end up dropping Charlotte's cake.' Lily smiled as Fanny mixed herself another stiff whisky sour from the bottles on the table.

'I'll take another small one,' said Margie with a wink.

'And me.' Lily's sister-in-law pushed her empty tumbler towards Fanny. Their attention was soon back with the cricket game being played on Lily's back lawn. All the kids were running around with their fathers and much cheating was going on, judging by the frequent calls of 'Oi! You're out!'

A picnic table had been set up at a safe distance from the pitch area and spread along its clothed length were plates of sandwiches and small iced cakes, plus a variety of drinks to wet parched whistles. At intervals the men would come over for a breather and a beer with their wives, leaving younger legs to take over scoring runs.

Margie had four children now. And Fanny three. Davy

and Angie had given Lily two nieces. Lily loved all these kids, treating them as her extended family. The girls – even the big ones – had decided to join in with the cricket rather than sit with their mothers.

'You must be proud as punch of her, Lily,' said Margie. 'Who'd've thought that one of us would end up with a brainbox like that in the family. University was always for posh people.'

'We're certainly not that.' Lily rolled her eyes. 'Charlotte swears like a navvy at times. Big as she is, I have to tell her off.'

'These flappers!' Fanny mocked. 'Don't know what girls are coming to nowadays.'

'You're a fine one to talk,' Margie snorted. 'You were the worst of the lot, Fanny Miller, in your prime.'

'I'm still in me prime, I'll have you know.' Fanny feigned indignation. 'I might be thirty-five soon but I'm wearing well, and you lot are only a few years behind.'

'I'll give you that, Fan,' Lily chuckled. Her friend's fiendishly red hair had lightened over the years as it became threaded with silver, but that apart she looked and acted as perky as she had fifteen years ago when pushing a street barrow.

Fanny distributed the cocktails then raised hers. 'Cheers.' The drinkers chinked together their glasses.

Lily settled back in her chair, enjoying the Indian summer sunshine filtering through the orchard leaves. Charlotte was in to bat, and Danielle bowled an overhand tennis ball that the lithe batswoman whacked up high in the air. The boys fielding charged after it, with some of the younger cousins giving chase. The two eldest girls engaged in a chat while waiting for it to be retrieved.

Charlotte and Danielle were best friends. The way the two of them carried on reminded Lily of herself and Margie when younger: dissimilar in looks, one being dark and one fair, yet like kin nevertheless. Charlotte had recently graduated from Cambridge University and turned twenty-one. Danielle had finished her education at the Pitman's secretarial college. Mrs Bloom had passed away, but Danielle had continued to live with her younger aunt, whose children had already flown the coop to set up their own homes.

'I was changing nappies at their age.' Fanny watched Charlotte and Danielle dashing back to position now the ball was sailing through the air in their direction. The men also stirred themselves from having a chinwag to show willing and get back into the game.

'Times are changing for women, Fan ... for the better. Girls coming through aren't settling for pin-money jobs. They want careers and a say in things.' Lily was also watching the younger women. It was a momentous occasion for Charlotte, and Lily felt a mixture of emotions: pride and relief to see her sister so strong and beautiful and well prepared for her future. Yet she was wistfully aware that this beloved person who had been such a force in her life was now a fully-fledged adult ready to strike out on her own.

'Good luck to all of them, I say,' said Margie.

'That's Evie, isn't it, with her husband.' Angie jerked her head at a couple heading through the side gate that led from the front of the house.

Lily jumped up and waved a welcome, then set off to meet the newcomers on the lawn.

'Oh, I'm so glad you made it from Kent.' She gave Evie an affectionate hug and Colin a peck on the cheek.

'Wouldn't miss this party for the world,' Evie said. 'The boys were going to come with us but then a rugby fixture scuppered those plans. They knew cake was involved too.' She shrugged, letting Lily know she couldn't fathom the workings of her sports-mad sons' minds.

'Never mind ...' Lily said. From the corner of an eye she had noticed another late arrival: a stooped elderly gentleman loitering at the side of the house. He was watching the cricket. 'Help yourself to drinks and food on the table. Fanny mixes a good cocktail. I won't be a mo; Charlotte's grandfather has turned up after all. I thought he might not come ...' Lily started towards the gate.

William Stone removed his hat with a palsied hand. The other was gripping a silver eagle's head atop an ebony cane. The walking stick was a relic from the long-ago days when he would swagger out of the gates of Whitechapel workhouse and imperiously shake it to hail a taxi.

'Come and take a seat. We'll cut the cake soon,' Lily invited. 'Charlotte will be glad to see you.'

'No ... thank you, anyway. I shan't stop. I just came to bring these.' He raised a hand clutching a small package and an envelope.

'I'll call her over to come to say hello before you leave.'

'No, please don't stop her enjoying herself.' His wrinkled face, dotted with liver spots, twitched into a half smile. 'How tall she's got. She looks so happy.'

'She is very happy.'

'If you'd give her those. Just something for her coming of age and to let her know I'm aware of her achievements. An honours degree from Cambridge. A wonderful double celebration for her today.' He inhaled noisily. 'Her late grandmother ... her father too, would have been so proud of her.' He put on his hat, pulling the brim low over his rheumy eyes. 'My thanks for allowing me to keep in touch with her all these years and to know of her successes.'

'You're her blood family too,' Lily said simply.

'Your generosity of spirit is humbling, Mrs Wilding.' He turned and shuffled back towards the road. Lily felt pity for him; a lonely man but still proud enough to decline a seat at a table where he knew he wasn't really wanted. It seemed impossible that once he had scared her; that once he had fed her skilly and now she offered him birthday cake.

She looked at the package and envelope. She imagined they contained more jewellery, more money. The sadness of it. The granddaughter he'd once wished didn't exist was now showered on every birthday with wealth he'd purloined from the Whitechapel Union. Charlotte knew only the bare bones of her parents' relationship and her unfortunate start in life. There had been more than enough sorrow and ill feeling, and Lily hadn't wanted to pass it on undiluted to the next generation. Charlotte would fly high, unfettered by bitterness.

'Was that Grandpa you were talking to, Mum?' Charlotte had removed her pumps and hared towards Lily, barefoot.

'It was. He brought you this but wouldn't stay.'

Charlotte swiped her perspiring face with a bare forearm. Her fashionable short frock had grass stains on the lemon silk and her blonde hair – earlier styled in a sleek bob when greeting her guests – had been curled by humidity. Still she exuded loveliness, and Jicky's floral perfume. She took her gift and quickly opened it. Her jaw dropped. 'Crikey. Fifty pounds *and* a gold bracelet.' She slipped her wrist into the bangle. 'Danielle and I have talked about getting a flat together now I've come down from Cambridge. The money will come in very handy. Should I go and catch up with Grandpa and say a big thank you?'

'I think he'd like that,' Lily said.

Charlotte set off, then hesitated and came back to give Lily a hug. 'Thanks for all this ... for everything. It's a super day.'

'You deserve it, love.'

She watched her sister trot off and disappear around the side of the house. Charlotte had started calling her 'Mum' when little, wanting to have a mum at the school gates like her classmates. Her big sister had fitted the bill. When older she'd carried on with it in a jokey affectionate way. Lily waited for her to come back so they could talk some more about a house move. University dorms had been different; Lily knew Charlotte would be gone for good this time.

Lily chuckled as infectious laughter drifted over from the crowded table. The men were back to tuck into food and drink, leaving the kids to carry on with bat and ball.

Davy had sat down next to his wife and immediately dived into the cakes. Lily's adored twin brother, once a skinny little thing, now looked like a portly gentleman. Only his calloused hands marked him as a costermonger. Margie and Smudger had drawn together like magnets, standing arm in arm. Always an attractive girl, her husband and children had brought out her beauty. Fanny was on her feet, pouring cocktails for one and all, while her husband Roger passed her the bottles. Evie's once petite shape had been rounded from babies and good living, and her Colin, now quite bald, was sitting opposite her, smoking his pipe.

People were missing from the table. Important people who should have shared in this day. No Adam ... beautiful soul that he'd been. The man who'd saved so many lives and limbs during the war couldn't cure himself during the flu epidemic that followed. No sweet Joey Robley, who hadn't returned from France, breaking his mother's heart for the second time as the war claimed another of her sons. No Eric Skipman either. He had come back but then moved up North to marry a girl and start his own green-grocery business.

Then she saw Gregory approaching the table with more bottles to replace the empties. He put them down and carried on towards her. Her heart quickened as her eyes locked with his and she thought again how much she loved him. And cherished him.

He played cricket with other men's kids though he'd love a child of his own. He'd paid for Charlotte's education and had done so gladly. He'd never been critical of his wife allowing a tramp to stay in a home he paid for. Because they were soulmates and he knew it was important to her without needing an explanation. Jake had stayed there for four years. He had turned up at the market every day to help sweep up and stack pallets. He'd refused all payment but had liked to receive a cotchel along with his colleagues. One afternoon, tramping up the lane with his fruit and veg, he'd collapsed and had passed away quite peacefully. He'd never said how old he was. Jake would never talk about himself. Nobody knew his story.

'Was that William Stone?' Greg asked.

Lily nodded. 'He didn't want to stay. Charlotte's run after him to thank him for bringing her a present.'

'Was she surprised to get one from her mother?'

'She was, and pleased. She's going to write and thank her for the scarf she sent.' Betsy Finch had also been advised of Charlotte's milestones. At Christmas, Charlotte would receive a card from her adoptive mother containing a ten-shilling note. Betsy had never visited, although she lived not far away in Kentish Town. Maintaining a distance seemed to suit Charlotte, who'd never asked to go there. Betsy lived alone, as far as they knew. Michael Vincent's death had occurred shortly after Greg came home, and had been reported in the paper as unexplained. A general assumption was that a disgruntled punter must have pushed him down a brothel stairway.

Lily held her husband's face between her palms and kissed him.

'What was that for?' he asked, his autumn-coloured eyes sultry.

'Just to thank you for all this . . . for everything, for being the best husband ever.' She touched the whitish mark on his cheek, the one that Charlotte, when young, had said made her dad look like a pirate. He was still the most handsome man in Lily's eyes. Scarred face and silver hair at thirty-eight, yet even now women's eyes followed Gregory Wilding in the market.

'I'm glad you're happy, Lily.' He nuzzled her cheek. 'Besides, you're gorgeous, so what's a man to do?' He looked her over from bobbed chestnut-brown hair to slender silk-stockinged legs. 'You've hardly changed since the day we got married.'

'Almost thirteen years. Can't believe it's that long.' Lily sighed.

'Unlucky for some . . . not for us, eh?'

'No . . . not for us.' Lily nestled against his side.

Seeing them canoodling, Charlotte trotted past towards the cricket with just a wave for them.

Lily slipped a hand through Greg's arm and unhurriedly they strolled to join their friends gathered around the table.

'Charlotte says she's moving out into a flat with Danielle.'

'That's good, I might set up a billiard table in her old room,' he chuckled.

'You won't. We might find a better use for that big bedroom.'

'What's that then?'

'It might need painting ... pink or blue.' She saw his disbelief turn to hope. After so long without even one false alarm she could understand how he felt. She turned towards him, hugged him tightly. 'I'm almost sure ... I wasn't going to tell you yet just in case ... but I couldn't wait. I know that lot think it won't ever happen again for me. I know they're all too lovely and kind to say so. I know you are too. And that breaks my heart. But I think in the spring we might all be back together around that table for another celebration. A christening.'

He lifted her up so their faces were level and kissed her, then gazed at the horizon, closing his eyes to murmur a silent prayer.

'Not done bad, have we, for a bunch of workhouse kids?' He sounded croaky and surveyed his house and garden with a thoughtful grimace.

'No ... we've done all right, Greg. All of us.'

'We can afford somewhere bigger next year, move out a bit to the suburbs, if you like.'

'No ...' Lily breathed in apple-scented air while listening to their friends' laughter and the sound of children's voices. 'This is where we belong.'

Author Note

UPPER NORTH STREET SCHOOL AIR RAID

The first daylight bombing attack on London by fixed-wing aircraft took place on 13 June 1917. The bombs began falling just before noon on Essex and numerous East End districts.

The worst incident was the damage done to a council school in Poplar. Upper North Street School was hit and the bomb fell through three floors of classrooms, exploding in the infants' class on the ground floor. They were making paper lanterns.

Eighteen children were killed and many more injured. The caretaker found his five-year-old son lying dead among the debris. About a week later one of the biggest funerals in London was held. Fifteen children were buried in a mass grave and three had private graves.

Funds were raised for a memorial. It stands in Poplar recreation ground and was unveiled in June 1919, bearing the names of the children killed.

ENDELL STREET MILITARY HOSPITAL

In May 1915 the only British Army hospital to have been established and run entirely by women was opened in a converted workhouse building in Endell Street, Covent Garden. Flora Murray was Doctor-in-Charge and Louisa Garrett Anderson was Chief Surgeon. As was usual at that time, none of the staff had previously treated male patients. It was generally assumed the venture would fail within six months. It didn't and the Women's Hospital Corps continued treating convoys of casualties up until the end of the war.

Acknowledgements

Anna Boatman, Sarah Murphy and the editorial team at Piatkus: thank you for your praise and support for the *Workhouse to War* trilogy. Thanks also to Anne O'Brien for her editorial input, and to Juliet Burton, my agent.